DEDICATED WITH LOVE TO MY

HUSBAND ROGER

OUR CHILDREN

DIANA, KAREN AND JEFFERY

AND OUR

GRANDCHILDREN AND GREAT GRANDCHILDREN

A VERY SPECIAL THANK YOU TO

JAMES AND MARY ROAKE OF BILLERICA,
MASSACHUSETTS, AND

MARY HURLEY OF WEST BALDWIN, MAINE

FOR THEIR UNENDING SOURCE OF ENCOURAGEMENT
THROUGH THIS TRUE

LABOR OF LOVE

AFFECTIONATELY,

THE AUTHOR

MARY VION HOOVER

# Contents

# CHAPTER 1

The bright sun warms my face as I lean against the window and gaze down into the beautifully trimmed garden below. My head is reeling as my thoughts spin faster and faster through my brain. It is as if every happening of my life is trying to crowd into my head so that not one small detail can be lost or forgotten. The whirling memories of years past become a collage before my eyes. The past, present, and my apprehensions of our future all become intertwined into a giant tapestry, one thought interwoven into the next. These thoughts are so tightly joined it is impossible to isolate or separate one from the other. The speed at which my life is passing before me is almost incomprehensible. I feel as if I am falling from a great height, spiraling downward in total darkness and I can't seem to find a way to help myself recover from this seemingly free-fall my life is in. In the silence of my bedchamber I am experiencing a deep feeling of loss and frustration. How will I ever be able to upright my world and put things back into some semblance of normalcy?

My eyes blink in an attempt to remove the moisture that has gathered in them and I wipe away a runaway tear. My particle self reminds me that these are very private thoughts, unspoken and to be held deep within my very soul for all eternity.

My eyes continue to stare downward not really focusing on any one object. I know I am only trying to escape, if only for a moment, from my present pressures. I seem to relax a little as I let my mind take over my senses, thus allowing me to remember the more pleasant things in my life. The wonderful smells of all those beautiful roses in the garden below as they sway in a light breeze, shaking the drops of rain from their pedals, looking so vibrant. It is amazing what a soft spring rain can do to revitalize the creations of nature. They were planted there so many years ago by past generations, to please the eye or to be picked and placed in one of mama's beautiful hand blown vases. She would use them for a centerpiece on a table or sideboard and we would all enjoy their freshness and beauty for many days.

Standing here and reaching far back in time and deep in my heart where my memories can be retrieved for my personal pleasure or displeasure, as the case my be, I come upon some of the more happy special moments. These are the carefree times of childhood. Oh not my childhood but that of my children. What a delightful sound the children made with their little voices, as they merrily called, back and forth to each other as they romped about. I seem to be trying once again to hear that special happy lilt of their voices, that told me just how secure and content they were. Oh what bliss the shimmering granite walls of this old house holds for me. This structure that I call home, has been called home not just for myself but also for many generations before me.

I can't recall having ever taken the time in my busy life, to fully appreciate what living here has meant to me. My childhood was also spent playing in that garden down there, just like my own children did. Yes, my very being is so intertwined with every element that surrounds me and I feel the two could never be successfully untangled or separated. From the ivy-covered walls to the worn fieldstone walking paths, they are all a part of me. Every inch of this beautiful estate is meshed together and in essence is all a part of my total self. We truly become creatures of our environment.

I know I should pull myself together and away from this window and continue with my day but my eyes just keep drinking in the view from up here. I have an overwhelming love for those flowing fields out there in the distance, looking like an emerald green jewel. The colorful wild flowers with their earthy sweet scent interspersed in the meadow area, which is mostly fenced with split rough-hewn timbers. Layer upon layer the texture and vibrant colors blend to present to my gazing eyes a beautiful masterpiece of nature. The railed fence is darkened with age and in some places in need of repair. Right now the repair of the old wooden fence is the least of my worries.

The thickly wooded forest, dense with both trees and foliage makes a wonderful backdrop to this picture nature has provided for me. I can feel a little smile that turns up the corner of my mouth as I remember how scared I was of the forest when I was but a wee bit of a girl. My parents and aunts and uncles had always told me that a big black bear lived in that deep dark place and the forest held all kinds of things that would jump out and eat me alive. Oh how those stories kept me from tromping out to explore for myself. All of these recollections impart my years here in this old manor house. Caswell, the place that has been a safe haven for my family, all these many years. So many dreams were born here and have come to fruition. It is hard for me to realize that those happy days gone by have lead to my own family of three strong, almost grown, young men and one very lovely little girl. I marvel at their eagerness for the future, with all of its challenges, its promises, and even with all of its unknowns.

In this half day dreaming state I am in, I wonder; what my children will have to look back on when they become the age I am today? Will they have found happiness, riches, contentment and will their wishes come true and their dreams be fulfilled? What affect will my decisions and those of John's have on their lives and their tomorrows? What a great responsibility each of us has for others as we trod along this pathway called life.

I have never really taken the time nor pondered the thought of how one small decision of mine might change, direct, redirect or merely be a confusing factor in the life of another human being. Oh my, when did life become so complicated? Perhaps I am making it much more complicated than it need be! In the state of mind that I am in today I cannot seem to help myself.

A wistful sigh seeps from deep within my body, but I ignore anything that might interrupt my thoughts and continue to wonder back in memory many years. These are years, which, in reality seem like only yesterday. I find myself shifting my weight from one leg to the other and leaning more heavily against the window casing, as if I am in need of more support for all these heavy burdens, I seem to be carrying. I am pleased that the thoughts pouring forth to me now are of blissfully, happy times.

I can see in my minds vision a truly scrumptious April morning.  It was a special morning where I awoke very early.  On that particular day I was very eager to greet a new dawn, with my heart so full of love and happiness I just knew it couldn't possibly hold any more.  My nerves were all a-jitter and I could hardly sit still as Katie combed the long tresses of my light, honey blond hair.

Mother had come in and out of my bedchamber a million times, wringing her hands together as she checked on one thing and then another.  Half of the time not uttering a word to me as she came and went.  I knew she just wanted everything, on this particular day, to be perfect.  Her words and those of Katie's, still ring clear in my mind.

"If you don't sit still, Miss Elizabeth, it is going to be impossible to wind these silk ribbons evenly through the curls," Katie chided.

"Please Elizabeth, do as Katie says."  Mother pleaded.  "You will never be ready in time if you don't."

"I'll try, I am just so nervous, I can't stop fidgeting."  I tried my best to explain away my jittery twitching.  A slight sideways glance at my mother let her know I was doing my best.

Katie was a master artist at fixing hair.  I knew whatever she did, my hair would look its best.  Yet I also knew that Katie was a perfectionist and would work until every strand of my hair was in the exact place she wanted it to be.  She had gone over and over the vision she wanted to create, she had explained she wanted my hair to cascade down my back like a glittering waterfall.  She had it all worked out in her mind and with every stroke of the comb she wound the ribbons around the headband covered with baby pink rose buds.

Oh how many times Katie had described to me just what she wanted to achieve.  As I sat as still as I possibly could I knew she was doing her very best to make it exactly as she had planed.  So I just sat there letting her weave her magic.  The aroma, of the sweet smelling roses were making me have a very tight forehead and swirling feeling in my stomach.

The next problem I had to face on this morning of mornings is how, in the name of the Queen, would I get my dress on without messing up my hair.  After all of this setting I surely did not want to do it all again.  I could never endure going through all of this twice.  My stomach was in knots.  But no need to fret, for little did I realize that with the capable hands of Auntie, Mama, Katie and my cousin Sue, nothing was impossible; without even one strand of blond hair being disturbed, on went my dress, and before I could blink an eye, they were all trying to button the tiny satin buttons that seemed to go on forever down the back.

Papa had fashioned for me the most delightful looking glass and I strained to see every inch and every small detail of my dress.  I am sure that it is prettier than any the Queen's dressmakers could make.  Besides, every stitch in my dress has been hand sewn with love.

3

My dress was made from the finest white cloth Papa could purchase. It was adorned with a beautiful embroidered design and many times the sharp end of the needle had pricked auntie's fingers as she skillfully guided the needle through the material in an exacting pattern. With precision and expertise auntie made the tiny handmade silk roses that encircled the slightly scooped neckline and she had finished her creation by covering the last button of the waist closure with a beautiful silk rosebud which she made a tiny bit larger than those found around the neck of my dress. This was a lovely finishing touch to the already wonderful creation of hers.

My auntie was so patient at all the many fittings, nipping and tucking, here and there, to make everything fit just perfect. She made petticoat after petticoat to go both under and over the bum-roll letting the material bellow its fullness as far out as possible. My chemise was made of the finest silk and felt ever so soft and light against my skin. I am sorry I can't say the same for the comfort of my tightly laced corset. It nearly took my breath away. Then there was the layer after layer of under garments. Auntie had insisted on creating fullness that flowed gracefully over the farthingale. She had a picture of perfection in mind too and she went to all lengths to achieve her vision just as Katie had.

Dear, sweet auntie, her greatest joy in life was to please, and that she had done for me. For on that my wedding day, I stood dressed in the exquisite wedding dress of my dreams. I think secretly I wished the queens' designers could see my dress they could have learned a few things in design from auntie. Yet I knew that would have been an impossible wish for a creation such as that would have caused quite a stir, fine or heaven forbid even imprisonment. Our station in life dictated what we should wear and woe to anyone that stepped outside those boundaries.

How ridicules it would be of anyone to think that any of us was trying to do or be anything but happy. My wedding day was just that, my special day and how could that hurt anyone else. In my way of thinking it was selfish of the Crown or any one else not to want my happiness anyway. My determination that the day would not be marred by the edicts of anyone, least of all jealous rulers and their henchmen was apparent as I glanced into the looking glass only to see a very determined look, frozen on my face. Hopefully all the Queen's men will be far away tending to some of the Crown's other dirty work and unable to spoil my happy occasion or cause any concern for my Papa.

"Oh puff!" I am letting my thoughts ruin my day, I thought to myself. I must not think of anything but my wedding and looking the very best I can for the man I love and intend to spend the rest of my life with. Yes a very special day indeed, the day, when John Curtyce and Elizabeth Hutchins would become man and wife. It was a day that would start a new beginning, of our family, John's and mine.

A deep breath cleared my thoughts causing me to take notice that I was reminiscing and reliving my past so vividly that I was reacting as if I was in the process of getting ready for my wedding right now. Closing my eyes momentarily I slowly brought myself back to this day and this time, but not before I tucked every detailed thought and every moment of our wedding day back deep in a special place in my mind so that at another time and place I could once again clearly bring them into focus for my pleasure.

Where had the years gone? How had I let them pass by so swiftly? We were so eager then, as my children are today, to go forward with our lives, unafraid of the future, for we were as sure as the sun rises that everything would be all right. Yes, positive of everything. The confidence of youth, giving us the strength to conquer the world, for it lay at our feet.

As I lapsed back into thinking of the past, I couldn't stop myself from murmuring softly, "our special day, and what a day it was." I can remember, oh so clearly, the wonderful smile on the face of John as I slowly walked toward him and the Vicar. He took my hand and we repeated the words from the Bible that would bind us together for life. How handsome, John looked, with his coal black shoulder length hair. His hair has a slight wave that seemed to cause his hair to defy manageability. His eyes the color of a gray winter sky with a twinkle of mischief causing me to wonder just what he might be thinking, at that very moment. These thoughts cause my face to flush with color for even today after these many years of marriage, John was still as handsome as ever.

There was the beautiful picturesque, Old Parish Church, made from stones pulled directly out of the hallowed ground. The church steeple seemed to stand especially tall on our special day. The bell tower allowing the beautiful bells to ring loud and clear echoing the joy in our hearts, for all the countryside to hear. That's where it all began, on April the nineteenth, sixteen hundred and ten.

Mama and papa had arranged a beautiful garden party for us. It was held in the garden I look upon at this very moment. Friends and relatives, from near and far, started arriving very early in the week. I can remember coach after coach and family after family ringing the big bell to let us know of their arrivals. Some were also on foot and others on horseback and they had all came to pay their respects to our family and to John's. They were an excited and happy bunch, there to join in the festive occasion. The house was already full by mid-week yet somehow there was room made for just a few more. Every time another carriage arrived or there was another ring of the bell at the door they were directed to the meadow. I feared that soon the meadow would be over flowing too. My thoughts were that some had just heard there was going to be a big celebration and fine foods so they just thought they would drop right in.

I wondered in amazement at the efficiency with which mama handled all the details of such a gathering. She seemed to enjoy the massive confusion and the entertaining of all these people at her home. One more person or one more family, it just didn't matter. She seemed to be having the time of her life. The comfort of her quests was always foremost in her mind and heart. She had a quiet, serene quality, which made everyone more than comfortable and so at ease. Her enjoyment of this special event was very apparent as I watched her move amongst her many friends, her skirts rustling almost singing a merry tune as she scurried about from one person or task to another. Her hair, a light color with golden red highlights was done up tightly into a bun at the back of her head which she neatly secured with a white lightly embroidered caul. The cap tied tightly to her head occasionally let a strand of her hair escape. With a quick push with her finger the hair was put back in place and without missing a beat she hurried along.

Our walk from the little church to Caswell Manor was only a short distance but as we walked along the cobblestones of the roadway pushed hard against the bottom of my feet. My soft-soled slippers were of little use against the elements underfoot. I remember now that most of my discomfort came from my hosen, which were hot on this warm spring day. I had even hand-knit them of fine silk threads all by myself and I was proud of my accomplishment. Yet I think I would have been smarter to knit them out of cotton thread, for they were slippery and they let my feet slide back and forth easily in the slippers. My slippers of satin were embellished with a shoe rose, matching those adorning my dress. I was clinging tight to John's arm, feeling his muscles tighten as he drew me close to his side and that made my heart race as we walked along. Arriving at the garden area John and I were greeted by a throng of guests. One by one they passed in a line, all echoing the same sentiment, "a happy life and with much love and many children as we journeyed down life's path." How happy we were then and how excited we were to face the rest of our lives together. Little did we know, that life did not always turn out as we anticipated? Nor did we realize that it was not always filled with happiness. Yet even if we had known, nothing could have dampened our enthusiasm for life with all its ups and downs, just as nothing could have happened to dampen the joy on that, our wedding day.

Now as I look back and think how swiftly the years have passed. Days blur into weeks, the weeks turned to months and the month's roll into years and they all have flown by with the swiftness of a strong wind. I wonder if it is that way for every human being? For my personal years have passed in a blink of an eye, and my tomorrows all too soon have become yesterdays.

It was only two short years after our wedding that we laid papa to rest in the beautiful little cemetery beside the Old Parish Church, and then just five years later, mama, beside him. It was a loss greater than any I had ever experienced, for it had never entered my mind that I would not have my dear parents at my side forever.

Papa had worked hard all his life and his endeavors had made for his family a very comfortable life. He had turned the clumped hard soil into rich farmland. This now rich soil produced great crops to sell in his store for others to buy and food for our own table at Caswell.

Caswell was situated just a short distance from London Town, giving father access to his business in town, without traveling many miles by horseback. Toward the end of his life he had been able to spend his days hunting and playing games, in general enjoying life to its fullest. Oh my, thinking back now it still angers me to think that my papa could have been taxed just for the beauty of my wedding dress had the Crown thought me dressed out of my station in life. Many were called into court back then and today many are still being fined for less of an offense than improper dress. I know that papa would have paid any amount of fine levied, for he hated being under the scrutiny of the Royal Fist. In the years between then and now the seriousness of the days, is much more real to me. Things have not really gotten a whole lot better. But papa was always respectful

6

to the sovereign, yet feeling that a man needed a bit more room in making his own decisions, than the courts of the Crown was allowing them.

It is well that he is not here today to see and hear what is going on in his beloved homeland. Knowing that papa had that little stubborn streak in him. That causes me to shutter at the thoughts of how he would react to the constant, persistent interference in our lives today. Especially where our belief in God is concerned.

John was so good and reassuring and took right over when papa passed on. He was used to stepping in when times got hard. So being thrust in charge of the business dealings of papa's was like second nature to him. His life had been one of taking care of his only surviving brother and sister, since the death of his parents. He had been a very young lad when his parents passed on and he was left with the decisions of manhood pressing heavily on his young shoulders.

I guess I should have paid more attention myself to the running of the household, the farm and papa's business. Being an only child left no one else to help mama handle our large land holdings. There was far more work in caring for the fields, the sheep, our large stable area and just everything that made our home a productive one. I guess I expected everything to take care of itself. I had just never given it a wink of a thought. I quickly learned that a person didn't just get up in the morning and do nothing. I quickly became aware of how important the bookkeeping for both the household and the business were. I know papa had done his best to educate me to the administrative side of Caswell. He had given me every opportunity to know the business also and of what it takes to keep an estate of this size running smoothly. Looking back I absorbed more than I thought, but probably not all that I could have. Being a girl didn't seem to put a damper on questions I asked of him. He always answered every question with a serious educated answer. I probably had plenty of chances to learn, at least more than most girls my age, for papa would usually take me along when he went to London Town. I was as familiar with a law office, a bank, a shop or an accounting house as anyone. Papa made sure of that fact. He wanted me to be as educated and well advised as if I were his son. Just because I was a girl made no difference to him. So I managed to be right there at his elbow observing his every move. So you can see it is not as if I knew nothing, but it was certainly wonderful to have John to take over. For my mind, was not at all emotionally un-entangled enough to make the kind of decisions that needed to be made, nor was mama's in her grieving state of mind. She could not cope with the loss of father in her life. She was only used to tending to the house staff. Mama knew nothing about financial matters anyway. So she couldn't be of any help there even if she wanted to. Dear, dear, John, he is always so hard working and capable of being up to any situation. What a blessing he was and is in our lives. What a lucky day for me, the day I married John Curtyce!

It is hard to believe that John Jr. is now almost seventeen, a man, and William, too, at fourteen, thinking he is as big as his brother, and woe to any who calls him a child. Yet, I still hold on to the youth of Thomas, though he will turn thirteen his next birthday. To me he will always be my tousle headed, brown eyed pet. He is the one who is always so willing to please, to calm the storm, or give that big grin at just the most inappropriate time and make you forget whatever is bothering you. He will never seem quite grown to me. I will always see in him the small child of yesterday.

It doesn't seem like it was more than a minute ago that young John Jr. was born. My vivid memory gives me shutters as I think of the windy storm that lasted for over a week. The clammy dampness giving us, great concern for little Johns health. The dark threatening skies seemed to never clear and had almost prevented us from taking our young son to see the Vicar for his baptism. My emotions became mixed every time I entered the little parish church. I had attended the same parish church all my life and the church had not changed one iota in all those years. There will always be a special place in my heart reserved for the memories I have acquired there. Its walls hold a history of our lives and within its sacred ground are the departed of my heart. We are so united with the church and our church leaders that it is not a matter of it being a part of our lives; in fact it is our lives. I doubt that any decision is ever made, in our daily activities, which is not first taken to God for guidance and affirmation. I do pray that as we endeavor to guide our children that it will always be with God's blessings.          John Jr. was but four years old when along came our darling little William, with his blond curly top and his steel blue eyes. He was so different from his big brother, who had the dark brown hair and deep-set gray eyes. The two of them, what a pair! They romped and played, learned to walk and talk and just in general had a jolly good time. I often wondered as they struggled to stand if they would ever be able to acquire the knack for standing upright on those little wobbly legs and be able to propel them forward. That is one quandary I need not have ever pondered, for when they finally found their balance they were off and running and getting into every kind of mischief they could possibly imagine. It seems they started life on the run and have not stopped or looked back yet. They were always on the go, eager to learn, excited to do any new thing that came along. I am sure they get that enthusiasm for life from their father, who always meets a challenge straight on, never doubting the outcome, and never questioning the task.

Two years later our darling sweet Thomas burst into this world with enough enthusiasm and energy for the whole family. He immediately captured our hearts with his cunning ways and darling little coos and smiles. He has been a blend of both the Curtyce and Hutchins families. Taking on the characteristics of both, John and I. We call him Thomas the adventuresome. He is always exploring everything he comes in contact with and asking a million questions. He will never take 'no" or "I'm busy" or even "I don't know" for an answer. He is just so different in his ways of looking at the world around him. I have to chuckle to myself as I remember back through our boys' growing-up years, for as time passed we settled into life with our delightful family and had given up any hope of having more children. We had often wished for a little girl but had not been blessed with one so didn't anticipate it would ever happen. We were more than content with our three very bright and lively sons. I have to confess, that deep down, a little girl would be nice, but God's will was being done in my life and I firmly believed that He did not want me to have that dream fulfilled. My fervent prayer at the end of every day is to do the will of our Lord.

What a surprise! Seven years had passed, when I found I was once again with child. At first I was skeptical and even in denial about what I suspected. So I was very careful to make quite sure that my suspicions

8

were correct before I breathed a word to John. I would not have wanted to get his hopes up only to find I had made a mistake. I knew in my heart of hearts that John would be as happy as I. This would truly be a blessed event. Increasing our family after all this time was something that had been put completely out of our thoughts. I knew we would both secretly wish for a little girl, yet a healthy baby is all we ever prayed for. We wouldn't want God to be angry with us or think us unworthy of this great gift he was giving us. After all these years with the boys I wondered if I would even know how to take care of a little girl anyway. It was really of little concern for we would be thrilled which ever it turned out to be. We would love, nourish and care for the new baby with all our hearts. I was so anxious to tell John the good news. It took me days and days to prepare in my mind just what to say to him and just when to say it. I was so enthused by my secret. I had planned all day just the exact words I would use and I pictured John's reaction as he listened to my great announcement. I definitely wanted to wait until we were alone and the worries of the day were behind us. I knew I wanted it to be a very special private moment, just between John and I.

As I remember it I retired a bit early and waited in our bedchamber for John to come up. When he finally opens our chamber door, he looked tired and pretty much near exhaustion. I considered waiting until another time, another day when I saw his strained face. I was setting at my dressing table brushing my hair and I watched him from the corner of my eye. He undressed and climbed right into bed. His sigh let me know of his weary state. I continued to brush my hair wondering just what I should do next? I asked myself the question. Should I just blurt it out or forget my surprise for now? I was really in a quandary. All of my hours of preparations for this night and they seemed to be for naught. I was deep in thought when I felt John's hand on my shoulder. He had finally gotten tired of waiting for me to come to bed and had gotten up and taken my silver backed brush from my hand without me even feeling the transfer of it from my hand to his. John turned the brush over and traced the "C" that was hand etched on the backside.

"Such a pretty brush for such beautiful hair!" I heard him whisper softly. With the brush in hand John started brushing, my waist length curls.

"Your hair is so beautiful, Elizabeth, as are you! You seem so far away tonight, is something troubling you?" He inquired as he looked at me in the looking glass. I had to smile as he had put the little mirror directly in front of my face and was staring into the mirror instead of looking at me. He had his head cocked to one side with a cute little smirk creasing his mouth.

"Oh no, John! I was just contemplating some news I have to share with you." I answered coyly. Still not sure I would tackle this task of telling John that he was going to be a new father right now. No, I was not sure tonight was the right time.

"Well, what is it? You know there has never been one thing we couldn't share. Elizabeth, what could be bothering you that is so bad you can't tell me?" John questioned again, with a concerned tone in his voice. By the sound of Johns voice I knew I had to make up my mind of what to do and make it up quickly.

9

"Now, who said it was anything bad, John? I just said something, not something bad." You are reading things into this conversation that are not there." I answered him quickly, not wanting him to worry so.

"Well, by your mood, I just thought . . .." I cut his questioning off in mid sentence.

"Well don't think any more!" I turned and looking straight into John's beautiful questioning eyes, I told him, that in about seven months, he would be a new father once again. Well with that, he picked me up and swung me around and set me down, than picked me up again, and then didn't know what to do.

"Oh, Elizabeth, are you sure?" He exclaimed, with tears glistening in his eyes. I answered him calmly, with a smile. "Yes, John, very sure!"

"I should be more careful with you." He said.

"I'm not going to break, John. I am only having a baby." I assured him. I knew John would react this very way and he would be just as happy and delighted about our new child as I was.

John carried me to our feather bed and climbed in beside me. Holding me close to his body I felt relief that he finally knew the secret I had been keeping from him. We were both blissfully happy and my last thoughts before drifting off into a deep relaxed sleep were of how wonderful my life had turned out. What more could I possibly ask of God? He had given me everything my heart desired. A beautiful home a wonderful family and I might add an answer to my every prayer.

My calculations were very precise. In seven months I was giving birth to our darling little girl. I remember thinking could it really be true? Did I really have a little girl? John would not consider any name but Elizabeth, and I must confess I was proud he wanted our baby daughter named after me.

She was born with the most beautiful auburn ringlets. The ringlets were curled tight and laid gently against her smooth, cream colored, skin. As I looked down at her in my arms I traced her tiny oval shaped face with my fingertip. She had the most beautiful green eyes, with long eyelashes laying against her little rosy cheeks. We both just looked in wonderment at this tiny bit of life. Elizabeth is God's creation, through us, to take care of and love. She is, of course, my pride and joy and the very breath her father breathes.

Oh how I love remembering back through the years. Those special times when John would come in from the fields or back from his shop in London Town, his first stop was to find his little girl, pick her up, swinging her high in the air and round in circles until she would squeal "nuff papa!" Then he would sit her down with a big hug and kiss and ask how his dear sweet little girl was doing today? Then before she could even answer, he would take a deep breath and exclaim, "Woe to any man who tries to take you away from your papa, little one." Little Elizabeth, would give him a big hug and kiss, and tell him she would always be papa's little girl.

What a true joy all our children are to us, each in their special way. We have truly had God's blessings bestowed on us. Again my memories have taken me many years back, letting me relive the moments so precious to me. How long I have been standing here by the window, with my head resting gently against the casing, I cannot tell you. For if it wasn't for the feel of John's strong arms about my waist and his sweet lips kissing the nap of my neck, I might still be in dreamland. I was so deep in my own thoughts that it was some moments before I realized I was not alone in the room. I had not heard or felt John come into our bedchamber and walk up behind me. It was just all of a sudden feeling the warmth of his body close to me that I realized I was no longer alone. His closeness gave me such a feeling of security. This oneness that we share, I have never grown tired of as our years together tick away. The sensations within me are as intense now as they were the day we were married, and I hope will always be, until our days together are no more.

"How long have you been watching me?" I asked, my voice so soft the words come out only as a whisper, breaking the silence in our bedchamber.

"Just long enough to wonder where my darling wife has gone in her dreams. It seemed as though you were a million miles away, Elizabeth, dear. Is something troubling you?" He asked.

"No, John! Just hold me close and assure me again, that what is about to take place in our lives, is going to be alright." I responded, wistfully.

"Oh, my darling, lovely, Elizabeth! What am I ever going to do with you? We have gone over this so many times, and we both know that the future is never ours to know, but we must live by the faith, that what we do will be for the right and good of all concerned. I know it is hard for you to leave the only home you have ever known and cross to a new land with all of its uncertainties, but Elizabeth, even though we have had a good life here at Caswell, it was your family's home. I do not mean to sound ungrateful, that is surely not the case. I have become a part of Caswell and it has become a part of me. It is just that I long for a place where I can build a future for you, the children and myself. It will be our home, one that we create for our future generations. I truly feel Elizabeth that the place for us is in this new land. This new colony is a place where my dreams can become a reality. And I look forward with eager anticipation to the day we arrive. Please Elizabeth, will you put all your doubts and fears away and try to regain a little enthusiasm for the journey that lies ahead of us." John tried hard to sound convincing.

I tried equally hard to be honest as I answered in a soft voice. "Sweetheart, I am trying, but it is just so impossible for me to turn loose of all we have. Caswell has been my life. Look at all we have done, and all the things that have happened here at Caswell Manor. What about the memories, John? What about all the memories of my childhood? The ones of my family, who have lived here for generations? The precious memories of our children being born here and growing up here, what am I to do with them? What about them, John this New Colonies are so far away and

11

so unknown?" I rambled on, not taking my gaze from the window as I spoke. I could not look in John's face for fear of crumbling into tiny pieces and falling apart, completely apart. Somehow I had to hold myself together.

John squeezed me even tighter as he tried one more time to convince me that this was right for us. "That is just it, Elizabeth, they are memories, and memories are always with you. You never have to leave them behind; they will be as close as your heart and you can recall them at any moment in time. Your memories are always with you as vivid as they are this day. That is the beautiful thing about our memory; it gives us the chance to move ahead, without leaving the past behind." His voice was pleading with me. "Please try for my sake, for your sake, for everyone's sake.

I know what John is asking of me and I know what is expected of me, but could I do it? I slowly turned from the window and tilting my face up at John, I smiled and said. "I just need a little reassurance from you, John, to carry me through the rough spots. It is exciting, and I am excited; I just start remembering and can't stop. Your brother and Sarah will be by later this afternoon, and it is always better when Sarah is here, for she is as bubbly as the children over this whole thing. She lifts my spirits so, with her childlike giddiness. Your brother is also as excited and I know when we reach the other shore, we will have some family with us. It won't be so lonesome that way. John, hold me close, for I need an extra bit of coddling." With that, we lapsed into a long lingering kiss. I did not resist, the warm moist passion of his lips against mine and rather enjoyed the chill his caress sent down my spine. John and I would probably still be locked in that wonderful embrace if Katie my maid hadn't knocked on the bedchamber door. I had not heard her and after several light raps on the door Katie had decided the bedchamber was empty and had cautiously opened the door. John and I both jumped, startled to find Katie standing there. We were all a little red-faced, even Katie with an arm full of freshly folded clothing for me to sort for the long voyage ahead. Katie's entrance into the room brought both of us back to the present and the tasks ahead of us. My special task was to decide what would be taken and what we would have to leave behind. I sighed knowing the grueling task must continue. I knew I had to dig deep inside myself and calm my inner thoughts and fears, for I knew I had no other choices. I had to somehow find the strength to make the best of John's decisions. As John's wife, I was obligated to obey. I had no real choice even though John tried to make me think I did.

"Scoot now, John, or the ship will be here and gone and I will still be packing." I ordered him out teasingly, with a pat on his back. John made a hasty exit after whispering that his desires, inflamed by our intimate moment, did not like having to wait. With a wink of his eye to let me know he did not intend to leave the subject unanswered for long, he left the room leaving the job and decisions, of what to take and what to leave, up to me.

"Sorry, Mum," Katie uttered, with her slight accent. I didn't mean to interrupt you and the master. I have a fresh load of things for you to decide about." I tried to put her at ease, for she still seemed embarrassed at walking in on John and I.

"Yes, Katie, I was daydreaming and John came in. I guess I needed a little reassurance about this whole thing. We hardly heard you knock. I just find it almost unbelievable, that in a few short days, we will be leaving this beautiful old home that has been such an enormous part of my life, and journey miles across the ocean, to a land I can't even imagine." As I talk and talk, just babbling on, first about one thing and then about another I don't know whom I was trying to convince, Katie or myself. It all seemed so unreal to me.

"I know, Mum, it is difficult, and you are uneasy about it, but Master John and the boys have not stopped talking about it for months. Now that the time draws near, their anticipation is even more heightened." Katie said, trying to give me some encouragement.

"That's true, Katie, you can see it in their eyes and hear it in their voices, with every breath they take, the excitement is there. You know I am excited, too. It is just that I really thought by this point of my life, I would be long settled down enjoying the fruits of our labors, not starting a whole new life ahead of me." I explained my feelings to Katie as if she were a stranger. I knew she was well aware of my every thought on this and almost every other subject. Through all of our years growing up together I have subjected Katie to many hours of recitation on just what I thought of things. She has always been there for me listening to all my babbling.

"Yes Mum, I know." Katie sighed, realizing that nothing that either of us said made me feel any better. "Oh! Katie, just put those things down on the bed, next to the rest, and I will get my mind back to what I am doing and worry about tomorrow, tomorrow. William and Sarah are expected this afternoon. Would you please tell Cook there would be two more for dinner? Thank you Katie, and thank you for always being there for me." As I explained the schedule of the day I glanced toward the door so she would know that she could leave and didn't have to stay and listen to my prattle any longer.

I thought of how easy it was to talk to Katie; she is far more like a sister than a maid. I think she really feels the same about me. Her family had worked for ours for years, and Katie and I had grown up side-by-side, learning to ride Blacky my first big horse together. The two of us were so close almost inseparable. My mama always said we were so busy always getting into some kind of mischief. Our leaving Caswell is probably just as hard on Katie as it is for me. She has never been anywhere but right here at Caswell Manor either. I know she will be well taken care of as cousin James will be here for her and she will be treated well. He and Katie have known each other since childhood and have always been very close. I hope for her the transition will not be as difficult as I anticipate mine to be.

As I look down in dismay at the items on the bed I see so many piles of clothing. There is one pile for the church to go to families in need, one to take with us and one to throw away. Laughing a little at myself I glance over at another very large pile and that one is for I don't know who or what. Oh my, how will I ever accomplish such a tasks? Every time I pick up a piece of the children's baby clothing, I get that sinking feeling all over again. It is all I can do to push the tears from my eyes. Determined, I say to myself, I must, I must, and at last, I do.

As I changed into a fresh chemise, my hand decorated underskirt, an overskirt, then add a fresh embroidered bodice with puffed sleeve attachments, I feel much more refreshed. I retrieve a girdle belt and placed my small purse securely on it. The little purse holds my mirror, a fresh handkerchief and a small fan. I had just finished securing it about my waist when I hear the big door-knocker. The family has arrived so I scurry to the top of the massive staircase and greet them as I hurry down. The conversation takes no time at all to work itself around to the voyage ahead. When we are all talking like this, the whole idea of this fascinating adventure becomes exciting. Just to see everyone wondering and surmising what the New Colonies is like, gives me chills of anticipation. I just can't help getting into the happy spirit of things. I overhead John and William talking, over in the corner, about some land that William has heard about not far from Boston Harbor, where the ship would be put to anchor. At least one thing I know, I would never have to worry about John taking care of his family. That I knew, he would always do, if it were within his power.

The afternoon quickly passed and much to our surprise, we looked up to see Samuel, our butler, standing at the drawing room door, announcing that dinner was ready to be served in the dining room. What a delicious smelling meal. Cook has out done herself, once more. The smell of the fresh baked rolls and the steaming hot leg of lamb wafted past our nostrils, causing our stomachs to growl with hunger pangs. Knowing that it would taste as good as it smelled, we all hurry and sat down to eat. By the time we had finished the main course we all agreed that our stomachs hardly had room for any more food.

It was almost too much to even think of the beautiful bowl of fresh berries and cream, setting on the sideboard, waiting to be served as the finishing course to our wonderful meal. Where would we find the room in our stomachs for them? I thought. But of course we would not think of leaving one drop of them in the bowl. When Cooks daughter, Sadie, came to serve them we all took a deep breath and commenced enjoying every tiny morsel. We finished the meal off with a cup of tea.

Breathing a sigh of contentment, John suggested that we retire from the dining room. We all left the table to visit and talk some more. John and William went into the library for an after-dinner brandy. Sarah and I went out for a walk in the garden to get a little fresh air and leave the men to plan and talk, and dream dreams that only men can dream.

Before we realized it, twilight had turned to darkness, and all too soon, the day had ended. The carriage was brought around from the stable to take William and Sarah back home. As John and I walked arm in arm, back into the house, each carried in silence, their own thoughts of this day, and all its happenings. One more day of memories at Caswell Manor, to tuck away in my memory book and pull out another day, to relive again and again, as I was sure I would.

The following day, cousin James arrived early. He and John withdrew to the library immediately to go over the books of the estate. They wanted to get everything in order so that the task of taking over the responsibilities of Caswell would be as smooth as possible for James.

James had always been a man for business, and the Old Manor being left in his hands was being left in the most capable there were. James's mother had died in childbirth and his father shortly after, in a hunting accident. Little James had come to live with us and had grown up as I, thinking there was no place else in the world but Caswell. It was only right that he should be taking over the house, for he would care for it as his own; for in many ways, it was as much his as mine.

As the day seemed to be winding to an end I am having thoughts of the boys and their whereabouts. They had gone riding on their horses earlier and now it was getting quite late and I am concerned for their safety. But before I have time to even wrinkle my brow in concern I can hear them and see them running up the walk from the stables. They are laughing and talking, without a care in the world. It is good they all get along so well. Thomas is not as accomplished a rider as his brothers yet they always take him along, and I know watch after him, as closely as I would myself. How lucky we are, to have three such handsome, strong, healthy boys. The pride of being a mother swells inside me as they came through the door.

As for Elizabeth, I need not worry about where she is. She stays very close at hand these days, seeming to be picking up my unsure feelings. This must be so unsettling for her. She is so small and so vulnerable. My heart aches for her the most. I try to give her special understanding I know she has many unanswered questions. Even if she asked them, I would have no answers. I am too full of unanswered questions myself.

I have almost completed all I set out to do today and I finally feel that I have accomplished something. It has been a long day, but I can see that things are finally starting to fall into place. As I walk past the open library door I pause, John is still laboring over the books, so I decide not to disturb him and I will go directly to my bedchamber. I summon Katie to draw me a nice hot tub of scented bath water. I sit myself down and relax so completely that I really loose track of time. I have no idea how long I have been in the tub. It seems like just a moment, yet as I open my eyes I realize that my hot steamy water is now almost cold. I quickly finish my bath and step from the tepid water. Wrapping a piece of knobby woven, wool cloth about me I shiver a bit and hope it will both absorb the moisture and warm my now chilled body.

Without any warning John burst through the door and in a boisterous voice almost loud enough to wake the King himself, he declared. "Gracious, how sweet you smell, like the first violets of early spring." He was sniffing at me like a bloodhound as he wraps his arms about me and holds me ever so close. I melted into the warmth of his embrace and hardly realized until my head hits the pillow, that he has picked me up and carried me over to our bed. He is looking deep into my eyes and I feel my heart start to pound. It never takes much for John to arouse in me the desires I hold for him. Oh the enjoyment and pleasures we have shared over the years. We were as God intended us to be, one, fulfilling our love, with the warmth of our hearts. The touch of his cool hand against my still moist body causes chills of passion to fill me. Holding each other close we fell into a deep sleep. What could be more perfect than falling asleep in the arms of your own special partner? Yes a perfect ending to a perfect day.

I slept as sound and comfortable as a baby, and when I awoke, the sun had been up for hours. John was already gone and probably halfway through his things to do for today list. I hurried to put on my linen partlet, busk, farthingale and petticoats and proceed to pick out a lovely bodice and skirt in a flax-blue color and tuck my hair back into my caul. Taking a quick peek into my hand mirror, I tie it along with my house keys to my skirt waist and proceed to the kitchen, where wonderful smells were oozing from every crack and cranny.

Cook, is robust in stature and jolly in nature had she has also started her day very early. By the wonderful smells all the meals of the day are well on their way.

"Morning, Mum! Can I be fixing you some breakfast?" Anna, being our cook's given name, greeted me openly.

"No, thank you, Anna. I will just have some hot tea and a fresh biscuit and be on my way." I answered, appreciating her offer. After satisfying my need for food I quickly leave the cooking area and hurry on my way.

The days seemed to swiftly melt into months, and all too soon for some, but not soon enough for others, the day arrives for us to leave Caswell Manor and close the pages of a book of history that may well never be opened again.

The morning began with a bustle of excitement. Everyone was scurrying here and there, trying to find last minute things, and trying not to forget anything. It is not a matter of just turning around and going back for something left behind. This is it, the very last moments, decisions are being made quickly, and the finality of it all seems so unreal. It is like a stage of players all doing their parts at once, forgetting their lines, forgetting their places, total confusion.

As I look around our bedchamber one last time for any items that I might have forgotten. I find myself almost running for the door. I gently turn the solid brass handle, polished to perfection, and stepped out, closing the door tightly behind me. I must act quickly before the flood of emotions start to tumble out and consume the very fiber of my being. I walk down the long hallway, taking one last peek into the children's bedchambers and then I close the door tightly and go on down the hall. I have not the time to stop and reminisce over their growing up years or even remember for an instant, any of the many memorable things that had taken place there. I rush on down the long length of the upstairs hall and I was about to run as fast as possible can down the stairs and out the door when I grasped wildly and clasp tightly to the large carved knob at the banisters top. It wasn't until I had gotten to the top of this beautiful curved mahogany staircase that I let myself pause and for one brief moment in time I let my eyes move ever so slowly from one portrait to another. I was etching their memory in my mind, for somehow I knew it would have to last me a lifetime.

Peacefully they hung there on the wall in their massive gold frames, like sentinels, watching over the great manor. Then my eyes stopped and rested for a moment on papas, and I could almost feel his presence beside me. There he sat, back straight, setting upright, not touching the backrest of the chair. His white ruffled shirt looking to me as if it was causing him some degree of discomfort as he posed for the artist commissioned to paint his portrait. A cold damp sweat clung to my brow. I felt a cold chill running down my spine. As my eyes move quickly over to mamas, I can't help but marvel at her beauty. Oh how serene and beautiful she was. And oh how she hated sitting for that portrait. The long, long days sitting on the veranda, while the artist tried with the painters stroke to capture the very breath within her and seal it on his canvas. His accomplishments were great, for her portrait is exquisite in every way, and he had certainly captured her beauty. As I stare deep into her pool blue eyes, I think there is one thing he could never capture and that is her personality or her feeling of unconditional love for her family and for life itself. The spirit that lived within her is what made her unique. That sprit is ingrained in the walls and woodwork of every room of this great house. I let my eyes slowly drift, once more, from one picture to another, as I slowly descended the long curving staircase. To me, in my minds eye, they would always be there, the overseers of Caswell.

My feet hit the flat, polished surface of the entrance hall and I knew the time to leave Caswell had finally come. I walk to the big front door and turned the polished brass handle, adorned at the top with the head of a lion, and step across the threshold onto the front stoop. As the massive door slammed behind me, the sound of it's closing reverberated through my body. I know deep down in the very pit of my stomach that this will be my last look at Caswell Manor.

Looking up I see the carriage pulling up in the circle drive and watch the trunks and carrying cases being loaded on top for the ride into London Town. Finally, everything is loaded and I find myself heaving another big sigh. I think the task of loading went much to quickly and it made me wonder if we didn't bring enough of our belongs? I have no time now to ponder such a question, everyone has gathered around us to say his or her goodbyes. As I give each a strong hug I see their eyes moist and glistening with tears and trying hard to keep their composure. Everyone is wishing us well on our journey ahead. Martin, our carriage man, helped us up into the seats of the carriage, before climbing in the drivers seat. With a quick flick of the whip, the big black horses step forward, snorting through their nostrils as they strain with all their might to pull the heavy burden. As the carriage, laden with our trunks, and us heads down the long tree lined drive, I can't help but look back one last time. I needed to take one last look at the home that means everything in the world to me. I never want to forget the sight of Katie, Anna, Samuel, and dear cousin James, standing on the cobblestone drive, with their handkerchiefs waving madly in the air, sending us off with a hardy goodbye. I watch until I can see them no more and their presence blurs into the dust behind us.

I can feel the tears welling up in my eyes and feel their gentle moisture as they start to trickle down my cheeks. I bite my lip so hard it feels like it almost draws blood. I have to do something to keep from breaking into a full-blown sob. If it wasn't for John's strong arm about me, I think I would just slithered right off this seat and be swept away into oblivion, meeting the same destiny as the tears streaming down my face.

17

# CHAPTER 2

The rhythmic squeaking sound of the carriage wheels and the thunderous clap, clap, clap of the horses hooves as they trudge along the rough uneven cobblestone road entices my mind into a semiconscious state. I gently place my head on Johns soft shoulder and close my eyes trying to shut out the over whelming whirling thoughts, that are racing through my brain and clogging my mind. This muddle of mess in my head is causing me to have a horrendous headache with severely throbbing temples. I know I must somehow shut out this mental activity that is bolting through my head like lighting or suffer the consequences. Perhaps my thoughts are trying to find a niche somewhere within the chasm of my brain that might offer some solace, amongst all the confusion in there, just as I am trying to find some place to rest and comfort myself in my mixed up existence. I feel mentally and emotionally exhausted. My body and mind are totally spent and I know that I am not capable of thinking straight anymore. How can I shut off this thinking process? There is just no more room in my brain for another question, misgiving, why, or what if?

The decisions we had to make, the sorting, packing of what goods we are allowed to take, the sorrowful goodbyes, and just about everything connected with this adventure of ours, thus far anyway, has surely taken a toll on me. I wonder to myself when this aching inside my chest will cease or if it will ever stop. I don't mean to be selfish with that thought applying it only to myself, for I know, full well, that this time of transition is hard on every member of our family and also those family and friends that are very close to us. I am sure for some of them being left behind made it clear that it is not what they really wanted. We all find the excitement of our future very energizing but the parting with our past most difficult.

I noticed these difficulties many times with the boys, especially as they said goodbye to their horses. I watched as they patted them gently, and spoke to them in soft tones. The boys all felt the finality of this goodbye. The horses responding with a whinny and a nuzzle; of affection for their masters. The horses perhaps only sensed sadness in the demeanor of the boys. How could they know or understand that the words being expressed to them would be the last they would ever hear from these particular human beings. Watching from afar I knew the finality of the moment and it nearly broke my heart. It was an extra hard goodbye for our boys, for each received his very own colt on his fifth birthday, and as far as the boys knew now, they would never see them again.

Even Big Blacky had a wild look in his eyes perhaps expressing confusion or maybe even sadness as he rolled his big round black eyes and perked his ears forward as if trying to understand the soothing words being said to him. Yes, these were hard times, exciting times, and happy times and sad times, all stuffed into our emotions at one time, and mine was not coping with any them very well.

John and I cannot make any promises either to the children or to each other, for we know so very little ourselves. Information is not plentiful about this new land that is so far across the big ocean and that would shortly be called our home. Our faith in God is all we have, and I fervently pray it will be strong enough to bind us together through whatever lies ahead.

I can feel my eyelids becoming very heavy and my mind seems to be indicating a willingness to give in to a period of truce. I think I can finally feel a little relaxation taking over my body. A welcomed feeling, for my drowsy eyelids feel very heavy. I find myself drifting, going in and out of a light sleep. I let this very welcomed respite take over for I am so very grateful that we are finally on our way. Matters that I had control of are locked away in those trunks bouncing about above me. I am so very glad that those duties of mine are finally finished. The relief I feel is very much appreciated and with a deep breath I relax even further reminding myself that this is the starting of our great new adventure. Of course the lingering question is always present; are we really going to do this? Well, it is completely out of my hands now and like a giant snowball rolling ever faster down the hill. I will just have to wait and find out what the future holds for me at the bottom of my hill.

Suddenly I am jolted back to consciousness with thunderous noises, rattling about our carriage. The loud noisy clatter that surrounds us makes me aware that our carriage is in a very different place than when I closed my eyes. A chill of fright runs down my spine at the thought we have been stopped by highwaymen who are here for no good purpose. These robbers are becoming more and more frequent as so many travelers are using the byways to London Town these days. This is just one of the many hazards our good folks have to endure in these uncertain times. It seems if it is not the Queen's Men themselves making trouble then it is some unscrupulous robbers relieving people of their jewels and purses. Frightening stories of these highway robbers have been traveling throughout the countryside. With so many people going to London Town with all of their worldly possessions, just presents a perfect time for men with a dishonest nature to take advantage and strip people of everything they have and some times even taking their lives when a struggle ensues. For a fact their motto in many cases is "your money or your lives."

I quickly look out the carriage window trying to take in what is happening around us. I can see that the quiet beauty of the lush English countryside is no longer the picture my eyes saw when they last looked out of the carriage window. The scene now is one of frenzied madness. Shouts, screams, excitement, fill the air and invade our private space here in the carriage. There is commotion coming in from every direction and it is beyond my comprehension. It seems almost impossible that we could already be in London Town but as I strain to get a better look I have to think that it must be, for there is no place else where we could find this throng of people, in the whole of England.

London Town is always a busy, bustling place, but today it appears that this ship that is to depart for the new colonies has brought out many more curious people. They are probably wanting to get a good look at us and see for themselves if we have gone stark raving mad or not. Rumors have it that many think it is just too big a risk to even consider such an adventure and to willingly go, you have to be mad. Perhaps they are right!

Reaching high into the air, being careful not to hit one of the children or John, with my outstretched arms I yawn and stretch, awaking my mind and body from its brief repose. I still find it hard to believe the time has passed so swiftly. Many times I have made the journey into London Town from our Nazing village but none ever seemed this short. Could it be the forces from beyond are pushing me faster in this new direction than I really want to go? Or maybe it is my incapacitated state of mind that keeps me wondering against logic, and asking the question where am I? I have to give into the reality that only London Town could possibility be this busy. Dubious me still ignoring logic of course it is London Town and we are here.

I have to stretch my neck to see out the small openings of the carriage. I just blink my eyes at the mob of people shoulder to shoulder on the walkways and muddy streets. It gives me a claustrophobic feeling just looking at them. I notice the small groups of men standing on every corner, chatting away, as we pass by. People seem to be spilling out of every shop door, like water pouring from a pitcher. I can't help but notice the rutted, garbage-strewn streets, receiving every foot with a splash as people run heather and fro, dashing from one spot to another. Our carriage is having a very difficult time proceeding down the main street of town.

"Where in the world did all these people come from?" I asked, speaking to no one in particular.

"I am just in awe of everything that is going on in town today. The arrival of the ship into the port of London Town has really brought excitement this time it seems! The exuberance about town rivals nothing I have ever seen before. It is so overwhelming! I can feel the excitement in the air. As a matter of fact I can feel it oozing its way right into our carriage." I neglected to add that it had also planted itself right in the pit of my stomach, which at this moment feels so mixed up that it is making me feel very nauseous. Getting no comment from anyone, I guess I will just look in amazement like the rest of the family are doing and try to enjoy the moment as much as I can.

Maybe it is more nerves than excitement, I surmise, as I stare out, returning my gaze to the sights visible from my perch on the seat. The clamor of the hundreds of voices is only adding to the mass confusion about us and it is next to impossible to hear each other talk let alone understand what is being said. I realize that is why no one is commenting or answering the many questions and statements that are spouting from my mouth. I really had not realized this until John tugged on my elbow trying to get my attention as he was speaking to me. I was concentrating so hard on everything; it took me a moment to redirect my mind in his direction.

"I apologize John, I didn't hear what you said. I guess I am so pre occupied with all of the sights and sounds that I hardly heard your voice." I responded very apologetically.

John was trying in desperation to shout over everything from just a few inches away. I must say that he is not being very successful at his attempts. The chatter coming from the children only compounds the problem. My facial expression boldly tells John of both my fear and my surprise at this sight before us. My eyes are not only as wide open as they could possibly be, but my mouth must be hanging open in a wide gape also. There is absolutely no need for belladonna in my eyes this day. They were plenty big enough from shear amazement.

The stench from the street is nauseating and I fumble with my waist purse trying to quickly pull my embroidered handkerchief from my pouch. With my nostrils covered it is still hard to breath in a good deep breath. My nose stings from the foul odor rising from the rain drenched mud. Looking down at my pearl trimmed slippers I realize that they are no match for this mud and gunk that is oozing beneath the peoples feet. I frown at the thought of stepping from our carriage and into this mess.

Frantically I grab for my chopines in the bottom of my pouch. Thank the Lord I remembered to put them in the pouch instead of packing them away in a carryall or trunk. Having them over my slippers will make my disembarking from the carriage a little easier. The streets look horrifying to try and walk on, I think to myself, as I let a small smile form on my lips and continue thinking to myself. If only I were a man, I would have high boots on and I would not have to worry a wit about a puddle of muck. Of course high boots would not be the proper foot ware for a lady but these slippers certainly are not the proper dress for these street conditions either. As I reach for my chopines my hand instinctively feels for the familiar household keys that I would normally have securely tied on my waist belt. My heart skips a beat when I realize they are not there and then just as quickly I realize why they are not tied there. It was just a reaction for they had been there for so many years. Knowing the reason for their absence causes me to frown and release a long mournful sigh.

Noticing my discomfort, John soothingly announces, "I will see that you and the children are comfortably settled in the Inn before I leave you, Elizabeth. The Whitefield Inn will be more than safe, as long as you stay inside. You know that whenever so many people are gathered in one place, there is bound to be a lot of ruffians around to cause trouble. I do not want you or Little Elizabeth out on the streets at all. After seeing to your comforts I will have Martin drive me over to the Registrar's Office and I will make certain that everything is in order and the necessary papers are drawn up so there will be no delays in our departure. Then, in the morning, we will only have to get aboard the ship. I also think Mr. Anderson wants me to take some important papers to Boston for him. I will want to have a bit more information as to whom he wants them delivered and maybe he will have a little more information on the land William told me about. That way I will not have to go to the land office for it. The land office is a little to far from my other destinations. I do not relish making my way through all these people. Every buffoon within spitting distance seems to have crawled out of their hiding place." I was glad that John did not know the real thoughts of my mind. The ones that had really caused that big sigh.

Hearing John's concerns about the state of the situation in London Town did little to abate my own fears. I tried to put on a good front and appear unaffected by his comments as I asked in a shaky little voice.

"Do you think it is a wise decision to concern yourself about land before we even arrive in this new place, John? I know you and William have discussed this subject before but I thought that the division of lands would come after our arrival or had already been done." My question

21

must have seemed very inappropriate to him; for he snapped back his answer in such a stern tone it almost brought tears to my eyes. I was not use to John speaking to me in that tone.

"I'm not making any definite decisions on anything, my dear Elizabeth. It is just a good idea to have something in mind. You know it is now the second week of June, and although we are experiencing fine weather here, we cannot tarry too long after our arrival in Boston, or we will not have time to secure land before winter. Winter will almost be upon us even if the crossing is a perfect one. If it is not, we will be in bad trouble. The time allotted us to get settled is going to be very limited in any case. Don't you think that is a good way of looking at the situation Elizabeth?" John asked in a much calmer voice, realizing he had almost jumped down my throat before. It seems as though he is more on edge than normal. Realizing this, I smiled up and explained.

"That is true, John. I know from our discussions with the others that the majority of the land was divided between the families that went in the company of people before us. Yet they have begged us to make this drastic change in our lives, so surely they will provide nice shelter for us when we get there. I am excepting a cozy and warm home nestled around a wonderful little village." I stated and then continued, "Whatever you think John I just thought that William had taken care of all of this and that most of your questions that he could not answer, had been answered by John Eliot in his last letter. It will be less worry for me if I don't have to even think about it. Surely one of those many papers that we signed was for our land and home." I left the rest of my thoughts right were they were originating, in my head. For all of the questions were what if this and what if that? Where would we find John Eliot? What if they have returned to England or died and we have not been sent word about their demise? We have signed on to this company and now we have no choice but to follow through with our plans. The look on my face I am sure is telling John of my inner most thoughts and exasperation of not being in control of our own destiny. I try to keep a calm tone as we continue to converse. John knows me so well and I am positive I am only making it worse for him and that is not my intention. I want so much to be brave and wish so much that I could once and for all put my misgivings aside. I know there is very little chance of that happening.

I try to calm my impulse to counter John's statements but he just continues talking. "Yes Elizabeth, one less thing for you to worry your pretty little head with. I bet it is packed so plum full right now that it is near to bursting. You are probably hard pressed to find one small inch of room for even one more thought, no matter how tiny it is." I am not sure if John's statement is just his way of joking with me to keep my spirits up or if that little bit of sarcasm I detect in his tone is his real feelings coming out. In any case I am almost sorry I came out of my own thoughts to hear this rhetorical bashing of Johns. I would like to lash back at him in my own defense but I really think that I should not push any subject concerning my thoughts any further. It is a fact that he thinks I worry far too much but this is not the time to counter his verbal attack on me.

I open my mouth to respond to John, I just want my statement to in some way alleviate some of the tension in the air. I was not paying any attention to what was going on either inside or outside the carriage. I was paying more attention to formulating my thoughts. This inattention only lands me in a very precarious situation. Suddenly I am jolted from my seat and promptly tumbled onto the carriage floor. Is this God's way of shutting me up? I think to myself as I grab in the air and find nothing to hold onto. I really think that John and the boys are so surprised at this sudden jolt of our carriage and my sudden drop to the floor that they don't know whether to be concerned or laugh. Thomas is holding so tightly to his sister that she is squealing for him to let her breath.

"Hush Little Elizabeth you will end up on the floor like our Mama if I do let go of you." He retorted at her crying out.

"Are you all right, Mama?" They all chorused together, carrying concerned looks upon their faces. I knew they meant well, but as soon as they could see that no harm had been done, they all burst into laughter.

"Yes! I am fine," I said, ignoring the humor they found in my situation, and at my expense. I am grateful for the break in the serious talk between John and I.

"I can not really understand why Martin is being so careless with his driving of the carriage? He is one of the very best carriage drivers in the country." I queried, concerned an accident might happen, much more serious than just me tumbling from my seat.

"No telling what Martin is doing out there. This crowd is fearsome. There is hardly room in the streets to drive." John said, answering my questions very matter of fact.

"I do wonder how we will ever find William and Sarah in all this mess?" John asked. I wrinkled my brow and wondered if John had these questions and concerns how could he expect me to have none? He is speaking his out loud while mine have to just roll around in my brain. I have to try so hard to keep mine from bursting right out of my mouth, just because he requested me to do so. It is true that John had perceived my many questions and had answered most of them before I could even speak them. That was just a matter of him knowing me so well.

John tilted my chin toward him so I would not miss his next statement. I interjected before he could speak, "John I could listen to you much better from my seat than from the floor." After helping me up he continued what he had started to say.

"Elizabeth if you will just listen, for a minute, I will explain the plans. William and I talked over all of this before we left Nazing this morning. We anticipated a very busy scene in town today. Maybe not quite as crammed with people as this but we talked out all of the possible scenarios. I was just wondering out loud thinking that maybe William might have changed the designated location of our meeting" John continued without even taking a breath.

"Sarah will be settled in their room, and my brother, if he has completed all of his own business, will meet us in front of Whitefield Inn." John looked at me and sighed as if to say are you satisfied? I guess I was happy that I had nothing to clutter my mind with and it is

23

probably better if I didn't ask any more questions or even think them. John and his brother seem to have thought of everything. I will just sit back and try to relax. A smile creases my face, as I full well know that would be next to impossible for me to achieve. Even in what I think is a relaxed state I find myself sitting on the very edge of my seat, straining every muscle in my eyes so as not to miss a thing.

As the carriage begins to slow I realize we are very near the inn. Both John and I look at the children and simultaneously realize that by the looks of elation on the boys' faces they intend to leap from this carriage and explore the town. They look like they are ready to spring like a cat out the door. They are ready to seek their freedom and be a part of this crowd and everything that is taking place in London Town tonight. I am afraid that much to their dismay, their father has other ideas for them. John interjects into their free wheeling thoughts with his request of them.

"I could use your help boys in getting everything done before we board the ship in the morning. The one thing that I need of you right now and the best way you can help is to stay close to your mother and sister. I will leave Mama and Elizabeth in your most capable hands, knowing that you will let nothing happen to them. Your Uncle William and I will return as quickly as possible and release you of your duties. You must not let me down now. I would hate to miss the ship because of trying to find a lost family member." John, informed the boys of his decision.

Their sighs of discord let it be known that they were disappointed in not being able to see the sights of the town on their own. I think that john has little worry as to our safety. I will probably lock the door to our chambers and not even let John back in. John knows though that once he asked the boys to do this he had no more concerns, for they are all very responsible and would follow his instructions explicitly. There was very little chance that anything would happen to us anyway. In fact, the boys probably won't let their Mama, Little Elizabeth or even their Aunt Sarah and cousins out of their sight. I glance over at John with a winkled brow hoping he will read my mind and let them enjoy a little of London Town on this one last night in the country of their birth. They may never pass this way again. I was capable of taking care of our daughter and myself. When I looked in the boy's faces I knew that the conversation on this point had come to an end. They were pleased to be needed and pleased to help in any way they could. With everything said, that I guess needed to be said, we sat in silence for the rest of the way to the inn.

Letting my mind ramble on in memories once more I fill with pride over our children. I am so very grateful for each of them. They will be such a big help to John and me as we start to rebuild our lives in this far off new land. The planting, building and what ever else it takes to get our endeavors completed in this new colony will surely require all of us. In my heart of hearts I hold more concern for Little Elizabeth in this great transition of ours. She is so young and vulnerable. She is inching ever closer to me here in the carriage and I instinctively put an arm around her shoulders and pull her close hopefully giving her a little assurance that everything will be fine.

24

As we pass the building that housed John's business for years and my fathers business before that, tears fill my eyes. I can't imagine how John must feel leaving behind his patrons, his dreams for the future and all his hard work building up the business after father's death. Many long hours spent both at the business and Caswell to create a lucrative business and farm and now he was abandoning all of it for what?

John's shop had always been a greeting place for old friends, and new alike. It has been a good business and his patrons have all extended him good wishes, with regrets of course, that he will no longer be around to get their goods for them. It was pleasing to John, to have them care so very much, but made it very hard for him to say goodbye. It has been extremely hard for him, I am sure, to give up everything. I must keep this in mind. Yes, he had made many friends through the years but John is an optimist and had told them he looked forward to seeing a lot of them in this new land of opportunity someday. It is true that many had voiced a hope of taking this same journey at a later time. There were many of his business associates and some of the town's people from Nazing that had already made this journey and we look forward to seeing them on the other side of the waters.

My head just keeps shaking back and forth. All of this is just too hard for me to take in. I keep wondering if I packed everything we will need. With the space on the ship being very limited our belongings had to be limited too. I have packed materials from John's store and yarn, along with cooking pots and utensils.

We were told of the small space available so I packed very tightly. I just can't imagine what these shipping companies expect of us. We are leaving almost our whole existence behind. I tried to follow the mandates given us as closely as possible but I really feel that some of their requests were impossible to even take into consideration. There are just some essentials we cannot leave behind, the minute I start thinking about this voyage my mind immediately starts through the list of what I have packed and what I have not. Let's see, I did put clothing in for everyone, yet I know I must be forgetting something. I can honestly say that as I packed the trunks I tried to keep everyone and their needs in mind. That thought brings a little crooked smile to my lips. I must confess that maybe there is a thing or two packed in the trunk that John would not consider a necessity; one of those would be my wedding dress that Auntie made for me.

As I sorted and piled and gave away things, it was the one thing I just couldn't bear to part with. It just lie there on the bed, no, I could never give it away. So at last, I folded it very neatly and tucked it, way down, in the far back corner of my trunk so it would not easily be detected. If John, were to ever see it he would reprimand me sternly for using up valuable space on frivolous items. My answer to that would have to be that I did not consider it frivolous and my reasoning behind packing it is so our daughter will be able to have it for her marriage. Doesn't that make it a necessary item I ask myself? It is a fact that I will never be able to find the materials in this new place where even the most essential things in life are in short supply or not in any supply at all. Those are the facts, as I understand them so that would be my answer to him. Yes even if Little Elizabeth is only six, and there are many years ahead of her before she will be thinking of such things as a wedding dress. I had to still bring it and it doesn't matter a bit what John

25

thinks.  He knows how sentimental I am; he will probably just laugh and say something like: "That is just like you Elizabeth; always thinking ahead and worrying about the future as if Little Elizabeth was going to settle down tomorrow and get married."

Now the rose plants are another matter.  I have no idea what this other place has in it.  I don't know if it has all rocks and dirt or all sand and swamp.  Maybe the earth over there has never even seen a beautiful rose.  So in it went as a matter of fact in several plants went. I will have to remember to keep the linen that I wrapped around the roots wet so that they don't dry out and die.  Woe is me, no time to think of it now.  It is done, and I will just have to work out the consequences when I come to them.

Besides, when I unpack my wedding dress and plant my new garden, they will be the two things that will bring the past up close to the present and bridge the distance that will separate me from my beginnings. I wonder how long it will take for us to get there so I can plant the roses?  I am anxious to get there and do so many things and yet in another instance I find myself dragging my feet.  I must always remember that I can always draw on john's strengths and enthusiasm, for he surely has enough for us both.

As the carriage pulls up in front of the Whitefield Inn, I have to put my thoughts aside and concentrate on the moment at hand.  As John had said there was his brother William standing there waiting very patiently for our arrival. He was right in the designated spot even like it had been marked off for him and him alone.

John and I greet William with a big hug and hello inquiring if he had been detained long.  William assured us that he had not, and that he had finished all his paper work and would be happy to help John get his papers in order, and the trunks over to the dock.  John was very grateful for the offer of help for it was getting late and darkness would be creeping in soon.  John gave his brother some instructions and explained what would be most helpful to him.

John's brother was an old hand at this.  He had helped to send John Eliot off on his journey to this new land, two years ago.  Since that time they had been corresponding, as best they could.  Sending and receiving letters or word of mouth messages from England to the new land was next to impossible.  Even if a message was sent from either place, it was never assured that it would reach the other shore or person it was intended for. Many ships were lost in storms or ended up docking far from their intended destination.  So it was just by chance anything went through.  Everything connected with this new place seems to be a point of concern for me. My brain just has to many things to ponder.  Like for instance, where might we end up?  Not a question worth posing to John.  He would just laugh at me, probably pat my head, indicating I was overworking my brain once again.  Blinking my eyes and relaxing the frown that formed on my brow.  I returned my attention to the things I have more immediate control over.  I didn't have much success at that either for as John and William stood there conversing, my thoughts turned to how this whole idea of this voyage to another land, across a large ocean had came about.

In my mind, time once again rolled back to the letter William had shared with us from his friend John Eliot. He had beckoned William to come to the new land and bring his family. William and Sarah had greeted this invitation with great exuberance and had very quickly decided to do just that. Then they approached John and with their enthusiasm had talked him into it very easily. Where John goes the family goes! That sounds simple enough, but I must assure you that it has not been simple in any stretch of the imagination. It seemed like such a good idea at the time. Now I am not that positive about it.

William was as jovial and optimistic as ever as he greeted us. His indication that the dock area was crowed beyond belief with people, trunks, chickens in crates, ships supplies and most everything one could imagine told us that time was precious and we should hurry right along, John would proceed with haste at taking care of the business at hand. With this summation of the situation in mind he wasted no more time.

Accepting his brothers offer of help, he directed Martin to go with William. It might take them a long time with all the confusion that William had described surrounding the docks. When I turned my head back in William's direction he and Martin were already gone. My searching eyes just caught a mere glimpse of them as they rounded the corner with a wave of their hands. Our trunks, satchels, our total worldly possessions, were teetering precariously balanced atop the carriage. I looked away quickly not wanting to witness them falling onto the garbage strewn street below and splattering into a puddle of muck.

John turned and taking me by the arm he escorted us into the inn. He continued to chat as we walked to the beautiful registration desk. He seemed to be trying to fill in the time with words. I couldn't tell if it was because he was anxious about all of this or if he feared I would change my mind at the last minute.

"Elizabeth, the town is really a buzz, isn't it?" He said, as he tried to make general conversation.

"You can say that again! I would hate to get lost in this mess of people. I don't think I can ever remember seeing so many people here before. I hope they are not all planning to get on the same ship with us. It would be a bit crowed to say the least. Don't you think John?" I questioned, finding that talking kept my mind a little more preoccupied from deeper pondering.

"I believe it would be at that," He replied giving a hardy laugh and answer to my question. His conversation led me to believe he was becoming a bit more relaxed now that we were finally in town.

True to my character I of course had to give him some last minute instructions as if he were as small as Little Elizabeth.

"John, please be careful on your walk over to the offices. I know it will be pleasant and feel good to stretch your legs after the long carriage ride form the country. I hope you can take care of the business at hand quickly." I tried to smile a reassuring smile as he gave me a sideways glance and hurried off. He stopped abruptly, as if he had forgotten something.

"I will hurry as fast as I can," he called back, as he waved and proceeded on down the street. John is so excited I don't think he really knows what he wants to do first. John spoke briefly with the innkeeper before leaving and we had been asked to step aside and wait while he finished with customers ahead of us. While waiting we stood and enjoyed the view of the crowds through the little multi-paned windows that surrounded the entrance to the inn. The outer panes of beveled glass surrounding the door frame were crafted with splendid stained glass which let the light from the street reflect in interesting patterns on the flooring and walls around us.

"Look, boys! Look, Elizabeth! The old lamplighter is just starting to light the lamps along the street. Also watch the stores start to light up as the storekeepers light the oil lamps and candles inside the shops. In the dusk of day a splendid glow is hovering in the air and the tiny windows look so different at night." I commented, as I tried to describe the beautiful sights before my eyes. I was hoping that Little Elizabeth would benefit more from my chatter and descriptive process than the boys for they had all been in town many times at night, but Little Elizabeth, being so young, would never have been allowed to stay up this late. As I glance down at her I can see her eyes are sparkling too as the lights dance in them. I can also see that she is as thrilled at the sights before her, as I am.

I hope she will always remember this special time in the years to come. This is the country of her beginnings. She has not been on this good earth long enough to have acquired too many memories of what England is really like. I do so want her to have happy memories of her childhood, just as I do. I somehow fear for her future and for her memories, far more than I do the rest of the family. The boys are grown for the most part and are on their own and have many years of remembrances. I know that we will endeavor to make our new home as secure as possible for her and for the rest of our family but that ever-present doubt that pops into my head cannot be alleviated. There is just too much unknown out there in our future.

John Jr. tugging on my elbow breaks into my thoughts. The innkeeper is beckoning us to follow him. Quickly I gather up our belongings as do the children and follow him as he leads us to our bedchamber for the night. Now that I am in our room I am beginning to realize just what weary travelers we are already and we are not really that far from home.

My first suggestion to the children is that we rest a bit before supper and their fathers return from the shops. They all seem ready to take me up on that suggestion but when I glance from one to the other I can see that no one is really intending to relax. It is just impossible! We are far too excited to relax that is for sure. I finally give up and leave the room to the children and their chatter and walk quickly out of the door and over to Sarah's rooms. Gently I tap on the door and listen for any sound from inside. I don't want to bother her if she has somehow been able to relax and is sleeping. Shortly I hear the lifting of the door latch and the door opening a small rack.

"Hi Molly, is Sarah asleep?" I inquire, quietly. Molly is one of Sarah's servants that will be traveling with her.

"Oh, no Miss Elizabeth; won't you come in." Molly replied, and I thank her as I step inside the door. "Just a moment, I will tell Miss Sarah that you are here."

As Sarah entered the room she was wearing a bodice, Bristol-red in color and she looks as radiant as a rising sun. This particular color of red is very pleasant to look at and not a harsh shade of red. There are a lot of unacceptable colors in clothing these days. It wouldn't matter if you looked fantastic in the brightest red shade available in cloth, you wouldn't be allowed to wear it out in the public. Just one of the edicts of society! Sarah is just beautiful and I marvel at just how fresh and unwrinkled she always looks no matter what she is wearing. With her petit figure I think she could wear just about anything and look absolutely voluptuous in it. The low and square cut neckline allows her smooth cream-colored skin to glisten in the glow of the lamplight. The bodice is pointed at the bottom of the front and the overskirt pleated around the waistband compliments her tiny waist. A split in the material up the front gives a very detailed look to her hand-embroidered underskirt, which is made especially to peek out from beneath. Sarah is a picture of perfection indeed. The rose flush of her high cheekbones only adds to her beautiful oval face. A bright smile shows her perfect white teeth as she stands here before me greeting me with a big smile. I only wish I felt half as good as Sarah looks. These are of course private thoughts as I rush forward to give her a hug. I do wish I possessed more of a positive attitude like Sarah. Why was it so hard for me to accept all of this? I just can't believe that this is going to be my very last night in England. The finality of that thought is starting to scare me.

In all the commotion and excitement of the getting ready for this new adventure I have forgotten to consider just how much the past and everything around me really means to me. I think I am realizing for the very first time how hard it is for me to leave everything behind. Oh my, this is not going to be easy, no not in the slightest since of the word. With each encroaching moment I realize more and more that sailing off to this unknown land is not going to be anything like John has made me believe it will be.

If only John were more understanding about this big undertaking. In all the rush and decision-making, I think he has almost lost his insight into the feelings of others, and that is just not like him at all. I know that he would never want to do anything to hurt or make any of us unhappy. His family is really the most important thing in the world to him. We have all tried our best to support him in this decision of his to the fullest. This great adventure as he calls it has consumed our lives. We have gone along with everything he has asked of us and nearly forgotten any wants of our own. I am sure he is truly grateful and I am also sure that he believes very strongly in what we are doing with all his heart and soul. If this is how I really think John feels then why do I still question his decisions? What is hard for me to accept must not be hard for him is the only answer I can come up with.

"Elizabeth!" Sarah's voice cuts sharply into my private thoughts. I can feel my face redden for not being more attentive to the moment. "My goodness Elizabeth where are you? I don't think you have heard a word I have said." Sarah tilted my chin upward and my face directly in front of hers.

"I am sorry Sarah; my mind just keeps wondering off. I can't seem to come to grips with this whole situation. I can't concentrate on any one thing for very long at a time before my mind takes off thinking of all the, ifs, ands, and buts that consume most of my thoughts lately. How can you accept all of this so readily? Don't you find this the hardest thing you have ever done in you life?" I questioned, as I felt the big tears starting to gather in my eyes.

"Elizabeth, you are putting yourself through far more than you need to. To answer your questions Elizabeth, yes I am very excited about this adventure we are partaking of. In the first place what choice do we really have? It seems to me that our husbands made up their minds a long time ago, and our duty as their mate's dictates that we do as we are told. We are very blessed that John and William give us as much say in the decision making as they do. We should be very grateful to them for that. It makes it easier if you just accept things as they are, and take one day at a time." Sarah voiced her opinion very strong and straightforward. She was never one to mince words. I felt as if she were actually scolding me. I know she is probably right and I also know I am not capable of doing what she suggests.

"Sarah, the problem is I don't think I have ever really accepted any of this, let alone all of it. Now that the time is so near for us to sail, there is something deep down inside of me that keeps pulling with all its might in the other direction." I tried hard to explain to Sarah how I really felt but knew as I shrugged my shoulders in dismay, that I shouldn't spoil her good spirits with my doubts.

"What am I to do?' I said, looking at Sarah with blurred vision.

"First of all you stop crying and feeling sorry for yourself. Second you do exactly as you have been planning on doing all these many months. Continue this path with as much happiness and good spirit as possible. If you don't you and everyone around you are going to be miserable." She said, her voice forthright and her answer to my questions very direct. I really felt like I was being reprimanded for a bad deed.

I know she is right and I know that I had better stop this discussion right now. My feelings are way to raw and I must change the subject quickly or erupt with words that might spill out of my mouth without me thinking before I speak them.

I know you are right Sarah and I will try much harder than I have been. I suggest we get the children gathered up and ready to go down to the dinning room for dinner. I am getting very hungry and the men surely should be back within a few minutes. It has been hours since we checked in or it seems, anyway."

"I was beginning to think about something to eat myself. I know that my family is very hungry and William gave me no indication as to when he might be back. He just said that it might take a very long time to get everything in order." Sarah added that we all have a very busy and early morning ahead of us and would need lots of good rest. So the earlier we could eat and go to sleep the better we would be for it.

I readily agree with you on that subject Sarah. I will hurry back to my room and get the boys and Little Elizabeth ready. It will just take me a few minutes." As I expressed my desire to do what ever would please us all, I rushed out the door.

I don't know if I feel better or worse for my visit and conversation with Sarah. The one thing I do know is that I am very hungry and once back in our room I found everyone in agreement. Indeed they were all starved.

As we meet Sarah and her family in the hallway and walked down the steps to the entrance of the dinning area. We seem to be quite a chatty bunch. It seems we are all commenting on how loud our stomachs are growling, each of us thinking everyone can hear them. It was no wonder we were feeling the pangs of hunger for the delightful smells are wafting out the door of the kitchen and up the stairway and they seem to be curling right under our noses. With each step we were truly being made aware of just how starved we really are. It has been many hours since we had eaten and all the bumping up and down in the carriage had literally used up what energy I had stored up, that's for sure.

We were standing about the entryway not quite knowing what to do next, for it was totally unacceptable for us to enter and dine unaccompanied by our husbands. But just as we were about to decide that our sons would certainly qualify as escorts, John and William came rushing through the door. With a quick greeting they hurried to freshen up, indicating they would be only a few minutes. Teasing them Sarah and I told them we could possible wait that much longer, but only if they really hurried.

"We will make it quick. You'll see; we will be back before you can blink twice." John exclaimed, and they both dashed up the stairs taking them two at a time. Sarah and I stood waiting and marveling at the beautiful massive staircase and the beauty of our surroundings. The large, crystal, candelabras standing on each side of the entrance to the dinning room is simply the most beautiful sight I have ever seen. The tiny candles that surround the massive gold base, with crystal droplets hanging all around it sends off such a warm glow. Such a homey feeling! The innkeeper and his wife are so hospitable to us and it is very much appreciated. They seem to be trying their best to make us feel at ease. I feel like everyone that looks at me can see the sadness I am feeling. I must be wearing a big sign saying, "Look at poor little me."

"This is really quite lovely isn't it Sarah?" I comment as I try to make conversation.

Yes, it certainly is, and it smells just as nice as it looks. I am beginning to feel my stomach gnawing at my insides again." Sarah replied.

With nothing else to do but wait I let my eyes rove over the elaborate furnishings and wall coverings about the inn. I was recording another memory to put in the pages of my memory book.

The clamor of John and William coming down the stairs was a welcomed sound. The innkeeper was most happy to seat us at a large round table near the window. We could look out and watch the people as they pass by. John and William were gracious enough to seat Sarah and I closest to the window; indicating they had just been through all that throng of people and didn't care to see many more of them right now.

The candle lit room was delightful, and the round tables set with beautiful white linen tablecloths and pewter tableware gave the dark-paneled room a real look of elegance. The chairs about the tables had tufted seats with beautiful needlepoint backs; each chair back was a scene of the beautiful English countryside.

The meal itself was something to be admired. It was more then sufficient, wonderfully delicious, and the conversation and company truly completed a most delightful dinner and evening.

John and William looked ever so handsome dressed in fresh white linen shirts with embroidered collar and cuffs. John's close-fitting doublet accentuated his most masculine torso as his whole attire presented a very handsome man. I was always pleased to see him dressed like this in his Schaube, which is knee-length. Such a handsome gentleman, my husband! I swell with pride as I let my mind wonder and take over my thoughts and dwell on more intimate times.

I look over at William who looks equally handsome. I am sure that he makes Sarah's heart race the same way that John makes mine race.

I could not think of any occasion that would have caused us to stay in this beautiful inn, except this one that brought us here tonight. This was indeed a real treat for there were many roadhouses along the way where John could have bedded us down for the night. I know that since this was our last night in our country that he wanted it to be extra special, and it was truly that.

The excitement of this event had returned to all of us, even me, by the time we had finished our meal. John is chattering non stop about how grateful Mr. Anderson is that he would hand carry his important papers to Boston. He did not want to leave these obviously irreplaceable papers to the whims of fate. Nor did he have the time to wait for months and months to get them there. It would take long enough for them to get there with John, and then an answer back if one was needed.

I was listening very intently to John relate how hard it was to go over to the stables and tell Martin goodbye. Martin had been a great help to John, from the moment of our marriage, when we moved into Caswell as man and wife. I know John would really like to take Martin with us to this new land. He could really use his help in this new place too. It was decided that it would be much more help to all of us if he stayed at Caswell and worked with Cousin James. John admitted it was like saying goodbye to a brother and then quickly stated that he was mighty glad that he wasn't saying goodbye to his brother and then he quickly added that he didn't think he could go if William wasn't going too. The same went for me! I could not imagine not having Sarah near by. She is a tower of strength to me. Families are just meant to be together, not all strung out all over the place. The more I listen to John, the more I do realize this is hard for him too. He like all men seems to find it very hard to express their true feelings.

As much as we hate to break up this pleasant evening we know we have to part for the night. We are all very much aware of what tomorrow will bring. We knew we are to arise very early to board this ship that will take us to our new home. So, with that in mind we say our good nights, and quickly go to our respective rooms. We are all hoping for a good nights rest.

Once in our beds my family found it very difficult to fall asleep. We all seemed to toss and turn and roll back and forth for hours. The much-needed sleep was slow in coming. The last thing I remember thinking was what would the ship be like? I could not imagine being on a ship, in that big expanse of ocean for a long period of time.

The morning broke early and the bright rays of the sun came blasting through an opening in the curtains and straight into my eyes. After a few minutes letting my eyes adjust to the bright morning light, I found that each little ray was dancing ever so lightly across the feather pillow, skipping gently over John's face. As he started to stretch and open his eyes, I quickly closed mine. I detected a slight frown on Johns face and I was not ready this early in the morning to have him be upset or something. This day was going to be hard enough as it is. Oh, perhaps John only thinks we have over slept. It took John a moment to fully realize where we were and why we were here. He knew perfectly well the innkeeper would never allow one of his quests to arise late. I opened my eyes and smile at John as he is about to smother me with a good morning kiss.

"My sweet, sweet, Elizabeth, I could never imagine being apart from you. You look so childlike, so delicate, and so, so very beautiful lying here beside me."

"Well John, what brought all of this on? You seem extra attentive this morning. Are you afraid I might change my mind and decide to stay at Caswell?"

"No Elizabeth it has nothing to do with that. I just want you to know that I realize what you are giving up and I appreciate you standing beside me and believing in my decision to make this voyage."

"John would you lead us in a prayer this morning before the children wake up?" I requested of him.

"Of course, Elizabeth, a prayer of thanks for you, our children and for this opportunity to start anew. Asking of our Lord a safe passage across calm waters. If I may make a special request, it is for the blessing of the Lord to always be with us. May we give thanks to him always for all that He does for us. For His protecting hands to guide us,

33

through all of our endeavors, in this new and unknown land. I ask in the name of our Lord and Savior."

I did not want this moment to end. John's arms in a loving caress made me feel so safe and secure. Being held like this was familiar to me, and I know the moment I step from this bed I will be journeying into unknown territory from there on.

Hearing the rustle of the children on their pallets across the room told us that our time for intimacy would have to come to an end. We would wait for another day another time for our special moments. As much as we both hated for the moment to end, we knew the day must be faced, time must move on. John's tight arms about me told me he too was having a hard time releasing this moment in time.

We were all very anxious to leave for the ship. We all had our own reasons for wanting to get to this ship and see it first hand. It was just a short distance from the inn to the wharf, and the morning was exceptionally beautiful. We all decided to walk over to the ship. We really appreciated the fact that everything was attended to last night so that we could truly enjoy this new experience with all its new adventures attached. The morning air is crisp and cool with a soft gentle breeze and the breeze is throwing a spray of salt water toward us as we approach the docks.

With all the noise about the dock area, it is hard to even try to converse. I am very content to just observe everything that is going on. For this early hour, the waterfront is sure a busy place. The area is cluttered with everything from man to beasts and all that a person could imagine, in between. The seamen all seem to be in a very big hurry. I would guess that they must have started their day many hours before us. I wonder if their breakfast was half as good as ours, for I am still more than full from the wonderful breakfast the innkeepers wife had made for us. I am very grateful for this walk to help digest some of the food I consumed before leaving the inn.

As we round the nest corner, there the big ship looms before us. So stately and so proud she looks, perched very high and serene in the slightly rippling waters. My! It looks huge sitting there. I stop for a moment, glued to the spot, watching the waves slap against her sides. The slight movement of the waves with little white caps on top of them slap gently against the ship. I was fascinated watching it bobbing up and down like a spider on a string not knowing if it wants to be up or down.

Well, I think to myself, so this is going to be our home for the next few months, not really bad at all. It was truly a beautiful ship. It did look a little ominous, there atop the rippling blue water. The ship was made of very dark lumber, polished to a high sheen. It looks as if it has been cleaned with a tiny brush so as not to miss even a small niche. The luster reflected the water and the edge of the dock on its side.

The front of the ship juts out to a point, like a needle ready to pierce a piece of fabric, while the very large section which I am told is called the understructure, sank way below the waterline, making it impossible to see just how far down in the water the ship really goes. It

34

has two tall masts, positioned in the middle of the ship, which seems to be reaching high into the heavens. All the ropes are neatly wound and tied, as if no one would be touching them ever again. Everything looks so perfect. I am finding everything I see quite interesting.

We all stared in awe as we walked along side the ship and I starred even more intently toward the planking that had been placed between the ship and the shore to assist us in boarding the vessel. I was not so sure I wanted to walk on it. It is only by Johns guiding nudges that my feet found there proper place, for my eyes are taking in all they could see of this marvelous structure. The walkway is a bit unsteady under my feet, and at this point, I am really about to turn around and go the other way. I really don't have much of a choice but to continue on for as I glance around I realize an eager husband and four very excited children would surely trample me.

The splash of the waves against the ships sides seem to very easily toss it hither and fro. None of this motion seems to bother the sailors, for they just go about their work as if nothing was even moving. I can't say the same for myself! I cannot find my footing no matter how hard I try. When I just about catch my balance in one direction the ship changes and moves in the opposite direction and I have to grab hold of John to keep my balance.

Little time do I have right this moment to conquer this balancing act, for the First Officer is barking out commands one right after another. His manner is very rude in my estimation. He is talking so fast that everything is becoming a muddle in my mind. What does he want from us? He is confusing me to no end. The Purser is asking John for an accounting of our belongings which we left on the dock last night and he wants to know what we have to bring aboard and down below with us right now. John with the patience of Job is trying to find out where our trunks and other personal belongings had been placed.

Things are happening so fast that it is hard to keep up. We are ordered first here and then there and it is hardly giving me a chance to collect my wits. It seems like the only words a person knows around here is, "Hurry! Watch your step! Step lively!" Almost every word out of the sailors' mouth is emphasized with force, causing the instructions to sound a bit strange. We quickly obey every word, afraid not to and follow a sailor down to the passenger area.

Entering the dimly lit between deck area causes me more panic as I trip over something on the floor. John quickly grabs my arm to keep me at least half way on my feet.

"Honestly! John, I can't see a thing. Where are we going?" I asked. I feel totally confused and turned around at this point. I don't know right from left, or up from down, I have to confess.

"Where ever they take us. I am as lost as you! Our eyes will adjust to the darkness soon and it will be much easier." John answered, totally amused at this situation. I can almost detect a slight bit of laughter in his voice.

I can guarantee to everyone, there is no amusement in my voice as I continue talking. "I surely hope so, I feel as if I am totally blind. I am hoping that we do not have to live in this darkness for the whole voyage. This is just an unbelievable situation! I don't think there is a bit of air down here either." My words are coming out in a sputtering sound as I am concentrating so hard on where I step and place my next foot. I can't do two things in the dark at one time. Either I talk or walk!

"Here we are sir. Your trunks are in the corner, over there, and it is quite important for all the passengers to find a settling place as quickly as possible." Stated the seaman.

I try hard to listen to the seaman, but I just can't when there are so many other things I need to do. For one, standing up has become my prime concern. It is most difficult for me with every thing beneath my feet either quivering or rolling. All the directions and instructions have swirled into a massive fog in my head. Just keeping track of everyone, in this throng of confusion, is almost more than I can handle, and for the life of me, I cannot see our trunks, or anything else, for that matter. I can hardly see my hands in front of my face. How was I supposed to find this settling place? I don't even know where I am let alone where it is. The manner, in which we are being treated, leaves my nerves more than a little on edge. John, sensing my tenseness, and knowing me so well, can tell that I am a little less than delighted with the way things are being handled. He tries to calm me down, as best he can.

"I have even lost Sarah!" I stated rather loudly. Turning to find her, our faces bump, nose to nose. "Oh my, there you are Sarah, I thought I had lost you!" We both started to laugh hysterically. At least this little comical interlude has caused us to laugh so hard it has brought tears to our eyes and relaxed the tension around us. As a matter of fact I just can't stop laughing now. As we continue our giggling I feel a lot of pent up frustrations leaving my body. I know John and William would lie to stifle this giddiness but they are laughing too. It seems to be contagious! We must look a sight with tears running down our faces. The people that are already in this between deck spaces must think we have surely lost our senses. Well, better tears of joy than tears of sadness.

Within a few minutes, our eyes begin to grow more accustomed to the dim lighting and we gain control of our laughter and stop fumbling around. I think I can finally make some kind of sense of this place. I feel for the sake of my family I must try hard to control myself and do some placing of our belongings so that we will be settled as the sailor has requested we do.

The corner, where our belongings were stored last night is just such a perfect spot. William and Sarah are against one wall and then there is a slight bend or corner in the ship with a slight division in the long wall starting down the side of the ship. The ribs of the ship jut out just past the space allowed for our family giving us a bit more privacy than it looks like most of the other passengers have.

This ship that looked so massive as we walked along the outside of it is looking smaller by the minute. I really have to take a moment to look around and try and get things down here situated in my mind.

The tiny lanterns that are hanging every few feet along the wall give out such a tiny bit of light. It is rather a soft glow more than anything. Cute little silhouettes sway and dance to a tune not audible to our ears. They seem to sway in a synchronized motion, gracefully doing their little pirouettes. It is amazing how clearly I can see now. I can actually pick out sights quite well. Hmmm, it doesn't seem dark anymore. I muse to myself.

I could use a little bit of fresh air though I wonder if those tiny porthole windows can be opened. They are so very little and only let a very small stream of sunlight come in. I am sure if someone would open them just a smidgen it would help a little. The air is so still in here and humid and wet against my skin. The odor bites at my nostrils and I retrieve my handkerchief and place it over my nose and mouth. It seem that the more people that arrive, the more stuffy it gets.

Hammocks are hung precariously here and there, and the belongings of others are tossed in untidy piles along the sides of the room and in the middle of the floor. I wonder if they intend to leave this very small living area in such disarray?

I so wish for my beautiful big windows, opening out into the beautiful garden at Caswell Manor. When I try really hard I can almost smell the beautiful roses, sending their heavenly scent high into the air. "Oh," I let a long sigh escape my mouth. This is not going to be easy, living in these close quarters, without any real privacy to speak of. Men never seem to mind these little inconvenient stumbling blocks that are placed in front of us at every turn we take. I am sure that Sarah and I will notice every one of them. John would reprimand me for even thinking ill of anything connected with this great adventure so I must once again keep my thoughts to myself and not speak one of them out loud.

Glancing around I cannot seem to locate the boys. They have taken to the motion of this ship like a duck to water. They must be already running about, finding more than enough to keep them occupied, I am sure. It will take them no time at all to explore every inch of this ship and report back to their father all their findings.

Little Elizabeth, on the other hand, is staying close by my side, holding tight to her little cloth doll her Great Auntie made for her and gave her just before we left Caswell. She was so excited and thanked her Auntie and immediately named her Katie Doll. Since that moment she has not let her out of her sight for even a moment. It is a true comfort to her; for how could any of us know what is going on in such a little mind as hers. If we thought our world is being turned upside down hers must be spinning totally out of control.

How I hope we are doing the right thing. How will we ever know? If it wasn't for our faith in God, knowing that we can rely on Him for our every direction, I am quite sure this whole move would be quite impossible. Yet, even with the assurance of our faith to guide us, it still will not eliminate the difficulties and hardships that are bound to be ahead of us. There are just so many unanswered questions to deal with. I cannot help wondering, even after hours and hours of prayer if our decisions are the will of God, or our own will being done. We try everyday to keep the Lord first and foremost in our hearts, as we strive

37

to do the right thing. Our sole purpose in this adventure is to take to this new land the very depths of our spiritual ways. We will continue to worship and believe, build our church and thank God for granting us this privilege to serve Him. Personally, I need to rely more on Him, then maybe I won't have to worry so much. John is always reminding me that I should give my burden and worries up to God to take care of. I wish I could do just that. But it seems I can't.

Well even with all my pondering thoughts it hasn't taken to long to put our belongings in place. We have managed to transform this little corner of the ship into our own private world. Yes it will be a very comfortable little living space indeed.

As I turn my attention to finding where Little Elizabeth is, my eyes settle on a tiny little form, curled up tightly in the corner, very sound asleep. Securely cuddled under her arm she tightly holds her Katie Doll. Such a precious child, her dark auburn curls, dampened by the moist air, cling tightly to her little oval face. I gently stoop down and kiss her on the cheek and cover her with a light wrap.

I continue to converse with Sarah and we decide to join the men up top for the big ship is about to set sail and we will be on our way.

# CHAPTER 3

Leaving little Elizabeth in the care of Sarah's maid, we edged our way toward the stairs that will take us upward to the deck above. Our minds had been so intently focused on this settling process we had literally lost track of time. We have no idea where to locate the men. Ascending the stairs, we make our way toward the opening and step jauntily onto the beautifully polished wood deck and into the glaring brightness of the forenoon sun.

"Oh, my eyes!" I exclaim, as I close them quickly thrusting my hands over my face to protect my eyes. I squeeze my eyelids as tight as I possibly can, and hold them in this pinched closed position, in fear the bright sunlight will once more invade my eye sockets causing me more pain than I can bare.

"I wonder where John and William are?" I inquired of Sarah. "I am afraid to take my hands from in front of my face to look for them. I hope they see us, and come to assist us soon. Have you located them yet? My feet are going one way and the rest of me seem to be confused as to which direction it wants to go. Mercy! Mercy!" I scream out in distress.

"Oh my!" Sarah's exclamation sounds as if she is just as befuddled as I am. "No, I cannot see a thing either. The light hurts my eyes, far too much. I have only been able to open one eye a mere slit." Sara admitted in disgust.

"Well Sarah, we seem to be having the same trouble as we had earlier, only in reverse. The difficulties transitioning from light to dark, and dark to light, will we ever get used to it? These adjustments seem to be insurmountable!" I conjectured, half making a statement to Sarah, and half trying to convince myself that this situation would surely get better, while contemplating what to do next. "I am teetering frightfully near the edge of disaster I fear. My footing is not very stable," I was trying to relate to Sarah just what a desperate situation I feel I am in. "I really doubt that I will get use to anything on this ship, quipped Sarah. "I wonder how the sailors do it, seemingly without any difficulty whatsoever? I am sure they must have a secret that they aren't willing to share with us. I surmise that their amusement at our expense must be great." Sara mused, trying her best to get a handle on her own unbalanced situation.

This was the very first time I have heard Sarah utter any dissatisfaction with our new adventure. She has done well to follow blindly with such cheerfulness thus far.

"Sarah, I feel at such a loss! It is as if I were in a total state of motion every minute. I can hardly cope with all this. This adjustment from the dimness below to the brightness above, the constant motion, first in this direction and then in that, just compounds my unsteadiness. I do hope it gets a lot better before this voyage is ended, or I fear they will have to tie me to the side of the ship just to keep me stable." I sighed, knowing Sarah had no answer to this predicament either.

As Sarah started to respond to my statement, an unexplainable fear clutched at my innards. Her voice seemed to be less and less clear and it was becoming more and more faint, until it no longer reached my ears. In panic and confusion I gasp as I drop my hands from in front of my eyes, and scream in shear terror. Now I had lost my hearing too. What else could happen to me was my next thought? But things were happening much to quickly for me to comprehend.

Just as I thought my eyes might finally be adjusting to the out-of-doors, the ship has taken a sharp lurch forward, which has caused my feet to break their bond with the deck. Now not only can I not see I can't stand up and I am being tumbled and tossed first in one direction and then in another on the slippery deck of the ship. Isn't there anyone out there that sees what is happening and can come to my rescue, my mind screams out in distress?

If I cared a wit about my dignity I might say I had lost it too, but it is the least of my worries right now. My very life is about to be taken from me. This awful fright that grips me and this dizzy sick feeling that engulfs me as I swirl and roll, whirl and tumble, first here and then there in every direction possible. I feel as if I am in a big barrel rolling heather and fro at someone else's will, for I know for a fact that it is certainly not my own will wanting to do this.

Where is John? Where are the boys? Where is anyone that can save me? My thoughts are spinning as fast as I am. I find it hard to believe that every person on this ship is so preoccupied that they cannot see the danger I am in. I find my voice and scream for assistance. I cannot see anyone moving quickly enough in my direction. Would I ever see my family again? Will I even survive this beginning of the voyage so I can reach the ships final destination? Before the questions running through my mind can be answered I find myself sailing headfirst across the deck toward a cluster of the ship's passengers. It was only Sarah, with her scream of concern that seemed to get anyone to pay the slightest attention to the seriousness of what was happening. Up until now all I could ascertain as I flew by the people were jeers from the sailors with an occasional laugh from a bystander. I lack the ability to see anything funny about what is happening to me.

What kind of a ship am I on anyway? Do they think that I am some kind of a court jester, frolicking about the deck, and my degraded state was not to be taken seriously? No one seems to care about my safety or my great embarrassment. I know I am completely out of control. What is happening to me is not of my making can't anyone see that. I can faintly still hear Sarah's voice.

What a spectacle I was making of myself! John's wife, in all my glory, sprawled out on the deck of the ship, tossing from one side to the other; unable to grab hold of anything to break the grasp this seemingly endless situation finds me in. How can any one in their right mind find this to be a laughable matter?

Seeing a foot close by I grab for it. But too late the ship has decided to roll in the other direction. I let a shrill scream erupt from my mouth and I force it to become louder and louder as I grab at whatever I can in a desperate attempt to stop myself and save my body from further harm. Finally I sight an outstretched hand and thrust mine towards it. No it is not to be! To my dismay my efforts are to no avail. I breeze right by, rolling to the other side of the ship. There just seems to be no help for me, I think to myself.

My skirt is folded around my head and my whole attire, is all glommed up with my petticoats twisted about my legs so tightly it leaves me literally tied in knots. There seems to be no hope for this situation and it looks as though I am headed right over the railing into the foaming deep, dark waters below. Bracing myself for the inevitable my body seems to relax as I look up to see two massive leather-booted feet standing astride, directly in the path of my head. As I slide headlong into them my shoulders collide with a hard thud against the black leather. With agonizing pain shooting through every inch of my torn and bruised body I am more than grateful to feel a strong hand gently lift me to my feet. I let the weight of my body fold into the comforting arms of my rescuer.

My nightmare is over! As I bury my head against the sailor's chest I feel my body tremble uncontrollably from its terrible encounter with terror. The tears pour from my unopened eyes. My body aches from top to bottom after its violent pouncing on the harsh wood decking.

I feel rivulets of moisture trickling down the side of my face. Lifting my hand I gently touch my cheek to remove the tears. I quickly pull my hand away for the pain is far too great to leave it there. My burning and stinging face causes me to look down on the deck and there appears a pool of blood, the sight of which causes me to get sick to my stomach. Instinctively I know there is a massive cut over my right eye and a large bump below it. No wonder that area of my face hurts far worse than any other part of me. I am concerned about all my bumps and bruises but this cut causes me the most distress.

Pulling my head away from the chest of my rescuer I can see where my head has rested. He now has a large crimson spot right near his shoulder. His shirt is soaked with my blood. What am I to do? I feel just dreadful. I am sure my attire is in shreds and the rest of my body a mangled heap beneath my chemise, for there is not an inch of me that doesn't ache.

With profound repugnance, a voice directly in front of my savior summoned my attention. I look with blurred vision for the bleeding is much more aggressive now and running into my eye. I fear the person behind the demanding voice. I am sure I am going to faint. I try to calm my emotions as I look into the unrelenting eyes and unsympathetic face of no other than the captain of the ship. His presence alone gives me trepidation I surely do not need him to speak in such a harsh manner. His ruff, raspy voice, sends chills through my mangled body as he ordered his mate to release me at once. The mate obeying a command by his captain does just as he was ordered. He let me go and down I tumble, crumbling to the deck like a rag doll. I am a mess of aching skin and bones with blood and tears streaming down my face and forming a second puddle on the beautiful deck.

Without so much as another word the captain himself reaches down and gently assists me to my feet. He is keeping a firm grip on my arm, which hurts so much I wish he would not squeeze so tightly, but I dare not

41

complain.  His manner seems to have softened some and he is much more gentle with me than the look on his face would implicate.

"Who's wench is this?" he bellowed above the shouts of the people and the veracious whipping of the massive sails.  I want to assure him that I am no ones wench, but the loving wife of John Curtyce.  Yet I cannot find my voice to express anything to him.  Trying extra hard I am finally able to choke out a few words.

"Oh!  Thank you, captain.  I thought I was going over the side," I respond gratefully, not waiting to be claimed by anyone.

Yes, you were surely headed in that direction.  It is not a good situation to find ones self in.  You must take a bit more caution, milady, when up on the top deck.  A pretty thing like you might get lost if you were to fall overboard and you would be a very tasty morsel for the hungry fish down there."  I appreciated the captains concern and also appreciated him calling me a lady instead of a wench.  Turning to the mate that had saved me from just such a tragedy as the captain had described, I tried to say thank you and express just how sorry I was to have caused so much trouble.  He was still standing very close to my side as if he expected me to start rolling about on the deck again at any moment.

"Oh!  Thank you, sir," I stammered once I found my voice.  "How can I ever repay you for your kindness to me?  If you had not been here, I surely fear that I would have gone over the side of the ship."  I tried to express how grateful I am and I wondered if he could possible realize just how thankful I am. Just saying thank you does not seem quite adequate for the saving of my life.

"Here now, let me be helping you over to a seat, Ma'am.  You look a little shaken."  The mate said, edging my elbow in his hand as he guided me toward a stack of crates near the big center mast of the ship.  I followed his suggestion very grateful for a place to rest my weary body.  Before I could even be seated on the crates, the booming voice of the captain once again startled me as he interjected his authority and stepped between the mate and me.

"That will be all, mate.  Your assistance to the lady is gratefully appreciated I am sure.  You have more important things to do on this ship than lallygagging around this lady.  The passengers aboard this ship will have to fend for themselves and cannot be expecting us to come to their rescue all of the time.  This is a dangerous place and the sooner they learn this lesson the better off they will be.  Go on with you now, before I find reason to put you in the brig for neglect of your duties."  The captain's voice rang out so loud that it echoed in my aching head and added dramatically to my embarrassment.  The sailor had saved my life and I was grateful even if the captain wasn't.  Why was the captain admonishing him so?  I cannot figure this captain out.  One minute he is as gentle as a kitten and the next minute he is roaring like a lion.  What in the world is the matter with him?

"Aye, Captain!"  Replied the mate, and hurried off to another area of the ship.  I was not sure of what the captain would do next.  His gruff voice with his stern wrinkled brow frightened me about as much as the fall

42

on the deck.  I felt I must vindicate my actions with some kind of an explanation.

"Captain, I am so sorry; I don't know what happened!  I just suddenly went flying about.  I am not normally as clumsy as this.  Please excuse me for any trouble I have caused.  The sailor saved my life, I am very indebted to him."  I stammered out my apology.

"Not to worry, milady!  It will be no time at all, and you will have your sea legs about you.  It is a bit tricky at first, learning how to keep your balance and keep your feet under you with the ship moving all the time.  By this time next week, you will be so used to everything, you will be thinking' you are the captain of the ship, himself."  With this statement the captain lets out a hardy laugh that shakes his whole body.  His demeanor seemed to soften once again and I managed a slight smile from my swollen lips.

"Thank you, thank you Captain, for trying to make light of the situation."  That is about all I could get muttered out of my half-lifeless body.  I was half filled with hate for the way he had treated my rescuer and half filled with admiration for his gentleness.  I could not decide which I favored.  Sarah had been stunned into a state of immobility.  John, hearing the commotion had come to see what was going on.  He resolutely shook his head in amazement as he looked down at me setting on the crate with the captain still standing over me.  As John addressed the captain he assured him that a closer eye would be kept on me.

Thanking the captain for coming to my assistance, John stood by the captain's side, looking down at me with a worried, but puzzled, look on his face.  I thought I even detected a slight grin at the corner of his mouth.  But if I do, he must be thinking better of making light of the sight he sees.  I know it isn't a pretty sight.  I do not know if I should be mad at John for his behavior toward me or his seemingly lack of concern for my welfare.  Perhaps it is just best to ignore it for now.  I have been enough of a spectacle for one day.  Looking up at John, I do see the tender side of him returning as he questions me as to how I am feeling.

"Are you all right, Elizabeth?  What in the world happened to you? You gave everyone such a scare.  Look at poor Sarah she is still in shock. By the looks of you, you took a pretty bad tumble.  I just heard Sarah scream "She is going overboard!" and when I looked up and realized it was you I ran to be of some help to you.  You really must be more careful when you are up top."  John said, half questioning and half scolding me.  His tone seemed to change as he chatted and looked over the bump on my cheek and the cut over my eye.  Perhaps he is more than a little concerned realizing the extent of my injuries and just how close I really came to going overboard.

As for me, I just want all this to be over and everyone to stop staring at me.  Most everyone on the ship is now crowded around me asking questions.  I smile up at John and conjure up enough strength to assure the ones of the company that stand nearest that I am not severely hurt. If the truth were known, I can hardly walk.  I brave the pain and push myself to stand erect.  I nudge John to walk me across the deck to join the others at the railing.  John does so automatically but keeps a steady grip on my arm. Sarah expressing her concern for my head wants me to go down below and get it taken care of. I wave off her suggestion as we all join in the jubilant moment of our departure.

The time had come for the big ship to sail from its moorings and the time had also come for us to start our great adventure with the sea. Most of us have never been on a ship before, so our expectations, of what this crossing will be like is just that, our expectations. We have literally nothing to be comparing any of this immense undertaking to. My personal experience doesn't seem to be starting out on sound footing.

With my moment of tragedy put aside we all join along the side railing waving, and shouting our goodbyes to those loved ones, friends, and well wishers who stand on the shore with their feet planted on that solid turf that my own feet so longed for. I am glad for this diversion for it is a relief to be in this small clump of people with their sights set on something besides me.

Tears stained every cheek and every face showed the strain, this departure holds for each of us. There is a lot of joy mingled with a whole lot of anticipation. We hold within us, close to our hearts, our own secret thoughts. I let my eyes rove from one face to the next and do not see a dry eye amongst us. As we stand in silence, tenaciously holding the railing of the ship, I surmise that some of this ships company, are sad and some are happy with this departure from our homelands.

We all have different reasons for taking on such a drastic change in our lives. One thing for sure, none of us can escape the momentous feeling of finality that hangs about us. Yes, there are tears to be shed by everyone, if for no other reason than the excitement about us as it plays with the strings of our hearts. We are all caught up in this special moment in time. No matter how hard I try to keep my own emotions to myself, tiny flutters dart around in my stomach and tears mix with the blood from the cut on my forehead and the fluids join and flow down my face. The huge white sails rustle in a slight breeze; we feel a slight movement of the ship. I cling tightly to John's arm with my fingernails digging sharply into his forearm while the other hand holds tight to the railing of the ship. I am feeling quite comfortable in this stance, when a strong gust of wind catches in the billowing sails and forces the ship to lurch forward in a jerky motion. Again I am afraid of loosing my balance, but John has a tight grip on me. The ship glides faster, and faster as the wind pushes us further away from the dock and I see my beautiful England fading into the haze and mist of the shoreline.

What a strange feeling, seeing the large mass of land slowly become smaller and smaller and eventually becoming just a thin line against the horizon. I squint my eyes as tightly as I can, without closing them altogether, but it was no use, there is nothing left to see. The shoreline of England is gone, another memory fixed in my mind, to recall at a later time, in a far distance place.

When I finally dare to release my gaze from the fuzzy line between sky and sea I find that my surroundings are more than just unfamiliar. It is probably the most frightening feeling I could have ever imagined. Here I am standing on something solid yet floating along in this massive expanse of water. The vastness of the ocean causes the ship to look dwarfed in comparison to what I saw at the dock this morning. There is nothing but water and more water everywhere I look. What a total isolated felling a person gets when there is nothing tangible to reach out and touch or see or latch onto. I am able to touch the ship, stand firm on its deck, or at least some of the company can stand firm on its deck, and yet we are so completely encompassed by nothing solid. Truly our lives, our very souls, are in God's hands.

Mr. Weatherford, being in charge of this company going to the New Land, realizes that most everyone on board is experiencing a feeling of anxiety. Standing on a barrel near the center of the ship, he is calling us together for a few moments of prayer.

We all kneel down on the weathered wooden decking beneath us, the men remove their caps and the children kneel in silence and the women cling to their families as the minister prays:

"Our most gracious Father in heaven we do humbly come before you today, asking that your guiding hands be upon us, Lord, as we journey far to unknown shores. We beseech you, Lord to help us be ever mindful that Thy will be done. Help us to share when there be but a crumb left among us. Help us to love without malice or hate. Let us strive to overcome when our bodies are too weary to attain the goals we have set forth to accomplish. Lord, help us be ever mindful of all that we do, for where ever life leads us Lord, we pray that you will always be at our side to guide and direct and protect us as we strive to do Your, will. May our lives be lived to the glory of God! Amen."

As we stand up, lifting our eyes toward the heavens, another strong gust of wind catches in the large sails. It is as if God had blown His own breath into them. The ship lunges forward taking us by surprise and very much off balance. Then as if He is taking charge of the situation the little ship sales ever so smoothly across the deep indigo blue waters.

My heart is pounding ever so hard in my chest, and I feel sure as I am standing here, God is already answering our prayers. It is as if He has come down and blessed our little company of people, and in so doing; He has touched the very depth of our souls. All of us on deck start stirring about, and we leave the railing holding our own thoughts within as we move on.

I seem to feel an oneness about us, as if all of a sudden we had joined our hearts and minds together. It was a good feeling, one that would help us to rely on each other and be there for each other. Isn't that what we are here for? Yes, it would be easier now! Why? I really don't know! I just know that we have been touched from above and what ever we do we will be all right. Yes God is good, yes, truly good! How quickly He has calmed the storms of my heart and set my mind at ease. I will hold these thoughts tight within me as I continue to walk along the deck, holding just as tight to John. The pain has somewhat subsided in my head and when we find ourselves at the stairs leading back down below deck, I hesitate, knowing what blackness lie below.

I need to sit down, for my body aches from the vigorous tussle with the ships deck. My head is so full of all the unanswered questions that are crammed inside that it is essential that I give both my mind and my body a rest. I will keep the thoughts and questions locked inside me for now for if I don't they will tumble out and like a giant snowball rolling down hill will just get larger and large and consume all my thoughts.

John's nudging has guided me down the steps to the lower area. Again going from the bright light above to the dim lights below causes a few moments of adjustment and more than a little confusion with so many people crammed into the between-deck area. Everyone coming below at about the same time, and all the talking has awakened Little Elizabeth. We find her cuddled close to Sarah's mad, sobbing softly. When we finally make our way close enough for her to see us, she jumps into her father's arms and begins to cry uncontrollably.

"Here! Here! Little princes. You are all right! Mama and Papa are here now, calm yourself down!" John is doing his best to quiet her fears. With a few soothing pats on her back from her father she soon stops her loud crying and it softens into a light snivel. When she realized how many others were standing around her, she hid her face against her father's shoulder, but soon returned to her happy little self. John put her back down and she picked up her Katie doll and began making friends with some of the other children.

"My! How easy it is for a child to make friends," I said, turning my conversation and attention back to Sarah.

"It sure is! I wish it was that easy for us." Sarah answered, letting her eyes move about the crowd of people.

"I am quite sure it will not be too hard, in close quarters like this. There is no room to spare down here and no room for discord." I added as my eyes roamed the room and moved from face to face also.

Everyone seems to be preoccupied in settling in. The men can always find a bit of something to keep themselves occupied and it is usually not close at hand. With making sure all of our things are together, my time is passing fairly quickly too. I turned from the task of getting a little place set up for cooking and see Sarah coming my way carrying a bowl of cool water. She has come to clean off the cut on my face. The cool water is very welcome as Sarah gently washes the bloodstains from my face and forehead. Assuring me that the cut is not real bad or deep and except for the black and blue coloring on my skin, she tells me that I do not look to worse for ware.

John and the boys were able to turn our corner of the cramped between-deck area into a quaint, almost homey area. With a bit of lumber left over from a previous voyage and some light coverings strung across the area with a rope, we are provided with a lovely sleeping area. Beneath our bed there is room for Elizabeth to lie close to the wall, and with her brothers grouped about her, she will be protected from rolling about if the seas get rough. We have a small area in which hot coals are placed, and on that we are able to cook a small pot of porridge to go with our biscuits. There is a large cooking pot at the head of the settling area. We were informed that this is for the entire company and it will be up to all of us to share in the preparation. John had spoken with the captain about this procedure and the captain had told him they had found it very useful on other voyages. He said that some of the passenger on

46

earlier passages had used all their food up very quickly and toward the end of the voyage had nothing to eat. Fights had broken out over the food or lack thereof and to keep that from happening this process of sharing had been devised. Portions of all the provisions are stored in the holding area below to be used for this purpose.

It really isn't taking us long to acquaint ourselves with others around us. Some we know from our own town of Nazing, and some are new faces that we will enjoy getting to know. I am sure in a very short time everyone will know each other quite well. These cramped quarters and the closeness of each family area leaves no room for doubt.

Across the ship from us is a sweet young couple. Newly married, they were starting out their new life together on this new adventure. John, William, and the older boys are trying to help them get their hammocks strung up. We all took a liking to each other right away. They very quickly became like a member of our family. On the other side of William and Sarah is a family that had lived a town or two away from us. She is quite far along with child, and I really wonder how she will ever manage such an undertaking as this in her condition. She is a brave girl in my eyes, for sure! She had two little curly heads running about and they are a handful in their own right. Little Elizabeth is finding them quite fun to be around so they seem to be keeping each other occupied. Just for them to have someone to play with gives their mother a bit of a break once in awhile.

Everyone seems to be finding a spot to settle. It is first come, first serve and the little area is becoming more and more crowed by the minute. More passengers are coming down to the between-deck area. I think we have squeezed as close as we possible can. Yet now we are being asked to squeeze together some more. I am concerned as it looks as if we have a bit more room than we need. Sarah and Williams family and ours are trying to save some space for Ann, who is Sarah and William's soon to be sister-in-law. I hope no one thinks that we are taking up all this space for our own comfort. Before I can worry about what the captain or anyone else might think of us any further, Ann has finally found us and scooted in her belongings. It was very important that she be near family members.

"Hi, Ann," I greeted her with a warm smile of welcome. Sarah had not yet spotted her.

"Hi, Elizabeth," shouted Ann, trying to be heard above the clamor of voices as everyone chatted loudly. "Where is Sarah?"

"She is about somewhere, Ann. Do you need something?" I replied, as I looked around for Sarah.

"No, I just wanted to see her and let her know I was here. I got a bit lost in the group of people gathered along the railing and was unable to find a familiar face," Ann explained.

"She was just helping with some of the smaller children a bit ago. I am sure she will turn up any minute now. There is such a crowd of people all-trying to find a place to put themselves and all their belongings. I wonder if this ship will hold all of us?" I chatted with Ann as we waited for Sarah's return.

"It sure is a tight fit, isn't it? Are you all right Elizabeth? I saw that awful fall you had on the top deck. I was so frightened for you. Your face is so bruised and scratched. You must be so sore," Ann commented, before being interrupted by Sarah who had finally spotted us.

"You say it is crowded, well it sure is, Ann, but we will make room for you under any and all circumstances." Sarah laughed, as she envelops Ann in a welcome hug. "I have been looking all over for you. We were thinking maybe you didn't come aboard." Sarah spoke and winked a sly cocked eye in my direction.

"Oh, yes indeed, I came aboard. You couldn't have kept me away. I am so anxious to see Eliot. It seems like far more than two years since he first left to go to this new place. It has been very difficult to communicate at such a long distance, with so few ships making the crossing. It was one of the last ships back from the new land that brought his letter asking me to join him. That was the same time he contacted William to make sure you were all going over at this time. I am so excited I can hardly contain myself! It is a real dream come true! Just think, in a few short months, I will be Mrs. John Eliot," Ann exclaimed. Her joy and excitement beamed from her face.

"How wonderful for you, Ann. I know it has been a difficult time for you and Eliot. Being away from the one you love is never easy. I know Eliot's work with the Indians is his calling from God, but the separation has caused an unbearable loneliness for both of you. Eliot has confided in William, many times, of his need for you and to be near you. This time apart has weighed heavy on his heart also." Sarah knew how lonely Ann had been while waiting for word to join her brother. He had kept himself busy with his work but poor Ann had been left, sometimes for months at a time, not knowing if he was alive or dead or if he had forgotten her all together. She had done well to push the doubts and fears far back in her mind and not dwell on them. She knew how important this cause was to her future husband and accepted it with a smile and cheerfulness. We all knew that Ann would work just as hard as Eliot and right along side of him as soon as this ship delivered her into his waiting arms.

Eliot had written his sister a long letter explaining the difficult time he was having, trying to teach something to a group of individuals who had their own gods and as far as they were concerned they didn't need any more. They had plenty of them in their native rituals and ceremonies. With the difficulty in communicating with these Indians it made the progress go very slow. These people had never heard of our God. The one God who watches over all the people of the earth! First Eliot had to learn the Indian language and then he had begun the arduous task of translating our bible into the language that the Indians spoke. He had to gain their confidence so that they trusted him and were willing to listen to what he had to say. Not an easy task with all these ships and strange looking people coming to their shores.

The Indians lived without boundaries and roamed as they pleased. They lived with nature as their constant companion and respected it greatly. Their thankfulness was to the winds, the sun, the stars, the moon and each held a great meaning in their everyday lives. We were the strangers and had to prove ourselves to them. We had to let them know that we wanted to be their friends. The only contact the Indians had ever had with persons outside their own tribe, were the early explorers or a few fur traders from areas far to the north. They were very cautious and suspicious of strangers. The Indians did not let anyone into their tribal confidence with out much scrutiny. Then when someone like Eliot appears and tells them that there is another God, one who is very different form the ones they believe in, there is even more skepticisms. When William and Sarah had shared this correspondence with us at their last visit to our home we found it very hard to understand. It was hard to imagine a people that did not think as we did and did not share the same beliefs.

"Is their language so different from ours that it makes it that hard to communicate with them?" I asked, trying to understand such a difficult calling.

"Oh yes! Exclaimed Ann. It is very different from our language Elizabeth. From what I have heard, it is not only the language but also their very different way of life. They see their existence with the world as one. They are the same as a bird, a deer or a rabbit. The animals of the forests are revered and some are deities to them. They coexist with all living things. Eliot had an Indian live with him for a while, so as to learn their language and be able to write a little of it. By now, he can communicate quite easily. They have such different ways of thinking. Their whole outlook is different. Eliot is so dedicated to this cause that he spends almost all his time outside, teaching them "The Way". He is learning a lot himself, I am sure. It is all so exciting; I am really looking forward to joining him. From reports, it seems to be a pretty place," said Ann, radiating with happiness as she spoke.

"Yes, by some," agreed Sarah. "But by others, the report is that it can be a very hostile place, especially in winter."

Sarah's statement was not meant to dampen Ann's enthusiasm; it was just a statement of fact. None of us really know what to expect. It has been twelve years since the first settlers landed on the shores of this new land and built the Plymouth Colony. They had many difficulties to overcome in that first year and even the second and third. Yet in my mind twelve years should have seen great strides in their community. Problems surely were fewer now. They must have learned to cope with the severe winter weather that had treated them so badly those first few years. They had lost many of their company of people to the brutal weather, fever and sickness. They had to deal with little food and the starvation of many. In listening to the tales that had come back with the sailors it was a fearsome first few years that those poor souls had to endure. Yes the stories told of families broken in body and spirit and those that were left feeling devastated and alone were hard to imagine.

How their faith must have been tested. But surely by now things were more like at home. Yes in my mind anyway I think there must be a lot of progress up to now. There would be shops now and homes for us to go to, yes everything should look more like what we left behind in our homelands. I know that my own thoughts are just my attempt to bolster up my own doubts. But surely it is true, there had to be enormous progress.

49

Many ships have gone over, and companies of people just like us have started new settlements. Yes, I am sure things are much better by now. There are always hardships that come along with anything that is new and different. But...my thoughts dwindled and my attention turned to listen to Ann and Sarah as they talked to each other.

"Yes, I have heard of the beauty and the despair. I really wonder what we should expect?" I questioned Ann, as the three of us stood around talking.

"You know, Elizabeth, that is what makes this voyage so exciting and yet so frightening. We have so little knowledge of what it is really like," Ann, continued thoughtfully.

"That is very true, Ann" said Sara. "One thing is for sure, we will be finding out in a very short period of time, won't we? And one thing I do know for sure, Ann Mountfort, if you had not gotten on board this ship, my brother would not let any of us off at the other end. According to father, he is as anxious as you, and father made it very clear that we were to keep a close eye on you, until you are safely handed over to Eliot," Sarah's teasing statement caused us all to laugh.

"Well, here I am, Sarah," Ann said, with a cute, little crinkled up look on her face and a curtsy. "Here I am, in your safe hands and it doesn't look like I could get very lost anyway. I don't know what I expected to find aboard this ship, I have never been on one before."

"We were at a loss, too, Ann," Sarah stated, profoundly looking around at our living quarters. "It is going to be very close in here, very close indeed. I just hope this voyage goes well and we are not delayed by bad weather. I can't imagine being on here any longer than is absolutely necessary."

Ann and Sarah continued their conversation and I turned back to our area and focused on putting some more of our family belongings back in the small trunk that we are allowed to keep here in the between-deck area. My mind continues to wonder as I first think that the closeness will not be any bother, it will probably give us a since of security. Then I look around at the crowded conditions and reconsider my thoughts. As my eyes rove over the mass of people squeezed into this very small area I know that some of them will mind it very much for we are already hearing grumbling undertones around the area. Consoling my thoughts I conclude that we will make it, if we all work together. When I finished putting things in place, I looked around for John. It had been a long time since I had last seen him, and I was glad when his smiling face was in full view. He was beaming from ear to ear. I could tell that he was really enjoying all of the excitement and newness of this very special day in our lives. I might call it confusion, but to John Curtyce, it is pure pleasure.

"John, where are the boys? I can't ever seem to locate anyone. They really are taking advantage of every opportunity to learn about this ship, or just be out of sight, whichever it is," I said as I smiled up at John.

"Well, Elizabeth, this is probably the most exciting thing that has ever happened in their young lives. There really isn't any place for them to get lost and as long as they stay out of trouble I want them to explore and enjoy and in general soak in all of this new experience. If you need them for something, I will try and find them for you," answered John, looking about to see if he could spot the boys.

"No, I was just anxious about their whereabouts. It must be getting toward late afternoon by now," I said, trying to seem unconcerned about the boys. John would tease me unmercifully if he knew I was anxious about their safety.

"I will be finding them soon if they don't show up on their own as Mr. Weatherford has asked all the company to meet so he can talk over a few important facts with us before nightfall. The boys will have to be here for that," John explained.

John had not detected my uneasiness about the boys and I was glad of that. I know I worry too much about my children but that is the prerogative of a mother.

"Are we to be in on this meeting, John? I mean the women, are they invited to this meeting." I asked John in a questioning tone and I am sure a questioning look on my face. In public matters women were often left out. It was just something that was expected.

"Yes, of course! I think he wants to just suggest a few things that might make this crossing a little easier and more comfortable for all of us. Like I told you before about the preparations of the meals and things like that. That pertains to the women so I am sure he will expect to see all of them at this meeting. He has made a couple of crossings already, and with each one, new things are learned and if applied on the next voyage they can be very helpful, I am sure." John explained to me what he knew of this meeting. I listened intently as John talked to me. Yes if there was anything that would make this voyage easier I would surely be for it.

"I will be interested to hear anything that will make this a more comfortable crossing." Chimed in Sarah who had been listening in on our conversation. Being that we are packed in here so close we were finding that there is no such thing as a private conversation. I didn't mind that Sarah was listening anyway. We both smiled over in her direction letting her know that we understood and felt very much the same.

"Me too!" Echoed Little Elizabeth, much to our surprise. We had not realized that the little ears of a child were paying such close attention. It gave us all a good chuckle, which was greatly needed to ease our tensions.

My, already late afternoon I think to myself. Since these first few hours have passed by so very quickly, my anticipation of a swift journey seemed attainable. That was very heartwarming for me. I do not want to be on this ship any longer than I have to. It has already started out with one bad incident. I just want it to be over as quickly as possible. I know that it will be important for me to keep myself busy

51

throughout this voyage so that the days will just pass by swiftly. Knowing my own nature so well I am sure that this morning has gone so quickly due to the fact that I had many chores to accomplish in getting settled. I must keep this in mind each and every minute of, each and every day. With this planted firmly in my mind I turn and continue to busy myself with attending to the personal needs of Elizabeth. Hearing a strangely familiar voice in our midst I look up and see the tall burly figure of Mr. Weatherford, standing at the center of the between-deck area near the bottom of the stairs. He seems to be making general conversation but as our fellow passengers look up and see him also they all begin to move closer. John placing his hand in the small of my back gently guides me over to the gathering. Everyone seems to be listening to what he is saying with great interest.

"Hello, my name is Mr. Weatherford and I just have a few things to discuss with you this afternoon, my fellow passengers. These are a few new ideas that might help in this crossing and new adventure we have all embarked on. We have learned from previous voyages that it is important to make sure, at all times, that you have your belongings securely fastened in place. It is not uncommon for the seas to get very rough and they are very unpredictable, and this can happen without a moments notice. You do not want everything to be sliding around or falling on top of someone. Nothing should be stacked atop anything else." Mr. Weatherford stopped talking as he had notice some latecomers gathering around.

When he was assured that everyone was present he continued. "The women will be in charge of the cooking for their own families and for the one company meal served at the noon hour each day. I have already discussed this plan with some of your husbands and they all agree to this arrangement. This meal will be served at the noon hour as I have mentioned. The way that you will know that the meal is ready to be served will be signaled by four sharp clangs of the bell. For those of you who are not familiar with a ship and its schedule, a bell is rung at the beginning of each watch. This is to let the men know they are to change watches. The Captain has been good enough to set up a schedule for us and will be ringing the bell one short ring every hour on the hour. Two rings are for the sailors aboard, and a steady tolling of the bells is a sign of difficulties, at which time all men should report immediately to the upper deck. This will be for assistance to the Captain. The crew on a ship this size is very small, and with any sign of trouble all hands on board are called into service and action. The children should be kept below deck as much as is humanly possible. They would only be in the way up top and have the possibility of falling overboard." There was a slight pause in the speech of Mr. Weatherford and a look in my direction. "I would not want another incident like the lady's mishap this morning as we were starting our voyage." Though not the child he had mentioned, it is very clear, at least to me, that I am the lady he is speaking of and my cheeks flush at his mention of the incident. Some of the passengers turn my way, which only embarrasses me more. I was grateful to the few who didn't turn and look at me for I had hoped by this time the awful accident had been forgotten. I looked down at the planking on the floor and returned my attention, if not my eyes, to Mr. Weatherford and listened to the rest of his instructions and suggestions to us.

"During the mid-morning hours, preferably right after prayer time it might be a good idea for the mothers or servants to take the children up on the upper deck for a brief walk and a breath of fresh air. It is going to get very closed in down here for everyone.  The older boys will be expected to obey the orders given to the men and assume the same responsibilities.  All of us have to do our very best to obey the rules of the ship and in all matters obey the captain as he sails the ship to our destination.  This is a dangerous crossing and I make this statement not to discourage or to scare any of you.  It is a fact and I must make you aware of what might happen so that you will always be on the alert while we are sailing upon these open waters.  Please remember our purpose for coming on this voyage.  It is our intention to always follow the direction that God leads us in.  I do hope that all of you will keep this in mind and keep a constant prayer on your lips and in your heart for His guidance and love."

My mind began to wonder at this point as I mulled over in my head what Mr. Weatherford was saying.  John looked down at me and nudged my arm giving me direction to pay closer attention to what Mr. Weatherford was saying.  With reluctance I returned my mind to the matters at hand.

"I will need to have a meeting with the men and the captain as soon as he has leave of his duties and enough time to meet with us.  We shall do our best to comply with his wishes.  He and his men are skilled at their jobs, and if not interfered with, will see to it that we reach the other shore in a safe manner.  This is a capable crew with an experienced master at its helm.  Are there any questions any of you have on your minds?  If so, air them now."  Mr. Weatherford paused from his address to the company and waited for questions.  No one seemed to want to say a word.  The air hung heavy in the silence of the room.  No one seemed to want to ask any questions.  Mr. Weatherford waited for a few more moments and then said a short prayer and excused us.  We all slowly went back to our settling places.  Some of the men stayed around to see when they would be meeting with the captain.

I mulled over every word that I had heard, over and over in my mind.  We would have to listen very, very carefully for the sound of the bells.  We wouldn't dare miss them and we would be severely reprimanded if we did, and I am very sure of that.  The bells would be our ship's crier.  Yes, that would be nice a small little ring of a bell telling us another hour had passed.  I would have Thomas keep track of the number of times the bell sounded and by that we would always be in touch with the time of day. He could scratch a mark onto the wall of the ship by our living quarters and we would not loose track of even one day.

Mrs. Griggs and Mrs. Seaver came over to say hello and discuss the preparations of a meal for tomorrow's midday.  It was too late today so each family would just have to be on their own until we all got used to this scheduling.  Since this is new to all of us we hardly know where to start.  We will have to plan carefully with so many people to cook for. We had thought everyone was going to be left to do their own cooking and in their own little cooking area.  We do think this is a very good idea though; it is just how to go about it.  Knowing that at least by this method every passenger would be assured of at least one good meal a day. That is a very satisfying feeling.  Some of the people who are alone on the ship will have a little camaraderie with all of us.  Also, if someone becomes sick, the rest of the family will at least get fed.  With the men huddled in one part of the settling place and the women seeing us conversing in another they all started coming toward us.  We all talked giving our opinions on how and what to do.  It was soon agreed that the best person to head the process of the one communal meal would be Mrs. Griggs.

The stores of food are kept below deck except for daily needs for each family. Mrs. Griggs right away took charge and requested that foodstuffs be brought up so that in our spare time we could get as much washed and prepared in advance as possible. She assigned tasks to all of us. Everyone went about there own jobs without a grumbling.

It is now late in the day and my family will soon be getting very hungry. Our stomachs are still very use to the schedules we had at home in Nazing. We had not had a chance to get use to a ships schedule, and today we have been involved in such a busy day that no one had really thought too much about eating. I am sure that the little ones are starting to feel that hungry gnaw in their tummies though. The children's built in time mechanism, never fails them when it comes to mealtime.

Mrs. Griggs and her husband had owned a small roadhouse near London. It had been used mostly for travelers who had not allowed themselves enough time to reach the bigger city, and had found at the close of the day that they were not where they intended to be and had to find shelter. It had not been a large place, but at least she was used to cooking for more than just her family and would be a great help when it came to putting together meals for a large group such as this.

Mrs. Seaver was used to cooking for a large group, also, just by the size of her family. She and Mr. Seaver had with them their seven children and three servants. The servants were a great help to her, and also, to everyone else. One of Sarah's servants had been trained in the instruction and care of children and had taken it upon her self to entertain and care for the smaller ones of the company. She was of great assistance to the mothers of the younger children.

Mr. Seaver was a robust man with a slightly balding head and eyes that twinkled and crinkled into little slits in his round, rosy-cheeked face. Mrs. Seaver on the other hand was quite slim and with her hair piled high on her head looked to be several inches taller than her husband. Both possessed broad smiles and seemed to be in compliance with anything asked of them.

Others who had brought their servants along expected them to help with the preparation of the meal and whatever else they could be useful at. There would be no time for idle hands on this voyage. Everyone would be expected to help where they could.

The day seemed to go quite smoothly, and before long we could feel night creeping in. The shadows on the wall of our living quarters, reflections from the flickering candlelight, grew larger and larger. After attending to Little Elizabeth and her needs, I covered the china pot and slid it into place. Making sure everything around our area was secured, I tucked her in her little bed. I knelt beside her and we said our evening prayers. Almost before her head hit the small feather pillow, her eyes were closed and she was sound asleep.

"Look, John, she has fallen asleep already! This has been such a busy day for all of us, and for someone as tiny as she, just the adjusting must have worn her out," I said, as I looked down on our beautiful, sleeping child.

"Yes, she is really a very tired little girl!" Answered John. "I am not so far behind her myself. It looks as if most everyone is going to be ready for a good night's sleep this night," he said, as he looked around the between-deck area.

"Yes, we are all a tired looking bunch tonight," I agreed, with a nod of my head. "My bones are a tired bunch too, bruised and aching."

I turned my attention to the rest of the family and seeing to their needs. Being far too tired to do much of anything else, I slipped behind the draped curtain of our bed knowing that John would follow in a short while.

I was just about to drift into sleep, when I heard John whisper to me. "Did I wake you?" He repeated softly. "No, I thought I was so tired I would fall asleep, just like Little Elizabeth had done, but once I got in bed, I am finding it very difficult to fall asleep. I was just kind of drifting in and out of a light sleep waiting for you to come to bed." I quickly added that it wasn't him getting into bed that was keeping me awake, it was just this ship and all these people and my aching body. I felt that I had to explain further so that he would not be upset. John started talking to me before I could even formulate my thoughts in my mind. It was like he was reading my mind again. "I am sure it is just the newness of everything and the strangeness of our surroundings," he said, looking at me as if that would really help the situation. I really didn't think anything would help. The motion of the ship, the strangers about and the crowded condition, all hampered my being able to relax. To keep from going into a long explanation of how I really felt, I merely said, "Yes, you are probably right," and turned over toward the side of the ship. Once John was in bed beside me and the warmth of his familiar body was close to me, it gave me the feeling of security I needed, and finally I was able to drift off to sleep.

Bong! Bong! Bong! Bong! I sat straight upright in my bed. What on earth was that? What could be the matter to be causing all the noise? John was not beside me. Where am I? What am I doing? Is that our Nazing Church bell clanging? What has happened? It took several moments for me to reacquaint myself with my surroundings and calm my pounding heart. Then I realized where I was and the noise had only been the ringing of the ship's bell. Strange, it didn't sound like anything I had ever heard before. The nice quiet ring I expected tinkling out like our church bells was in reality enough to bring the whole Queen's guard to attention. Was it really necessary at this hour? I thought to myself. Then I realized the schedule the captain had set up. Something must be wrong. The men were gone and everyone seemed to be scurrying about. No matter what I thought, it really didn't seem to matter, for anyone who had been asleep was now awake and the day had begun. We were all relieved that nothing was terribly wrong, just a bit of toppled cargo and an overzealous bell ringer.

The days seem to roll quickly by, one right after another. They seemed to all kind of merge into one. Day after day we move about, doing the things that have to be done, trying to keep the children happy, playing little games when they got tired and cross. It was hot and stuffy, and the sea breeze that passed by the small porthole windows didn't seem to come in, or stay for long if it does manage to squeeze by the opened glass.

After a while, I looked forward to a few minutes on deck, just for a breath of the fresh, salty, sea air. I would never have imagined just how scarce the fresh air is in the between-deck area we are assigned to live in for the duration of this voyage.

Time moved on, and the keeping of time seemed much less important to me than it had the first day of this long sailing adventure. I really didn't seem to care anymore if the time is kept or not. One moment in time is not that different from the next moment, and it seems to march right along no matter what I think anyway. At this very moment I am thinking just how much I am looking forward to being up on deck and I intend to take the very next opportunity to be there.

The air felt cool against my cheeks as I sat upon a crate, on the top deck and looked out across the vast deep blue water. The span of this great body of water and the reflections of the great billowing clouds on its sleek surface gives me a very lazy feeling. Allowing myself a brief respite I let my mind take me back in my memories to my beloved home. My mind pictured our beautiful Caswell Manor and my heart longed for all of her comforts. In my memory I relive the sights I so vividly remember of the beauty of the fertile English countryside. They swam before my eyes, in an ever-moving panorama. As I walked in reminiscence through the rooms of the old manor house I can smell the all to familiar, tantalizing aromas of things cooking on the kitchen hearth. I can wonder out into my beautiful rose garden smelling the wonderful perfumed air supplied by the delicate roses. Oh my I think to myself, these are the things I loved so much. These are all the things that are such a part of me. Oh, how I am missing all of them, and how I am hoping the small shoots I have taken from my beautiful roses will be alive and grow in this new land. It is strange how at times I feel so alone amongst this company of people. All things familiar to me are gone. The touch, feel and sounds of my homeland are all distance memories. I am lost in a strange new sphere. This is the first time; I have either taken the time, or had the time or maybe allowed myself a moment in time, to reflect on what we have left behind. I somehow wonder what it is that causes some of us beings to go forward to new and unknown things?

There are some human beings who can never change; they seem stuck, glued to a certain spot in time. Yet, they are happy with their lot in life, or at least seem to be. I guess people like us, have either become unstuck from our intended places in life, or maybe we have never really been permanently attached anywhere. Just wonderers, free to roam, explore, and expand our horizons. Yes, that is what I like to think; we are like a giant puzzle many, many, pieces, not having found our place in this patch work, life yet. Someday, yes maybe someday, this puzzle of my life will be completed.

# CHAPTER 4

The howling wind is screeching like a banshee, as it angrily whips and pounds with an undeniable force against the ship. The mighty gusts make the vessel creak and crack, as if her strained seams are going to burst at any minute. The menacing sounds combined with the fierceness of the rain, which beats hard against the side of the ship, cause us below deck to quake in fear. Is this the dreaded cry of death reaching out to grasp us within its evil talons and throw us into its big cauldron of frothy sea? Is it going to encompass all of us on board and take us down, down, in a swirling mass, to the very bowels of the ocean?

I am shaking with trepidation as the forces crash about me. My emotions are triggered into a frenzied state. As I look up toward the only light visible from our quarters, I can see a tiny line of grayish green light showing near the steps that lead to the top deck of the ship. A small portion of that upper deck is visible through the steamy air. This dreary dismal storm is causing a quite heavy mist to hang in our between-deck area. Our living quarters hold the thick moisture like a cloth that has sopped up a puddle of water. The dense air is stifling my breathing and I stand frozen to this spot as I survey my surroundings. It looks as if the air, in our area, is about to release droplets of water at any given moment. We appear to be unprotected from this storm even here below deck.

Looking around the room I see that every ones hair is moist and damp. As I instinctively reach up and feel my own scalp it seems much more than just damp. It has a very soppy feel to it. In fact my hair is quite wet and matted to a point of feeling like the moss that grows on a forest floor. It makes me wish my hair were not so long so that I could more easily care for it. I have piled it high atop my head in a tight knot securing it with pins and I thought I had done a rather good job without the assistance of my hand looking glass to assist me. I am sure it would help if I could see my reflection. No need to worry about it now, everything is put away for safekeeping and this morning as I set about getting ready a hand mirror was not my prime concern. Yet now as I try to keep the loose strands of hair in place I do wish I could have seen what I was doing. Again and again I must push the loose strands from my face and eyes in an attempt to see more clearly.

I feel so unkempt and dirty! What I would give right now for a nice hot bath, with the beautiful lavender scent and Katie to bring me a fresh pale of hot water to pour over my head and whole self. Just the thought gives my mind refreshment, if not my body. Standing here in our corner living area reviewing the past few days leading up to this unsettling situation, I reach for my hairline, subconsciously once more, checking for a strand of hair that has again fallen into my eyes. My skin feels cold and clammy as my fingertips brush my forehead. I suppose that the conditions down here are not nearly as fierce as what the sailors and men are laboring in on the top deck above. To be directly in the enormous elements of this storm is not comprehensible to my mind, yet I feel that their one salvation is the fresh air that they can fill their lungs with up there. Ah, for a gulp of that fresh air right this very moment. Oh how I would love just one good long deep breath.

I can't help but ponder our fate, as I stand here in our little closed in world. I watch, wide eyed, the steady deluge of green, foaming, seawater pour down the steps and into our living area. The ship seems to be setting very low in the water giving more credence to my thoughts that the ocean would soon overtake use. The enormous waves seem to envelop the ship in their giant curls and the gale pushes and pulls us at its will. The gale force wind roars on and on seeming to be never ending. My eyes ache as I stare in disbelief at the sight before me. My heart is pounding with dread at the thought, of things to come. The sea is the hunter, I think to myself and we are its pray. Will it devour us? My mind questions but receives no answer.

With a loud thunderous bang, the ships crew slams down the hatch door that separates us from the outside world. They have entombed us in our tiny quarters. We are imprisoned and helpless in our cave-like setting. The cries of the sick and the screams of the terrified children are haunting reminders of how all of us feel. Why are they locking us in this God forsaken area with no way of escape no fresh air to breath? We will surely die! I am sure this is a question in every ones mind but we keep our thoughts to ourselves as we have been told to do.

The captain hailed the men very earlier this morning to help with this foreboding situation. There are sure none to be found on this deck area, except for a few of the very young men. They have been put to the task of bailing out the water here in the living quarters. They do not seem to be making any headway against the rushing water as they perform their arduous task. The morning hours are fleeting away so quickly and there is no apparent lessening of the totality of our situation. The young men seem to be fighting an unconquerable foe. Only time will tell who the victor will be.

I squint my eyes and peer through the foggy air looking at one family after another. Only the ones nearest me can be seen clearly. I try hard to focus my gaze directly on their faces. As I move my eyes from one face to the next I am made aware of their quiet, pensive emotional state. Some look almost skeletal as we have not been able to cook any of our communal meals and even if we had I am sure there is not one of us that could keep food down. My eyes keep moving from one gray hazy area and one questioning frightened face to the next, as I will my eyes to adjust to the dark, dull scene within my vision. I wonder what I am really hoping to see in the expressions on their faces. Perhaps I am looking for some sign of hope so that I can draw off of their strength.

As the clarity of my vision becomes more apparent, I let my eyes wonder with no definite destination, moving here and there over the walls, the sea of faces, the flooded plank floor, noticing that there are no signs of hope, just the panic and distress in each persons in this company of people and the immense amount of water continually flowing in. The small drains along the side of the ship seem to be totally inadequate. They are unable to keep up with this overwhelming inundation of water.

As I turn from my thoughts and observances I automatically try walking around the area. I am sloshing forward through the water, not walking. The water is just too deep to allow a true walking stride. Not being able to make my way even over to Sarah I turn back to my own area and start putting our belongings up out of harms way. My attempts are futile; there is just no place to put anything that would possibly keep it dry and safe. The water is just getting deeper and deeper with each passing moment. My arms are left weary and aching as I strain to lift the water-laden items. I feel defeated in my efforts and I finally concede to the great strength of the sea. My bones ache from the dampness and a chill creeps through my body as I tremble in the humid, moist settling area. Pulling my shawl close about my shoulders I lift Little Elizabeth upon our bed hoping to keep her out of the path of disaster.

A moment of bright light shines into the area and I turn around to look toward it. I am pleased to see John returning to our area. I am really anxious to hear the news from the upper deck and what the captain might think of this storm and can he predict its end? I wonder if the situation as a whole is getting better and that is why John has returned?

John had no more than stepped within earshot when I burst forth with a barrage of questions. "The water is almost knee deep, John! What are we to do? What is it like down below where all of our belongings have been stored? What is it like up above? Are the boys all right, John? Is this storm, going to be over soon? Where are the boys and why didn't they come back with you? Are we going to live through all of this or are we going to die?"

"Whoa there Elizabeth, we are doing our best! Everyone is working as hard as they can. It is a real mess below deck and almost impossible to stand or move about on the upper deck. The water is coming in faster than we can bail it out down below and on the main deck the winds force a man to hang on for dear life. Every man on board this ship is working as hard as is humanly possible. The captain tells us that this is not a very strong storm. If it were later in the season we would be in for a much rougher time. He told us that some of the late season storms wash over a ship and it is never seen again. Just try and get as much put up as possible. I think the captain was right; we are in for a good one, though not the worst he has ever seen." John answered in a shout, in order to be heard over the crashing roar of another onslaught of waves.

His response to my questions reached my ears as a whisper, but I could see by the strained expression on his face that every word had to be forced from his mouth. I shrug my shoulders half in understanding and half in question to what was being shouted at me. I had already done most of what I could hear him tell me to do and what ever else he said would have to just go undone. And what was this about the captain telling them this was not a really bad storm? I could not envision any worse storm than this, and if there is such a thing, I surely do not want to experience it. I think the captain is trying to scare us and he need not do that. The storm is doing a really good job on its own.

"I have stacked all our belongings up as high as I dare. It just isn't safe to put them any higher. Besides the captain said we were not to stack our belongings. With the ship tipping from side to side and from stem to stern, it is really no use; everything is falling about. I fear they might be thrown down on top of us. I am going to put the ones I did stack, back down. I am afraid that Little Elizabeth or some of the other children will get hurt if we roll one more time.

Everything is starting to float here and there across the floor, I am trying to keep our things contained near me." I am trying to answer John as calmly as I can but with my heart pounding as loudly as it is in my chest he surely can hear it and can feel my tension. I am sure he can easily detect the panic in my voice. I feel so very inadequate in this predicament we are in.

We are about to conclude our conversation, such as it is, when I hear the snapping and ripping of the big sails that are our only source for moving us forward in our quest. It sounds as if they are being torn to shreds. The sound is horrifying! I envision them being completely ripped into tiny pieces.

Fear holds me in its persistent grip once more, as I wonder what our fate will be? Why was God so angry with us? We must have done something terribly wrong for Him to bring His wrath down on us like this.

"John, this noise is terrifying; the material the sails are made of is so heavy, how could the wind be ripping it like this?" I questioned John as if expecting an answer to all my questions and fears and yet knowing that John had no more the answer than I do. I know the words pouring forth from my mouth cannot be answered, at least not at this time.

"I am sure the crew will be able to follow the captain's orders and take care of the sails before the wind can take its toll." John replied. I know that John is trying to reassure me as best he can. I want to be hopeful but things sure don't look too good. Maybe the damage will not be too great. But what if it is? How can we sail without sails?

Suddenly my body is flung into John's arms and we both fall onto the slop-laden floor. The violent fury of the storm had increased in its intensity, if that could be possible. Liz falling from our bunk nearly tumbles atop us and I reach out and grabbing her by the arm to keep her from being flung across the floor. "Oh my, are you all right Elizabeth and you Liz?" John questioned.

"How can we be saved from this destruction? What is to become of us? How can our little ship ever overcome this fierceness of nature?" My questions came faster and faster as I lay in the slime, entwined in John's arms, with my arms wrapped around Liz holding her tight to my chest. I want an answer to everything that is happening to us. There are no answers, not a sound is coming from John. As John uprights himself he reaches down to assist me in getting to my feet with Liz cling to my neck in a death grip. Without so much as a single word John turns away from us proceeding back across the floor to return to his station up top. I didn't care a wit any more what the captain or anyone else thought, there was no distance, between us that could blank out the questions spewing from my mouth. One after another formed in my mind and immediately sprang from my voice growing louder and louder with each sentence.

"I wonder what we have done to deserve such retribution as this from our Lord?" Not waiting for an answer from John even if he had one, I continued, "We are trying to do what the Lord wants. Surely this is not his will, for us to die in this vast, wet, water wilderness? It just seems like there is nothing we can do to help our situation. We have

60

prayed, and prayed some more. Can God not hear us over all this clatter and clanging?"

John rushed back to my side not wanting my outcry to upset the other passengers anymore than they already were. "We just have to do what we can Elizabeth. Our will is hardly our own under these circumstances. I am sure the storm will calm itself soon. Do what you can here and I will go back to helping the others." With that he left the area and my questions or the answers to them went with him.

All of us here in the living area were reacting to this stressful time without thought as to what we were doing. It is an automatic mode we find ourselves in. The situation is constantly changing. We are swinging about as if tied to a rope. We try our best to make the children safe and the many sick as comfortable as possible. The sick are many as our stomachs have been tumbled upside down and rocked back and forth until everything inside us has come up. All we can do is react moment to moment and do what we can for the ones who need help the most.

Everyone is clutching to everything and anything that seems to be the least bit stable. We had come to a point in this storm where we were attempting to just do one thing, and that was to stay alive. I wonder if we will be successful? Nothing we do or say is making any difference. It is not human nature to sit idly by and do nothing to save ones life, yet there is just nothing left to do. The forces that surround us are far too strong for us to deal with. Mother Nature has won this battle I fear. My hope of salvation has left me.

With John gone I feel so alone and afraid. I am just left to take care of Liz and myself and fend off the forces of evil that try to encroach upon us. I wonder to myself if I will have the strength to endure all of this as I feel the storm intensify. I am sharply reminded of my duty to my family as Little Elizabeth is flung from her perch on the bunk once more. It is not safe for her up there.

"Little Elizabeth you almost landed on the floor again." I shouted.

"Mother please, I am too big to be called Little Elizabeth any more. Please can you call me Liz like the other people on the ship do, please! Sometimes you remember but other times you don't and I hate to be called that." Her pleading with me made me smile as she had her hands on her hips in a position of desperation.

"Yes I will call you Liz like the other people on the ship do. I realize that you are growing up now and want your own identity."

I just forget once in awhile Liz. I don't mean to upset you. I will try as hard as I can to think before I speak your name. I knew by the look that Liz gave me that as far a she was concerned she was not growing up she was all grown up. I smile to myself knowing that she had a long way to go before she was all grown up but it was all right for her to think of herself that way, it really doesn't matter. John and I will make the change she requests of us more easily than her brothers will. I know they will still call her Little Elizabeth just to tease her. They enjoyed seeing her wrinkle up her face and stomp her foot and declare that they are oafs for not doing as she requests. It makes her so mad she burst into tears. Then of course they pick her up and apologize and try to make everything better until the next time. I am sure they will get over their teasing soon and comply with her wishes.

Realizing that she is safe in my arms and no real harm has come to her, I quickly balance myself against the wall and try to assess our situation. Liz is heavy and her weight had almost toppled both of us into the slush under our feet. Her arms are tight around my neck in a death grip that impairs my breathing. I try to calmly unlatch her arms and assure her that she will be fine. Her soft warm body quivers as she weeps in fear, the terrified little girl that she is. The haunting look on her face startles me as I wiped the tears away.

"Honey, don't cry; Mama is here! We are going to be alright," I said, trying to comfort her as best I can, for I am nearly as frightened as she is.

"I'm scared mama, what is happening?" Liz screamed out in such a hysterical manner that it sent chills down my spine. We both felt that there was no hope for us. I knew that I had to in some way put my feelings aside and assure Liz that God would not let us down.

"It is just a storm, darling. It won't last long." At least that was my fervent prayer; at home a storm blew by in a matter of hours. Surely that would be the same here at sea. We would just have to endure this gale a bit longer. Yet as hard as I try to show Liz the strong side of me, the more panic I feel in the pit of my stomach.

The rains had started so softly, seeming so serene. We had all commented on what a welcome change it was from the hot, sticky, and dense air that had surrounded us for more weeks than we cared to recount. In previous weeks the air had been ever so still moving not an inch, giving not a whisper of a breeze. The air had stayed close, seeming to track our every move, like a hound chasing a fox. We could never seem to be rid of the sultry heavy feeling it delivered to us.

Our skin stayed moist and clammy, as did almost everything in the between-deck area. The children were all crying, unable to breath in the confines of our living area. The conditions were just unbearable. We prayed, again and again, for the Lord to deliver us from this unbearable oppressive situation. Yet, day after day, the same conditions persisted. Was this His answer? Were we now to have more water than we needed? More wind than is necessary to move us to our destination?

We had welcomed the soft rain as an answer to our prayers, a miracle. A few soft drops of moist water giving us hope. It was a welcomed relief from the heat. The coolness of the air that the soft raindrops brought truly seemed heaven sent.

The captain had warned us against the possibilities of a bad storm ahead, but with no experience with the sea, we had no idea what to expect. The heat of the previous weeks had caused some of our fellow traveling companions to become sick. We moved about the between-deck area very slowly.

We tried as best we could to preserve what little energy was left in us. In most cases there was just no energy left at all. It just took too much effort to do even the lightest of chores.

Two of Sarah's boys had taken sick with a fever and had been put to bed. We were all fearful that the next victim might be one of our own. The mood had become quiet, pensive, and somber. Somehow we managed to make it through those sultry days and now this new experience was introduced into our lives. Another new link in our chain of life was being connected. Our mood has now changed to fear. Fear for our very lives. Fear that we would never again see the light of day.

A sharp crack rang in my ears and I look to my right where the sound is coming from. The hatch door has slammed down hard against the deck as it is being pulled open by the captain. A very eerie gray colored light is being emitted from the outside. My heart is leaping with joy at the thought we might get some fresh air into our quarters. But the commands of the captain quickly dash all of my wishes. Not knowing what is going on, we quickly obey his orders. The children are to be lashed securely to the side of the ship. In their wildest dreams they could never have imagined anything like this. The fright of having their mothers tie them up is unbelievable. Their screams can be herd above the roar of the thunder outside. Liz's tear-stained face, upturned with her questing eyes probing my face for an answer to her many thoughts sends chills down my spine. There is nothing I can do but hold her tight, and sooth her fears to the best of my ability. I have no words to express to her that I am doing this to protect her and keep her from further harm. I just have to convince her that I will not leave her under any circumstance.

I glance up at the small porthole window near our settling place. I know that it cannot be opened for any reason. The water would come pouring in if it was opened even a small crack. But oh how I needed one small breath of fresh air. I look around the between-deck area and as my eyes search through the dense air from one passenger to another I see just how desperate our situation is. We will surely die! If we do not die from drowning then we will surely die from suffocation.

I try to turn my thoughts to a more pleasant subject but find it very hard to find anything pleasant to think about. Many hours have passed since John left my side. It seems like hours since the captain had given us his last orders. When he closed the hatch door it was like closing the lid of our coffin. We were enclosed in a coffin of murky slim with air thick enough to cut with a knife. The air truly has become so thick with humidity I can see droplets falling from it. It is no wonder we are having so much trouble breathing. Looking down at Liz I notice that hers and my breaths have become more like gasps. It is like hard labor to even get a small amount of air into our lungs. Again I wonder where my God is and silently ask why he has deserted us? What have we done that is so terrible to cause our situation?

What has happened to make the sea so angry, turning on us, like a mad dog turns on a loving master? I rest my head close to Liz's and I try to understand the events of the past weeks leading up to the beginning of this storm.

63

The elements of the weather had at first teased with little swells of white capped water moving more briskly around the ship. The wind picked up at times but always returned to a more normal even flow. Then all of a sudden without much warning it swung around with such a vengeance that it shook every timber in the ship. It was a wind greater than I had ever seen in my entire life. The winds attack on us was like a full army of men, set to conquer and destroy. It blew at gale force causing the ship to almost stand still as the captain tried to sail headlong into it. His success at forward movement was very limited. Then we found the ship being swirled and whirled from one direction to another. We are rocked first this way and then that. Just about the time we catch our balance in one direction everything changes and we find ourselves almost tipped over. We scream and moan begging in our prayers, "Please Lord, stop this torture, save us from our deaths. Please, please save us." God does not seem to hear us. I fear our doom is set in stone.

When the men had been called to the Captain's Quarters early this morning, for further instructions, they had all left in a rush there was no time for questions. I grabbed at the shirttail of Thomas as he slid past me and followed his father and his older brothers. It was no use, for Thomas was determined to go with the men. I could not detain him! There was no time for any arguments, for they were gone much too quickly, and have stayed gone much to long. Needing a pause from my thoughts I try to get Sarah's attention. Calling out as loudly as I possibly can in her direction, I strained to be heard over the clamor around me.

"Sarah! Can you hear me? Sarah! Sarah! Can you hear me at all?" I shout as loud as I can. Sarah has her back to me and just can't hear above the noise from the storm.

"Sarah, Sarah," I try again and again. She was only a few feet away from me, but the noise of the storm overrode my effort. I could not make myself heard. There was no possible way of communicating. Now it seems like everyone in the between-deck area is either crying or screaming. My heart goes out to the poor little ones; it was bad enough that they are all sick, never mind this awful noise and now being tied up. What must they think? They are all so confused and now they even mistrust their mothers. There is just no way to make them understand it is for their own safety.

The stench of the close, steamy, closed off quarters begins to affect the very strongest of stomachs. It is almost worse than in the beginning when everyone was seasick from not being used to the motion of the ship. I thought that was the worst it could ever get. Boy was I ever wrong! At least then we could keep up with the mopping up, but not now; the floor of our tiny living space is a mass of mixed liquids, sloshing from side to side as the ship gets tossed about. The smell permeates our nostrils. The slop jars had not been emptied for days except the ones that have spilled onto the deck and now ran mixed with other bodily fluids in a swirl about us. We are standing in ankle deep muck. The conditions in here are much to our making but defiantly not to our liking.

"Sarah!" I tried one last time to get her attention. Putting as much strength behind my shout as possible, I yell out once again.

64

"Elizabeth, is that you calling me?" Sarah is finally answering back. She probably noticed my frantic gestures more than hearing my voice.

"Yes! Is everything going alright with you?" I responded as loudly as I can.

"I think so; the fever has just about left the boys but this storm is about to make us all sick. I wonder how the men are doing?" Sarah yelled back. I could only hear about every other word.

"I wonder too," I shouted back. It was no use; there was just no way to carry on a conversation with all this noise. I just wanted to know that they were all right anyway, and I had very little energy to waste.

The furious, relentless storm just keeps lashing away. It has been seven straight days. Some of the passengers have scratched marks into the sidewalls of the ship so they can keep track of every day this vicious storm is with us. I wonder to myself, what is the use, who will ever see them down at the bottom of the ocean? And that is where we seem to be headed. The sooner it all ends the better and praise be to God, if I or anyone else survives this horrid ordeal. As far as I am concerned the storm never seems to give us a moment's peace. My ears actually hurt from all the booming, creaking, smashing, crashing hideous sounds going on around me. I want to give up, give in and have some peace once again.

Almost simultaneously with my thoughts comes a quietness around me that seems quiet strange. I momentarily feel I may have lost my hearing. Not a sound is coming from beyond the walls of the ship, not a stir of any motion is penetrating the air. This must be the end of the world. At least the end of my world as I know it now. Perhaps my hasty silent prayers have finally been answered.

Not knowing what to do or what to think anymore, I give myself body and soul, into the hands of God. I am much to tired and desperate to care what happens to me. I closed my eyes in complete surrender to whatever my fate is to be. All I can do now is just cling to Liz and pray, prayer after prayer.

It took me some time to realize that my body was tightly tied in knots and my eyes desperately crunched closed. I was clutching so tightly to Liz that I was literally squeezing the life out of her.

My mind is trying to comprehend the recent state of our existence. Do I dared open my eyes and look at the others around me. We were all struck dumb with fear. The absence of the noise has caused all of us to catch our breath and has lessoned the cries of the children.

As we listened more carefully the creaking of the ship was still audible and the wind was still blowing but nothing like it was and we were very grateful for that. The smell in our area sickened me but I had to put that aside for by some small grace of God we were still afloat. The prayers on our lips now were that this storm was really over for good.

Just like that, a simple click of the fingers and it was gone. As meek as a kitten, the storm disappeared, slipping from our sight, swiftly and quietly, leaving us shaken and ill, but still whole.

The hatch door was opened and we could once again see the blue sky above. The great clouds, still looking threatening, soon scattered and slowly drifted toward the horizon. The hot, bright scalding sun returned and the muggy, humid air, once again, hung close about us. We knelt on bended knees, in the slimy mucus of our own making, and gave thanks to God above. We had truly been spared!

We had not seen the men folk for most of the week, and we were happy for any time they could spare us. There was still a lot that had to be done. When the captain finally had time to come and talk to us he advised us of what damage the storm has caused and it was far greater than any or us could have imagined. The stores below had been thrown and tossed about so badly that the men were spending almost every waking hour getting everything back in place. The main hold below our deck had taken on an enormous amount of water, and it had to be continually bailed out. This required many hours of arduous backbreaking work. Many of the animals had drown and were tossed out to sea, fodder for the fish.

We could not be sure of just exactly what our losses were. Captain Rylick had taken a quick perusal of the supplies and stores. He assessed the damage to the ship and determined it was minimal. The repairs can be taken care of by the crew without too much loss of time. Our stores are another matter, as are our personal belongings that were put in the lower holds of the ship. We would not know until our docking in Boston Harbor just what has survived and is worth keeping and what is not any good and will have to be thrown out. We are all discouraged at that bit of information but when compared to the loss of lives it is little of nothing. We had not lost a single person in our Company and none of the crew had been lost or hurt.

Realizing how very blessed we were, everyone set out to do their part in getting our living quarters back in some semblance of order. Busy hands are keeping our troubled minds from thinking on the, what could have been. We all started to pitch in wherever needed.

As I watched John, William and Thomas, I thought they were really enjoying the dangers of this voyage far too much. As a matter of fact, they don't seem to see any danger at all. Every time they returned from a task, they have a new tale of a ship's life to tell, mimicking the sailors as if they were their shadows. The women in contrast wash the soiled clothing in salt water, as the fresh water supply is very low. The cloths dry stiff with white salt deposits clinging to them. They will be harsh to our skin when we put them on, but clean.

The fun the boys and John are having is wearing heavy on my nerves. The excitement for me has turned to nothing but work and drudgery. I find Thomas, almost too good at this ships life. He has taken to this sailor's life far too eagerly. He is fascinated with every little detail of the ship, the ships crew, and the daily routine. Everything about the ship, the ocean and this voyage is of interest to him. His questions are endless. He has even inquired of the captain as to how he can learn more about sailing.

The captain told John of Thomas's interest, and they agreed that a little learning in the ways of the sea could not be harmful to him. He will be like a cabin boy. That was how John explained it to me. That didn't sound too bad; what could that hurt? Might even be fun for him since he seemed to love it so much! John and I agreed that Captain Rylick could ask Thomas if he wanted a position as cabin boy for the rest of the voyage.

When Captain Rylick finally got around to asking Thomas to take part in more of the duties aboard, to say he was excited would be an understatement. His eyes lit up brighter than the stars in the black night sky, and he wore a grin upon his face as broad as the ocean we travel upon. I agree with John, that this will help him to pass his time while aboard.

Little do I realize that no matter how hard I try to hold on to Thomas or how much I try to convince myself that this is just a passing fancy, I know instinctively that I am loosing my young son to the call of the sea. Each day that passes lets a little more of the salt air seep deep into his veins. He takes on the likeness of every sailor he happens to work with. Even at times, pretending to be the captain of the vessel himself. Cautioning him that this, being a cabin boy, was a very temporary situation doesn't seem to deter him in the least. He is truly enjoying every moment and everything he does. It is a challenge to learn everything quickly and exact. It is obvious from his actions that Thomas has taken to the life of a cabin boy quite easily.

I could not let my thought dwell on Thomas any longer for it is that time of day which requires a meal to be fixed. As evening approaches, I open and look in our little trunk. Searching the contents for something to nourish our bodies. I find very little, but there are a few of Cook's biscuits left in the tin. They are a bit hard, spotted with green/blue mold yet we will eat them with gratitude and relish their taste as if they had been freshly baked only hours ago in the old brick oven at Caswell Manor. They will taste good with a bit of broth and a piece of cheese. Our daily needs will be taken care of once again, as our Lord has promised. The supplies are very low, and not wanting to risk running out, rations have been set up. It doesn't really matter what we eat, even the daily meal cooked by the women has become a mere salted broth looking more like hot water than stew. There are a few greens being carefully doled out.

No matter what the food, I still consider this mealtime our special time. Time for us all to talk over what this day has meant to us. I really cherish it, realizing that time is not standing still. In the not too distant future, the boys will be on their own, with families and farms to care for. I will miss little privileges like these I am enjoying today.

As I listen intently to the talk around our family cooking area, I can't help but smile, for the feeling of love and compatibility oozes from each member. The chatter tonight seems to be mostly about the clean up from the storm and who is sick and who is getting better. Just general talk, nothing but communing with each other. What could be better than this, I thought to myself.

67

Clinging to the serenity and love that enveloped us as we sat close about, laughing, talking and eating, I neglected the apparent fact that Thomas had been exceptionally quiet for quite some time. He seemed to be mulling something over in his mind. It was with more force than he really intended that the next few words came flying out of his mouth. He surely had decided to take part in our family conversation with gusto. I will never be able to forget how profoundly his statement emerged from his mouth or how outlandish his announcement sounded to my ears.

"You know, someday I will own a ship like this, only much bigger. A ship that can sail in any seas, setting high atop the white capped waves, with big white sails bellowing out, saluting to the wind as it passes by!" Thomas's surety in his statement caused me to lose my want for food.

A chill creeps into my bones and tiny dots of perspiration bead upon my brow, for something tells me that this is not an idle dream of a young boy. No, indeed it is no dream; it is the goal of a man who would stop at nothing to obtain that goal. In my thoughts I imagine the great sea god, Neptune, pulling hard in one direction as I pull in the other, and Thomas is, in the middle, and somehow I know who will win. For as I look into the eyes of Thomas, I see a look of determination and adventure.

The salt has already reached his heart and he wears that wanting look, the one that says: I want to somehow capture the unknowns of the sea, explore its depths, and rest on the sands that it brushes against. The tales told by the sailors have found a home in Thomas's imagination, and no talking at this time would or could change his mind. Any arguments only seem to fuel the fires that burn within him. He revels in the thoughts of far off places, of danger and intrigue. The seeds have already been planted, and the only thing left for them to do, is to grow. I must keep my thoughts to myself and try to get my mind off the subject. That didn't seem to work for back my mind went to thinking again. Had this whole voyage been a mistake? If we hadn't come, Thomas would not have known of the sea and its mysteries.

As I start cleaning up around our area and getting Liz ready for bed I attempt to keep the thoughts of Thomas's future out of my thoughts. Looking around the ship I notice the lights along the wall. They are getting very dim and look as if they are ready to go out. The candles are burned down to little nubbins of almost nothing. My thoughts and movements have been so preoccupied that after putting Liz down the boys had curled up on their pallets around her and they were all fast asleep. They had experienced a long hard day. Their pallets, must feel awfully good to them.

As I stop my fidgeting about, I flop myself down beside John atop the trunk and take a big deep breath. There is no need to speak a word for we are very much aware of each other's thoughts and the thoughts of most of the people around us. We are all exhausted, weary travelers. This long voyage has taken its toll on this little company of ours. The enthusiasm has been knocked out of us by that destructive storm and now as we slowly drift on toward our final destination, the little ship, like a crown, setting atop a huge, green-blue pillow of water, seems like a mirage in my mind.

68

We have been afloat for a little over a month and a half now and who knows how much longer it will take for us to reach land? Who, but God, knows for sure where we are? The way we were tossed and blown about, we could be most anywhere. I had very little confidence left in me at this point.

It had been a very long time indeed nearing two months-without even sighting the smallest speck of land. How much longer could it possibly take?

I wonder if we are ever going to get anywhere. What if we had been turned around? We only had the captain's word to go on. What if that bad storm had blown us way off course? Was this our destiny, to drift forever, never setting foot on land again?

"How much longer will we be on this ship? Oh John, what is to become of us?" I cried out. The words came bursting forth from my mouth, sounding almost in a panic. John tossed me a sharp glance. My thoughts had been so strong, I felt as if he had been in on them. John, sensing the urgency in my voice, didn't inquire as to what was the matter with me, he just answered: "It really shouldn't be too much longer. You must not shout out like that Elizabeth. Captain Rylick assured us, in our meeting today, that we were on course and should be sighting land just any time."

"Land, what does it really look like? It has been so long," I said wistfully. The thoughts that had been rolling around in my head could not be contained any more. I am just too full of questions that there never seems to be a good answer for.

"Yes, it has been a long voyage Elizabeth. It will be good to touch God's good soil again-to take a big hand full and let it sift slowly through my fingers," John responded, with a distant look in his eyes. I could tell that he, too, was feeling the effects of the voyage. He longed to plant his fields, get us settled in a home and once again be a productive farmer and father. Right at this moment, we would both welcome the sight of land, any land.

The women had been kept extremely busy since the storm, for as badly as the lower decks were disturbed, so was our living area. It had taken many hours of cleaning to remove the odors of the sick, but with a few days of having a nice sea breeze and being able to open the small portholes, the air finally gave way to semi-freshness. Surely it could not be much longer!

"Oh, John, please let this be over. I don't think I can endure another night upon this water," I exclaimed, knowing I should not say such things, as soon as the words left my mouth.

"Elizabeth, don't talk like that; others will hear you. It just takes a small seed of thought to get everyone down. We are all a tired and weary lot at this point," John admonished.

"I can't help myself, John; I seem to have forgotten all the reasons we had for this whole undertaking." I tried to explain as best I could.

69

"Elizabeth, darling, let's go up on deck and get some fresh air. I think a walk about the deck will do you good. You have been cooped up down here far too long," John said, hoping that a bit of fresh air would help my mood.

"Thank you, John! That sounds so nice. You always know just the right thing to do," I said, giving him credit for understanding.

"Not always, but it is nice of you to say so, anyway," he answered with a half shy smile on his lips. As we mounted the steps and walked out onto the upper deck, my first action was a long, deep appreciated breath of fresh cool, night air. We walked along the rail, listening to the wind blowing about us, and the flapping of the big sails above us. I looked up to watch the rustling sails flying against the deep, dark, midnight sky. The ladies had mended the torn areas and they looked very used, but strong. The stars in the heavens, twinkling like a million jewels, looked as if an artist had flung them carelessly upon a darkened canvas letting them fall where they may. "John!" I whispered. "Yes, Elizabeth!" Came his soft answer.

"I have missed our special times together. I miss the privacy of our bedchamber at home in Caswell. I miss you close by my side." I sighed; as I looked around to make sure no one was standing close to hear my confession of love to my husband. "And I, too!" John responded, taking my hand in his.

"Really, John? Do you miss being close to me, as much as I miss being close to you?" I inquired, excited to have him admit his feelings to me. It was nice to be reassured of John's feelings for me even though I did not ever doubt him.

"What kind of question is that, Elizabeth? You are what keeps me going, you give me the very reasons to endure and strive to accomplish whatever God's will is for me in this life," John whispered, as he pulled me close to his body and leaned against the polished ship's rail. No other words were needed. It was enough to just be together in each other's arms, enjoying the silence of the night and the beautiful glow of the bright moon above, as it shimmered and glistened on John's dark hair.

"Oh, John! I love you so!" I exclaimed, looking into his deep-set eyes.

"I pray, you always will, my darling!" He whispered into my ear as he took my hand in his, and we slowly traversed around the ship once more. We paused often on our short walk around the deck to take in and enjoy the fresh coolness of the clear night air.

"I hate to think of going down below again, don't you John?" I ask, hoping he would want to stay up on deck just a little longer. He didn't answer; he just kept walking. When we reached the steps, we again hesitated, not quite ready to give up our moment together; we delayed our return to the between-deck area as long as we could. It was really quite late and most everyone has gone to sleep by the time we descend back into the closeness of our living area.

Slowly we walk back to our sleeping family, doing our best not to disturb the others in the area. It seemed to be so terribly quiet in the living area. The hammocks were swaying as the ship rolled from side to side. The people asleep on the floor seemed unaware of our movements as they dream of having better times ahead. I ready myself for bed as John tucks the curtain tightly about the corners of our bed. Leaning on one elbow, he gives me that familiar little crocked grin. The one that always signaled he was in the mood for more than just a quick good night kiss.

"John, this is hardly the place!" I exclaimed, responding to his look.

"Why, whatever are you talking about, Elizabeth dear?" John replied, trying to seem coy with his thoughts.

"You know perfectly well what I'm talking about, John Curtyce. We have been married far too long for you to try and fool me! I know you and your little smile. That twinkle in your eye is a dead give away, John Curtyce, and you better be for getting thoughts of that sort right out of that head of yours," I said in a soft teasing voice.

"Now, what thoughts would that be, my darling Elizabeth?" John retorted, seeming to be having fun at my expense. Knowing that restraint at this moment was the best decision either of us could make.

John and I fall asleep, entwined in the warmth of our special embrace. When daylight finally shows through the little porthole, I find myself still wrapped in his strong, muscular grasp. He is so handsome and I do love him so very much. I let my mind wonder to years past and other times of great enjoyment. Oh how I love this handsome John Curtyce, even after all these trials and tribulations he is and always will be the love of my life. Our conversation becomes a whisper, as most of the company is still fast asleep.

"John, I will never be able to deny you a thing. I am completely lost, entwined in this spell of yours," I confess!

"I truly hope so, for I would never want you to lose your love for me, for I know I shall never lose mine for you," John whispered. I smiled up and squirmed out of his clutches and proceeded to get presentable.

The rustle of the children below gave us a start, and we quickly emerged from our sleeping spot. It was difficult to interrupt this intimate moment, but the day had begun and was in full swing. I found it sad that our special moments together had to be so brief and secretive. We had never experienced, up until now, a separation of any kind in our married life. Our days had always been filled with togetherness. John would do his chores and I mine but we always seemed to have a few moments in each and every day to share ideas and have small talk between just the two of us. I suppose this was just another reason for me to dislike this voyage. It is just keeping John and me apart in so many ways and I don't like it. I suppose no one on board this ship likes the situation they find themselves in, but what can we do about it now?

"Mama, I'm hungry," moaned Liz. "Well, I guess that means that this day has to get rolling along." John I stated, with a little crinkled smile. "Just a few minutes Liz, and Mama will be up and fix us all a bite to eat. Are your brothers awake yet?" I inquired.

"Yes, mama Thomas has already gotten up and so has William," Liz stated, sounding quite grown up for her age.

"Where is John Jr., I ask as I slipped a skirt over my shift and brushed my hair back with my hands.

"He is just getting his cloths on, now," Liz, informed us, seeming her same happy little self.

"John, are you already dressed?" I asked just to make sure. Sometimes he seemed a lot harder than that to get up in the mornings, here lately. All their hard work was catching up with them. They really didn't get the rest here on the ship that they were used to. At home they were busy, but nothing like this. It will not be getting any better either. I foresee the future as a very hard one.

"Yes, Mama, I have stirred the coals and the warming area is ready," replied John Jr.

"Thank you son! I will be fixing us some hot mush shortly," I said, nudging John to hurry and get dressed.

"Yum, that sounds good; I feel extra hungry this morning. Could we have some biscuits with it, with some fresh churned butter?" Asked John Jr.

"John, you are making us all hungry. It won't be long now until we can have some of the things we have missed so much.

This voyage has made us appreciate those little things we took for granted, hasn't it?" John answered his son as he slipped from our sleeping area with a broad smile on his face. I felt like private conversations on this ship were impossible. John and I would have to be more discrete when expressing private thoughts.

"It sure has, Papa, it sure has," said Liz, as she jumped in on the conversation.

When Thomas and William returned, the meal was ready. We sat down and said our prayer of thanks for God's loving kindnesses and His watchful care through the night. We prayed for His loving care through this, another day aboard our floating home. Our mealtime was as enjoyable as ever. The chatter seemed to take on a special air this fine morning. Everyone must have had a nice sleep last night, for all were in good sprits. There was an extra something about everyone's mood. Maybe it had something to do with the captain's announcement that land should be sighted at any time. Everyone was anxious to go to the upper deck and be the one to sight it first. Even the little children were scurrying about,

72

without much fuss.  Would this be the day?  Would this be that long awaited day?  The words would be like music to our ears. "Land!"  "Land!"

All day long, most of the company sat atop crates or barrels looking, searching, and seeking for that tiny, dark dot of land on the horizon.  There were many sighting throughout the day but most of them were figments of the imagination.  That did not keep us from continually letting our eyes search the vastness of the ocean between the ship and the edge of nowhere for the elusive land mass.  Very much to our dismay, there was just no land in sight.  The anticipation of all of us on board heightened, as the afternoon grew further and further along towards evening.  Our eyes blurred from the constant staring across the glassy blue surface of the water.  No matter how much we wanted to see land there was just none out there.  Hour after hour we waited and watched and still nothing.  Watching the little whitecaps upon the surface of the ocean was mesmerizing.  As the wind whipped and puffed and filled the big sails we glided along almost effortlessly.  Was this new land really out there?  Doubts and disappointment was felt so deeply by everyone. Finally we all started ascending to the between-deck area and we all went to bed with a real heaviness in our hearts.

Several more days passed.  The spirits of the little company of people became more and more depressed.  We just couldn't help ourselves anymore; this had to come to an end, it just had to.  Even the sight of the graceful dolphins jumping from the water like the acrobats that perform before the King were not appreciated. There was nothing that could amuse us or cause us joy like the sight of land.  We waited and watched until our eyes grew tired of the glare from the sun on the water.

The time of day I do not know, for time just didn't mean anything to me, but the excitement of the day will live in my memory for a lifetime.  Those beautiful words came bellowing down from the sailor on watch:  "Land!  Land Ahoy! I see land!"  Captain Rylick came from his cabin and looking through his long telescope, calmly announced, "Aye! It is."  We all gathered about to see this great, long-awaited spectacle.

This journey seems to have taken an eternity.  Was it really true?  Had land really been sighted?  Now that it had happened, it seemed quite like a dream, for it wasn't there; anyway it wasn't there for the naked eye to see.  We squinted, and looked, and scanned the line between sea and sky.  For hours and hours we starred out at the horizon.  There still appeared to be nothing.  When we asked the captain again, he said, "It is there all right, just a little out of our vision for now."

My! I thought; this must be an awfully tiny place if we can't even see it.  What were we coming to?  Would it even be big enough to hold us all, let alone the many who had gone before? Had we been given the wrong information?  I was more than a bit apprehensive, to say the least.  I kept my thoughts to myself, remembering how John had said:  "The slightest seed of doubt could cause panic amongst us."

It wasn't until almost dusk that a very thin, grayish-black line formed between the blue of the sky and the green-blue of the water.  "There it is!  I can see it!"  Someone yelled.  "Where?" "Where?"  We all yelled and came running to take another look.

73

"There, right on the very edge of the water and sky," one of our company said, and pointed far, far out.

"Oh, yes! I can see it too," many voices echoed at once.

What a relief it was, to finally be able to see land. I felt a renewed hope; a new breath of life had just been extended to me. I would make it after all. I would see this new home of ours. Yes, we were almost there.

Little did we know that sighting land and being close enough to walk upon it are two entirely different things? Yes, it was sighted, but it would take us at least three or four more days to reach it. So we watched with eagerness, as it grew closer and bigger, looking now like it might accommodate us. This tiny strip of God's earth with its sharp cliffs beautifully topped with green trees and laced with long sandy beaches that tried to hide lush secured coves, had mesmerized our gaze. There were rocky cliffs, high above our heads that seemed insurmountable. The vastness of the coastline is nothing like I had imagined. It seemed to go on forever, and the closer we got the further we had to go. These thoughts of mine led me to wonder if our final destination was attainable after all. Sometimes I feel the ship is close enough for us to easily swim over to the shore, then the ship turns slightly and again it looks far away. It is like an elusive dream, just out of reach.

It had now been four long days, since the first sighting had taken place. We grew ever more anxious to touch our feet on solid ground. The captain rang the bell for an assembly of the people, and we all hurried around to hear what he had to say.

"I have called this meeting to let you know that the time for docking in the Massachusetts Bay is about to come forth. We will sail into the harbor tomorrow, late evening. It is my advice, to Mr. Weatherford and all of you, to stay put for the night. It would not be advisable for any to leave the safety of the ship until daybreak. The area is unfamiliar to all and can be very dangerous and hostile. When morning breaks, I will awaken you with the ringing of the bell, and you will be free to take leave of the ship at that time. I know this is a bit of a disappointment to you. I know you are all anxious to be off the ship, but please heed my warnings." The captain explained the situation with a grave look on his face, for he knew what our thoughts were.

Mr. Weatherford responded to the captain's statement. "Thank you Captain Rylick; we will, of course, do as you advise. I too would not recommend leaving the ship so near nightfall. We are grateful to you and your crew for a safe arrival and to God, we give thanks!"

Another night on the ship! Could I really stand it? It seemed that every time the end of this voyage was near, something popped up to extend it. How much longer were we expected to endure these crowded, stifling conditions? There really must be an ending point somewhere! My gigantic sigh brought me a wrinkled brow and a fierce glance from John. I knew it was no use voicing my thoughts, for they were very near the thoughts of all aboard. There was nothing to be done but endure another night aboard ship.

74

As the ship sailed, now very close to land, we could see the beautiful trees and dense foliage. The landscape was not too different, coming in to this new area, as it had been going out from England. There were many boulders hanging to the sides of the cliffs or balanced precariously atop the land. We all stayed on the top deck and strained our eyes, so as not to miss anything. It was truly a beautiful sight. The sky, a deep, clear azure blue, with a few white cloud puffs scattered here and there was dotted with big white sea gulls as they flew over head, and occasionally swooped down to grab a fish from the waters below. The fresh cool breeze was like heaven to us. We were now passing some pilings, from an unused dock jutting out from the water, and the great white birds perched atop them looked at us with as much curiosity as we looked at them. We were close enough now to see a few people about the wharf area situated along a small islands edge. We seemed to be gliding along so effortlessly and as we get nearer to the Boston Bay docks, I sigh disappointed to see buildings in such a tattered and half-put-together state. Surely there is more to Boston Town than this? My mind seems to be seeking an answer to what my eyes are seeing.

A few small dinghies attached to long ropes are tied close to land, while another ship sets at anchor not far away. Nothing of real excitement around the bay or on the shore seemed to be going on. Much different than when we left England with its throng of people. I wonder if the other ship has just arrived or is it getting ready to sail back to London. If I wasn't so tired of being in this ship I might be tempted to jump aboard and go home.

Home! The thought was tantalizing. I just let my mind wonder as I looked out upon this new place. We were in a cove, or bay with land on both sides of us. It was not really close yet, but the way it curves, gives me the feeling of giant outstretched arms being wrapped around me, giving me a huge hug as I am surrounded, in a welcoming embrace. At least that is what my mind wants to believe.

As the sun gently drifted downward, it looked like a red ball of flame in the western sky. It reminds me of a very sleepy eye, closing ever so slowly, too tired to raise its lid, finally falling to sleep. Then it was out of sight.

Again, we joined the others down below deck. This would be our last night aboard. The mood was not a somber one, for there was many things to be accomplished this evening in order to ready us for the departure at daybreak.

What once had been a neat little corner was now a home setting, in miniature. After seeing to food for the family, I started the task of putting things back in the trunks and making sure all clothing and utensils were in place.

"Elizabeth, are you packing already?" inquired Sarah.

"You can be sure of that! Sarah, I want to be off this ship as quickly as possible . . . first crack of dawn," I replied.

"You sound as if you didn't have too good of a time on here," Sarah said teasingly.

"Just about as fine a time as you had, I'm sure," I retorted, knowing Sarah was just having a bit of fun. Then I looked over at Mary and asked, "How are you making it, Mary? Is that baby going to be waiting to be born on land?"

"Yes, I think there is still time. Although, during that storm, I had my doubts," she responded with a heavy sigh.

"I truly admire you, Mary; this had to be such a burden for you. It was most uncomfortable for everyone; I can't imagine making it in your condition. You are a very brave women!" I told her, truly admiring her grit.

"You are both so kind. I am very tired and will be very glad to be off the ship. I must say that Liz was a great help to me. She kept the two little ones entertained most all the time." Mary continued chatting as she gathered their belongings.

"I am glad she was not a bother to you. It was fun for her, too," I assured her.

As I turned to look at the other passengers, it is a delight to see that there is not one bit of space that was void of happy voices. The discontent and disagreements that had at times come between us was now gone, and nothing but excitement and enthusiasm flowed amongst us. We had arrived-safely and in general good health.

To God " be the Glory!" Amen.

# CHAPTER 5

The gentle rocking under foot, combined with the outstanding sights that filled every inch of vision, in every direction, brought to me anyway, a renewed feeling of hope. This little company of ours has finally reached our destination and we are safe from the clutches of the monsters that inhabit the sea. I don't know how much longer any of us could have endured the rough, rolling, angry, seas, especially after that frightening, devastating storm. To see one slight puffy cloud in the, other wise, clear blue sky brings great concern to my haggard mind.

Standing here on the spotless, polished deck, of this little wooden ship, enjoying a moment of quiet serenity, my thoughts reach out to a time when I feared we would never reach these shores. But as I was told we would, we have. I stand here more than a little amazed, enjoying the sea breeze as it gently picks up water and ever so gracefully sends a soft spray of moist and cooling air over my body. I don't even mind the dampness it leaves behind as it moves onward. For with it has come a calm, welcomed dot of hope, a spark within my heart, a baptism reviving and cleansing my mind, giving my soul great expectations for a wonderful life in this enchanted little bay.

The journey to the shores of this new land is now a thing of the past. The doubts of our making the passage alive now behind us and the prospects of what lies ahead lurking in our hearts. Each of us taking in this special moment in our own way, as one feat of my life's journey ends another looms ahead.

I have envisioned so much in the past few months. My mind has been a constant panorama of pictures floating, swirling in a deep fog. I was unable to really imagine what this new place might be like. My minds eye was continually seeking a vision of our future. I am skeptical as I look at the beautiful scene before me, for so far nothing in my wildest dreams could have prepared me for the voyage we have just concluded. And I know there is no way to prepare for our future here either.

The long boats have finally started to take some of our company of people to the sandy shore. What a delightful sight! I am eager to be amongst them so I too can be off this ship. I hope our turn will come soon. There is nothing I can think of that will make me happier than getting off this ship. We will be able to shop in the newly established stores of Boston Town and move into our new dwelling. The sigh that escapes from within me, tells it all. Pure delight! The only question in my mind is, am I really ready for what lies ahead? Is this small group of adventurers, who have journeyed and endured, this long arduous passage, with such hope, ready? Only time will answer all the questions that fill my mind and the minds of those that came with us. As always, I will have to wait, live each day as it comes and then look back to see if my memories bring fulfillment of all my expectations.

"Come on, John! Come on! I can't wait to get off this ship! I want to look around," I shouted to John a short distance away. I hadn't intended to sound so demanding, as I spun from my thoughts to the actual goings on about me. The scampering feet, gleeful laughter and exuberance

77

of everyone still on board the ship emitted energy into my soul that said move on. And I was surely ready to do just that.

John rushed toward me with a scowling face. "What is it Elizabeth, that demands such immediate attention? We are here to stay and as I look at it we have plenty of time on our side," he stated, hoping that I would calm down.

"I can't explain this feeling inside me, John. I have an urgent need to be away from this confinement that I have such distaste for. I am anticipating the scurrying of many feet in this busy port of Boston Town. I do hope we will have some time to look around all the quaint little shops, like we would in London Town. Oh John please understand my excitement and get us off this ship." I begged for John's help, I did want to see the shops, and the happy smiling faces of the shop owners that would be there too great us.

Yes it will be so nice after all these long months at sea to be settled once again. Set up our home, cook for my family, plant my garden and live life once again with purpose, love, and security. All these thoughts sent a wave of urgency through my whole body and my voice was its release. All I know is that I want off this ship and now! But this is a demand in my thoughts alone. For I know I should not speak my feelings out loud. If I could swim to shore from here I almost think I would attempt it.

"Yes, yes, Elizabeth, it has been a long voyage, we will gather our things up quickly, and be on our way. I just thought you would rather wait until we could get to the dock. The long boats are more hazardous. But if you must go now it is fine with me. Grab what you can carry, boys, and we will have the rest sent ashore." John directed the family, finally coming to the realization that I could not be detained here much longer.

"Come on, hurry! Hurry! Mama, I want to go, you are too slow." Liz cried out, jumping up and down with excitement.

"Well boys, you better grab as much as you can safely handle and lets get off this ship before Mama and your little sister burst," John exclaimed, laughing at the excited family around him. Even if he didn't want to show it, I have a feeling this is a picture he has conjured up in his mind for a long while and a welcomed scene indeed after all the complaints and doubts that had been hurled his way in the past. The smile on his face let me know that he was happy, extremely, extremely, happy.

"Papa, they are not the only ones that are anxious. I can hardly wait myself. I want to see what our new home looks like," came a wistful and excited response from John Jr.

"I think we all feel the same way, "echoed William, who already had his arms laden with our bags.

"Well then, you two, William, Thomas, grab hold of that trunk, William pile those light pieces on top and let's be on our way," commanded John.

Liz tucked Katy doll under one arm and tried hard to pick up a heavy flaxen bag, expecting to tuck it under the other arm, as she proudly announced, "I'm ready." We all had to laugh, for she couldn't have possibly taken one step without falling flat on her little turned up nose. At least she was willing to help.

"Here little sister let your big brother carry that. You hang on to Katy doll and stay close to Mama," John Jr. said, coming to his sister's rescue. He was always so good to Liz, perhaps spoiling her a little too much. He really took being the eldest son quite seriously. William, on the other hand, got very exasperated with John Jr. William being only a few years younger didn't think John Jr. should be so bossy. But we are depending on all our children's help as we strike out on this new adventure in our lives.

There would be little time for them to play as I had, under the shade of the old elm tree and to dip their toes in the cool pond, while they watched the horses graze in the beautiful fields of the lush English countryside. No, those were my childhood days, and most certainly would not be theirs.

"My! My! What a sight to behold. The water looks so far down. I don't know if this is such a good idea after all, "I expressed my insecurities to John. But I had to quickly put everything out of my mind and just concentrate on this disembarking business. It is finally our turn and from the looks of that unsteady boat below me I wonder if this will be as easy as I had anticipated when I made the request to leave the ship this way. I think maybe the ones who are waiting for the ship to be maneuvered up close to the dock are perhaps the wiser. Now that I'm here, teetering on this rope ladder above the water, I don't think I am as anxious to go ashore, as I thought I was.

"Go on, Mama! Don't stop now!" Hollered the children, as they ascended onto the teetering rope ladder directly behind me.

"I'm trying. Please watch Liz, John, this is going to be too hard for her," I said, feeling very uneasy about this way of departure, now.

"We'll watch her, she'll do fine," John replied. I reached to grab the sailors outstretched hand and held tight for fear of falling into the dark green, murky water that swirled beneath me, looking much like the open mouth of a wild animal, licking its chops as it awaited its dinner. What a relief to finally feel something solid beneath my feet, even if it was wiggling back and forth.

When everyone that could fit were safely aboard the long boat, the sailors started to row for shore. The distance between the ship and the sandy beach did not seem far. The rhythmic stroke of the ores as the crew heaved to, caused the long boat to glide effortlessly through the water making for a very pleasant ride to the land. It is almost as pleasant as a lovely summer row down the beautiful river Lee in my wonderful homeland.

I am in a very relaxed state and I let my eyes rove over every inch of the shoreline visible to me. The jagged rocks are so beautiful as they seem to be caressed with a kiss as the water laps up at them. The water is groping at the sand as if trying to catch hold, only to loose its grasp and return outward and wait patiently for another try at this game of the sea. The sea gulls are swooping down and skimming the top of the water in search of a noonday meal. Which reminds me that I too have an empty feeling in my stomach. I must keep my mind on the things happening around me for this is all too fascinating for me to really think too much of food right now. Sitting here upon a wooden crate in the boat I feel as if I am already becoming very much a part of this new and wildly beautiful place that I find myself in.

Upon reaching the shore, the sailors secure the ropes to a stand of pilings and with our feet fairly flying we all scurry out of the boat, not caring one bit that we are wading in knee deep water and getting our clothing sopping wet. We hurriedly fight our way through the retreating waves.

"Land! Land! Solid earth beneath my feet." I shouted, as my feet lit on the sand causing small clusters of sand and pebbles to move around in the water as I wade in. The water was becoming very cloudy as we pushed our way forward.

Looking around I am finding everyone who has come in our long boat, with happy faces and heaving sighs showing their joy after our journey and tug-a-war with the sea. We are finally here standing on land and it is really hard to believe.

My personal joy, I was off the awful ship, standing in water that covered my shoes and on pebbles that hurt the bottoms of my feet and it only brought me elation. The swirling water felt as if it wanted to take me back out to sea but I fought hard and dug my toes deep into the sand. I would not let the sea win.

I was having as much trouble standing on this solid ground as I had standing on the moving ship. Now that I no longer had to contend with the movement of the ship on the water, I now had to work at just standing still. My legs feel like soft taffy, wobbly, mushy, and unable to hold my weight.

"Look at me John, I am having problems standing up. I can see that I am not the only one either. The others are also trying hard to find their land legs. Everyone is walking about as if they have had a dram too much ale." I conversed with John, as we walked along hoping the circulation would soon return to my limbs.

"It might be a problem for most of us, but look at our Thomas, he is having no trouble at all." John stated as we watched Thomas walk about as if he was still trying to portray a seaman, swaggering from side to side, accentuating every move. I had to chuckle, at his whimsical antics.

"Isn't this wonderful? Here we are, finally! I can't seem to make myself believe it. The fluttering in my stomach makes me want to dart about like a dragonfly, from here to there, taking a quick peek at everything that surrounds us!" I exclaimed finding myself caught up in these simple joys of life, and forgetting momentarily all the little apprehension nestled deep down inside me. I knew they would return they always do. I would deny them to John and the children but I cannot deny them to myself. But for this, very special moment in my life, I will not let them creep in and spoil my happiness.

Immediately we started up a small incline toward a rutty dirt road, which we were told lead to Boston Town. We take our time and leisurely stroll up the hill only stopping briefly here and there to take in our surroundings along with a deep breath. The hill was steeper than it looked. On one such stop I found my eyes locked on John's and realized he was standing in silence staring at me.

"What is wrong John? You are looking at me with such a quizzical expression on your face, I asked, shading my eyes and squinting, as the glare from the noon sun off the water was bright. Seeing him more clearly now I could see the impish grin on his face and knew he was mimicking my own facial expression as I viewed the scenery as we passed. He was thoroughly enjoying every minute of this new experience, as much as I was.

My how he loved life! He had a God given way of turning every experience into a pleasant one. Nothing was too big to conquer or too small to enjoy. The simplest things brought him pleasure and he always had a smile on his face and a soft, happy whistle, coming from his lips. I thank the Lord above, for bringing him into my life.

"Elizabeth, the look on your face is breathtaking. I hope you will always hold this enthusiasm, you look so happy and that makes me happy," John said, with a broad smile across his face.

I had not the heart to tell him of all my misgivings and fears, nor did I want to. I too wanted to revel in the enjoyment of this moment.

"I am happy, John. I look forward to wonderful times in this new land. We have our whole life ahead of us and it is up to us to make it into whatever we want. Now just how many people have an opportunity like this? See I still remember the reason for leaving our homeland, this chance to begin anew. I bet you thought I had forgotten everything, didn't you? I haven't, I just have lapses every once in awhile and it takes me a little time to get everything back in perspective. It will be nice to make our own decisions and accept the challenges ahead. Oh! I am sure we will make plenty of mistakes along the way, but we will have no one but ourselves to blame for them," I answered John, knowing full well that I was drawing a lot of my strength from one of the conversations I had with Sarah before leaving England. Like she had said, "what choice do we really have?" Sarah's profound words ring truer with each passing day.

It is just hard to imagine all these changes taking place in my life. Me, the un-traveled, settled one, born and raised in one place, from a family that had not journeyed any further than London Town. How had my life turned around like this and how did I end up here? I never would have thought that anything like this could or would ever happen to me.

Looking around I find the docking area very small and the men unkempt and scraggly looking. They look much to thin to be working the docks; not at all like the burly, strong men that work the waterfront in

London Town. The shipping area in London Town is also a lot larger than this one. Warehouses line the streets and there are always several ships in port at the same time. Here it is very empty and as I look around, spinning in a circle, I fail to see anything that resembles a town. Where can the shops be? Where are all the throngs of people? Surely this is not Boston Town. It looks very deserted and different than I had imagined. Yes very different indeed! Afraid to ask for fear my suspicion to be correct, I just have to say nothing and walk on. I'm in total amazement though at the lack of, of, my mind cannot find words to express my feelings. My thoughts were stuttering in my head. I swallowed hard as the realization severely hit me. I can't hold my questions in any longer.

"John, where are the shops, the houses, the people?" I stammered in a squeaky voice. "I really expected more. We have reached what seems to be the main street and there is still not much to look at. There are not nearly as many people milling about as I had anticipated," I questioned, as I surveyed this Boston Town.

Everything is put together in such a haphazard way. The few buildings I can see are scattered here and there and don't seem to be in any sort of order. I let my eyes roam further ahead of me, but found much the same sight. "Perhaps this is just a temporary docking area. The town must be on over the hill. That would explain the lack of people." I prattled on, blinked my eyes in disbelief at this assemblage of leaning buildings and the only person in sight, a small boy running by, rolling a big hoop with a stick. He did fascinate me. He possessed quite a skill to keep the big hoop turning on the rutty, rough road.

"That looks like fun," said Thomas, breaking into the conversation. "I must try that sometime. It must take a special agility to accomplish what he is doing. Looks like the hoop would just stop and fall over. Look, there are ruts and holes big enough to loose little Liz in, he continued grabbing at his sister and teasing her into a squeal as she dashed off ahead of him.

Thomas was exaggerating somewhat, but his description quite accurately fit the boy and a few of the holes in the pathway did look quite large.

We must be getting very close to the main part of town by now, don't you think?" William ran up beside us asking the question of his father.

Then turning in my direction, looking as if his mind was rejecting what it was seeing he went on. "It looks so different here, than at home, Mama!" He exclaimed, with almost a total blank expression in his eyes. William looked from one lopsided shack to the next. "Where is everything? There is not even an inn to stay in! This is strange." He echoed the bewilderment that I held in my own mind.

"No, boys, there has hardly been time for the families here to build a town." Their father interjected as quickly as possible. "They have been much too busy, trying to get their homes built and plants in the ground so they would have food for their tables. There are not too many tables either. We are going to find that we will not have a lot of things that we had at home either. If we do have it, we will be making it ourselves. Our tasks ahead are many, and few of them will be easy." John's stern reply to the family left us with a wrinkled brow and little to say. I felt empty inside like I had as a child when I had been reprimanded for a bad deed. I had left everything behind in England, thinking we would at least find some of those things here. Now I'm told there isn't anything? Have I been lied to?

"Papa, where is our home? Is it going to be here in Boston Town? William asked, trying to ease the tension that shrouded all of us. John's jaw was taut, I could see the tension showing in his face, and feel his concern at our apprehensions.

"No, William, it is several miles away from where we are right now. I am not too sure myself. Mr. Weatherford has just described it to us and has laid out a plan for the division of the lands. We will all be going out to this place together, for our safety, and the safety of all our company. He made that point quite clear to us.

They have lost a lot of people, who came in ships prior to ours, to other areas already. Some of our company has insisted on staying in town and a few have decided to return as soon as possible to England. It is too bad everyone had to split up so much. They had hoped for a larger, stronger company. Our being here will help fill part of the void but the ones insisting on going back will leave another one. We will have to make do with what is left over. I guess you never know just how things are going to affect someone. It is better that the people let us know their decisions early and the ones from our own company that already want to go back, well at least we know just where we stand. I'm sure we will make it with the ones that have decided to complete this venture.

From what we are told, most of the native people right along these coastlines are friendly but they can be very unpredictable. You must keep close by and watch out for your mother and sister at all times," John explained, trying to warn the boys of a few of the dangers that could be lurking close at hand.

"I see Mr. Weatherford is calling us to assemble over there by that building. Come, let's hurry, we have a long way to travel, we must not keep anyone waiting," John said, waving for us to follow him quickly.

"Welcome, welcome dear friends. Our first act in this great new land will be to give thanks to our loving God for a safe passage. Let us pray!" Mr. Weatherford proceeded.

We all did as we were instructed and I for one gave an extra thanks to my Lord, for I really doubt I would be standing here in this exact spot at this exact moment if it weren't for His good graces. We do have much to be thankful for. Our God has been good to each and every one of us. I knew without anyone telling me that. It was a miracle in itself that I was here at all. I don't need anyone to tell me to keep that thought foremost in my mind. It is permanently seared in my brain.

"We are going to be starting out for the area that has been granted to us and the company we are to join. Later we will have plenty of time to look around after we are settled a little more. It is very important, now, that we all get our things together and it will be up to each head of family, to take care of their own families, servants and their indentured ones. We have a wagon being loaded for us it will bring the supplies that we were able to save from the storm, also the heavy trunks. Most of the other belongings will have to be carried by individuals, so let everyone do their share. It will make it much easier for everyone, if we all work together.

It is extremely important that we all stay together; do not stray off the path as we head for our new home. We are all anxious, but we want to arrive safely, so we must follow orders. When you hear the ship's bell, please assemble right back here. It will probably take a couple of hours or more for the ship to be unloaded. Anything that is left behind at this time will be brought out to us in the days and weeks to come.

If there is anything you want to do in town, you had better do it now. It will be some time before you get back this way. There isn't really too much here, but help yourself to whatever it is you need," he said, as he bowed slightly at the waist and gestured for the people to disburse.

"I need to deliver these papers before we leave the waterfront. I know for sure, it will be sometime before I get back. I will be far too busy getting us settled and getting some land cleared and plowed, to make a trip back to town. Will you be all right here, for a while?" John questioned, letting us know that he was uneasy at leaving us alone and yet had to take care of business. But with so many people standing about it is hardly likely that we could get lost.

"Yes, we will be just fine. Go and do whatever it is that you need to do, and hurry back. This will give the boys a little time to look around and Liz and I also. We will keep our flaxen satchel, small trunk and Liz close by," I told John as he started on his way.

As we waited for John to take care of the business at hand I kind of wished I could go with him to see the barrister and his office. Everything else here, was so different than at home I was sure it would be too. I was curious but I knew it wasn't a place for a lady to visit. I would just have to be content to chat with the folks around me and watch the children as I had been instructed to do. The general conversation led to our disbelief at what we found in this new port compared to what we had dreamed it to be. We chatted on and on and let our eyes rove from area to area, trying to understand how we could have all been so wrong about this place.

I sat atop our belongings and leaned against the side of a building. The wood building was rough, splintered, darkened by the weather and made of mud and wild grass stuffed between the hand chopped logs. It was not at all comfortable to lean against. All the buildings in town were similar. The only thing that resembled home was the thatched roof setting atop each building.

As I scanned the immediate area I noticed a small group of huts that looked very different than anything I had seen before. These huts were nothing but bent poles, with grass like matting attached with heavy vines. What a curious way to put a structure together, I thought. Surely

84

those are not a business of any kind. I shuttered at the thought that those huts might be what they call a house in this odd new land. I blinked the thoughts right out of my mind and only thought good thoughts and how glad I would be to have a house again, strong walls, heavy doors for security, and a nice big fireplace, for warmth and cooking and our own bedchamber. Oh! How nice it would be to feel secure once more, in a place of our own. I closed my eyes against the bright sunlight and while letting by body rest; I gave my mind free will to remember just how this had all begun.

It seemed like such a long time ago yet actually it hadn't been. In the midst of the entire discontentment over our spiritual future, much talk and many deliberations with countrymen had taken place. The areas in and around London Town had become the center for these discussions. After much thought and prayer, a patent was procured from The Crown. This was the beginning for the people who accompanied John Endicott, to begin a new plantation in a new far off land. I wonder if they were as devastated then as I am now with what they found those four years ago. I am sure it must have been even bleaker then than it is now. Why in four years has there not been an attempt to make this place a real town like London Town. Why you can hardly call this more than a slum area. Surely they could have done better than this? I just cannot believe what I am seeing no matter how hard I try.

Seventeen ships so far had been outfitted with supplies and people for this same voyage to the "New Land," as it is being called. I never, in my wildest dreams, ever thought our family would be joining them, yet, here we are.

The people of Nazing, in England, had been informed of all the decisions and were aware of what was taking place but I myself gave it very little thought. I was content, secure, and very happy, so I could think of no reason why we might even consider such a change. With all the incoherent stories that had reached our ears from the returning sailors, why that just gave me more cause to stay where I was.

Their stories told of some who had gone to the new land on one ship and returned right back on the same ship, or the very next ship that they could secure passage on. With this kind of information, I could see no reason at all for me, or my family, to be involved in any way. It seems ironic to me as I sit here waiting for John, that some of our own company will be doing that very same thing. I cannot imagine any discouragement that would get me back on a ship, at least today. It would take a King's army to do that.

I do remember the captain telling us of how one ship sailed into Salem Harbor, another port to the North of where we are now and found the people there in a very dire situation. They were in such a desperate condition and the captain's ship being near the end of its journey had very little provisions to offer them. So all they could do was give them a few sparse supplies and put out to sea once more, looking for a better place to drop their anchor. Now that our journey has been completed I can understand much better how those people felt. If they had not found a port better than the one in Salem Harbor, then perhaps I can see why they would risk the dangers of the sea once more and return to England.

I am glad decisions like that are not left up to me. It must have been so disheartening not to be able to help those poor people standing on that sandy shore. Knowing what little is left of our stores after this long and laborious crossing, I hate to think of what decisions we would have had to make. I would not have been able to deny one of those poor creatures anything they wanted.

This human drive within us is strange. Even with all the adversities, we are still willing to take chances, struggle, fight, endure, and for what? What is it we are really searching for? Do we know? We give our reasons: a better life, more freedom to make our own choices, our children will be able to have much more than we ever dreamed. Is it really true, though? Or, is it just a human weakness to always want more, uneasiness within us all to seek out the unknown and conquer it, if we can? We are strange creatures indeed, we seem to have an unquenchable thirst within us for knowledge of what lies beyond. Even with all the stories we had heard, and with all the fears we had, we still have answered the plea to come, to join in the freedoms, to partake of the prosperity.

When word reached Nazing, from the first few ships, it was not good. They had lost most of the cows, horses, and chickens in the crossing, and many were sick. There was a great need for more people to go and colonize. There was a need for merchants, artisans, and people willing to train others in all facets of life.

There were some important changes being made in this latter company of peoples. If more were to come, they would be expected to be able to take care of themselves and their families for at least eighteen months, and have the means to build their home and start a farm. They would also be expected to establish for themselves and others a means to achieve the needs of the people already in the new area plus those yet to come. I am sure all of our people were not able to meet every single requirement but we knew it was of the utmost importance to come as close to these expectations as was possible, for our own well being.

We were told there was plenty of fuel for warmth, materials for homes, seas and rivers to fish in, and good ground to farm. The incentives were all there and I surely pray what was told to us is true; it is evident there is no town like I envisioned.

Oh, I sighed, where is my beautiful Nazing, with the neat little gable fronted, and thatched roof houses? Where are my beautiful cows grazing in the lush, emerald green, open fields, the neatly piled stonewalls, and split rail fences, our beautiful stable, with my horse Big Blacky? Where were Katie and Cook and Martin? Where was my beautiful home, nestled close to the beautiful river Lee, with the bustling town of London, a short distance to the east? Where has my life gone? What am I doing here?

These memories, flashed before me like a painting in my mind, flooding my thoughts and senses with the smells of the fresh cut hay, Cook baking in the early morning hours, the big beautiful willows that lined the creek, and my very colorful and delightful rose garden, with its beautiful scents, so strong and sweet, reaching the heavens. Oh! It smelled so good in early spring, as the buds burst forth into delightful big flowers.  Where was my quiet little village?  I could picture the parish church so clearly in my mind and the graves of my loved ones.  The view from the hill, so serene, as it overlooks the Hertfordshire and Middlesex countryside.  As my lovely memories surfaced, I felt the tears of sadness well up inside me, and I swallowed hard to keep them back.  I must not look back, I am much to weary, and I must look ever forward.  I opened my eyes to the present, blinking back the tears, and blocking out the flood of memories, that were persistently trying to come forward in my mind.  I busied myself with attending to Liz, trying to compose myself and get my emotions back in tact.  This is not easy; it is something, I am afraid, I will struggle with until the day I die. I cannot turn loose of the past with ease.  Just when I think I have everything under control, up pops something to remind me of days long gone by.  Oh my what am I to do? I continued leaning against the building and letting my mind reach many miles, across rough green seas to a place I longed in my heart to be.

It was a welcomed reprieve from my thoughts when Sarah and John's brother joined me; it was just what I needed.  I had to put all my focus on the present, I needed to break up this time of daydreaming, and focus on what was going on around me.

We were all waiting anxiously with Ann.  Eliot had not arrived yet. Where could he be?  We all knew he would be as anxious to see Ann, as she was to see him.  Ann could not wait much longer.  It was Eliot, who had written to William and Sarah, beckoning them to make the journey and accompany Ann, so that they could get married. William of course, had rushed over immediately to talk to John and the wheels were set into motion and they have not stopped grinding away yet.  Eliot's first step onto this shoreline must have been much more astir than we perceived ours to be.  After all, he had come to this land with some of the first.  He had plodded on, with his strong determination to preach the gospel.  My, I thought it has been almost two years now that he has been preaching to his small congregation and to the Indians.  It has been a fulfillment of his dreams.  Dreams he now wants to share with the one he loves.  His endeavors must have kept him very involved and busy, for teaching to a lost people, such as these natives we have heard so much about, must be quiet a task.  Savages, yes.  That's the word they use to describe them. It sounds so harsh, so inhumane.  Sarah had told us of how Eliot had felt a burden for the salvation of these lost souls.

Eliot had learned their language and spent as much time as possible with them.  It was very hard for both he and Ann being apart so long.  As we all stand here together we seem afraid to ask out loud the question of where he might be, for fear something has happened to him since last Ann had heard.  What an awful thought!  So we all continue to stand together and wait.

I wiped the perspiration from my brow, and looked about to see if perhaps John was returning.  Seeing no one walking our direction I once more turned my attention to the family about me.

"Where is Eliot?  This is something you would not want to be late for."  Sarah spoke loudly, rebuking her brother's absence.

Concern was beginning to creep into the expression on Ann's face. Sarah had not meant to alarm anyone, and certainly she had not meant to shout out her concerns so loudly.

Only a few moments more elapsed when we heard Eliot hollering out to Ann and Sarah. It was a welcomed relief to look up and see him running toward us as fast as he possibly could. He actually reached us almost before we recognized it was his voice coming to our ears. Picking Ann up in his arms, he swung her around and looked at her with tears glistening in his eyes and an expression of such great admiration.

"You are like a vision, Ann, a virtual dream come true! I am so glad to see you, each and every one of you. This is truly a blessed day," he said, turning and shaking hands with William, and giving his sister a big hug.

"My! The children, they can hardly be called that anymore. They have grown so much in the past two years, I would hardly recognize them," Eliot exclaimed. Letting his dark brown eyes, flecked with tiny pinpoint dots of gold, rove lovingly from one face to the next.

"That, they have," agreed Sarah. "Where have you been Eliot? We were beginning to think you were not coming for us at all," inquired Sarah, admonishing her brother for his tardiness.

"Hello, Elizabeth! Welcome to your new home," Eliot said, as he turned to take my hand and deliberately ignore his sister.

"Why, thank you, Eliot! We are mighty pleased to be here," I responded, with a curtsey.

"Where is John?" Eliot asked, looking a bit concerned. He knew well the hazards of the crossing and was concerned about his friend. "I hope no misfortunes have befallen you?" He continued to inquire.

"No, we thank the Lord for our blessings. He has just gone over to deliver some papers to the Law Office, from Mr. Anderson, in London Town. Mr. Anderson was most anxious to have these papers hand carried. John should be back shortly," I answered, assuring Eliot that he had arrived with us and was quite well.

"I am anxious to see him, and see how he liked the voyage," continued Eliot. Showing his excitement at having friends and family about him.

"Not to spoil his telling you himself, but I think he and the boys delighted in every minute of it. I am sure he will have lots of tales to tell," I stated, but before I could continue John, rushed up and interjected, "I sure will have!"

"Well, hello there, John! How was your voyage? We were just talking about it," said Eliot.

"As I heard," said John. "It was delightful! Just delightful! We hit the most exciting storm, except for the fact that we lost a lot of our stores, it was very exciting." As he continued to explain, Sarah, Ann, and I just glanced at each other. There was no denying, it was exciting. John just neglected to add fearful, long, distressing, and a few of the more important details that caused all the excitement.

"Sarah, where has William gone?" Eliot inquired. "Is he tired of my conversation already?"

"No, I'm sure not that." Sarah answered as she laughed, then continued. "He was just here a moment ago and has gone down to the dock to see that, all of our things have been unloaded." Sarah paused and then continued. "I am sure he will be right back."

"Well, I hope he hurries back! I am thankful God has been good and you arrived here safe. I have so much joy I can hardly contain myself. I have brought a couple of my neighbor boys, to help carry some of your things back, and you will all be welcomed at my home, and the neighbors too, until you can locate your plots of land and get a shelter built. We don't have very much in the way of houses, it is not anything like you came from, but what we have, we wish to share. We look forward to helping you get started," Eliot said, as he introduced his neighbors to us. That statement "we don't have much in the way of houses!" seems to startle my brain.

"We surely do thank you. We look forward, with great anticipation, to our new life here. I am sure we can use all the help and suggestions you can give us. You have already struggled through so much. We appreciate this fine welcome, indeed. We are all weary from our travels. At this point, it is just the hope, excitement and anticipation, which are keeping most of us going. We all need to put our backs into some hard labor. Our bodies are stiff and weak from the crossing," John continued conversing as we waited for William to return. John seemed to be trying to fill in words knowing that I had taken note of what Eliot had just expressed.

"You will get plenty of that, from now on. You should enjoy your brief reprieve, for it is not to be a very long one. Settling here is like nothing you have ever experienced before. There are no stories, that have reached your ears, that could amply describe what is ahead for you," Eliot told us.

We all had a questioning look on our face after that statement but Sara was the only one who spoke up to her brother. "That sounds quiet ominous, and bleak Eliot,"

"I don't mean to scare anyone off, I just don't want anyone to have a wrong idea of what it is really like. We have had some newcomers arrive at Boston Harbor, expecting to have houses built, towns built, and all the conveniences of England. The disappointment was so great for some, that, they returned to their homelands on the next passage they could find. Others were not prepared for the hard life, and sickness quickly took over their bodies. We have lost many people to disastrous illnesses. Keeping their spirits up was most difficult. We tend to forget what it is that we

89

are here for, and the reasons for which we left, in the first place.  I felt as if Eliot was reading my mind.

William came up from the dock area and informed us that we could proceed on our way as soon as we were ready.  Eliot was anxious to know more about the rest of the company and continued to ask questions of the ones that were close by us.

"Is most of the company in as good shape as you are, William?" Eliot asked of his brother-in-law.  I have only seen a few of you standing about.  Hopefully there are more passengers somewhere." Eliot looked concerned as he conversed.

"No, some still have the fever, our boys had it, but are feeling fine now.  Sarah and the girls, managed to keep it away.  Griffin and Mary Graft are expecting their third child any time now.  She is very heavy with child, isn't she, Elizabeth?"  He answered looking over at me.

"That she is, indeed, it is beyond me, how she made the voyage at all.  I thought for sure, we would loose her and the baby, during that storm.  She is a brave women," I said.

"Yes, we all have a great deal of admiration for her," Sarah explained to her brother.

"Well, we will see to it that she has a proper place to stay, until they can get settled.  We have to look out for each other around here.  It might not look like we have accomplished much in the past two years, but we really have.  After you have been here for a few months, you will appreciate our effort, more.  With the Lord constantly at our side and with His many blessings gratefully received, we have marched forward with confidence and pride in every small accomplishment.  It is not an easy life, for anyone, but it is a very rewarding one.  God has opened many doors, and provided us with all our needs.  We are, truly, thankful for Gods many blessings," Eliot said, and continued telling us about this new place.

The ringing of the big bell quickly brought our friendly conversation to an abrupt halt.  We all quickly gathered around Mr. Weatherford.  "Welcome once again to the beautiful shores of the Boston Bay!" He said.  "It was good indeed to dock on her beautiful shore.  As the days and weeks pass, you will become better and better acquainted with it.  But for now, it is of great importance, that you follow every instruction given you. "

"We are but three miles from Roxbury, that is the place where we will settle.  We have a few wagons to haul our stores and the heavy trunks.  The rest will have to be carried as I stated to some of you previously. Please, everyone, do your part.  It will not be a big burden on anyone man, if we all work together.  Some are sick, so it is up to the others, to take up for them.  We have all come through a very trying time, and a very long voyage.  The path to Roxbury is narrow, and in some places, heavily forested.  We must all stay together, taking care not to stray.  Keep close watch of the children, as there are many wild animals.

The natives are very curious and could be lurking about, most anywhere. For the most part, they are friendly. There are some that are quite rebellious, and have been known to attack without provocation; on occasion they can be very unpredictable. Well, if everyone is here, now, we will be on our way." Mr. Weatherford spoke in a clear, concise manner. We knew what was expected of us.

As Mr. Weatherford, continued we hardly dared to even glance at each other. The conversation and instructions gave me chills. I turned my attention back to what was being said. Nodding my head, as if in agreement with every word.

"Eliot, since you, and your men, know the road so well. We will let you take over from here. I will stay at the back, to make sure no one wonders too far off the path or gets lost. We have plenty of daylight ahead of us, and our God has provided us with a beautiful, sun lit day for travel," he said, conversing further with Eliot as to the direction we would take to our new homes.

"Yes, Mr. Weatherford, I will take the lead; let's be off," announced Eliot.

With that, we all started down the road, following Eliot's wagons, laden with a good majority of our goods. Eliot sat Mary upon the seat next to one of the drivers. She deserved to ride. Even though it was a bumpy, narrow path, I doubt if she could have walked very far. She looked so tired, as if she was going to have that baby any minute. Poor thing, she must be so scared, and trying not to show it, or be of any bother to anyone. I marvel at her strong will.

The scenery, as we passed by, was quite intriguing, and beautiful. The wild flowers were scattered about the forest floor and dotted the meadow with vibrant colors. They added so much lovely contrast to this new landscape we feasted our eyes upon, as we walked along. The trees were extremely tall, and the forest area thick. The deep dark green foliage emerged from every corner of my vision.

The big white birds, along the seashore are gone and to take their place are beautiful small birds, of many kinds. Some are as scarlet as a setting sun, and others, as blue as the sky above. Sweet chirping sounds, and long melodious trills, fill the air all around us as we walk along the path. I can't help but admire all the beauty that surrounds us and strain my eyes to take it in all at once. It is hard to keep my mind focused on putting one foot in front of the other. There is so much to see, and it is all wondrously breathtaking. I cannot help but think, this great God of ours, is truly the Master Sculptor, the Master Artist with His canvas, being the breadth of the universe.

"There are sure a lot of rocks around here, aren't there, Sarah?" I commented, as I noticed more and more of the bold outcroppings emerging from the rich dark soil.

"I was noticing the same thing, they are sure rough under my feet," answered Sarah. "Look over there! In that clearing, the boulders are huge, it would be impossible to move one that size," Sarah exclaimed, in amazement at the gigantic granite formations.

"I sure hope, for John and Williams sake, that all the land is not like that," I added, looking in amazement at the size of some of the boulders.

"Eliot, is all the land this rocky?" Sarah asked of her brother. Stopping momentarily with her mouth agape in wonderment. "The field stones are much bigger than at home in England." She continued as she surveyed this unique coming together of sky and earth about us.

"No, but a lot of it is. You have to pick your home spot and farmland very carefully. Some of these rocks are small and easily moved, and others, that just break the top of the ground, go down, it seems forever. Some of our people have had to give up their chosen plots to the rock, and move to another spot," Eliot continued explaining to his sister and any close enough to hear as we walked along. "In some cases, the plots were just not suitable for building, planting or much of anything," he spoke, still with an excited tone to his voice.

"I sure hope we have some good land, for I am very anxious to get started," said John, with a sideward glance toward the boys. His thoughts were pretty much readable by the look on his face

"John, I think you will be pleasantly surprised at this area called Roxbury. Don't let the name scare you. It is like a garden of Eden!" Eliot, answered John, with an expression of merriment on his face.

"I think you are a little prejudice, John Eliot," Sarah, interjected. Sarah still thrived on teasing her brother and it was quite apparent that she had missed the closeness and fun they had always shared. She had not wanted him to go, when he first brought forth his plans and she had voiced her opinion profoundly to him. Now, here she is, right along side him with us close behind.

"You could be right, Sarah. I have really fallen in love with this great land. It offers so much," Eliot replied. You could tell by his voice he was totally enthralled with his new wonderful home. He wanted everyone within hearing range of his voice to take heed of his enthusiasm.

"Well, I must agree, it is beautiful, I have enjoyed this time, to walk along, and take in all the sights," I said.

"We are very close now to Roxbury," informed Eliot, turning and waving back toward the rest of our people.

"Really! The time has passed so quickly. I hardly realized we have traveled very far at all," Sarah, commented.

The look on Sarah's face was not one of surprise, but one of consternation. "If we are so close to this place called Roxbury, then where is the town, pray tell?" Sarah whispered to me, so no one else could hear. We both scanned the countryside, and saw nothing. As Sarah glanced in my direction all I could do is shrug my shoulders as I saw a lot of beauty but no structures. Sarah must not have listened to what here brother had said earlier.

We walked on and on, my eyes never seeming to tire of the wonders about me. Everywhere I looked, there was something prettier, or more interesting, to look at than in the area we had just passed. Just ahead, was a great open area, the ground was covered with hundreds of tiny multicolored, wild flowers. The colors were so vivid; they gave the area a look of a gorgeous quilt. Sometimes, a brilliant yellow came shining through the velvety green background. Then a little further, there would be a whole field of bright crystal blue flowers. Sprinkles of white and red were dotted here and there. My! It was breathtaking. The sweet summer clover, like a thick blanket, thrown atop the damp, darkened brown earth, enhanced the air with its fresh smell. The scenery changed so fast. It was just a few steps back, we could see nothing but rocks; now, this. How blessed we are! I thought as we walked on.

"I guess I am expecting to see the town to soon." Sarah speaks up again. "It must be farther along this path. I am glad I didn't question Eliot, as to where the stores and houses are. He would have thought me ungrateful perhaps." Sarah chattered again. I knew then she had not heard a word of what Eliot has said to us back in Boston Town.

"Tommy!" Eliot spoke to one of his neighbor boys who drove the lead wagon.

"Yes sir, Mr. Eliot," he replied, as he slowed the wagon almost to a stop.

"We are going to stop up here in this little clearing. Where the fresh water pond is. The horses need to get a drink and I think some of us would like one too, a short rest would be welcome," he informed Tommy.

"That sounds good, a chance to cool off a bit," William, Eliot's brother-in-law, said as he trotted a bit faster to catch up with Eliot.

"There are some beautiful, big willow trees along the waters edge, and we can sit under them, in the shade," Eliot continued to explain to the ones nearest to him.

"That sounds like a welcome idea, doesn't it, William? I think we are all a bit out of shape. I can feel the strain, of not being active, my legs and feet are starting to ache." Admitted John.

As we got closer to the meadowland, we could see a small clearing. A bubbling, darting stream, was rushing and winding down the hill, where it emptied into a lush, tree lined pond.

Standing near the edge of the pond, was a beautiful mother deer, with her small fawn at her side. Oh, what a wondrous sight! Nature at its finest I thought to myself. The colors of the deer blended into their surroundings so perfectly. As we approached the mother deer, ever on the alert, pricked her ears high and nudged her little one, and off they bounded, into the thick, dark green forest. Even though I tried to keep sight of them, they had eluded any detection. They had completely disappeared in seconds. There was absolutely no trace of them. It was really a shame we had to disturb them, but we were all thirsty too, and were glad to have the pond and stream to share.

The water was clear and cool. We could look deep down and see big rocks, and large fish swimming around. Some of the boys jumped in. It was so refreshing to wash our faces and drink the cool, blue, water.

"I would just like to stay right here. This is such a beautiful spot," I exclaimed to John.

"Yes, it really is that, Elizabeth. Maybe we can find us a place, just like this, to build your home," he commented. There that word is again build. I think my mind might be starting to comprehend what it is hearing.

"Our home, John," I corrected adding that would be most wonderful, but I won't hold him to it. I would be grateful for any place right now. It seemed like it had been such a long time since we left Caswell.

The respite was over much too soon, and we were back on our rutty dirt path. The rest of the walk did not seem to go as quickly as it had before we stopped. I guess we were all so anxious to get there, and we were beginning to tire. I must say, my first impression of this new homeland is very favorable, and I believe, well worth the sacrifices thus far made. I think? I find my inner self-questioning its own thoughts. I know that thus far we had seen only the natural, wild side of this landscape. There was nothing to indicate any sort of civilization.

Then as we came around a little bend in the road, climbed up a rather steep hill, we all came to a rather abrupt stop. There we stood, lining the ridge, looking out over the most wonderful sight our eyes could ever behold. Before us was a lush little valley, clinging very close to another winding, bubbling stream, which was lapping its way through another beautiful meadow. There was not a sound to be heard, from any human source. Complete silence encompassed all of us.

As I let my eyes scan the breadth and depth of this serene, beautiful setting, my eyes came to rest on a most gorgeous pond. Oh my! What a beautiful sight, I thought. The meadow and pond, where we stopped to drink was breathtaking. Yet this one far surpasses it.

"Oh Eliot! You were right, it is a Garden of Eden," I commented, as I turned around and around in a full circles, trying as hard as I can to not miss one speck of the view. I wanted to see and remember as much as I possible could.

"Yes, Eliot, it is everything we expected, more than we ever anticipated in our wildest dreams, and totally indescribable," Sarah added in agreement with all our comments.

We all stopped for a very long time and just enjoyed what our eyes were beholding. Our wonderment was justified. But were all our reasons for coming to this strange new land?

# CHAPTER 6

As the days slowly move on, I find that the change in the season is beginning to bring a welcomed relief to my psyche. The humid air of the hot summer days, is finally giving way to a cooler fall breeze. I can't remember a summer that has ever hung on as long as this one. Not being used to the climate in this new region, I am never sure what to expect, or even sure it is fare to compare it to that of my homeland. It does appear that the heat and humidity has been with us for such a long time. It is leaving with reluctance, and I can finally feel the cooler temperatures associated with the oncoming of winter getting near.

Just the heat produced from the cooking area, in our confined shelter, is enough to make our sleeping or even trying to rest unbearable. Maybe it is a blessing that we are required to be outside, working for the settlement, so much of the time. Our duties require an enormous effort from each company member. Our obligations bind us to this "Company", we signed on with, and our personal choices are set aside as our days fill up with chores, meetings and prayer services that sometimes-stretch long into the evening hours.

I am left with little time to call my own. John and the boys have worked everyday from dawn to dark in order to finish a shelter for us before the winter months do arrive. Now they are hard at work helping others to complete theirs.

The shelter is adequate. I need not say more! I dare not complain for fear of retribution from our leaders and God. I do confess that in my dreams and in the imaginations of my heart, I had pictured something more than a half dug out hole in the ground, with little more than a pile of fieldstone's for a cooking place and a grass mat for a roof. I am trying to take John, at his word. He says we will once again have a real house, and assures me that this shelter is just temporary. The family's being bound to our duties as we are, gives us few choices as to the decisions of our own lives. We are obligated to take care of our family needs after our communal chores are completed.

While outside I enjoy watching the very young children, for they seem to be unaware of danger or cares. They spend their days playing and the ones a bit older look after the younger ones. By the time they reach Liz's age, they will be hard at work. Every bit of help and strength is needed to survive in this wild, untamed land.

Personally, I could use a few more hours in my day, just to keep up with everything that there is to do. It is impossible to keep the shelter clean. Living in mud and dirt, damp with moisture and mildew leaves much to be desired. The smoke from the stone cooking area fills the air with soot and leaves its smoldering stench, deeply embedded, in everything. I am finding this a most difficult living environment.

There is always mending to do and usually I take the time to tend to that late at night, by the light of the coals. Our clothing has not held up very well and as it gets colder we will have to wear everything we brought with us, just to keep warm. I think back now of the many piles of clothing I gave away or just left behind, and wish for just a few of them.

My men folks are looking shabbier by the day and Liz is looking, no better than the urchin children that roamed the streets of London Town. Those children sadly had no place to go, but mine have a home and it grieves me deeply to see my own family in such a state as we are in here. If I were still at Caswell, in my beautiful village of Nazing, Liz and the rest would be provided for in a much better manner. The only consolation I can find is that everyone in our area looks the same for every ones clothing is in a needed state of repair.

On a brighter side of my life, I have found time to plant a small, late summer herb garden, and a few vegetables. It will truly be a miracle if we have one thing from it for winter. It is no wonder that food is so scarce. The settlers have put other priorities before their gardens and then find it to late to do anything about it. I wonder, to myself, of course, as to their reasoning. I dare not make an utterance of my own against anyone or anything they do.

The dirt floor is damp from ground water seeping in from the little stream that comes near our shelter. John explained that it couldn't be helped as this spot, was purposely picked because it was on the bank of the stream and perfect for a shelter such as this. The stream is just a wild brake-away thread of water from Stony Brook. I do often bless it for being so close when I have to haul water for the small garden, or for cooking.

There are times when all our belongings are covered with a green fuzzy mold that carries a pungent smell and burning sensation in our nostrils as we breathe. This condition is caused by the very design of our shelter and with no way for air to circulate through our dwelling place, we our doomed to live this way. My only repose from the situation I find myself and my family in comes from my faith that God, we are told, will provide better and greater things for us, as long as we hold steadfastly to his commandments and teachings.

I have made it my goal to find something to be thankful for each and every day. Today it is my little kitchen garden. I have a moment in my day to work outside and am enjoying it so very much. I know I have gotten started far to late, but I see the small plants popping their little green heads through the brown, damp soil and it brings great joy to my heart. By the time of the first frost, the tiny plants will be barely big enough to harvest. But harvest them I will, and the few fresh vegetables that grow, will be consider my first garden in this new land, a success, and great blessing. If the Lord finds me steadfast and blesses my garden, I might even be able to dry some herbs for use during the long winter months.

As I take the time this day to ponder upon the many things we have done and the accomplishments of our "Company" of people I concede to the fact that they have been many. I realize that we have, truly secured the blessings of God. The storehouse used by the whole community is partially full and without any great catastrophe, our leaders assure us it will carry us safely through the winter. John tells me that they have collected, quite large stockpiles of essentials and not to worry.

Every meeting we have sounds better and better, until our leaders come to the closing, and end by saying, "no matter what we have stored up,

97

it is still going to be a long, cold, hard winter and we must conserve and care for what we have been blessed with." Then we go into sometimes days of long prayer sessions, fasting and wailing, beseeching our God, to hear our cries, so that we can be assured we are in the good graces of He who watches over us.

No matter what confidences I have stored up they all seem to be destroyed by the end of our prayer meetings. I leave for our dwelling place with chills down my spine and unspoken fears in my heart. John chastises me and says I have taken to many of the old tales and stories that were brought back to England by the sailors, to heart. He thinks I have way too many preconceived ideas and that I had them before we started this new adventure and I have brought this fear of doom upon myself. I dare not say he is wrong, but in the few short months since our landing, I find most of them to have been true.

It doesn't make any difference what I think or feel. My fate is set on a much different course than it was in my homeland. Recognizing this as a fact of my life, I will still give thanks for my very own kitchen garden and anything else I can find that is pleasing to me this day. I will go to my Lord in prayer tonight, as I do every night asking for guidance and forgiveness. Praying He will hear my prayers, even the ones I hold deep within and see me, worthy of an answer.

When I am able to harvest the few things that are here I will know the Lord, has heard my prayers. And when the family warms their cold bodies by my cooking fire and feels the warm trickle of fresh steaming vegetable broth, roll down their gullets, I will hear them say, "job well done Mama," that will be my just reward. Liz is about the only one that seems to take notice of anything that is done around our settling place. The boys and John don't care a speck about the garden, now. I will remind them at those meals of how they laughed at me for even trying to grow anything this late in the year and that if I hadn't, they would not be feasting so fine. My thoughts bring a smile to my lips as I can almost visualize the moment in advance.

I know that this Roxbury place, I find our family in, is but one place in the vastness of this territory. As numerous new ships arrive daily I wonder where the people they bring will find a place to settle. The shores are beginning to become crowded to overflowing. Yet each and ever person is as needed a commodity as the animals and food. For that fact alone I know they have to find someplace to plant their feet. When asking questions that enter my mind I am constantly reminded that it is not my worry and that they will settle somewhere even if families have to double or triple up to accommodate them. I am daily reminded of our need for these new arrivals with their wide diversifications and especially for their skills. We would not be able to exist here without the talents and expertise of each and every creature that has given up almost all that they had and come to these untamed, harsh shores. Within these few short months, I have been able to comprehend the need more clearly. The continual changes taking place in forming something out of nothing, has to be due to a great dedication and effort on the part of each person here. We are told by our leaders daily to remember what we are here for.

To say that we are the same, as a family, as we were in England, would be an untruth. We are living together yet separate and I find it

98

very discouraging to cope with our lives, as they are in this new colony. In England we were so close that every phase of our lives intertwined with each other. We would progress through each day, with complete total togetherness.

Now we are each in our own little world, coming together for brief moments, then much to quickly we are directed to a separate path, required to accomplish yet another task.

What has happened to us? I sometimes think that I am the only one that sees, that something has changed in our cohesiveness, as a family. Our entire way of life has been cracked and shattered to slivers. The threads that have always bound us together are strained almost, to the breaking point. I feel as if I am losing touch with John and the children. It is a scary feeling and leads me to hold tighter to Liz. Without her I would feel totally alone. This isolated existence is not what I want for us and it is not what I dreamed our lives would be like.

As I look up from my garden tending, I realize how much time has been idly dwindled away with my daydreams. I really must set my uneasy feelings aside, for this is much to nice a day for dreary thoughts to bog me down. I must not be glum! I chastise myself within my own mind, knowing that John would surely reprimand me if I were to share my thoughts with him.

I am thinking to myself that since my day started so early I should not waste a beautiful day like this on daydreams. I am extremely thankful for this bright warm sun. This is the kind of day I need for the washing of our tattered clothing. It is a task that I have put off to long. This gift of nature shall not be wasted in a dingy, hot, stuffy, living quarter!

John and the boys arose early, leaving in the still damp darkness of early dawn. What a special time of the day that is. The big red ball of warmth called the sun, popping over the horizon gently pushing the darkness of night clear out of sight. That special moment of stillness just before dawn breaks and life is renewed for another brief day. Off John and the boys went to help another neighbor finish up their home. If I had started my wash shortly after that, I would be about ready to take in the dried clothing by now but my wondering daydreams have surely delayed that. Today, for Liz and I, was like all the others that had come before and would no doubt be the same for the ones that follow. Daily chores came first and as John and the boys strolled off to accomplish their jobs we were once again left alone to tend the fire and do our "normal" duties; the "woman's work," as it is called.

How strange, when I think back on my life in England, to have pictured our family as it is today would not have even entered my mind. Especially in the early days of our marriage, life was simpler or at least it seemed to be.

To have conjured up any kind of a picture at all, of this strange new place, would have been a mistake, and probably near impossible as I see it. I try not to be disappointed in my life or in us coming to this new land, yet a small nagging feeling deep down inside me keeps recalling all we left behind.

To put my finger on the exact cause of my dissatisfactions with our life here in the New Colony is very difficult. For I really don't know what it is that is bothering me. I do know that I am tired, and life seems bleaker and bleaker as the days seem to grow longer and the cold reaches deeper into my bones, causing them to ache and my body to chill.

The very thought of winter frightens me. The stories have been horrendous, frightful tales of starving, death and people freezing as they slept in their beds. Diseases that wracked the body with high fevers and insane minds were the stories brought back from the sailors and survivors that had returned to England. Oh how it makes me shutter to remember these stories. It makes my fear even more what might be in our future here in Roxbury.

The people who came the year before us and a few who came even earlier, tell us there is really not to much to look forward to but the cold, sickness and then they add, the probability of very little food. Sometimes I wonder if they want us to leave or stay? I can find plenty of reasons for going back to England already without them trying to frighten me to death but John can find none. Perhaps, they tell us the worst, so when things turn out to be not that bad, we will really think a blessing has been bestowed upon us. Isn't that deceitful, trickery? Or maybe truths we don't want to accept.

God forgive me for thinking such hateful thoughts! I pray quickly to myself, for fear I might be struck by the mighty hand of God for letting my mind dwell on bad evil thoughts. Our elders have warned us not to look to the bad, but find good in all things. They forgot to tell me how to accomplish this. The fear for my family's safety is what causes these thoughts.

I am afraid of what might happen to us, and not afraid to admit it. I keep thinking of what if this and what if that? No matter how reassuring John is I cannot eliminate these thoughts from my mind. What if God has forsaken this new territory we have come to? This is my biggest "What if?"

It does amaze me that the days have passed so quickly. With all our hard work, getting our dwelling completed, we have not been allowed the time, to stop and look around. We have worked hard and struggled daily, to beat the winter cold. When the sun comes up, we automatically get up, having much more work to do, than the day ever allows us to finish. There is absolutely no excuse for wasting one moment of daylight, and our leaders have made sure, that we are aware of that fact and that sanctions will be taken against us if we should let it slip our minds. Where are these freedoms, we came in search of? The personal ones still seem far out of our reach.

The special moments of my life, the ones I hold so dear are few and far between. John and the children seem to be, enclosed in a fog in my mind. I have trouble bringing their features into focus when they are away from the settling place. Whenever we can find time for one and other, they are precious times to be tucked away, and pulled out of my thinking bag another day. My good memories are the pleasures of my future.

100

I realize as I think over these past few months since our arrival, that I have already stored many good memories since coming to this new place. One of my very favorites is the day we first went out to locate our land. It was wondrously exciting, and how enthusiastic and anxious we were to get started. A day bright and sunny, as today is. Yes, the mood was much different just a few short months ago. At least my outlook on life here was much different then, than it is now.

Why my enthusiasm has waned and I have to reach deep down inside my bag of memories, more often than I care to admit? I have no single excuse or answer. It is just a deep seeded feeling that reoccurs in my mind and settles in my soul on a daily basis. I am afraid the tattered edges of my memories, are far to frayed to pull out many more times. To loss them completely would destroy my existence. Today I must try to refill my bag, find the good in this day and restore some of that lost enthusiasm. This is something I must do for my own sake and for the sake of my family. I have got to turn this experience around into a positive factor in my life. At least I have got to try.

As I go inside to retrieve the soiled clothing I find one very good reason to be grateful. It is the wash. If I didn't have the wash to do, I would be stuck in this horrible smoke filled room. I smile, at the thought of a chore giving me such pleasure. This stale air is certainly not where I want to be on this bright, glorious, autumn day.

I hurry with full arms toward the brook. The bright glaring sun blinding me momentarily as I step from our little sod abode. I clutch at our worn soiled clothing, trying to keep them from tumbling from my arms, as I race down the well-worn path, which leads me to the waters edge.

The lovely little stony brook winds its way across the velvety green meadow. It bubbles and leaps its way forward, making that energizing rushing sound that seems to say, "Get out of my way, get out of my way, I have a busy, busy day." Like a rhythmic song, it chants to me whenever I am near.

On and on it rushes darting over, under and around every rock and pebble in its path. It seems much like a child busy at play, without a care in the world. I like to listen as it passes by. I think the sounds it makes are happy ones, laughing sounds that make me happy and carefree inside. It always gives me great pleasure to sit upon the bank and enjoy its splendor.

Doing my washing within its clear waters, as I am doing today, helps to relieve the doubts I have inside. While here by the brook I loose myself in the beauty that surrounds me and it gives pleasure to my life. Yes, this is one of the more pleasant of my many chores.

Placing the clothing in a deep, hallowed out pool, just right for this particular task, I leave the clothing to soak in the clear blue water. I turn and walk through the tall grass and bramble toward a stand of trees and breath deeply enjoying the cool air as I enter a shaded area. Leaning back against a tree, I let my back slide down its rough bark, as my eyes rove over this beautiful spot, we have picked for our permanent home. The small rise in the land is going to provide a perfect view of the surrounding countryside.

The placement of our house will be such, that it will overlook the beautiful crystal blue pond. I can feel the excitement flow through my vanes as I envision what it will be like when it is completed. Oh what a blessed day that will be. I draw in a deep breath and let it out slowly and a sigh seeps from deep within me as I do. I feel at peace when I am here alone with my thoughts. There is no human around to tell me what to think or if what I am thinking is right or wrong, good or bad. I can be me, totally me.

John's plans are to someday have horses to graze in the meadow, and we will be able to watch them drink from the pond as we rest under the shade of our big beautiful Elm tree. Of course the elm tree isn't here yet, but when it is, we will place it right there, right in the middle of our lush green rolling meadowland.

I know these are just dreams today, but they will become the realities of our tomorrow. Anyway without them what would I have? Nothing, that's what I would have, nothing to look forward to at all. I know all these things won't happen right away, but they will, someday. John assures me of that and says, for now we have to concentrate all our efforts on the present and that means shelter and food.

How many times have I been told these words that roll around in my head right this moment? Yet as we struggle daily to accomplish the smallest of fetes, I find myself leaning more and more on John. I keep his promise to me, locked tight within my heart, for it keeps me going. I am one of Gods' creatures who will always find she is in need of something to look forward to. Hope in my heart and soul is what keeps me going.

Letting myself dwell too much on the past is not good and I try hard not to, but I often find myself looking wistfully into the past, allowing myself to recall things that have happened long ago. If I didn't look back, I wouldn't be remembering the special look in John's eyes, as he holds me close and assures me with his loving, kind, words.

"Elizabeth, please don't ever doubt me. You are so easy to read my darling! Your fears for our future are written all over that pretty face of yours. Everything I do is for you and the children. All you wish for is not possible this very minute, but I promise you, by all I believe in, I will build you a dream."

How does he read me so well? How does he know what lies in my mind? I hate for him to see the disappointments I hold so tight inside me. I am ashamed that I think the way I do. I will keep praying for God's help and surely He will hear me and give me the strength to endure the things I cannot change.

Our shelter is really not all that terribly uncomfortable. The room is adequate, square in shape with a dirt floor and a roof that is part mud and part straw. Everyone has a warm place to sleep. The neighbors have given us lots of help, just as John and the boys are doing for them today.

The wood for most of the structures is cut from the stand of forest growing on the property. It is nice they don't have to go far for what they need. It saves them time and strength they dare not waste. My hope is that the trees are not wasted. I love them so and know that as fields are cleared for planting and trees are cut for buildings and firewood, that we will loose so much of the beauty I am looking at today.

With all this cutting and building, I fear that I will look from my window someday and they will all be gone. The trees bring me a bit of comfort when I look out wishing to see Nazing again. Those times when I get lonely, when I long for a vision of Caswell, with its rolling hills and beautiful stands of trees, gracing the countryside.

Today feels to me like the many wonderful days I spent in my lovely English home. It is a quiet, private day, one in which I can let my mind reach as far back as it wants. It is a day that allows me much needed peace in my soul as I dip into my wonderful memory basket and relive each and every precious vision. It is like having a secret treasure trove; one I keep hidden, deep back in a dark place, where only I can go. I can pull them out one by one and touch them again and again, within my mind. I never let them get far from the forefront of my mind, for they must be close at hand for me to view, for they are my life line to the future, my connection with my heritage. They hold me together when times seem unbearable, without them I am nothing, and without them I would have nothing.

My memories are the arteries of my existence, my bloodline to tomorrow. Without the present there is no past, and I must step boldly into the future to keep time marching on. But for today I have let my memories carry me far away, for far to long. I have many things to do and my daydreaming has again wasted much precious time. I will try to do better I promise myself. It is not good for me to live so much in my memories. If I do that, it won't leave me time enough to make new ones and I surely want to be able to do that. So I must hurry on my way.

As the bright sun dances off the beautiful colors of the changing leaves, I find them breathtaking. This sure is a perfect day to be out here, along this lovely silver blue water. The stillness of the air lets the water move at its own pace. It does not seem to be stumbling over the rocks as it does when a hard wind is blowing. Occasionally I can see it rush just a bit and take with it the deep black soil of the embankment. The sounds the water makes is very calming to me as it hurries on its way.

I stand to stretch my back as it hurts from bending over so long doing the washing. I really don't even remember getting up from my perch near the tree and going back down to the waters edge to continue with the wash. As I look around, out across the great expanse of the pond, it appears like a very large looking glass, reflecting the entire world that is within its realm. My eyes rove once more over the magnificent landscape and I take in the loveliness that it offers. It is a vibrant refreshing sight.

How could I be so callous and unappreciative of all God has given me? All this beauty that encompasses my world as it exists today. I would have to be blind not to notice the brilliance of the red maple trees set in contrast against the deep glorious green of the pines. The beautiful white birch dotted here and there in small clusters adding to the spectacle of colors that are blended so perfectly, forming another masterpiece, painted with nature's paintbrush.

I wish again, as I have many times in my life, as I look upon a special scene such as this that I might have the ability to put what I see on canvas. Woe is me, an artist I am not, so I will just have to enjoy what I see and remember what I can, for it won't be long until this beautiful multi colored landscape will change to white and never again will it look just as it does, here for me, this day.

The fall foliage, in all its glory, looks like a bright colored bonnet, atop a pretty mistress's head. With the ponds reflection it gives me double pleasure. That's how I will remember this special day. Every time I see a beautiful new bonnet, I will see the glory of this blessed day and recount Gods love in sharing it with me.

I wonder if next year these wonderful, bright reds, yellows, greens and all the other colors will be back to bring pleasure as they have today? The crisp fall air is invigorating and being able to look out upon Mother Nature's handiwork, is special. There must be every shade of red imaginable. There are some leaves so dark red that they almost look black and others so yellow like the sun that they have an illuminating brilliance. It is these times that seem to make all the work and toil worth the effort. I do give thanks for these my many blessings and ask forgiveness for the lack, of tolerance and gratefulness that I often find within my sole.

John has laid out the plans for the house very much like the small cottages around Nazing. He has also explained to me at least a thousand times that this house cannot be very big. I can never seem to make him understand that the size of the house doesn't really matter. I just want a house, a place to call my own. Hopefully by this time next year I will be watching the progress with eager anticipation and constantly wondered how it will look when it is finished. Now that will surely be a time for celebration. I will bide my time for now, and will fill the void with dreams and wait.

I am startled when the weight of someone breaks a branch under foot. I turn and quickly look up. My heart is pounding so hard it is ready to jump out of my chest. I am relieved to see John and not one of the wild inhabitants of the forest. "Oh John, it is only you! You startled me. I didn't hear you coming down the path from the fields. Are you through with our neighbor's house already?"

"Elizabeth, what in the world is wrong with you? What could you possibly be thinking about that would take you so deep in your thoughts and far away as to not even hear me approach? You did not even know that I was walking up on you, until you heard the branch break beneath my feet and looked to find me standing right before you?" He chided, with a questioning look upon his face. "It is very dangerous for you to be so unaware of what is going on around you. You have been warned and warned of the dangers that linger in the forest. You really have to be more careful. You never know when Chickatabut, or some of his Sagamore tribe might be lurking. They could conceal themselves most anywhere in this wooded area. One of their favorite fishing spots is just a short distance away.   You know of his dislike for the English and all of the new inhabitants of this land." John continued.

"Oh, John, you worry about me too much.  I'm not far away in my thoughts at all.  I am right here, wandering what my new home is going to look like when it is all done?"  I told him, trying to alleviate some of his apprehensions about my being in the woods alone.

"Well, I ask you not to expect more than I can build, but I assure you, it will be warm and comfortable and it will be ours.  Will that make you happy, my love?" He asked, as he put his arms around me and held me close to his body.  I wonder how he knew my thoughts so well? My private thoughts of what I wished our home to look like. Again he was reading my mind.

I pushed my thoughts aside to answer his question.  "Oh yes John! It will make me very happy.  Tell me again, just where will everything be when you finish?"  I begged, for I loved to hear every little detail, over and over.

"Well, let me see now, the walls are going to be over there.  You will cook on a big fireplace centered in the middle of the room.  It will be a fireplace like you have never seen before, and will not only be for cooking but will warm the whole house.  We will all enjoy setting around it and talk over our days just like we used to do back home in England. It will be the central gathering place for our family.  Above the cooking area, will be a loft area for the boys to sleep.  Our sleeping area will be on the backside of the fireplace, with Liz's sleeping area toward the other end of the room.  That way we can all be warm and make use of the fire.    There will be large windows across the front with little crisscrossed windowpanes to let in all the bright sunlight.  I am hopeful that by winter next year we will be enjoying that fireplace and also our private bedchamber with a nice down comforter to keep us warm." John looked down with a wink of his eye and continued talking before I could comment.

"William and Sarah's' home is coming along quite nicely. Everything is starting to fall into place. They will be well settled by the time the deep winter cold reaches us.  I think that William will also have a good garden next year.  He is so excited and already talking of his future plans.  A good harvest will help to replenish some of the stores for the company.  They are very much needed." John gave me a progress report and only paused momentarily and then he went right on talking.  I well knew the status of Sarah's home for she and I talk about it every chance we have.  They would probably have a fine harvest of squash and a wonderful garden of greens by this time next year.  I was happy for them and knew they would be helping us and just as excited for our family when we finished our home.

"I am not going to wait for the house to be finished to prepare our fields either," stated John, and then looked wistfully off into the distance.

I knew how much he missed his farming. I wanted so much to give him some kind of reassurance, letting him know that I understood and though I seem much to impatient at times I knew John and time would take care of all my uneasiness. We did need to contribute back to the essentials of the company for with all of the new families things are surely getting scarce.

"John, I will be ready for the harvest of our first crop of millet, and melons and what ever else God sees fit to grace our farm with. By then we will perhaps have some farm animals to feed and a nice harvest of rye, for fresh bread will be a much-welcomed commodity. Life will be different in a year. Won't it be nice to have our very own garden right near the house? We will add our stock a little at a time, and much sooner than we think, we will open our eyes and there before us will be all we left behind."

"Elizabeth, you will see, dreams can come true. We will have a cow, a few chickens and a sow or two to start with, what more could we ask for? I know we could use a few more animals and I do want to get another cow as soon as we can. But for starters that should be fine." John rambled on and on, and I listened intently, enjoying the warmth of his arms around me. He seemed to appreciate the sharing of our dreams. His excitement for life and his assurance always served to calm and ease my doubting thoughts.

"John, this is really hard, I mean, to start all over again, isn't it?" I half questioned and half stated a fact. "You know John I am one of those people that Eliot spoke of the ones getting off the ships expecting to see towns and homes built. I am very saddened to see that those things are not here for us."

"I sensed your disappointment Elizabeth from our very first steps off the ship and I am very grateful you did not voice your displeasure there and then. Yes, I can't deny that this starting over is very hard, but it will be well worth the effort too," John stated as he kept me firmly in his grasp.

"I know we are all looking forward to the Lords' day. We will give thanks for our many blessings, but it will also give us all a much-needed day of rest. Everyone has worked extra hard this week in order to secure all our winter supply. We could not have achieved any of this on our own.

The boys, you, Liz and all the others, it is wonderful to see everyone pitching in to help out. By the way Elizabeth, how are Mary, and her new little one doing? She really didn't wait to long, after we got here, to have that baby, did she? The baby really came fast, it is a wonder she didn't give birth while we were still at sea," John continued, not changing his position in the least. He seemed to be perfectly relaxed, just enjoying life as usual.

"It was so sweet of her to name the baby John, after you. They are really going to be fine neighbors! She and the baby are doing very well, and the place they have, is just right for all of them. I was glad to see them get their home started and up so quickly, for I know she didn't want to be living with someone else, with the new wee one,"

"I guess the next thing to be built, after the houses, will be our new meeting house. Won't that be exciting? So many new things," John said, as he turned me around toward him and kissed me upon the tip of my upturned nose.

"Will we have that done before the end of next winter or not?" I asked, not moving an inch away from him. I was enjoying this comfortable closeness that seemed to be eluding us of late. He let his chin rest against the top of my head and continued talking. I could hear the rhythm of his heart beating as my head rested against his warm chest. It had been a long spell since we had any time alone just to converse, relax and enjoy each other. Leisure time was not a commodity that this new land had a lot of.

"Well, as far as I can tell, it should be done within the first part of spring. At least, that is what Eliot and William told me. They are in charge of that project. I am thankful for that. I have my hands full."

"You know John, it is very important, that we get the meeting house established as quickly as possible. We are growing in numbers so fast, we are really running out of space in the temporary building, and we need room for storage. Sarah was telling me, that some of the fields that were planted before we arrived are really abundant in their yield, and some of the kitchen gardens promise to have a large crop. Not mine, I know, I planted way to late. The soil is so good here, that is, after the rocks are removed. We must take advantage of what God has given us and not let anything go to waste. At this point everything is doing so well. We really have to keep a good eye on what crops we have big or small for we can't afford to let any of it be a loss. I am afraid we would be chastised by God if we were to do that!" I explained my reasons for concern at having the meetinghouse done as quickly as possible. It is our duty to God and this company of people to do our part and take up what others lack and do theirs if necessary.

"I know that your concerns are well founded, Elizabeth. Do you think there is more I can do? It is true that more and more people are coming over, now. That is why I need to get started with my business as soon as possible. As you know there are many things that people have left behind. Supplies are essential for our survival. Since it looks like it will be next spring before I can be of any help, I fear even more crowded conditions will lead to fierce competition. Look how crowded it has gotten in just a few short months," John said, voicing his feelings about his expertise being needed or not needed.

I was sure he would have no trouble in getting started. We would just work hard and it will all turn out good. The influx of people and their needs for goods will assure him a good business.

"I think you will be able to accomplish your goal by spring, John. Everything seems to be falling into place very nicely, don't you think?" I asked, needing his opinion to reinforce mine. After all, his decision to come to this new land took in many factors, God being the first and his business being the second. We seem to have our first considerations under control but I know John is worried about the second one. He has said nothing about his business for such a long time now. But this is probably not the time to bring it up. He has enough to worry about right now and I know I surely do so I will just keep my thoughts to myself.

"Yes, very nicely, very nicely indeed!" He answered, giving me a tight squeeze about my shoulders. Yes, John was always there for me. And in most instances things turned out just as he had said they would.

"John, you had better get back to the fields and I must finish this wash before the current takes what little clothing we have left down stream." John's reluctance to release his hold on me to posterity was apparent. Just as I requested John turned loose of me and gave me a quick kiss on the forehead. Running at full speed up the embankment he almost tumbled and fell as he turned to wave and shout, "be careful and mindful of the dangers Elizabeth." Then with a few of his quick manly steps, he was out of sight.

I must hurry now and finish this chore and get back to the settlement myself, for this day is passing much to swiftly for me. As I stoop to wring the water from some of the clothing, I notice my reflection in the water. It tells me that my personal days have also passed swiftly. As I look at my face looking back at me from the water below, I rub it gently, I suppose hoping to rub away the aging lines of which there are many. It tells me that I am surely not getting any younger. I could not expect time to stand still for me, or for anyone else. I really wouldn't want it to, but it could slow down a bit, couldn't it? It is funny but today I do not feel as old as this reflection depicts and yet other days I feel so much, much older.

I have to admit that I am not used to doing all of these chores. The cooking, mending, tending to this wash and all the other things that go on in my day where for the most part done by someone else in England. I would not be telling the truth if I didn't admit to missing Katy, Anna and the others back at Caswell Manor. Yet, doing these things for my family, and myself does give me a good sense of being useful and a real feeling of accomplishment and pride.

I am amazed at what I can do and what I have learned to do in the few short months since I left my homeland. No one is going hungry and our clothes are clean and our shelter is finished. I was able to use a good portion of the cloth I brought from John's store and have made quilts with most of it and stuffed them with the fathers from our neighbor's chickens. They are soft and warm upon our beds. Just right for these cooler fall nights.

As I continue to finish up the wash I realize that these small special accomplishments in my life are the things I want to write in my journal for Liz. I want her to know all these little facts and remembrances of my life and our lives as a family both in our homeland and here in this new land. It is these simple things that bring to our existence, pleasure and happiness and sometimes doubts and tears. Someday many, many years from now, my children, especially Liz, will read it and learn from it the truths behind the upheaval in our lives and what brought us so many miles from our beginnings.

The chill in the air is letting me know that to much time has been lost to my reflections on life and I had better get my cake of soap and quickly retrieve these thoroughly soaked cloths. I had not realized just how cold the water in the stream had gotten for it now is about to freeze my hands as I wrong the last drops of water from the last of the clothing. I will have a hard time getting them dry if I terry much longer.

Finishing this task with a little reluctance, as I enjoyed my solitude and special time with John, I slowly climb the embankment and walk back to our sod shelter, enjoying the songs of the birds as I trudge along the path with my heavy burden. I stretch the clothing along the fence as I pass to the door of our humble abode. Leaving them there to soak up what warmth they can I enter the cooking area and it feels extra warm compared to the cool outside. I find myself trading one good thing for another here. This cooking area lacks the wonderful freshness of the outdoors I just left. It is a fact that none of the air in here is fresh. As I walk over and stir the embers lightly I marvel at how the slight touch of the stick causes them to burn bright red. I add more wood to the coals and see the flames jump higher. Content I hum a soft tune and start our mid day meal. Surely the men would be coming back any time now. Liz had put some bread in the warming oven while I was gone and placed the big kettle over the fire.

Liz was becoming such a young lady and quite capable for her tender years. As a matter of fact she has left many of the things of small children behind and has become quite a little lady. I am sure her young years are passing by much to swiftly. The responsibilities that go along with this new life have developed all of our children's minds and bodies into strong, responsible young people. Even Thomas seems much older than his years.

Turning from the fire I notice Liz standing by the window with her little pug nose pushed against the waxed paper covering that was stretched so tightly it almost gave the appearance of a real glass pane. She seemed to be deep in thought and looked so small and fragile as she stood there. I do worry that she is growing up far too fast. At her age there should be nothing to trouble her young mind. All her thoughts should be like bright rainbows. I just stood still watching her until she realized I was doing so.

"Mama, I miss the kitchen at home and Katy and Anna and everyone. Anna always used to make us such delicious things, and she always let me help her. I want to go home, Mama, I want to go back to Caswell, to England." Liz cried out as she ran across the room and into my arms.

I was overwhelmed by her sadness and the yearnings in her heart. My arms encircled her and I held her close. "Liz, we can't go home, precious one. I know you miss everything, so do I! We just have to trust in God and do the best we can with what we have here. You are such a big help to me, I could never get along without you." I said, expressing my love and trying to reassure her that her world would someday be put back together. I fear I have left her alone far to long today. It has given her to much idle time to remember. I held her close and we continued to chat. Slowly she pulled away and we automatically started to prepare our meal and waited for the men to come in.

Neither Liz, nor I were prepared for the burst of excitement that at that very moment broke through the door. John running in, hollering at the top of his voice was enough to give anyone the fright of their life.

109

"John, what is wrong, what has happened?" I screamed, thinking something terrible must be going on.

"Happened! Happened! Well, just wait till you see, Elizabeth Hutchins Curtyce. Just wait till you see!" Responded John, with such joy, he was about to burst.

"See what, John? What are you up to now? Pray tell what is going on? John what is going on? Quickly, quickly, talk to us." I requested getting very excited too and not knowing exactly why.

"Well, we had to go into town for some supplies and while we were there, the captain of a newly arrived ship, was inquiring as to how to locate us. It was just a coincidence, us running into him. He has just arrived with another shipload of our fellow countryman and cousin James sent us a few things, he thought we might need. Oh! It is so wonderful; I can hardly wait to open the big trunk he sent. Hurry boys, bring it in and set it down, right here in front of us. But, first, close your eyes, Elizabeth, quick," John, ordered, in an excited voice. I did as he said, not wanting to spoil any surprise he might have. I could hear the door open and close. I could hardly wait to see what was going on.

"Now! Now!" They all yelled at once. Before I could even open my eyes, I heard Liz gasp. Quickly my eyes flew open and my mouth followed. "Oh John!" That is all I could say, for there before me, placed in front of the big fireplace, sat my very own rocking chair. It was the chair that Papa had hand carved, just before I was born. I was speechless. Cousin James could not have sent me anything more precious and loved than the old rocking chair. I just stood there with my mouth wide open in amazement. He knew when I left, how much I wanted to bring this rocking chair with me but couldn't, due to the limited space available on the ship. He had promised me he would get it to me somehow and as always, he had kept his promise.

"Well Mama, aren't you going to sit down in it?" The children said, as they watched with broad smiles. They knew how pleased I was, for as always, the tears started to flow. I sat down, my legs feeling very wobbly under me. I just couldn't believe that James had managed to ship my favorite chair over to me. The excitement continued.

"Well, now that Mama is sufficiently surprised, lets see what is in store for the rest of us?" Announced John. "We will open the trunk right now. Oh look! Here are some of the tools, I had to leave behind, and they will come in handy when we start working in the fields in the spring. Elizabeth, here is another gift for you, from Anna and Katy. Open it, hurry," he ordered, so excited now, he could hardly contain himself. When I opened the wrapping there was the most beautiful silver locket.

"Oh, look, it is too pretty to wear. I am liable to lose it or something," I cried, my hands trembling, as I held the shining heart locket in my fingertips.

"Look Mama, it opens. Open it, see what's inside," said Liz. My hands were trembling so hard; I could hardly grasp the tiny heart shape between my fingers. When I got the two sides to separate, there were two tiny, miniature pictures of my Mama and Papa enveloped inside. I could not contain my joy.

"Oh, how wonderful! Look, John, look, pictures! Just like the ones hanging in the great hallway. They are painted ever so tiny to fit on the inside of the heart. What a wonderful surprise and what a wonderful gift!" My tears of joy were shed without shame.

"Here, Liz, here is something with your name on it. See what it is." Her father commanded in a loving voice, obviously enjoying all this very much.

"Oh, it is a new dress for Katy doll. Auntie must have made it. It is so pretty. I will put it on her right away. She needed a new dress," exclaimed Liz, as she ran to get her doll. Liz had put Katy doll away in a secret place thinking maybe she was getting too old to play with dolls. But now she had lapsed back into that little girl state and was eager to bring her out and dress her up. How good it was to see the happiness return to her eyes. They were bright, not at all clouded with the unhappiness of earlier this afternoon.

"This is wonderful, here is something for you, John, and you also William, and a package here for Thomas, too," John said, as he let his voice trail off at the mention of Thomas's name.

"Thomas.... Just where is Thomas?" I inquired. In all the excitement, I had not noticed that he was not with John and his brothers. No one answered my question. The eerie stillness of the moment left chills running up and down my spine. I stared at first one face and then another, patiently, but with apprehension, waiting for someone, anyone to answer.

"John, where is Thomas? Why did he not come in with you? Is he tending to something outside and missing all the fun?" I tried for an answer once more. No one in the room could seem to find their voice. I was becoming very agitated and just about to scream out when John finally said something.

"Oh, Elizabeth, that is some more of our good news. Thomas is staying on board the ship, with the Captain. When the Captain found us, he told us he was looking for a cabin boy for the return trip. That was all Thomas needed to hear. So he signed up, and is off to merry old England! The Captain was pleased, that Thomas has some experience, and he took him right out to the ship. Thomas will return with him in about six to eight months. Whenever he brings another ship full of people to this new land. He will probably see the family while there and he has been instructed to tell them that we got the trunk, chair and all the wonderful gifts and were very thankful for them. Isn't that wonderful news?" John exclaimed, excitement written all over his face.

"Wonderful news, John Curtyce! How could you call something as absurd as that, wonderful? I can't believe I am hearing you correctly! Thomas is going to do what? You go right now! Right this very minute and get Thomas, you bring him home where he belongs. I can't imagine, in my wildest dreams, you letting our little Thomas go off in a ship across the

111

rough old seas. I, I, I, I am just speechless. I am at a loss for words," I screamed out in dismay.

"Children, I think you had better step outside for a few moments. Your mother and I have to talk a few things over," John insisted, in a steady tone.

"Yes, please do go outside and your father will be joining you, so you can go get Thomas," I counter instructed all of them, shaking all over at the thought of what was going on.

"Now, Elizabeth, calm down! You are getting far too upset over nothing, nothing at all! This is a great opportunity for Thomas and it is what he wants to do," John stated in favor of this arrangement. As he tried to explain he reached for my shoulder. I jerked away.

"Calm! Calm, you say! Well, let me tell you John Curtyce, I don't think I will ever be calm again in my life. Thomas is hardly old enough to know what he wants and what he doesn't want. He is but a child and you have cast him adrift in a precarious little ship, without friend or family about, to look after him. I am still at a loss, as to whatever possessed you to even think such an idea as this, to be a good one." John tried to speak but I continued, ignoring his half formed words. "I am sick, my body has been stricken with pain. I want Thomas back now, now, right now, John, do you hear me? Now, John, right this very minute!" My voice grew louder and louder and I knew I was on the verge of collapse.

"Elizabeth, calm down, you are getting hysterical! I am sorry you feel this way, I really didn't anticipate you getting so distraught," John said, once again reaching out to me. I pulled back, away from his touch and continued to speak my mind.

"Distraught! You think I'm distraught? You could not possibly know the meaning of the word, John Curtyce! This is nothing compared to what you will see if you do not bring Thomas right back home, this very instant!" I reiterated my stand on this subject.

"Elizabeth, this is such a great time for Thomas! You know that he loves the sea and it is his dream, to someday have a shipping fleet of his own! This won't be forever, he is just going over and coming back," John again spoke; trying hard to convince me this was the right thing to do.

"He is just a child, John, not at all used to the rough ways of the sailors," I retaliated, trying to lower my voice

"No, Elizabeth, you are wrong, he is not a child, and he is a young man and he will do just fine! Besides, there is no way to get Thomas, even if I thought it a good idea to do so. The ship set sail a few hours ago," he announced profoundly. I thought I could even detect a slight bit of arrogance in his tone.

This only stirred the fires within me. "Set sail, you say! Do you mean to stand there and tell me, that my son has gone on a ship and has not even come to tell me good-bye? What in heavens name is happening to this family? It seems I am not a part of the family or any of the

112

decisions made anymore? What is going on?" I questioned, totally bewildered by this turn of events.

"Now Elizabeth, settle down! I am sorry this has made you so unhappy. We really didn't mean for it to happen this way! Everything happened so fast! There was no time to consider anything," John replied, trying even harder to make me accept his view.

"Well consider this, John Curtyce, if anything happens to Thomas on this voyage, I will have none but you to blame for it and forgiveness will not be one of the things in my heart!" I stated with a ferocious tone to my voice. I turn, and ran out of the sod house as fast as I can, down to the stream, with the tears falling from my eyes in great abundance. As I run faster and faster down the hill my toe hits hard against a large rock and the next moment I find I have landed hard against the ground. I am unable to move. The cold earth is very uncomfortable beneath me yet my sobbing body has no strength in it to upright itself. Great sobs pour forth from my mouth as I beat my fists, pounding harder and harder against the ground. The earth is not my enemy but I cannot stop myself. The more I pound, the harder I sob. I scream at the top of my lungs wanting the whole world to feel my agony and pain. I cannot live without my child; a part of me has been ripped and torn from my bosom. There is a big gaping hole in my heart. "Oh Thomas, Thomas, please don't be gone, please, please come home," I plead over and over, crying to God above, please let this be a dream, please let me wake up and this be a dream, a bad, bad, dream.

But it isn't a dream, and Thomas is not coming back. Not now anyway, not today. Something deep down inside, tells me this truth. I sense John coming came down by the little babbling stream; he put his arms around me and helps me stand on my feet. I pulled away and ran for the house. I was seeking a sanctuary from my misery and I couldn't seem to find it anywhere.

I methodically fixed our meal and cleared away the trenchers. Our family talk around the table is hardly heard by my ears. I work about in a daze, and ready myself for bed. I think if I can only go to sleep, the hurt will stop, but it doesn't and sleep does not come easily. My mind is constantly turning, trying to figure out a way to get my son back. What if he was cold and hungry? What if there was a wreck at sea? What if? What if? My mind whirled and whirled about, searching, seeking a way to recover my loss. If only I was a big bird, I could fly over the ship and swoop him up in my strong talons and carry him to safety. He could be home then, in the comfort of his mother's arms, safe from harm, safe from the clutches of that awful ship and its crew. My body is still racked with the silent sobs it holds within. My joy had been taken out of my life. My baby boy, by tousle-headed, brown-eyed pet was gone and I could not do one thing about it. Would I ever be able to forgive John for this? Could I ever find forgiveness for such a heinous hurt? These are the thoughts in my mind as I fall into a deep and restless sleep leaving all the many unanswered questions whirling around in my head.

# CHAPTER 7

The light, soft, snowflakes drift ever so gently through the cold crisp winter air. Each touching the earth with a likeness, akin to a kiss, a mother places on her sleeping babies cheek. I watch the snow come down hour after hour and stare into its blinding whiteness until my eyes can no longer focus. The icicles hang from the eves of the house, clutching tighter and tighter as they slide further and further down toward the ground. They freeze long before they can reach a safe destination and run away to safety. It is like a big game, could the melting ice get away from "Mother Nature?" No, she is much too quick. It would have to wait for another season to come before it can drip, skip and run tumbling down the hill to join in the fun at the pond.

I will have to wait for another season too, before my heart can laugh and sing, and leap with joy. How long would it take for my happy season to be here again? Weeks? Months? Years? All I can think about is Thomas, somewhere, way out there. He was communing with the grotesque sea monster and his beloved Neptune. While I, his mother, sits and looks out a small, winter stained window. Wishing all the while he would walk up the front path. The whys, in my heart have never been answered and the days drift ever onward, piling up like this snow before my eyes.

My fear for Thomas's life never ceases, nor does the aching in my heart. John has tried in every way he can to explain. He has tried to compensate, whenever he could. He has tried to reason with me, but to me what happened is beyond reason. There is nothing to do; whatever he does now is to no avail. There is no consoling the loneliness that dwells within my body, or the emptiness Thomas's departure has caused within our family. His parting has saddened everyone, but for me, the beating of my heart was thrown off course, the day he boarded that ship. I am at a loss to put into words, what I feel inside. For me, his mother, it is an unexplainable experience. A part of my very person seems to be missing. I have no one to express my thoughts to. I would be strongly censured if the elders were to even surmise my thoughts. Until someone experiences the emptiness, of a missing child, they could never really understand. I must remain alone with my turmoil and disbelief.

Now the full force of winter is upon us, with its relentless winds and the seemingly never ending cold and snow. Our company of people has tried to prepare against the onslaught of its furry, yet none of the stories that reached our ears before leaving England, portrayed it quiet like it is. For a fact, they were not even close in the description of its physical powers.

The walls of our crude built shelter, is like a thin piece of muslin that offers, very little resistance to the strong winds that whirl and whip about us, squeezing through ever crack and crevice. Slowly the cold creeps through our skin and settles deep in the marrow of our bones.

We keep the fire roaring day and night, moving ever closer to the blaze, defying its scorching singe, as we huddle together hoping our closeness will give us some comfort. We move within the fireplace enclosure itself and feel the soot drop off, onto our heads. We are forced to breath the sooty, smoke thickened air, choking us, as it fills our lungs.

The constant fear that we will run out of wood haunts us. We watch the neatly stacked woodpile dwindle downward with each passing day. The scarcity of the wood that was so plentiful during the spring and summer months is frightfully low. We wonder in our minds if we will make it through this winter, but dare not voice our thoughts aloud, for fear we will scare Liz. William and John know full well the dangers that surround us.

I am thankful for the lean-to John built against the back of the house. It has kept the feed and the chickens and goat within our sight and out of harms way. The goat has at least provided us with milk and the chickens with meat and eggs. The snow has been far to deep for any of the men folks to go out hunting. The grain is getting very low, as are most of our other supplies. Perhaps we can get a small amount of grain from the gristmill. We need just enough to tie us over the winter months. I am so thankful that Mr. Dummer was able to get the mill going before winter set in.

Perhaps, if the snow lightens up a bit, an occasional fresh fowl, or a rabbit now and then, can be gotten by the men and what a blessing from God, that will be. My wonder at our existence is overwhelming. How have we managed in less than a year to totally reverse ourselves so completely?

Now mind you, I am thankful for the shelter we do have and what food we managed to store up from this meager existence. Yet when I do take the time to look back, I am amazed at where we are today compared to where we were and how we were living a year ago. It doesn't seem possible that everything has been used from our company supplies. It looked like so much at the beginning of winter. I thought we would have many things left over come spring. How could we have been so wrong in our judgment of our needs? Because of the extremely bad weather, we are not free to go about and visit with our friends. We have become almost isolated, except for those extremely close by.

This time, of almost total solitude, has allowed me to study John and his moods. He does not seem to be completely at ease with his surroundings. He has not been able to do really much of anything since we got here. It is hard for him. He has always been a man in control of his own destiny. Now, others have taken over and we seem to be like lost sheep, following the leader.

Even the church has not been quite up to the expectations of some. It is as if the feelings of the people are still not being listened to. Much of the dissatisfactions are still with us. It takes so much of our resources to sustain the meetinghouse and the leader of our congregation. Not that we feel that it is not our duty to do so. It is just that everyone is struggling to get started, there are only a few that are really doing well.

Only those that came before us who had their fields planted and their harvest was good are really secure in their feeling of having enough to eat this winter. We have to draw all of our food from the company and are very fortunate to be able to share in others good bounty when it is offered.   It is unfortunate however, that we are not one of the ones to contribute instead of taking.   John says it will get better by next year, then we will be able to plant and harvest and sell or trade some of our goods for other things we need.   I suppose he is right, yet I fear it could not get much worse, if those things didn't happen.

The bleak, idle time of winter is so hard for me to deal with. Being cooped up inside with little to do, doesn't make it any easier. Again such a thought has to be kept forever unto myself, for the consequences for bad thoughts could be so mistaken and misconstrued if heard by others.   That seems strange to me also as I personally think that most everyone is probably thinking the exact same thing for we are all in the same situation here.   It is an awful feeling for me to even be afraid to voice my opinions and thoughts to John.   Yet on occasion that is exactly how I feel.

Why does it have to be this way?   We have always had such openness between us.   Not that we ever talked in the public about our ideas, but we could at least talk to each other.   Now it seems difficult to talk at all. There is always the fear someone will over hear us or the meaning of our words be misunderstood or that maybe we have no right to our opinion at all.

I wonder sometimes if John has noticed what a strain this coming to the new land has put upon our family?   I think men don't notice things as much as women do.   There is a great difference though and I don't think John could help but see it.   Maybe he doesn't really care about what I think anymore.   After all these years, could that be true?   I wonder could that be it?

Why can't I ask why anymore?   I am still the same person I haven't changed.   It must be that John is not sure of himself in his new surroundings and doesn't want to do anything until he gets used to the people and places.   That is probably it and I am seeing problems that aren't even there and making too much out of nothing as usual.

My how the snow is coming down.   I hope the men have not gone to far from the shelter.   It would not be hard at all to get completely lost in this blinding, white stuff.   They will be frozen to the bone when they return and ready for a warm grog, to soothe their cold insides.   I must keep the fire going and not let the flame get to low.   I don't think it would take too much for us to freeze right in front of the fire.   I hesitate to think of any reason for the minister to call them out on a day like this.   If I knew what they were doing out in this raging storm, I would only worry more.   Maybe I am finally realizing that for me, not to know something, is sometimes best.

I have been leaning against this window looking out for such a long time that my head is almost frozen right to the cold paper covering.   I must have been standing here much longer than I imagined.   It does feel good, almost a relief, to just let my mind wander aimlessly.   But the fire will be out if Liz hasn't put a bit more wood on it.   Before I can turn to see how it looks in the cooking area, here Liz is tugging at my elbow bringing me right out of my deep thoughts.

"Mama, what are you thinking about? You have been standing at the window ever so long, just staring out into the air," Liz questioned, her upturned face searching mine for an answer.

"Oh Liz, nothing really, I am just thinking. It is well into the month of December and the days of winter are still long before us. I guess maybe I was wishing for a small breath of spring to come blowing by the window as I look out," I replied, grateful to have her care and grateful to have her here to talk with me.

"Mama, are you watching for Thomas to come home?" She asked with a worried frown creasing her brow.

Her question startled me but I tried to keep my voice calm as I answered her. "No, Liz, I know it will be a long time before Thomas can return," I had known that since the day of you fathers great announcement. And very little had been said on the subject of Thomas since then. It was a subject that was better left not talked about. I guess in my misery, I hadn't realized how perceptive Liz really is.

"I know how you feel Mama. I am sorry you have to be so sad! I miss Thomas too! I know what will make you happy, Mama! Just wait and see what I have for you. It will take all your troubled thoughts away," Liz exclaimed as she ran to her sleeping area.

I hardly thought there was any chance that anything could do that, but whatever Liz was up to, it was making her happy that was for sure.

Much to my dismay, I was greatly surprised when she came back to the window. My eyes were wide as I viewed her with outstretched arms, as she hurried toward me with an apron full of brightly colored leaves.

"Oh, Liz, they are so beautiful! Where did you get them? The snow has covered all the leaves that the wind did not blow away, long ago!" I exclaimed.

"Mama, I collected them because they were so bright and pretty. Now I want you to have them, they will make you smile Mama, really they will," She said, as she reached out to give me her collection of pretty leaves.

"Yes, Liz, they will make your Mama smile, they are ever so pretty," I thank you for them and for your kindness and your thoughtfulness in sharing them with me.

"What will you do with them Mama?" She questioned. Looking about the room.

"Well, let me see, something as special and pretty as these leaves, they should be in a place of honor. Where would that be?" I said, putting my finger to my chin and twisting my mouth as I looked around the room for just the right special spot.

"I know, I know, put them there on the table, all around the bowl of red apples and fresh squash. Sprinkle them all around, so everyone can enjoy them. Won't that be nice? It will brighten up everything, don't you think?" Liz said, with so much enthusiasm and happiness in her voice, you just couldn't help but smile.

"Yes, I believe it will do just that, Liz, lets put them all about and sit a small candle in the holder. We will pretend we are having a grand party, and maybe the Queen will come," I suggested, beginning to enjoy playing her little game.

"Oh yes, Mama, and Auntie and Katy too, this is so much fun, when Papa and John and William come in they can pretend too, they will see what a fine time we are having and want to join in," she said, as she danced about the room, placing a hand full of leaves here and a handful of leaves there.

Yes it is a fine time, Liz, It reminds me of the fun times we used to have at Caswell," I explained to her. Then I bent down and gently gave Liz a kiss on the top of her pretty chestnut curls. It took this magnificent gesture of love, from the imagination of a small child, to bring me out of my self-pity. She had done it with a smile and the gift of a few dried leaves, but it was the greatest gift of the year for it had brought to me a warm glow and made me realize that I had neglected my family so very much, and all because of my grief over Thomas' leaving. I must never let that happen again, for seeing the shear delight in the face of this tiny little girl, as she gave up her treasure of leaves for the hope of making her mother smile, is almost more than I can bear.

Why had I been so blind to the needs of my family? It is not like me to let myself indulge in such self-pity. I will try to do better in the days to come. I know that I cannot forget Thomas, but I must tuck my thoughts far back in my mind and concentrate on the family that is here.

"Liz, lets surprise the men and when they come back from whatever it is, that has kept them away all day we will have a fine meal fixed for them. We will make a fine bunch of vitals and we will not pretend we are having a party we will have one. All that we can do for this year is done, we will enjoy the beauty of the winter, for with spring will come long days of hard work and then we will be wishing for a day like today." I said, encouraging her good cheer.

I think the snow has about quit, and while it has, I am going to put on my cloak and walk over to your Auntie Sarah's and Uncle William's and invite them to join us for this fine gathering. They will love some fine soup and bread and we will enjoy each other, as we should. I will not be long now, you stay in the house," I instructed her as I grabbed my cloak and quickly went up the street.

I pulled my cloak and hood around me tight as I hurried along. I feel light within my heart, like I have not felt in a long time. This would be fun, we would have guests again, and why had I not thought of this before? The children would come too and all the cousins could enjoy each other. The more I thought about this great idea, the faster my feet flew. I was more skating than walking. I had to remind myself to be more careful on the ice, so I slow myself down a bit, but only a little for I had a mission to accomplish, and I surely didn't want to waste too much time.

When I reached the gateway to William and Sarah's, I was completely out of breath; I paused and leaned heavily on the gate. When I looked up, I saw William chopping some wood. He looked up and saw me leaning on the gate. The look on his face was one of shock at finding me out in this kind of weather. He came running with the ax still in his hand.

"What is wrong, Elizabeth? What has happened to bring you out in weather like this?" He inquired, looking at me rather strangely.

"Weather like what, William? This is beautiful weather, don't you think?" I said, and chuckled at his concern, acting as if I didn't even know it was cold outside.

"Elizabeth, get inside before you catch a fever and tell us what is going on." He demanded and ushered me toward the door.

"Sarah, look who I found about our front gate." He announced as we entered the door.

"Oh, Elizabeth, what has happened, is someone sick, has someone gotten hurt?" She sputtered out.

"My! My! What a greeting I receive from the both of you. What is it that makes you think I am the carrier of bad news? I have come here to bring you a personal invitation, an invitation to dine with us this evening. Now is that bad enough news for the likes of you two?" I responded to their questions.

"Oh, that does sound like such fun, we have not been together in such a long time, it will be our pleasure, our pleasure indeed." Both answered at once.

"Thanks to you both. You don't know how happy you have made me. I really need to do something like this. I have missed our special times of sharing and family gatherings. I must hurry back to Liz now, for she will wonder what has taken me so long.

The men all left early this morning with the minister. I supposed they were asked to do some fowling or hunting of some kind. They are still out and will probably not be back for sometime. I will see you all in a short while." I said, and pulling my cloak about my shoulders and my hood up close to my face I backed out the door and started down the lane.

As I walk back to the house, I feel no need to really hurry; at least not as fast as I had going to their house. I am thinking now of just what we will fix and what we would do and how much fun it would be. I couldn't believe myself; I am as giddy as a child. I vowed to myself, at that very minute, not too ever let the traditions of my family get lost in this new land I found myself in.

119

We were still required to be so careful not to offend anyone by our deeds or actions and never knowing how others might think of traditions, I knew I would have to keep most of my thought to myself. I don't believe it to be wrong; it is just that things are so different here. It is as hard here as it was in England to know whom your friends are and who they aren't.

If someone hears of what I am doing tonight and thinks ill of it, I could be deemed unworthy and bring disgrace to my family. And I do not want to do any such thing. I know Sarah's thoughts on the subject so I have no worry about her. She is as confused as I am, as to what is going on in our lives. I do find her more in compliance with everything or at least she doesn't question things as often as I do. That is just the difference in our make up. I have a need to know or at least be considered in some way. Sarah on the other hand has learned to take each day, one step at a time. I admire her for that and wish I were more like that.

I could see no harm in my family traditions, or where they would cause harm to any others. I want them to be remembered, as I remember the ones from my childhood. I will just have to incorporate as many of them into our daily life, as I can. At least that way our children will hold them in their minds and pass them on to their families as I wish to do. At least for the sake of Liz, who is much to young to remember the festivities of Caswell Manor? Yes, somehow I will find a way.

Liz and I spent the rest of the afternoon tending to our vitals. We sat out the wooden trenchers, carved by John and the boys, from wood pieces left over from the forest cuttings. They are much appreciated and are serving us as well as any of my pewter or blown glass pieces, left behind in Nazing.

With the trenchers in place the table looks as festive and colorful as any that I remember at Caswell. The little candle is flickering a soft light from its wick. As shadows dance around the tiny room. Everything in the room seems to be joining in with our happy mood. Liz's beautiful leaves are indeed doing what she intended them to do, they are making her mother smile.

The rough, hand hewn table slab, looks as beautiful as any table at the old manor house in England. This one might not be as highly polished or carved and crafted as meticulously, as those in England, but it serves us with as much style and grace as the ones there had.

With the table looking especially nice we set our minds on the food we wanted to prepare. Some Indian pudding, a pot of fresh squash and the bread was already in the warming oven. I am just finishing up putting a big pot of soup to cook and steam over the hearth fire. Mmmm, I am already hungry, I admitted to myself, as my tummy grumbled at me.

It was some time later, when John and the boys returned. They proudly carried several rabbits and a couple of fowl apiece. That was their portion for participating in the hunt. What amazed looks they ware upon their faces as they see the drastic change in the house. They seem even more amazed at the change in me. John finally stammered out a few words and the boys just stood staring at the table.

120

"What is going on here?" John burst forth with his first understandable words. I was quick to explain what had transpired while they were away from home. I was in such fear of a reprimand from John for even thinking of having some fun and laughter in our life and home. I don't know what I would do if he were to tell me we could not have this family gathering. But I need not have concerned myself at all for we were all quickly caught up in the excitement of the moment.

"Perhaps, John, we could put a couple of those rabbits on the spit and really have a fine meal for your brother and his family. Wouldn't that be a real treat for us all? You don't think that the elders and others would object or think that we were misusing our foods do you John?" My questions were voiced because of my great fear of our family being chastised for a wrong done against the company of people. I hate this fear that lingers over us all of the time.

"If that is what makes you happy Elizabeth, then rabbits on the spit it will be. William and John get them cleaned right away and I will move some embers over here under the spit and we will have a fine rabbit supper in no time." John said, letting his enthusiasm seep from his body through the twinkle in his beautiful steal gray eyes. He quickly went to work building the fire. He was doing just as Liz had predicted he would. He was playing our game and pretending just like she said. It made me happy to see everyone in such a jolly spirit.

"John, do you really think it is all right to have a celebration like this? What if someone thinks it is not an appropriate thing to do? I have been told by some of the ladies that many of the families are becoming dissatisfied with the way things are being done. I do not want anyone to think bad of us." I asked the question of John one more time. I am truly concerned and fearful of the consequences.

"I hardly think that a family gathering requires the sanction of the minister or anyone else for that matter. People are just too quick to judge others. We will not worry about that tonight, we will just enjoy ourselves, for after all we have been through, we deserve some rejoicing. It is so good to see you happy for once." John stated, as he stirred the coals and continued his chatter. "We are just sharing what we have with other family members who could not join in the hunt today."

Finally everything was ready and I glanced about to make sure that everything looked just perfect. You would think this was the very first time I had ever had guests for dinner. I guess I felt like it was for the excitement felt in the pit of my stomach was causing it to jump with joy.

I turned and looked out the window seeing that it was starting to get dark and William, Sarah and the family weren't here yet. I grabbed a candle stub, placed in a tin holder and headed for the door. As I opened the door, the wind came rushing in and almost blew out the flame. "Oh, that won't do, I will get the lantern and use it." I exclaimed.

"What are you trying to accomplish, Elizabeth? Why do you need the lantern? We only have one." John questioned me. I was afraid he would laugh at what I was trying to do.

121

"I just want to use it for tonight, John, please get it for me. I want something that the wind will not blow out. I am going to put it right there on the fence post next to the gate. It will be a light to welcome our guests. It will light the path to our door, it is so terribly dark out now. This way our guests will be able to see their way and not slip on the ice. I want to make tonight just a little extra special, John. It will be alright just for this one time, won't it?" I asked, a bit sheepishly.

"A splendid idea, Elizabeth, I will go get it. Why don't you put a couple of small candles in the two front windows and we will be all lit up?" He said, as he fetched the lantern for me. I thought he was making fun of me but it didn't matter. I was far too happy to let anything spoil my evening.

"I will do just that, John Curtyce, that is a fine idea yourself." I tossed back at him. We both chuckled at each other and at the fun we seem to be having. The boys returned with the cleaned rabbits and John put them on the spit and hung them over the fire. Each took turns turning them round and round and soon had them roasted, to a perfect golden brown. The juices were dripping down onto the coals, and the flames, were leaping up as if to devour our meal. The delicious smell of the cooking juices caused my stomach to gnaw away at itself. It was almost more than I could tolerate, being so empty. I was glad when I could hear the sound of happy voices coming up the path. Rushing to the door, I opened it, welcoming our loved ones to our humble home with great pleasure.

"Greetings, to you all, this is such a wonderful idea. I can't believe it has taken us so long to do this. In England it was such a natural thing for us to get together. We have missed it greatly. Come in, hurry out of the cold. Son, put their coats on the pegs and let them come close to the fire and get their cold bodies warm." John's voice rang out with such good cheer.

"Burr, it is really cold out there!" Announced Sarah, as she rushed toward the fire. Not even taking the time to remove her cape.

"Uncle William, rub your hands together and blow into them, it will help the cold disappear," coached, John Jr.

"That it does, young John! I can't believe it is so frigid cold." William echoed Sarah's sentiments. "It looks like it has started to snow again, Aunt Sarah."

"Has it?" I asked, as we took the wraps from around the children.

"Yes, Elizabeth, it has. The wind is not as bad as it was earlier, though. What a great idea of yours to put the lantern out by the gate and the candles in the windows, it helped us to see the house in the blinding snow. It makes your front entry look as if it were smiling at us as we approached. The reflection of the light on the ice and snow looks so bright and cheerful, on this bleak winters night." Sarah commented.

"Oh, thank you, my mind has been running in a whirl all afternoon. Thinking of things to do to make this a really special time for all of us," I answered.

"Well, it looks like your mind has done a fine job in both the greeting of your guest and with the cooking. It smells so good in here. What have you made that smells so delicious?" Asked Sarah, poking her nose high in the air and sniffing deep. "It smells so yummy!"

"Well, the men did a fine job today while they were out fowling, they were able to snare a couple of rabbits, so here we are with fresh meat upon our table, our family about us, and many, many blessings to be thankful for," I announced, clapping my hands together, in a gesture of glee.

"John, lets sit and eat now before everything gets cold," I requested.

"Yes, Elizabeth, a fine idea," John agreed. We all found a place at the big table and when everyone was quiet we bowed our heads and gave thanks for the fine food, our loving family and the many blessings from our loving God.

As always when we were all together, the time seemed to pass by in a blink of an eye and far too soon, it was time for the family to be going back to their home.

"I really hate to see this evening end, it has been such a blessing and brings back such pleasant memories of our times together in our homeland." I said, giving a wistful sigh, as I helped them bundle the children snugly in their coats and hats.

"Yes, that it does and we must have many more times like this so that our children can grow up and look back on these special times as we do ours." John offered.

"Thank you, Elizabeth, for thinking of it. And for the fowl and rabbit, you are sending home with us." Said Sarah, as she gave me a hug then added. "Those little parchment rolls with your poem on it was a wonderful added touch Elizabeth."

"You know, Sarah, it really wasn't my idea at all. I have to give Liz the credit for all of this. It was her love and imagination that brought this all about. I of course did the parchments and thank you, but I will have to tell you sometime later, of everything that took place today. Sometime when we are just setting around doing our embroidery and mending and have much more time than we do this evening. Bundle up now and keep warm. Be careful on the ice going home. Good night now and Godspeed." I called out, as they made their way up the path and down the lane toward their home. I watched until I could see nothing more than a gray/white blur in the night.

As I cleared away the trenchers and put away the vitals, I felt satisfied within myself for the first time since landing on these distant shores. The light talk turned to the men's day of fowling and soon we were all ready to go to our beds for the night. John got out the beautiful bible that John Eliot had given us and read from the scripture. We said our daily prayers and a loving good night to the children as we watched them go to their respective sleeping areas. I helped Liz ready herself for bed and then gently tucked her in.

"Mama today was such a fun day. Could we pretend we are having a big party again sometime, and maybe Cousin James, and all the other friends you left behind can come? Could we, Mama, could we?" Liz Squealed, with a look of great anticipation on her beautiful little face.

"Yes Liz, we will play your game often, and even if there is no one but you and I, we will have a wonderful time. We must always dream of better times ahead and be thankful for our loved ones in far off places. You made me very happy today and your special gift of the beautiful leaves was the best part of the whole day. Thank you, Liz, you surely did make your Mama smile and you made her heart very happy too. Go to sleep now dear and with God's blessings, sleep well . . ."I kissed her upon her cheek and quickly left her sleeping area.

While I was tucking Liz in, John retrieved the lantern from the front gate and I snuffed out the candles in the front windows. I was glad to finally have the candles snuffed out. It was beginning to worry me having them burn for so long in the windows. I didn't want to be wasteful with our low supply of winter rations; I just wanted to be happy and cheerful for once.

"John, I hope the elders of the church did not think us to frivolous tonight, with the lantern out front and the candles in the windows. With the storm blowing as hard as it was, I think it really did help, but they might not see it that way. With all the supplies so short, someone is bound to complain. So many things have changed, I am afraid to think or do anything. Is it always going to be like this?" I asked, hoping for an answer I could accept.

"No, I am sure it is just us, Elizabeth. We had so many freedoms at Caswell. Freedoms others were denied. We were far more fortunate than most of the people that have come this long distance, all of them seeking many different things. We must remember that here we cannot get lost in great numbers of people like at home, for there are not great numbers here. Everyone must obey the laws of the church the same." He reminded me.

"I realize that John, but my question is to why we must give up all our family traditions, be afraid to even enjoy them within our own homes. Besides they are nothing to be ashamed of and certainly there is nothing wrong with them. I sometimes feel, that people believe something as simple as just being happy is a sin. I want Liz and the boys to have some remembrance of what it was like in my family and our home, before coming to this new land. If it hadn't been for the Archbishop, sending spies into our homes and listening to the private devotions of the families, we would still be in England and I would be enjoying my family and the special things that I grew up with." I stated, sounding a bit bitter, I'm sure. And if the truth were known I am, but I must not let even John know that. He would be bound to tell the minister and I would be punished severely for my bad thoughts and actions. I must play by their rules no

124

matter how bad I feel or how wrong I think they are. I will just have to find a way around the silly things they expect of us. I don't want to be made an example of before my family and the whole company of people. That would be even more dreadful than enduring the rules in silence.

"Elizabeth, are you all that unhappy here?" John asked, tilting my head up so he could see my expression as I answered.

"Not really unhappy!" I bit my lip, as I knew that was not quite a truthful statement. I quickly tried to explain in more depth what I meant. "You must admit our lives have really changed and one of our sons is not even with us. Do you think that would be the case, if we were at Caswell?" I questioned.

"Perhaps it would, for we never know what our destiny is to be. We just follow the leading of our Lord and Savior." John said, again looking for my reaction. He still held my chin firmly in his large, rough hand.

I twisted my head so as to release myself from his grip and continued my thoughts. "Yes, I too believe that we are to follow God's teachings and I always try and do my best, but when, what I do is within those practices and teachings, what makes them wrong?" I asked, for I really wondered what we were doing that was so bad. I also knew that my questions would probably never be answered to my satisfaction.

"Well, I don't have all the answers to all your doubts and fears, Elizabeth, and I am sorry you are so unhappy with our life here. We are here now and we must make the very best of it. We made a decision to join this company and by doing so we pledged ourselves to follow by its laws and rules. We must keep our promise Elizabeth, we just must. We have no choice unless we are to return to England and forget this whole new life. Is that what you want? Please tell me how I can make you understand how great the opportunities are here in comparison to England, for both our children and us and everyone involved. What is asked of us is not so hard to follow. It is just a great deal different from what our life was like in Nazing. In many ways it is much better, for the majority of the population here." In his own way John was trying to reassure me that life would someday be acceptable to me. At least that is what he hoped.

"I know some of what you say is right and still I fear for the way things are. We never had to take up arms and keep such vigilance at all hours of the day and night, like we do now. I am afraid for the boys and for you, John. I am concerned for Liz and me too. It is not a good feeling to not even feel safe in your own home. I never felt that way in Nazing. It is like we are always on a constant alert, always looking for that unknown predator lurking somewhere out there in the dark. Is it always going to be like this?" I questioned, wanting him to consider my views too. While he was forming an answer in his head I continued. "You know John we never had to live with a stockade around Caswell, now did we? Our guns were for hunting and a walk in the woods was a relaxing experience, not one immersed in fear for our lives."

"Yes, that is exactly what we are on, a constant alert. This is not a civilized land by any stretch of the imagination. There are many hostile elements out there and we do have to be on the lookout for them. It is for our own protection and for the protection of our loved ones and

125

friends, that we all take our duties very seriously." John explained, or at least tried to explain. But he was telling me something that I already knew and just didn't want to accept.

"Well, I still wish that Archbishop Laud and the Church of England would have left us alone, then my world would still be upright and not all topsy-turvy as it is now" I said, shrugging my shoulders. I feel better for letting some of my thoughts out in the open. My independent nature is, surely going to get me into trouble someday. I hope I haven't said too much already. It is not good to go against your husband's wishes and John did wish us to be right here where we are.

"Elizabeth, you had better be careful as to whom you voice these opinions of yours. It is very dangerous to go against any of our leaders or the rules by which we are bound," John warned. It was as if he was reading my mind. Could I trust John not to say anything? I had never had doubts about my husband before. Why was I having them now? I am afraid this is a very bad omen.

"I am only talking to you, John, and if you take my thoughts no further then this very room, then that is where they will stay. We have always been able to talk things over before. Now I am afraid to even do that. These are the very things that are wrong with our life; we cannot even be truthful with each other. There is a constant nagging feeling that someone is always about that will be offended by what they hear. So what has changed John, can you at least tell me that? Wasn't that at least part of our reason for coming over here? To be able to get away from someone else telling us what to do and say every step of our lives. Wasn't it because we wanted to be able to worship and believe without the scrutiny of the Archbishop? Didn't we find their ways of dress, their wearing of long hair, the spectacle of some of the things they did, things they requested us to do, not to our liking? Wasn't one of the most offensive things they did was think for us? Now, we are afraid of the same things here. We are afraid to even enjoy a family gathering, for fear someone will accuse us of being frivolous. It seems to me, we have brought many of our problems and dissatisfactions right along with us. I cannot really see the difference sometimes. We have traded one set of obstacles, for some very similar ones. I do not want to go to any extremes or go against the word of God! I just want our home to be our home and be able to feel at ease with what I want to do within its walls. Is that too much to ask for?" I stated my feelings openly for the first time in a long time and drew in a deep breath after my long dissertation knowing John would surely have an answer for me.

"No, it is not to much to ask for Elizabeth, but if the leaders feel it is going to disrupt the unity of the people of our settlement and cause God's wraith to come down on us, then they will take steps to rid the town of those elements." He stated. Emphasizing every word so, that it made me sick to listen to him. I just wanted to lash out at authority in general.

"Oh, John, this discussion is getting us nowhere. I don't feel that one little lantern lit and set upon a post to light the path to our door is going to cause any in the town any harm. If our home is dark because we used too much oil or tallow then that should be our choice." I said, looking at John for conformation of my thoughts.

"No, not harm, but it could be considered a waste, and that is a sin, Elizabeth." John said, as he turned away from me and walked toward the fireplace. He knew his statement would infuriate me. And that it did. I felt he was siding with everyone else and it made no difference to him what I felt, what I liked, disliked, wanted, didn't want, thought or didn't think. Why had he let me light the lantern and put it out at all?

"So, now, by my lighting up my home, I have sinned, is that what you think, John Curtyce?" I countered his remarks. His attitude was so infuriating and I was almost trembling I was so mad.

"No, I don't think so, but some could. That is what this bedtime talk is all about isn't it? Aren't we talking about others and what they might consider unnecessary?" John reiterated, once again.

"Oh, I just don't know anymore, I don't think that I can live without being able to think for myself. I pray every day for the guidance of God and always try to do his will in all that I undertake. I can't completely change my ways after all these years. I do not think I am such a bad person for trying to bring a little bit of hope and cheer into such a dreary, desolate, winter night. And if anyone else feels that I have done wrong, then they will just have to confront me with their feelings." I said, determined to have some say in my own life.

"Elizabeth, you have really turned this little discussion into a much bigger problem than it ever started out to be. There probably will be nothing said at all, I was merely trying to point out the fact, that you must be careful with your free spirit. You know that even your most trusted friend and most loyal relative could turn on you." John advised.

"John, are you suggesting?" I was cut off mid sentence. A sharp rap on the door spun both of us out of our thoughts and into action. My face paled at the thoughts of who might be standing on the other side of the door. John finished his sentence as he went toward the door. My thoughts and words were caught somewhere between my mind and my mouth. "I am not suggesting anything Elizabeth, I am just saying, be careful." He warned again, in an almost whispered tone, as he carefully took his gun down from the rack above the door. It was late, very late for someone friendly to be calling. John eased the door open a small crack. It was the Reverend, standing shivering in the cold of the night.

"Why, what brings you to our door at this late hour, Reverend? John asked with a surprised and questioning look on his face.

"Well I was just having prayer with one of the sick and afflicted of our settlement and as I returned home I heard voices coming from your home and had seen a light at your gate and in the window as I went by earlier. I was curious to find out if something was wrong or if someone was sick and if you needed prayer. I thought it was rather late to see your home so lit up." He stated giving us an explanation for his late visit.

"Everything seems to be fine here but we thank you for your concern Reverend. I just built an extra large fire this night and that is probably what you saw as you passed. Little Liz seemed to be a bit cold

127

and we didn't want her to catch a chill. Earlier this evening my brother and his family came for a visit. They arrived just at the peek of the storm and I put a few candles in the window to show the way. We could not even see the front path at that time. It was good to talk over the plans for our home now that his is done and they are settled. We are anxious to get started on it." John kept up a sort of one-sided conversation but stood his ground with the Reverend. Just how much had he really seen and just how much of our conversation had he listened in on?" The next thing I knew John was inviting him in to warm himself by the fire. I couldn't quite believe my ears. I was glad when he declined the offer and John once more bolted the door with the long wooden slide, and returned the gun to its place above the door.

"John, do you think he heard our discussion? I know he saw the lantern and candles from earlier." I questioned. This discussion with John and the unexpected visit from the Reverend had unnerved me. Maybe I should go back to England. I really don't know if I can live this life here in this new land. I was not ready to give up everything I had enjoyed before coming here, especially if it doesn't go against God and his teachings.

John readied himself for bed and crawled in and in seconds he was fast asleep. He had not even answered my last question of concern. I also readied myself for bed, but I am not quite ready to turn in, not just yet. I bent over the bed and listened to John's breathing to assure myself that John was totally immersed in sleep. Happy to see that he was I went directly to my secret hiding place and retrieved my journal and began to write all of the happenings of the day. It was at this very moment in time that I realized just how important these little journals would be. I will pass all the family traditions on to Liz, through them. At least some of the answers to my questions were lying right there in my lap. I can record what ever I please, for it will be for her eyes only. At the right place in time, I will pass them on to her. It will be her heritage, passed on to her from her mother. I gleaned a new spark of excitement and hope within me and I could hardly wait to write more in my little book, now my writings seem to have a real purpose. The feather pen fairly flew across the pages as I recounted in my mind this whole day. My eyes are growing tired and the light dim and my bones are aching for rest. This discussion with John has taken its toll on me. I will have to stop writing for now I will remember though, to always keep my journal in a safe and secret place so that I can always write my true thoughts and feelings and not be frightened that someone might look upon them and think ill of me.

As I look over at the little stool next to my chair I can see that the candle in the dish is just about to flicker out. I don't want it to burn low, for I feel a need to start right this very minute and go back, many, many years, back to the very beginning of my remembrance, and write to her all about her wonderful grand parents and the wonderful lessons they had taught to me. All with love and gentleness for they were the kindest two people in all the earth. I wanted to explain about my childhood, my womanhood, the trip across the big ocean and why we had to try this new life. I wanted her to smell the fresh green clover of the English countryside and experience the life I had known. I wanted her to feel, touch and sense the importance of our past and what it means to her future. I somehow had to convey to her through this little book all the secrets of life, with its sad times, its happy times and all that goes into making a family a very special thing. I do not want to leave out one single thing, for I want her, to have at her fingertips, the creation and heritage of her family.

The little candle flickered once more, telling me this is not the time, and I will bend to its truths, for I fear, within a short time, I will be in total darkness. So my thoughts for now will truly have to wait. There will be other times, and I am far too tired to think anymore tonight. I must make myself put these remembrances aside and get some rest.

The floor feels cold against my bare feet as I proceed across the room to put my journal back in its secret hiding place. Knowing that the books are safe is now paramount. I will let nothing happen to them. Feeling that they are now securely hidden I think I can finally go to sleep. Mmmm, this nice warm spot where John has moved over feels especially good. I need both the love and the feel of John's warm body tonight. As the tiny stub of the candle flickered its last sputtering of light I pushed it back on the little stool and settled in for a long nights rest. The deep darkness enveloped my surroundings. As I settled into my bed the glow of the small pile of coals was the only visible light in the room. I spontaneously place a gentle kiss upon John's forehead. His release of a soft moan as he draws a little closer allows me to snuggle up and draw some of the warmth from his body. But his warmth was not the only thing that I needed; I also need his love and understanding. In my desperation over the loss of Thomas, I have locked John out of my life. I have closed off the door to my heart and for that, I pray God's forgiveness. I think John knows that I will eventually come to my senses. And I do know in my heart or at least I feel that Thomas will return home.

Oh, what is the matter with me? Here I am letting my mind roll around and start thinking again. I am never going to get to sleep and get the rest my body so needs. I just can't get John's haunting words out of my mind. His warnings tonight were not against me, he was only trying to protect me. He knows me so well and knows that I possess such a strong will. He just doesn't want any embarrassment to come to the family or me.

My Mama and Papa had instilled in me, the will to survive on my own and be strong. Now I seem to rely on John and I sometimes get confused. I want to be dependent and independent all at the same time. Oh, sleep when will you come? It seems like it is extra hard to shut off my whirling mind tonight.

I will pray, maybe that will help. God's guidance in my life is needed and forgiveness for all my bad thoughts and needs is a constant prayer. God must help me to keep my determination under control. I sometimes go to far to prove a point letting my stubbornness override my good upbringing and good sense.

Still searching for that place in time called sleep gives me a chance to be thankful for so many things but tonight especially for the wonderfully warm bed cover. I pull it up over the tip of my cold, half frozen nose and glance about the room one last time before closing my eyes. I yawn and think to myself, yes Elizabeth you are exhausted, go to sleep.

129

I don't know when I finally drifted off to sleep. I just kind of slipped into dreamland without even knowing it. But my waking up was not quite as gentle. The bright rays of the morning sun and the cold in the air brought me out of my restful sleep, with quite a start. John's strong arms were still about me and in the comfort and security of them I hardly want to get up into the cold room and start the day.

Finally convincing myself that without a larger fire in the fireplace there would be no morning meal and surely no warmth, I have to ease myself out from under the warm covers. My morning coat is freezing and feels like it has ice particles on it. I wrap it close about my shoulders and rush to stir the coals and placed a few pieces of wood atop them. I gently apply air from the big fireplace bellows we had brought from Caswell with our crest on the front and soon the small flames were lapping up into the air and warmth began to come forth. With it came the smell of the drippings burning off the stones and that brought the household awake. Somehow sleep had doused my fears from the night before and I was ready for this bright sunny day and I greet it with a renewed fresh outlook.

# CHAPTER 8

The drifts of snow have grown higher and higher, as natures winter caretaker has poured drift after drift of white ice over the rolling landscape. The long months of winter have taken a toll on the once beautiful sparkle of the ice. The stark white, is now a dirty, dingy, gray color and where man has left his imprint, splotches of mud mix with the snow and cause a more dreary, drab, scene, before my eyes. Only areas untouched, by man or beast, seem to retain the pristine beauty originally seen, when the first white ice crystal flakes, fell ever so softly covering the frozen, shivering ground.

The icy water that drips from the warm edges of our thatched roof, seem to have been held captive by the cold grasp of old man winter and now with a few rays of warm sun, it is racing against time to leave the crevasses and edges of our home, continuing the journey downward and onward, fulfilling the law of nature. I am amazed at the large frozen icicles along the very top edges. Some actually reach from the tiptop of the thatched roof to the ground below. At first glance one might wonder if it is growing up out of the ground or dripping down out of the air. I know for I watched with wonder as the liquid runs for its life, only to be trapped by the bitter cold and frozen in place to wait for warmer days. It doesn't really matter how it got there, for in its wonderful beauty it looks very much like a waterfall, in miniature. I am sure that the ice formations have now reached their greatest potential and the demise of their existence will be forth coming as spring edges its way into view. For today, they touch the hard frozen ground and in the days ahead they will be melted into a memory. I will miss them, for never more will I see this beautiful sight exactly as it is this very moment.

The winter days pass slowly and they are long and bleak. I try hard to fill them with happy thoughts and I busy myself with things about the house. It is nice to look out the small, smudged panes of the window and see the first signs of spring breaking through the winter cold. I am glad to see the days bringing forth more warm sunlight and see that a few of the trees scattered about are starting to put on a light green hue. This is the first indication that the beautiful leaves will soon be covering them, and like a light cloak the leaves will stave off the lingering chill. These same beautiful leaves will soon be protection against the hot summer days that will be upon us far too soon.

After a long winter, we wonder if summer will ever really come and after a long hot summer we look forward to the coolness of fall and a peek into the cold recesses of a beautiful winter scene. As I stand here shivering in the chill of this room, I wonder if summer will ever really be here? As I sigh my mind repeats its thoughts. Will it ever really be summer again?

Why did winter always seem so long, when our seasons of life just seem to pass by much too swiftly? One might say we humans are never satisfied. Always wanting something completely out of our control. Looking, reaching, wishing for something different.

131

As I draw in a deep breath, I feel as if today has been an exceptionally long day; somehow longer than the others. Could it be that I am not as busy as usual? Having time to spare has given me time to think and for me is not always the best thing to do.

Thomas has been gone for the most part of a year now and my heart still aches for him. I wonder every minute, if he is still alive? Is he well? Is he on land or still at sea? Had he ever reached England? The ship will be returning this spring and until then none of my questions can be answered. I wonder if I will want to know when spring is really here or will I want it to pass me by, for fear that Thomas will not be on the ship? If that happens I don't know what I will do, I am so afraid of that moment. Why did he have to go to sea? Why, did he? Why did he? The always unanswered question, whirling incessantly in my mind. Even though I try not to think about him, I cannot seem to stop. The empty feeling grows vaster with each passing day. Maybe, just maybe, I will look out this window one of these days and there he will be, coming up the path, with that big, wide smile upon his face. What a joyful day that will be. Oh yes, a blessed day, the day my many prayers will be answered.

"Mama, are you thinking about Thomas again?" Liz questioned, as she walked up behind my chair, placing her hands gently on my shoulders. She rubbed my back gently and the warmth of her hands felt good on my chilled shoulders.

"Oh, Liz, how can you always tell?" I questioned, for she always seemed to catch me when I was doing just that.

"Well, Mama, you have such a sad look about you and you seem to be looking out the window at nothing." She answered.

"I try hard, not to be sad Liz, I really do? Someday when you grow up and get married, you will have children of your own and then you will understand just how I feel. It is hard to explain. Sometimes it is even hard for me to understand. There is just something inside you. It is emptiness, a giant void that nothing can fill. I just pray that Thomas is in God's safe keeping. It doesn't seem to matter to a mother, if her children are far away or right near by. Mothers always worry about them. You know we only want the very best for you. It is just part of being a mother. Yes Liz, someday you will look back and understand your Mama better." I hope you will, anyway.

My explanation seemed to sound shallow but my feelings run very deep. How could I expect her to understand, when I sometimes find my own sullen moods hard to comprehend? As I reached up and gently patted her hands, as they rested on my shoulders, I was silently but gently asking her to try and accept my feeble attempt at explaining the complexities of her mother's inner thoughts and feelings. Somehow in her little girl mind, she could put things together so that they made some kind of sense to her. I turned and looked into her eyes and as our eyes met she bent and kissed me upon my cheek. A kiss of warmth, of love, a kiss of caring. An unspoken response that talked many words, said many things, without an utterance of a sound. Oh, the complexities of this grown up life. Far to soon she would be a part of that world.

"Will I have lots of children, Mama?" She questioned. The questions of a young girl expecting life to be like playing with her dolls. Little did she know, little did any of us know at her age, and far be it from me to burst the enthusiasm of her young heart.

"Well, I can't answer that darling Liz. Only God can answer that question, and he will in time. You are young Liz and have many years before you have to worry with thoughts of babies and a home to keep. I do hope you will have a happy life Liz and a life full of all your dreams come true." We chatted on aimlessly as if we had nothing else to do.

"I want to have lots of babies Mama, a hundred of them!" Liz exclaimed with excitement in her voice indicative of a young child.

"My, my, little one, that is a lot of children to take care of." I said, as I lifted her onto my lap. Oh the dreams we dream when we're young. The innocence a child displays. How trusting in life, no wonder Jesus said to believe like little children, they are so pure in their thoughts. "You have much to learn about life Liz, much, much to learn, before that time comes." I tried to explain, that only much later in her life, would the questions of her own family be answered. She had plenty of time between now and then. Hearing footsteps entering the house we both look around to see John and the boys came in, so our mother-daughter conversation has to come to an abrupt end.

"Well, well, what do we have here? I see before me two very special ladies sitting by the window, looking ever so forlorn. What might it be that you two are talking about so earnestly?" John's eyes sparkled with mischief as he inquired as to our thoughts.

"Oh, Papa! Mama and I were just talking about when I grow up and have my own family. I just told her I wanted a hundred children. Won't that be fun Papa, won't that be a wonderful family?" Liz said excitedly.

"Indeed it will be Liz, a fine family." John answered, with as much enthusiasm and excitement in his voice as she had in hers. John was so good to play along with Liz's childhood dreams, knowing most of her talk was just make believe. At her young age, one or one hundred, what did it really matter? Far be it from us to tell her any different. At least she had dreams to look forward to, she might as well enjoy them now, for far too soon, the realities of life would overwhelm her and all her dreams would be much harder to realize than on this day. I could tell her from my own experience, but what is the use of spoiling her thoughts with the truths of life, they come to all of us soon enough. We have nothing to do when that happens but face them and work through them, as best we can.

"Mmmm, what smells so good in here?" Asked John, as he peeked about the fireplace kettles.

"Oh I don't think it's the cooking that you smell John. I brought in a few sprigs of herbs from the storage area and hung them up about the beams by the fire. The heat from the fire must be making their scent stronger. I like it too! I do have some nice squash in the pot and will be putting something to eat on the table shortly." I answered, leaving my

133

seat by the window and entering the cooking area. I did notice that the herb smell was much stronger, the closer to the fireplace I get.

"There is no hurry Elizabeth. We are not all that hungry. Our day was a good one and the meeting was most interesting." John was so nonchalant with his statement that I almost missed what he had said.

"Meeting, what meeting John?" I asked, quite surprised when the word meeting finally reached my brain. I had not known one had been called.

"Well, it seems that some of the company are going to be going to Connecticut. I was thinking it would be in our best interest to join them?" John was facing the fire with his back to me. I could not envision the look upon his face. I was grateful he could not see the stark expression of surprise on mine. Maybe astonishment would be a better word to describe my response.

I could not control the rage building up inside me and burst forth in uncontrollable anger. "Connecticut, join them, what are you talking about John Curtyce? Have you completely lost your senses? Do you mean move, leave our home, where is this place called Connecticut? Is it a long way away? Why do you want to move? What about all we have done here?" The questions just kept spewing from my mouth. What if, when, why? "Oh John, all the questions I have, I don't know what has gotten into you. Whatever it is, it is making you so dissatisfied with what you have. You always want to look in another place for your dreams. They seem to be somewhere over the horizon and just a little out of reach. I really can't understand John, I really can't." I cried out and through up my hands in disgust.

"Now Elizabeth, you've got to hear me out. Don't jump so quickly at what you think is going on. We do not have enough room here to grow the things we need. The opportunity for my store is not as good here, as it would be in Connecticut. You must trust my judgment on this, Elizabeth; it will really be better for us, for all of us. The boys will get a much better start in Connecticut than they will here. This place is already getting over crowded. Most of the establishments were already started before we arrived, and the land is not suitable for what we want to do. If we are to be able to raise enough to supply others and sell and trade for a profit, then it is going to have to be in another area." John was trying hard to explain his position on this subject. But he has not convinced me, and I doubt if he can.

"It sounds like you have already made up your mind John. Do I not have any say in this matter, none at all? Our lives have sure taken on a strange change since we came to this new land. I know you are the head of our family and always will be, but we at least used to talk over our plans before anything was decided on. I felt I had an input of some kind into what we were to do with our lives, maybe I was fooling myself all along, and maybe I really didn't. Was it because Caswell Manor had been in my family that you seemed to allow me so much say in the business decisions of the estate? Is it now such a whole different way of life that I am completely left out? Now, since we came here, I seem to have no say what so ever, I just move about at your command. You seem to have everything planned far in advance of telling me. Why, John? Why have things changed so much?" I questioned him over and over. I needed to have some answers.

"Nothing has changed Elizabeth, we still talk things over, and I still want you to know what is going on. It is just that sometimes things happen so fast that there is no time to mull over a decision. Especially since everything and everyone moves at such a rapid pace in this new place. Everyday a new area is opened up and if you are not the first to get there, your chances to succeed are that much less. I just want the very best for us and for the family. Our reasons for sailing across the vastness of the ocean in the first place was to try and give our family the very best chance in life that we could, wasn't that it Elizabeth? Weren't those our reasons and dreams? I always thought we wanted the same things." John just looked at me.

John was stating the truth. We did want the very best for the family. "Yes, that was it, at least part of the reason John, but we cannot be ever on the move. There is always going to be new things to see and new places to go, better opportunities in other areas. From the reports coming back from the fur traders, who have ventured much farther than most, this is a vast land we are in John, probably much bigger than we could ever dream. If we kept our feet moving every minute, for the rest of our lives, we would still not be able to see it all. I feel that at some point we have to take a stand and work at what we want right where we are. It is not going to fall into our lives out of the sky. If we are not stable for a period of time, we are not giving ourselves a chance to know if we have succeeded or failed. Some of us have to stay put and get established. We cannot always be looking for things out of our reach." I countered his arguments thinking my reasoning quite stable.

"This place called Connecticut is not out of our reach. It is just a new area and you will love it, Elizabeth, it will be your new home. I promise you, I will build you a fine home and you will have all your dreams come true there. Oh, Elizabeth, it will be so wonderful you will see it will really be a special place. Our place Elizabeth, we will make it our home, yours, the kids and mine. The company will be leaving in the early spring before the waters of the big rivers get to full and impossible to cross. We will have to have everything ready and be available to move when the time is right." John's voice was authoritative, informing me as to what he expected of his wife.

A chill ran down the length of my spine. The excitement in his voice held the same tone it had when his brother had first approached him to journey to a new land, far across the ocean. Not finding everything here as we anticipated only gave me more reason to think that no matter where we moved we would still find the fulfillment of our dreams hard to locate. John had accomplished so much in England and given up so much when we left. I know he did not dream in his wildest dreams that life in this new land would be like it has been this past year.

"John, no more promises, please, no more, I am tired and weary, I am sad and disappointed, I am tired of talk of a better life and always somewhere else. Please John, please no more. At least right now, it is hard enough to face the next day, let alone think about a month or more from now. Have you talked this over with your brother at all? Are they up and ready to move to this place called Connecticut?" I questioned with a bit of sarcasm in my voice.

"Yes, we discussed it, but he is not in favor of that kind of move for his family. He wants to stay here in Roxbury, he has some good ideas for his future." John turned to face me. His voice becoming quiet, probably thinking of what might be going through my mind on hearing that William and Sarah would not be leaving this area.

"Well, that sounds very sensible to me John, why doesn't it sound good to you?" I asked, trying not to get angry.

"I'm not William, I have other things in mind and this Massachusetts is not the place to put them into being?" He said, with a very matter-of-fact tone in his voice.

"Well, perhaps this is not the time to discuss this any further John, the food is about ready and we best eat it while it is hot. With all this cold weather it only takes a few minutes for it to turn to ice." I countered and turned to place the trenchers on the table. Hearing them thud as they hit the hard oak tabletop.

Though our discussion had stopped, the thoughts in my mind kept coming at an unbelievable speed. For the life of me I could not understand this unstable feeling within John. He was always such a settled person always the one that was methodical and sensible. I could not find it within me to really push him for answers to my questions. There seems to be a place in his being that is empty and he is trying to fill it will something, but he himself doesn't seem to know what it is he wants? I am doing my best to cope with the everyday changes this new life has brought and at the same time trying to understand the changes that are taking place in my husband.

I feel confused, I hardly know him sometimes, and I really can't figure out what it is that could be troubling him. This quest, this search for whatever it is, I wonder if it will ever stop. Will he ever fill that void in his life, or will he always be looking for bigger and better times? I must try harder to understand him. Maybe he feels that this whole idea was not so good for us after all. Maybe he misses home as much as I do and can't really tell me about it. He would never admit this was a mistake, and I knew that. So whatever it is, I will have to guess and make the best of it. If this is my lot in life, so be it. I love John Curtyce far too much to fight against him. I would follow him to the ends of the earth; I want to always be at his side. No matter where he travels I know I will follow him, for without him I am only half a person.

As we eat in almost total silence and the few subjects that were raised were quickly answered and put to rest. The boys glanced at each other and then looked over at their sister. Liz seemed to know, as did the boys, that this was not the time to ask questions. They all finished their meal without looking up. The unsettled silence was thick about the room. I cleared the table and washed the trenchers in silence with my mind roaming through miles and miles of past events in my life. I felt tired and old, small tasks seemed big, days were long and nights too short. What was happening to me? The little joys of life were passing me

136

by much too swiftly. Nothing more was said about the move and I went about my evening chores methodically.

The days grew longer little by little and with a few warm days mixed with the cold, I finally felt I would make it through this our first winter in this strange, beautiful but confusing new place.

I had not really wanted to entrench myself too deeply in this Roxbury, Massachusetts, for as the days passed, it was ever more apparent that John really meant to leave, come spring. Our only argument over this new place and long journey was the timing of it all. I would not move one foot without Thomas, if he was not back, I would not go. There was no power on earth that could take me from this spot, until I see my son come off that ship and back into our home where he belongs.

John, knowing me as he does, had better not fight me over this, for as sure as I am standing in this very spot, he will loose the battle. I cannot go anywhere without my whole family, it is either all of us, or none of us. This is the one decision I have made in all this and the one I will not bend on. I do not care what anyone thinks, or what anyone wants to do to me, my family comes first and it always will. When I say family, I mean each and every one of us, not just a part. John calls me stubborn, and that is all right, he can call me whatever he wants, I call myself a mother, a very determined mother.

The thoughts and remembrance of the past few weeks resurface far to easily. Each and every day brings a new question to mind, about this place, Connecticut. But today, I must put these thoughts from my mind and concentrate on just today. It is a fine day. A nice sunny day like this cannot be wasted on daydreams. I have much too much, to do. The winter damp has left our clothing and bed linens musty and dirty. Today is a day for airing them out and tending too much needed family chores.

The warm sun against my face makes little beads of sweat upon my brow and I find myself lifting my hand more and more often to wipe the tiny droplets from my brow. The walk to Stony Brook was well worth the effort for the enjoyment of being out in the crisp cool air and washing our clothing there was invigorating. I didn't even mind the trek home carrying my arms full of heavy wet clothing. It is a relief to enter the little gate and I put the freshly washed cloths over the little fence in hopes the sun will be warm enough to dry them before the cool air of afternoon comes rushing in. It is hard to find a good day to put the wash out, but this day held prospects of being an exceptionally warm one and being out and being able to feel and smell the newness of a bright spring drawing closer gives me renewed hope.

I had forgotten how beautiful the country around us was, the winter had kept me in far to long. As I look about I realize how much I long to work in the garden, to plant the seeds and see the tiny green sprouts, pop their heads through the rich brown soil and reach their tiny arms toward the crystal blue sky.

Oh how I long to feel the earth, warm and moist between my fingers and see the colors of the flowers, bright and beautiful, as the plants reach their maturity and bring forth their beautiful, budding flowers and fruits.

137

My one dream is to, once again, be able to pick a fresh, beautiful bouquet of roses, with the fragrance of an angles breath, to freshen the air. I will place them in a beautiful vase, upon my table, and enjoy their beauty and lovely scent. Just as I had done in Nazing and Mama and Auntie had done years before I was ever born. Yes, that will be a special day for me, for I truly miss my gardens and my beautiful flowers. I have barely been able to keep the little twigs, from England, alive. They are in the little shed potted in soil just waiting for the ground to be warm enough to plant them. If we move again I wonder if they will even make it?

As I look about and let my eyes rove over the little scattered homes and family plots, my eyes are squinted up tight, for the glare of the sun off the piles of snow left here and there, melting a bit at a time, is blinding. It is hard to shield my eyes against the brightness.

An ominous feeling suddenly overtakes me as my eyes caught a glimpse of someone coming up the roadway. As I let my eyes stop to study the figure momentarily, I think how curious, the figure looks very much like William coming home. A smile broadened my lips, and then quickly turned to a thoughtful frown, for he would not be coming home at this time of the morning unless something terrible had happened,

There are many trees to fell and haul out of the forest area where the men are working today. We are very short of wood; I hope the men haven't had an accident of some kind.

I could feel the apprehension creep into my body and stiffen it with fright. As I watched intently, the figure was getting closer and closer and I still was unable to make out the features. Finally deciding it is not William, for the color of the hair is not like his, and the walk, looking familiar yet not quite the same, made me wonder even more. Who is it? I squeezed my eyes tighter, but that didn't really help a lot. I don't like strangers coming near the house when John and the boys are away. It always gives me a concerned feeling being alone, just Liz and I. There are so many Indians still about and some have not been too friendly lately.

The figure approaching did not give me exactly a scared feeling, yet I must be cautious. I had Liz to keep from harms way. I moved toward the door of the house almost automatically. I think I shall go in and at least get the gun before this person gets any nearer. I don't want to be left standing here without any kind of defense.

As I backed into the door I almost fell over Liz, quietly setting on the floor playing with her rag doll. "Liz, you stay right where you are and don't come out of the house, no matter what happens, do you understand?" I ordered, not realizing how sternly I was speaking

."Yes Mama, I understand, but why are you taking the gun down?" She asked, only looking up for a moment from her play.

"There's someone I don't know coming up the roadway and I just want to be ready. Your Papa and brothers are too far from the house and would not hear me call to them. It is up to us to protect ourselves in case

138

this stranger is unfriendly or has any ideas, other than good ones, in his mind. Now, do as I say, Liz and stay put." I explained quickly.

"Yes Mama, I will." She answered, very unconcerned with any thing but her doll.

As I walked back into the sunlight, it impaired my vision so much I couldn't readily locate the man again. He must have already gone past the house. Oh how I hated the dimness of the house. Once again I found my adjustment to the light hampering me. The house was so dim compared to the bright sun out of doors. When I finally got my sight back, there the man was right in front of me. So close, I hardly had time to raise the musket. I gasp of fear escapes me. My intent is to protect my little girl and my home with all my strength. How had I let myself be so careless, as to have this stranger sneak up on us? I raised the musket to my shoulder knowing full well that this person was much to close for me to really aim the weapon. I only know that I will shoot if he intends us any harm. "Stop, Stop, right where you are, before I use this musket. I do know how you know and I will if you proceed any further."

"Whoa, whoa there, Mama!" Strange words to be coming from this stranger, I thought to myself. Yet there was an ever so slight familiar tone, to his husky voice, as he rushed toward me.

"You don't want to be shooting your own son, do you?" Came the next question from this man, who was standing far to close now for me to have any defense whatsoever.

"My son, my what? The sun was playing tricks on my eyes. This could not be Thomas. I must be dreaming. I have prayed for this moment so often, I am having illusions about it.

"Mama, Mama, it's me, Thomas, you haven't forgotten me, have you? I haven't been gone that long!" He said, as he reached to put one arm around me, and retrieve the musket with the other.

"Oh Thomas! Thomas! I can't believe my eyes or my ears either, is it really you Thomas, is it really you? It seems like you have been gone a lifetime. I can't stop shaking! You left a little boy and within less than a year you have come back to me all grown up. So tall you've gotten. I just can't believe this. Please tell me I'm not dreaming for I never want to wake up if that is the case. I have waited far to long for this day, for this very moment." I squealed my delight, and half crying and half laughing, I threw my arms about his neck.

"Yes Mama, it is really me, and no, you are not dreaming." He pushed me back, momentarily, and then dropped the gun to the ground. His arms again encircled me. My son's arms were really around me. It was true he was really home.

What a happy day this is for all of us. I will not try to contain the tears of joy running down my face, as they half freeze to my lashes and face, in the cool, early spring air. I was far too happy to care what I looked like or what happened to me now, far to happy. God had been good, he had brought Thomas back, safe and sound, a quite grown up, handsome young man. One that I hardly recognize, I have to admit.

"Liz, Liz, come here, come here! Come and see who is here." I called out. At first I heard no response from the house. Then a meek voice asked.

"Who is it Mama, is it all right to come out, really all right, Mama?" She asked, as she peeked around the door and looked out. She was heeding the stern warning I had given her, when I retrieved the musket from the house.

"Oh yes, darling, it is probably the most all right thing I would ever call you for." I answered, as Liz, timidly stuck her head out the opened doorway. I reveled at the look in her eyes at seeing her brother standing there. Liz, recognized him in an instant and fairly flew into his arms, like a bolt of lighting flying across the night sky. His outstretched arms caught her up and she hugged his neck so tight he thought she was going to strangle him. His strong, bronze arms, bulging with muscles, lifting her with such ease, high into the air. He swung her around in a circle and held her close to his chest once more.

"Well little sister, haven't you grown up since I went to sea? You have gotten heavy too. I can hardly lift you up." He commented. Giving a hearty laugh as he eyed the change the months away had brought.

"Yes, I am a whole year older now Thomas, I am a big girl." She replied, as he sat her back down on the ground.

"That you are, little sister, you are a big girl indeed." He answered, as he took her hand and put his arm around my waist and walked toward the door. "The air out here is still cool you both will catch the sickness if we don't get you inside and I need to soak up some of the warmth from the hearth myself. I have had a long walk from Boston and the dock area, and the chill of the air has about gone through me." He admitted. "Oh, we must not forget the musket." Thomas added as he picked it up from the ground.

"Of course, of course, I don't know what I am thinking. I still can't believe all this we will go inside. When your father and brothers return from the woods they will have the surprise of their lives. This is a most wonderful day for us all, Thomas. We have feared so for your safety and have longed so for your return home. I know you must have a million stories to tell and I want to hear each and every one of them, but for now, I just want to feast my eyes on your handsome face and enjoy the sight of your presence here beside me. My days have been so empty since you left, and my nights full of prayers for this very special home coming." I confessed my loneliness, unashamed, that had been caused from his brush with adventure. I was not the least bit shy about letting him know just how very much I had missed him and longed for his return.

"Well, I am happy to say that not only your prayers, but mine also, have been answered, Mama. I too, am glad to be home and in the safe haven that you and Papa have built for your family. It sometimes takes being away to make one appreciate what they have left behind. I know for myself

140

Mama, I missed each of you very much and don't want to go anywhere for a long time. No, I think I will be plenty satisfied to settle right down and work on the farm. The adventures of the sea are great, and I am glad I had the opportunity to go with the Captain, but I am ever so happy to be home once again." Thomas commented, as he looked about the house, and warmed his hands by the fire.

"Thomas, you have grown up so much. Not just in your height, you are not the child that left here; you have truly become a man. When your father sees you he will not believe his eyes either. I still can't believe I am standing here talking to you. I just can't believe this is really true." I could not help repeating myself as I shake my head in amazement at having my son, standing here, before me after such a long time.

Thomas, Liz and I spend the rest of the afternoon, talking and laughing and listening to the stories, brought back by Thomas, of the islands he visited and the people there. He told of strange fish in the ocean, of how schools of dolphins would sometimes follow the ship for days. He marveled at how they would leap high out of the water in graceful flight through the air, dipping once again into the sea, only to spring back into the air. His descriptions were so realistic. Liz, and I felt we were right their beside him. Seeing all that he had seen so vividly. There were so many adventures to take in all at once. We were talking so fast and long that the light in the room has grown very dim and we do not even move to light the oil lamps.

Suddenly realizing the time, I hurry to put some light about our home and started fixing something for the men folks and us to eat when they returned. They would be starved after a hard day of cutting wood. I rushed to retrieve my half frozen cloths from the fence, and laid them about the room to warm them before folding and putting them away. Her brother and his stories spellbound Liz. Neither of us would let him out of our sight hardly for a moment. I could not wait for John and the other boys to walk in the door, yet I wanted to be a little selfish and keep Thomas just us Liz and I for a little bit longer.

What a selfish thought. He had been gone for so long, I didn't want to have to share him at all. He was like a treasure that I wanted to keep all to myself, and yet, he was so special, I wanted to share him and the news of his return with the world. How mixed up my emotions are?

As he sat there, with the fire glowing about him, I noticed his face; the deep bronze color of it, his hair was streaked from the effects of the sun. His features looked weathered, and the maturity about him was apparent. He looked much older than his years. His voice had taken on a manly huskiness. I stood there watching, as he soaked in the warmth of his home. I could see much of his father in him. He had left us a boy and returned to us a man. I watched him thoughtfully, as I scrutinized his expressions, marveling at this, miracle, this very special day.

When I heard the latch on the door spring up I looked over to see William and John walking in chatting aimlessly to each other, their father close behind. Thomas had his back to the door so it took several moments before they even saw that anyone other than Liz and I sat here in the house. It was William who saw him first or at least recognized who it was

141

setting there, but he couldn't seem to get any words out of his mouth. His mouth just hung open, his eyes growing wider and wider. When John and John Jr. turned to see what was going on, it was instant pandemonium. "Thomas, is that you, really you?" Someone stammered out.

"I'm afraid so, your long lost, missing part of the family, has finally found his way home." He said, as he turned and got up to greet them.

"Well, I'll be! It really is you, Thomas, it really is you, isn't it? What a happy day this is. This is truly a day to count our blessings. Welcome home, son, welcome home. You have grown into a fine young man." John greeted his son with joy and happiness and a gleam upon his face that I had not witnessed for a long, long time. With hugs, and hearty handshakes all-round, we tried to settle down long enough to eat our meal. This was completely impossible, for we could not keep our mouths closed long enough to chew. The excitement was much too great and finally overtook us so much that we gave up on the food and just concentrated on talking and being a family again, a real family.

As I watched, listened and joined in on the conversation, I realized that this was what I had missed all winter, this, all of us together, setting around the table, talking over our day, our thoughts, our wishes, our dreams. Yes, my void was filled and I prayed silently, Dear God, I give thanks to you this day for the answer to my prayers and the fulfillment of my dreams. I am so blessed and so thankful for your care and love dear Lord. Thank you for this day and for bringing my son safely home to me. Over and over again, I repeated this prayer in my heart, over and over for fear that I might wake up and it all really is a dream.

The oil lamps grew dimmer and dimmer and the little lights started to flicker and go out on their own, we still found ourselves talking and laughing and enjoying this moment more than words could ever express. As much as we hated to, we were all very tired. Thomas, especially, needed to get some rest. He had not only had a long walk today, but from his stories, he had endured many long months of hard seas and hard work.

I looked over at Liz; she had fallen asleep with her head on her brother's lap. "Thomas, she has really missed you. When you left here almost a year ago you truly left a void in our family that could not be filled by anything but you. We are so thankful and happy you have returned to us, and safely too." My informing him was a needless act, for he could easily see what joy his return had brought.

A special joy was heard in John's voice as he announced the reading of the scripture. Our prayers of thanks we offered up to the Lord. It was hard to retire for the night, the boys still chattering away as they climbed into the loft. I heard them talking long after we had turned to our sleeping places. I knew we all needed a good night's sleep after all this excitement. But I too, found it hard to fall asleep.

I had to keep reminding myself that we would have many days ahead to get caught up on everything. We have all been asking one question after another as fast as we can formulate them in our minds. There was just so many things we wanted to know and it seemed that Thomas couldn't answer them fast enough for us. I didn't even get to ask him if he had gotten to see any of the family at Caswell. Oh well, my questions will keep until later.

I looked over toward the fire to see if John had remembered to bank it so that we would have warmth through the night and enough of the coals left to start our morning fire? He had! I glanced toward Liz's sleeping area she was fast asleep. What could I find to look at now? I could not possibly go to sleep. I turned to face John. He was curled up, and by his breathing; I knew he was sound asleep. I tapped him on his back.

"I don't think I will be able to go to sleep, John, I am far to excited. I can still hear the boys, they cannot settle down either. We are truly within Gods loving caring John; he brought us back our Thomas. Oh John, isn't this something, I still find it hard to believe? I just looked up and there he was, right in front of me. Just like that he appeared out of nowhere." I said, reliving the moment over once again.

"Well, since you can't sleep, I guess I can't either. I hardly think he came out of nowhere, Elizabeth. From the story he tells, you met him with a gun in your hand and he hardly knew whether he was welcome or not?" John chuckled.

"Now John, don't tease me, you know I was only trying to protect Liz and myself and you can't tell me you would have recognized Thomas at a distance either, and besides the sun was in my eyes and I couldn't see to good. You must admit he has really grown up, don't you think so?" My comments and questions kept flowing from my mouth.

"Yes Elizabeth, he has indeed and I will not tease you for I know how you have longed for his return and how happy this day has been for you. I would not spoil this moment for you, not for anything in the world. I am just as happy as you are at our son's safe return. Now lets close the curtains about us and get some sleep. We have the rest of our lives to enjoy the children." John's, suggestion was welcomed and I snuggled close to him and tried and tried to go to sleep.

There always seemed to be something that jumped into my thoughts, just as I was about to drift off. Once again, John's breathing told me that it had taken him only minutes to fall back into a sound sleep. I tried to lie still, but I couldn't. I would wiggle and fidget and fidget and wiggle. Finally I peaked out of the sleeping area at the coals in the fireplace. I don't know what I expected; perhaps I thought the warmth might bring on sleep.

The fire seemed extra bright, and the embers sparkled like jewels. Tonight was a special night, I wondered to myself if even the fire knew just how very special it was? Was the fire happy too? What a silly thought, but why not? Right now I think everyone and everything should be happy. The whole world should rejoice, for my son is home. My Thomas is really home!

I felt an urgent need to write all my thoughts down and since sleep was evading me I might as well do it. I slipped from my bedchamber and took my little journals from their special place and sat close to the coals. For a long time the thoughts of today spilled forth from my mind. I put them all down, one by one and then closed my memories and put them away. I crawled back into my bed and found that time had caused it to get quite cold. I moved closer to John and he stirred slightly but did not come fully awake. I know that tomorrow will be a day that I will be eager to awake to. A deep sigh told me that I was much wearier than I thought. I closed my eyes and for the first time in almost a year, I fell into a deep comfortable sleep. Sleep came fast and my thoughts of the day became my dreams of the night.

# CHAPTER 9

I am happy to greet the dawning of each new day, for my life seems whole now that my family is complete once again. I am realistic enough to know though, that there are many changes about to take place. But for now, I am quite content and I wish it could always stay just as it is this bright, warm, and wonderful early April morning. The last traces of winters white snow can be seen holding fast to the north sides of the trees and a few patches of the now dirty snow, can still be seen lingering in the depths of the green forest. There are a few of the very early and hearty wild flowers popping up here and there, once again doting the earth with their beautiful vibrant color.

I continue my days as usual, doing the same chores, the same way, as always, yet they seem a trifle more enjoyable. There is lightness in my heart and a spirit within my soul today that makes me feel like I can conquer the unconquerable.

As we sit around the hand-hewn table, this wonderful, happy day and eat our morning meal, the chatter of my family fills the air and is almost deafening. Our questions for Thomas have been never ending since his return and he has answered each and every one with such enthusiasm and excitement. This morning is not any different we listen and question more and more, never tiring of the stories Thomas is telling us. We are all of course anxious to learn any new bit of information from our family and friends in England.

It is most gratifying learning that he had really done quite well and had even had a little time while the ship was docked in London to go out to the country and visit Caswell and all our loved ones at home. The messages from relatives and friends are many and they are surely the next best things to being there.

One of the biggest surprises he had for us on his return was the fact he had been able to bring back a cow and a young mare, sired by Big Blacky. Oh how beautiful she is and how excited we all are to have her. Cousin James must have done some fine talking and probably paid more than a mere pittance in order to arrange their passage. With Thomas on the ship he made sure the animals were well taken care of and that they arrived here in fine shape.

It was more than two weeks after his homecoming that the horse and cow were brought out to Roxbury. He had not made mention of them at all, so when some hired men came up the lane and stopped at our cottage door, I thought some mistake had been made.

The men folks were all away from the house that day and I hardly knew what to do with them, except perhaps just stand and hold their tethers until someone arrived to take care of them and secure a place for their safe keeping. These animals were really a luxury and a necessity. There are just not to many available over here. So many are lost in the crossing and because of the severe winter cold a lot have died. Having these two plus the goats and chickens will help us to be even more self-sufficient. We are eternally grateful to cousin James for his foresight.

145

The days are getting warmer and warmer as April swiftly passes by. I revel in the heat of the sun and marvel at the beauty of nature. I find myself busy enjoying the grandness of spring and the wholeness once again of my family. I am so wrapped up in my own thoughts and deeds that I am momentarily unaware of a great sickness that is stealing its way into our village.

There have been rumors that other towns had been affected by this sickness, but it had not affected us so far as I know. I had put it far from my mind. It was just in the last few days that word had come to the members of our company that it was very near. The talk had made me take notice. Without us fully realizing it, it has crept slowly from one house to the next. There seems to be none of us that are being spared this dreadful sickness. It is really a very grave situation.

Our elders have warned us not to mingle with one and other too much for fear of it spreading further. We do not want this fever to spread to others like the great epidemic of smallpox. The smallpox epidemic had come upon settlements with such swiftness. We could never prepare for such a severe infirmity for they seem to be much swifter than we are. Many, many of this company we joined had died. I shutter just to think of all the heartbreak that has come to this little village.

The smallpox traveled from one house to the next and then out into the Indian villages. The loss of life to our own company of people was mammoth but the loss of lives in the native villages was even greater.

The Indians have held us to blame for this. Some have turned against us. They say it is the fault of the new people off the great ships that brought this great tragedy to their villages. They are a frightened people and some are coming into the towns and outpost areas, terrorizing and stealing.

Now this new illness has spread to the Indian's and we are getting word that once again we are being blamed. They have already sent war parties to our neighboring villages. The men are guarding our outer gates day and night.

I have to be ever so cautious to watch after Liz, John has warned me to keep her close for fear that she might be grabbed and taken away to some far off Indian encampment. The Indians can come upon us with such ease; it is almost impossible to detect their presence.

I am more than apprehensive when John and the boys have to be very far from the house. I am thankful that the plowing of the side garden is being done today and that our back few acres is the first priority, for that will keep the men folks close at hand in case of a surprise attack.

A sharp rap on the door casing startled me. My thoughts were on the Indians and the dangers they were causing. Many had seen them of late, milling around the settlement. I approached with caution and was happy to see one of Sarah's youngsters standing there. I don't know what I would have done if I had opened the door and come face to face with a fierce native.

My happiness quickly turned to concern as I took one look at the sad eyes of Thomas, their second eldest boy, and immediately knew that the message was not a good one. All I could really understand as he babbled it out, half crying and half trying to talk was that everyone was sick at their house. All the children had been stricken with the fever and his mother and father were both sick.

"Does your mother need me to come and help Thomas? Is that what she sent you to tell me?" I questioned and tried as best I could to calm him enough to understand him. All I got was more sobs and a shrug of his shoulders. I continued to talk to him but was getting nowhere. Finally I sent him back home with instructions that I would be there as quickly as possible. I put some hot broth in a kettle and sent it home with him.

My mind was a blank. As soon as he was on his way back up the hill I readied food for their evening meal, put some more on to cook for my family and questioned myself as to the likelihood of us getting this sickness again. Our family has recovered from what we supposed was this same fever, so I don't think it will hurt if I go and see them. Sarah would do the same for me.

I wouldn't want to have it again, for the first time was bad enough. Now that everyone is back to the tasks at hand I would not want to jeopardize our spring planting by someone getting sick again. John is so thankful that we were spared the dreadful severity some families had to endure with this epidemic. He and the boys have gotten right to the task of tilling the ground while it is still soft and pliable from the winter.

So many of our company have been completely bed ridden by this illness and they will be so far behind with their farming. It is hard for us to understand why God has chosen such an awful sickness to fall upon us. We must pray for his mercy. What have we done to deserve such wrath to fall upon us? We will pray for the strength of the sick to be given back and their health to be restored quickly. We will pray for forgiveness of our sins and pray that God will once more grant us our health.

I felt the urgency of getting over to Sarah's. As I turned to give Liz instructions I knew I had startled her, but she said nothing, only listened wide eyed.

"Liz, I want you to help me today with the feeding of the chickens and the other animals. I am going to take the chicken I have cooked for our evening meal over to your Aunt Sarah and Uncle William. They have sent word that they are all very sick. I will put another one in its place for our supper and leave everything in your care. I want a hot meal to take over to them. I have never known your Aunt Sarah to send for help I feel I must leave right away. I don't think I should waste any time in getting over there. Cousin Thomas was so upset just now.

It has been a hard time for them with all your cousin's sick and by the look on your cousin Thomas's face things are not improving as they did with us." As I talked with Liz of my plans she hurried to grab her shawl before going out the door to feed the animals. "I will help as much as you want Mama." She answered as she lifted the latch and went quickly on

147

her way.  Liz, knew far to well how listless and week she, felt when she had this fever.

As Liz, slipped out the door I hurried to put the chicken into something I could carry over to their cottage.  I am very anxious to see for myself just what the situation is.  It is so unlike Sarah to send word of an illness.  It must be quite bad.  I surely feel uneasy about the state of William and Sarah's family.  Even little Thomas's face had a pallid look to it.

Finding a pot that would do just fine I lifted the lid on the big black iron-cooking kettle that hangs over the small flames in the cooking area.  Testing the meat for tenderness I am finding it is not quite ready yet.  I really wished I had started it sooner.  I wanted to leave right away.  I will just have to take it as it is.  I can just hang it in their cooking area and it will be done long before suppertime.  What I sent with Thomas can be fixed for a midday meal.  I will take what I have ready for our meal and while I am gone more will be cooking and there will be plenty of time before my men come home for our evening meal.  Liz is perfectly capable of getting all of this ready.

My thoughts were flying around in my head.  How easily that problem was solved, I thought to myself, I don't know why I didn't think of it before.  I could have been there and back by now, I don't know why I was muddling around so.

I grabbed my wrap and as soon a Liz entered the door I told her my plans and gave her instructions for getting our meal well on its way before I returned.  She was a bit disappointed, as she wanted to go.  I felt she should not be exposed to this illness again and promised I would tell her Aunt Sarah and family she wanted them to be well real soon.

She pleaded with me once again as I reached for the door latch.  "Oh, no Liz, you must stay right here inside.  It is far too dangerous for you to be near the other children while they are ill and you know what your father said about the Indians."  I stated firmly.  I need not remind you of your father's stern warning and instructions do I?"  I continued talking as I picked up the vitals.  All this talk about the unfriendly Indians had peeked Liz's curiosity.

"Are they really going to hurt me, Mama?  They have never bothered me before.  I have seen them many times as they traveled through the woods.  They hardly noticed."  She said.

"I really couldn't say what they might do, Liz.  We must do as we are told and stay close to the house and take all the precautions we can.  You are old enough to understand these things now, and to obey your father when he tells you something.  You must trust his judgment; he has a lot of things to keep his mind busy right now, and doesn't need any added worries.

It seems the Indian people are upset over so many of them being sick.  They blame us.  Their anger causes them to do things they wouldn't normally do."  I tried to explain as best I could.  It was hard for me to understand myself.  I had no ill feelings toward these native people and

148

do not know why they should toward me. But I had heard the gruesome stories of the kidnapping and murders and of how they had stolen children and young girls and had taken them far away to their villages, never to be seen again. Knowing some of the stories to be factual gave me reason enough to heed the warnings of the elders and my husband.

"I understand, Mama, and I will do whatever it is you and Papa want me to do." She answered, and turned toward the door. "I will get some vegetables from the storage area and prepare them while you are gone."

"That's a good girl Liz, I knew I could count on you. "I did know she would follow every order her father or I gave her. Defiance of authority was not one of Liz's faults. She awoke every morning with a happy smile and a determination to please. Her whole personality was one of giving and caring.

The early morning hours had gone by swiftly and afternoon shadows were beginning to creep upon us. The livestock and the chickens were a great blessing but a lot of added work. Soon the ground would be warm enough to start the planting and we would have a garden full of vegetables, not just the few half grown ones we were now using. And herbs, what a blessing they would be. Liz's reference to the vegetables in the storage area jogged my mind to the fact that we were still eating off of last years harvest and fresh anything would be a marvelous change for our taste buds. Perhaps having something totally fresh will help to cure some of our ill and fatigued families.

There is so much preparing of the ground here before we can even plant one seed. I will be glad when the earth is warm enough to put the little seeds in the ground, but for now I will have to be content with what we do have and count it a blessing that there is anything at all. I must hurry and get on my way to see Sarah before it gets any latter in the day.

As I walk along the path, I find the beauty of spring overwhelming. The brilliant colors of the trees and flowers are so pleasing to the eye. The air smells fresh and cleans, as if it has been laundered and hung out to dry. How I loved the feel of the still cool air against my face, such a clean fresh feeling. I marvel at the colors so vibrant and bright, I wonder if their brilliant look is just an illusion, after the dreary dimness of the past winter. Whatever the reason for this beauty I feel that I am seeing nature at its best on this beautiful late afternoon.

My mind was not at all on what I was doing as I trudged along my way. I was so in awe of the wonder of nature, I almost walked right past the cottage. Returning a few steps back, I opened the gate and walked up the front path. I had chills up my spine as I approached the front stoop. A strange almost weak feeling overtook me. I approached the stoop with trepidation. There was something wrong; I could feel it deep inside of me. I stepped close to the door and could hear crying coming from within. I rapped lightly, my heart pounding so hard; I could hardly catch my breath. The front door opened ever so slowly. Reverend Eliot, Sarah's brother, was there and Sarah was crying, uncontrollable sobs. I walked in very cautiously and stood in the middle of the room, unable to move. I knew, by the look on my brother-in-laws face, that something terrible had happened. William's arms flew about me, and he laid his tear-streaked

149

face on my shoulder, his body raked with great sobs. He tried to choke out an explanation between the sobs.

"William, what is wrong? What has happened? Please, please Sarah, someone tell me what has caused you all such grief, and sadness?" I questioned them both. Looking from one to the other. I had sat the pot down right in the middle of the floor.

"Oh, Elizabeth! Tell me it isn't true, please tell me it isn't true." God would not take my sweet William from me. No, no, it can't be. Please, please wake him up." Sarah pleaded to me for help. Her arms outstretched to me and then turning and stretching them toward the body, still and dark, lying on the bed.

My eyes followed her hands, my mind craved for an answer to these statements that it could understand and yet as my eyes rested on the still body of William, I gasp, clasping my hands over my mouth. "William, what? Sarah, are you telling me that something has happened to your William? Oh no, this can't be. Tell me it isn't so. Reverend Eliot, tell her it is all right. Tell her that William is going to be all right. Dear God, please do something and help us, please help us!" I cried out in disbelief. The muffled words tumbled from my mouth and the tears dripped to the floor as I run to Sarah and held her in the tight grasp of my arms and our tears mingle together.

I want to tell her I know how it feels to loose a son, but I don't. Mine had gone away, but always with the hope of a safe return. Her son was gone forever, not to be seen by her again, until she, herself, parted from this earth and joined with him in the Kingdom of God.

Guiding Sarah to a chair she sits down and I sit beside her, hardly able to comprehend what is happening right before my eyes. The shock of this great tragedy has taken over my body with trembling and disbelief fills my mind. If I thought my Thomas's sailing away had torn me apart, it was nothing, no nothing compared to what Sarah and William were going through right this moment. By the shaking from within Sarah's body I could tell she felt like her heart had just been ripped from her bosom. She sat there unable to understand this tragedy that had befallen them. She had just lost her first-born and no amount of soothing words could help her at this moment. Her questioning came through her sobs, "why, why, why did God choose our son, our William?" I had no answer, but there must be one.

"God does have a reason, doesn't he, Reverend Eliot? Why did this have to happen?" I questioned Eliot, knowing what his answer would be before the words poured forth from his mouth.

"We cannot question the ways of the Lord, Elizabeth. He knows our every need and His promise is ever with us. He is our Great Comforter at times like this. We must rely on His love and strength to carry us through. We must pray for His guidance in this and all matters. Let us bow down on our knees and pray." Eliot said, taking Sarah's hand in his, he began to lead us in prayer.

As we prayed for peace within our hearts and answers to our inner most questions, I wondered at Sarah's strength. She looked so tired, the strain of the family sickness and the death of her son showed in dark, black circles beneath her eyes. My heart was being torn into shreds watching the agony she was going through and words offered in sympathy seemed to be empty and meaningless.

William came and sat beside her and took her in his arms and they cried together, they cried for the loss of a son, for the empty spot in their family. They cried with the memories of a small child that had so filled their hearts with happiness, they cried for the loss of the wonderful young man he had grown into and they cried for the years of happiness ahead that they had just been robbed of. It was impossible to console either of them.

Reverend Eliot said it would take time. I wonder if time can really ever heal a wound as deep as this. I don't think that there is any amount of time, no not any, that can heal the wound that is brought by the death of a loved one. Time might ease the sorrow but it is never totally gone. No there is never a total healing. I am almost sure of that.

I knew if John were here he would reprimand me for even thinking such thoughts. Our beliefs teach us differently. That little seed of doubt that lingers is not good I know. But John has never been a mother, nor has William, nor has Eliot so how could they possibly know just what a mother feels deep in her bones. Time is a healing of sorts, but to what degree?

I walked back home slowly. The shock and sadness weighing heavy on my shoulders as I trudged back up the hill. Somehow the beautiful spring day had turned into a black ugly spot in my world. It was an effort to lift my feet and move forward. I could not help the tears that streamed from the corners of my eyes, tumbling down my cheeks. Death had crept in like the thief in the night and stolen one of us away. The tears dropped slowly to the ground beneath my feet. I was still in a state of shock, as I lifted the latch on the door and entered the house.

"Mama, what is the matter, why are you crying?" Liz ran to me and threw her arms about me.

"Oh Liz! My dear, sweet Liz, something dreadful has happened at Aunt Sarah's and Uncle William's. Your big cousin William has died of the fever. It is just so hard to understand. Sarah and William are so devastated and their hearts ache so." I talked to her as gently as I could, but found no words to ease the shock. Liz's tears dropped in silence from her long brown eyelashes. The news was even harder to break to the men when they returned from the fields and we all moved about each having to deal with the loss in our own way and with the ever unanswered question of why, upon our lips.

The funeral for William was held in the new meetinghouse with the whole company in attendance. Reverend Eliot, giving a very glowing and inspiring sermon. What a beautiful eulogy to the memory of such a wonderful young man. He said, "William, like all of us, a child of God, had returned to be with his Heavenly Father. The purpose for which God had placed William here on earth had been completed and it was now time

151

for him to return home, to the loving arms of God." I listened intently as Reverend Eliot, continued. "We are all saddened by God's choice to take him from us in the prime of his life. I know that he will be very much missed by our family, and I pray to our merciful God above, that He will grant Sarah and William peace of mind and ease the sorrow of their hearts."

As I looked at young William's, sisters and brothers I could see what a void this loss had left in their young lives already. He was one they had always been able to look up to. This was so hard for them, how could we expect them to find understanding within their young hearts. If we as grown ups had a hard time understanding, how much more difficult it must be for these children.

William was an inspiration to all the children for he was a scholarly boy who, some said, promised to be a great leader here in this new land. He had come here a year before Sarah and William with his Uncle Eliot and had learned far more than most, from Eliot's teachings and guidance. He was a true inspiration to all who met him and the leaders anticipated that he would be that one special person in so many of the younger children's lives. I guess God had other plans for him.

As days passed, we tried to go on with our daily chores. Though we will never forget our loved one, the brutal task of survival in this new country of ours, kept our minds and bodies hard at work. We did not have time to dwell on anything, either good, or bad, for we were far to preoccupied with trying to stay alive ourselves, and providing for our families, the meager substances our lives required. This was a never-ending job.

Time passed as it always does and I planted my kitchen garden and could now see the first signs of new life, as the heads of the tiny new plants broke through the crusty brown soil. What a wonderful miracle of God it is, to see new life in any form, whether it is in the plants we grow or in the birth of a child or one of the new small baby creatures in the barn. It is always a miracle no matter how many times we see it happen.

It has taken several months, but Sarah has finally started coming out more. She is trying hard to put the death of William as far back in her mind as possible. She has been so ill herself. At times we feared for her life as well. She still wears the sadness upon her face, but the intensely hot sun of summer has brought some color onto her cheeks. I am beginning to see how, as time passes, the hurts of the heart start to heal, and one is better able to cope, as days and weeks go by. God does take care of his children, if we give him the chance.

I seem to be finding myself more outside than inside here of late. I do enjoy the fresh air and weeding in my garden. It is a labor of love for me and it is a diversion, from the confines of my tiny abode. My bonnet shaded my head from the rays of the sun and I worked about the small plants with ease. We would soon be able to pick a few of the young carrots and turnips. The squash and pumpkin would be a little longer on the vines. How nice it will be to have some fresh vegetables from our own garden, once more. I busied myself with my work; I was unaware of anyone standing near me. When a voice broke into my silent thoughts, I jumped, startled to find Sarah standing close to me.

"Why Sarah! You almost frightened the life right out of me. How did you ever come upon me, without me knowing it? You are as quiet as the Indians here about. It is so wonderful to see you up and out of the house again. I am honored at your visit." I babbled on at the embarrassment at being so surprised.

"Elizabeth, I have had such a hard time getting over the death of William. I can hardly talk about it yet. If I am to cry, please do not think badly of me, for I cannot help myself. I had to come and talk to you today, for I have something within me that needs to come out. I want you to hear it from me." Her statement was so profound I just nodded my head as she continued to talk. "I have brought some sewing with me and if you could spare but a few minutes from your work, I would appreciate it ever so much. Will you be so good as to, listen to me?" Sarah looked at me, her eyes looking big and round and full of expression.

I knew by the urgency in her voice that I must stop what I am doing and be with her. She is in such a need for someone to understand her feelings.

"Sarah, what is it? I hope it is not bad news, for I fear that I cannot take any more of that?" I said. "Of course I have the time to spare. A nice cool drink of water too, sounds good. Please come in out of this hot sun." I directed Sarah, toward the living area and retrieved a tin cup full of cool spring water.

"Thank you Elizabeth. No, it is not bad news, as a matter of fact, it is quite good news. I think it is anyway. I am with child, Elizabeth. I am going to have a baby." Sarah looked up with a sheepish grin, as she blurted out the news.

"Oh! Thank God! Thank God!" I praised the Lord in earnest. "This is the most wonderful thing you could have ever told me. I am so excited for you Sarah; this is just wonderful. Have you told William yet?" I questioned her excitedly. And what do you mean by, you think it is good news?"

"In answer to your first question yes I told William just today. He is quite thrilled about the whole idea. This will be our first child born in this new country. William thought that it was very exciting news. My brother, Eliot, says this is God's way of filling the void left by William's death. Maybe he is right. And that brings us to your second question. There is no one that can take the place of William in my heart. I have thought about this a long time. I don't want another child to take his place, for his place in our family was a very special one. Can you understand what I am trying to say Elizabeth? Nothing could ever take William's place, but a new baby in the family is always welcome." Sarah looked at me for a long while. She didn't really need me to answer her for she knew I understood her feelings.

For the first time in months I could see a sparkle of light, returning to her eyes. I reached over, putting my arms about her shoulders and I gave her a big hug.  That was all that was needed between us.

"I can hardly wait to tell John and the boys.  They will be so happy for you both.  And Liz, well she loves babies so much, you know what she will think."  I said, trying to break the silence that lingered between our words.

"Elizabeth, I must get back to the family now, I have stayed much longer than I told them I would.  I just had to tell you in person."  Sarah said, as she stood to leave.  The smile on her face reassured me of her inner peace and I felt good about life, a feeling within myself I had misplaced when William died.

"I can't tell you how much it means to me, to have you walk down here and tell me, Sarah, nor can I begin to express the joy your news brings to me.  Please pass on our congratulations to William."  I hugged her once again and waved as I watched her walk the path back to her home.

"Bye Elizabeth!"  She turned and waved just before rounding the hill and disappearing on the other side.

"Bye Sarah, and God's blessings."  I called after her knowing she could no longer even hear my voice.  I kept my eyes fixed on the last spot I had seen her figure and breathed a silent prayer of thanks.  It was so good to see her spirits up lifted once again, and something for both her and William to look forward to.  This hard life in this harsh place gave us little hope, yet once again God, had touched our souls and blessed us. He bent down from His, mighty throne in the sky and touched our family, healing our sorrows with His ever-present love.  Why did I find this so hard to believe?  I guess I wonder how He always knows just what to do at just the right time in our lives.

Sometime even as hard as I try I cannot understand all that is taught to us by the Reverend.  I know I question to often.  How can I learn if I don't?  I am just one of those mortal souls, that quests for an answer.  I should know by now that the Great Comforter is always with us. He has never failed me.

Summer was in full force now and everyday was filled to the brim with work.  The talk of leaving for Connecticut had not been put by the wayside.  It was still a very prominent subject about the supper table.

Thomas had been quite surprised at his fathers' first mention of another move.  He had many questions to ask and even put forth some good ideas.  John Jr. and William worked hard with their father and for once, when the conversation turned to moving on, I was a part of it and after a time, even looked forward to it taking place.  Maybe at first I was shocked, but now I think it would be a welcome change.  A part of me longed to seek the adventures of the unknown and the other part of me held fast to the security of our present shelter, such as it is, with our family and friends close by.

It was obvious that it would not take place until next spring, at the earliest.  We had all agreed to make some very definite plans and to

154

be prepared when we did go. Again we would be going into an area of few people, and hardly any settlements were established. A party of a few men and women had left about a month or so back, to secure a good place to settle our new company. When word was sent back that this place had been found, then we would all make our final plans to move on.

John had made several trips into Boston with John Jr. He was determined, this time, to have everything set. He would start supplying the people of this new area with the needed goods to sustain and better their lives. With the help of Thomas and his familiarity with the dock area and a few of the shipping companies, John had been able to secure a ship of his own and at this very moment he and Thomas were in town making arrangements for all the legal papers to be properly secured.

I don't think I have ever seen John so happy in all his life. He was in control, once again, of his own destiny and had the support of his family behind him. If John were to be involved in this new shipping venture, I would have a large responsibility for the farm and crops and animals. That is all right with me. Those are the areas that I feel most comfortable in.

A ship is just not my way of life. I know they are a necessary way of transportation, especially since so many of our needs have to be sent to us from far away places, but I am very sure that God made my feet for solid ground. As much as I would love to go someday and see my family and my beautiful Caswell, I think as long as it is by ship it will never be. My first experience with the sea I hope was my last.

John had tried to coax me into coming into Boston and going to the harbor to see this great new ship of his. Even offering me a personal inspection of the ship and crew and maybe even a short ride out on the open blue ocean. My reply being, "Oh no, John Curtyce, you got me on that sleek, green reptile called the sea once, and once only it will be. I will leave the secrets of the ocean to you and Thomas. I will tend to my home, garden and livestock." I responded and scurried them out the door and on their way. The two of them had left for Boston, a smile upon each face from ear to ear.

John Jr. and William were busy in the fields and Liz was doing some sewing. She has become quite handy with a needle and thread. She must take after her Auntie, for with very little effort, she can come up with the nicest creations. At first I was pleased and encouraged her to make dresses for her rag doll out of scraps of cloth from our tattered cloths. Then when I gave her an old coat, I had caught on a berry bush and torn almost to shreds, she created from it, a beautiful new coat for herself. I was amazed at her talent for sewing and began giving here more and more to do. I was proud to see her taking so naturally to something that would be very useful in her later years. These past few years have molded her into quiet an accomplished, young seamstress. She is such a great help to me.

It seems we all are looking forward to this move and having more room for everything. I think the livestock we are able to take along will also enjoy being spread out just a little bit more. I would like to bread the mare. Since horses are in such strong demand. I might even be able to sell the colt. When I approached John on the subject, he had agreed,

155

even thinking we should do it before we leave this area to insure a good match for her. We really don't know what we will find in the Connecticut wilderness. He is keeping his eye out for a good stud. Perhaps we can find one before we move on.

Today is a special time for me. I can finally harvest a small portion of the garden. I will pick the herbs first for I can dry them all and put as many of the vegetables and berries as I can away for future use. Next we will have to slaughter a couple of our pigs and dry the meat. There is just so much to be done, when I think about it. We seem to never really finish one thing before it is time to start another. Since we will not be taking all of our stock, we can trade for other necessities we don't have. There are always newcomers who need chickens. They are really great as they supply both meat and eggs. My mind is continually thinking of ways to take or transport our goods and us to Connecticut. I can just not face not having anything when we get there. John assures me we will have plenty. I will try not to worry so. Knowing it is some time before we leave hasn't stopped my mind from exploring every conceivable idea, notion or possibility in advance. I feel it is never too early to start preparing. I now knew how hard it was to begin again. I will not be caught unprepared a second time.

I have worked this tiny bit of soil long and hard, and have spent many long hot hours down on my knees planting, weeding and cultivation. Every usable inch is filled with plants. It has not been easy to grow this much, in such a small space and it has been next to impossible to acquire good livestock. If it hadn't been for cousin James and Thomas we would not have what we do now. Yes I know the difficulties in starting anew, with nothing, and my intentions are to leave nothing behind this time. Even a small blade of wild grass has become important to me. I chuckle to myself and think, I will not ask John to take the grass, hopefully Connecticut will have some of its own. John will be glad to hear of that decision I'm sure. I find this small amusing thought lightens my burdens and I have to chuckle to myself, for I know full well that John does think I am to attached to insignificant things and I guess he is right.

Since we are not contending with the long voyage, I can't imagine it being so far that we could not carry everything with us. Not at all like when we left Caswell, I pray! And I am getting more organized and familiar with what is of use and what isn't in this new place we now live in. Perhaps that has helped to make this decision to move a little easier for me. Whatever it is that makes me excited about a new adventure, so soon after the first one, I am grateful for. I doubt if I would really have much to say in the final decision but at least John is trying to do as I ask and at least converse with me as to what he thinks. I know his mind is already made up and I could never change it. It is just nice to be considered a little. I am careful not to assert my thoughts and opinions out in public; I would not want to be an embarrassment to John. No I am looking forward to a much better life in this Connecticut. For one thing I want a bigger garden and hopefully a more comfortable shelter. I just hope I'm not expecting too much.

As my thoughts passed through my mind I continued to pull at the tiny weeds that had tried to choke the life out of my plants. I pulled them with a vengeance and had become so engrossed in clearing them all

156

away I had not noticed dusk creeping up very quickly. It would be dark very soon.

I wonder where the men folks are? Even John and William have not come back from the lower fields. I must get myself up from here and get back inside and prepare a meal of some kind. As usual they will all arrive with the appetite of a bear. I stood up and looked over the garden and was pleased with what I saw. The fruits of my labor were many. I sighed expressing my love for the rich brown earth. My smile showed my pleasure for it had repaid my love with fine growth and beautiful, delicious vegetables. My wild berry vines held lush plump fruit on them and the few fruit trees we planted were over burdened with fruit, large, succulent morsels. In fact, the whole of all our labors have been rewarded with plenty. We would have enough to trade with our neighbors for goods that we did not plant ourselves and in that way we will have a better and more well rounded supply for winter. I gathered the picked herbs in my arms and concluded my garden work for this day.

The fields of rye are going to bring a bountiful crop too. Grain is a greatly needed commodity. When the men folks make the first harvest it will be such a great pleasure to take it down to Mr. Dummer's mill and have him grind it for us. For the small area we have, the boys and John have done a marvelous job in using every inch of space available to its best advantage. I am proud of my family and of our progress in this new land. It has been a continual struggle and a valiant effort by all and I am convinced the more effort we put in the results will even be better.

To my surprise as I entered the door, I saw that Liz had already started frying the fresh fish and had set the trenchers out. The gruel was made and the bread warming in the side oven.

"Why Liz, you have done so much. There is not one thing left for me to do, but put out a bit of cheese from the storage room. This is very nice indeed." I thanked her and gave a warm smile, a smile of pleasure at seeing our daughter turning into such a lovely young homebody. The best part was that she thoroughly loved every minute of it. The pleasure was truly all hers.

"You are welcome Mama." She replied. "I enjoy doing things about the house, I find it great fun to cook and make the meals." She said.

"You have grown up to be a fine young lady Liz, Papa and I are very proud of you." I stated, telling her she took after her grandmother, who always loved to do things in the house and the more there was the more she liked it.

"Thank you Mama, do you want me to go get the cheese from the storage room?" She questioned.

"No, that is all right, I will go, I must contribute at least a little effort to this fine meal!" I answered her and turned to go back out.

While I was out in the storage area the men slipped in the door. They had already washed up by the stream and were ready for a hearty meal.

157

Everyone was surprised when I told all of the men that this good meal was the contribution of their little sister. They all still think of her as to small to do much, but after tonight, their thoughts of her will be much higher, and their praise will be never ending, for I have already tasted of this fine food. Being the youngest and only girl has given way to a lot of love from her Papa and big brothers. They do like to tease her, insisting it might not be fit to eat. Liz just smiles and is most eager as ever to serve them no matter what they say or how they act. She knew better and was anxious for them to taste it.

John and the boys chatted amongst themselves for much of the supper meal. Talk of harvest and grain, of slaughter and curing of the meat. Selling of our over stock and trading for things we might need. Nothing had really been said about this ship of ships. I wonder when the great subject will come up. Far be it from me to bring up anything about the sea. It is really not my favorite subject in all this great big country. I know though that they cannot keep their mouths shut for very long. I can tell by the grins upon their faces that they are about to bust their buttons.

I was right, it was no time at all and John burst out, "Elizabeth aren't you going to even question, us about the ship?" You couldn't be that disinterested in it. You must be a little bit curious, aren't you? He blurted out, with a puzzled look on his face. He seemed more than just a little disappointed that I had not inquired before this.

"I was trying to be patient, just waiting for you to come forth with some pertinent information on your own John? Surely you have had a busy and fun filled day by the looks on yours and Thomas's face." I answered him, with a coy smile.

"You are such a sly one Elizabeth, you knew all along we were just about to burst, wanting to tell you all about our day and the very first of our fleet." The excited words came tumbling forth from his mouth. He could not contain his happiness and enthusiasm for this new adventure. He was finally doing what he does best. He is a businessman; a man of his caliber needs to have just that, a business. He has missed all of that since we left England. Just seeing him this happy made me happy too.

"Fleet, what is this fleet John? You didn't buy more than one ship did you? What ever would you do with more than one anyway? Surely one is more than enough, isn't it?" I questioned. I was concerned that in his enthusiasm he had put us far too much in debt. We would be in such arrears that it would be impossible to pay any of it off in our present state.

"Yes for now it will do quite nicely, but in the very near future, if all goes well we will acquire another and maybe even another. Trust me my dear, we do know what we are doing." He explained, in a very serious tone. Wrinkling his brow to show his determination.

"I certainly hope so John, it sounds like a mighty big venture to me. If this is your dream of dreams, then so be it, I wish you nothing but success in that vast big ocean, John. I hope all yours and Thomas's wishes come true. As for me I will be content to stay home and enjoy the solid ground beneath my feet." I commented, extremely enthusiastic as long as their plans upon the high sea did not include me in them.

"Mama, you have no idea what you will be missing!" Chimed in Thomas. "The life of a sailor is a good life, free and open and full of all kinds of things. You see different ports and different people, you are never tied down to one place, things are always new!" Thomas's comment made it almost seem like fun.

"Thomas, you never cease to amaze me, you really do love that vast big ocean out there, don't you?" I said, turning to look at my young son with astonishment.

"Yes Mama, I really do love her, but most of all I love you for letting me choose my lives work for myself. That is special Mama. You and Papa have given us all so much. The most special thing though is the love and encouragement you have both given all of us to try what ever it is we want to do. You never discourage us and always support us. That means so much to all of us you know?" Thomas's expression of his feelings brought tears to my eyes. I never thought of us doing anything more than just our best for our children. No more than any other father and mother would do for their family. I loved him for his thoughts though and for thinking us special. It meant a lot to me.

"Well that is very nice of you, Thomas, and all of you, for your thoughtfulness. But somehow I feel as if I am being softened up for a big blow. What is it that you are all up to now?" I said, looking at each of them one by one to see their reaction.

"This time nothing my dear, really nothing. The children really do appreciate all you have sacrificed for them, and I appreciate you too. We do not express ourselves nearly enough and we felt it was about time that we did. Another way of expressing how we all feel is written right here Elizabeth. Here read it." John said, as he handed me a folded yellowed sheet of parchment. I unfolded it gently and begin to read. It was the papers on the ship they had just acquired, and there filled in for her registered name was, "The Elizabeth."

"Oh how marvelous John, this is really a surprise, how exciting. A ship named after me." How exciting, I would never have dreamed of an honor such as this. Thank you both so very much. I am truly overwhelmed at your thoughtfulness.

"Now, no matter were we go, we will always have you with us, Mama. You will always be there to look after us and take care of us. Your name on our ship will bring us nothing but good seas and bountiful cargos; "The Elizabeth" will be the pride of the ocean. All will know her by name and honor her when ever they come upon her." Stated Thomas, almost in a shout.

"Well, I must say thank you, for indeed I am the one that is honored. Of all the names you could have selected, it is a great honor that you chose mine. I know how proud of her you are and how much you love her, this tells me just how much you love and care for me and I do

159

thank you. As a matter of fact I thank all of you." I said, patting William's back as he sat closest to me.

As the supper meal was cleaned up and the trenchers cleaned and put away everyone retreated to their places of rest. The day had been long and laborious for all of us. I was not quite ready for bed yet. I wanted to write in my journal. It had been awhile since I had taken it out and I had vowed not to let one important happening skip its pages. I sat down by the last tiny soft light of the only candle left burning. I must write fast before it burns out. The embers of the fire are not nearly bright enough to provide enough light to write by.

I had just finished putting the very last of the days exciting events onto the pages of my book when the light of the candle flicked off. I quickly tucked my book away in its secret place and retreated into the warmth of my bedchamber. As I lay my head upon the soft, feather stuffed pillow and closed my eyes, my mind once again relived this day and I fell asleep somewhere between a beautiful green garden and a beautiful blue ocean.

# CHAPTER 10

A giant wave rose above the sides of the tiny ship; it lifted its head out of the depths of a green, frothy mass and roared angrily. Held tightly within its curl, snarled a frightening, grotesque, green sea monster, with eyes that glowed like the embers, in the hearth fire, and a great gapping mouth from which sparks of fire ascended. It slashed and snarled, coming straight at me, I was unable to move; all I could do is hang on and let its full force hit me, devouring me, forcefully taking me away. I scream for help and scream some more. I cannot catch my breath I am going to drown. I am drawn down, down to the oceans depths and I am being washed out to sea, and taken captive by the demonic creature of the deep.

"Help! Help! Help me!" I scream. "Help me!" My hair was wet and tangled, sprawled about my shoulders in wet matted clumps. I lash at the monster and wipe the tears of fright from my eyes. My eyes sting from the salt in the water. I claw and scratch, seeming to make no headway against the strengths of the sea and its companion. My cries for help are falling on deaf ears; my life is in the hands of God. My outcries turned to soft sobs of defeat.

"Elizabeth, Elizabeth, what is the matter? What has frightened you so?" I could hear John's voice crying out to me. But I cannot find him. His voice is coming from a far off corner in my mind. I reach a trembling hand toward the sound of his voice and envision in my mind, him lifting my wet lip body up out of the water, dripping and disheveled, clinging desperately to what life is left in it. My eyes I keep tightly closed from fright and pain, and I doubt if they would open anyway as they seem to be glued shut. My clothing is a mass of wet cloth, now wrapped tightly about my body from the wreathing and slashing, at my capture.

Hearing John's voice again gives me a split second of added strength and I shove hard against the slimy scales of the monster and swim hard, flailing my arms in desperation to get away and reach the safety of my husbands arms. When I feel a somewhat reasonable calm has been regained, I slowly opened my eyes. Perspiration is dripping from my brow, my hair wet and sticky but the trembling of my body continues. It takes me more than a few moments to realize that the tenacious grasp that envelopes my body are the loving arms of John's. He has somehow rescued me from the sea and its monster.

"John! Oh John! Hold me I am so shaken. It was awful; this great green monster came out of the sea, wrapped in a giant frothing wave and tried to carry me out to the ocean depths. Oh John, I am so frightened. If you had not come in time and I had not heard your voice, I would have been lost forever." I cried, holding tight to John's neck.

"Elizabeth, darling, you have had a frightful bad dream. The Devil is trying to overtake your thoughts. He is working on you because he knows your ill thoughts about ships, sailing and the sea. All this talk of the ocean, the ship and getting ready to sail has caused you to have this fearful vision. You are all right; see you are right here in our bed. Except for the sweat upon your face and a bit of damp hair, you are fine. Take a deep breath now and rest yourself against me. I will hold

161

you here within my arms while you calm yourself. Your heart is beating so hard it is about to jump from you chest and you are ashen white. By the looks of you have seen death himself." John said, soothingly rubbing my back and holding me close.

"John the monster had eyes like burning coal, and a great large mouth, with fire pouring forth from it." I said, still trying to explain the reality of what I had experienced.

"It is not real Elizabeth, it was just your imagination coming forth in a dream. Stop shaking now and try to relax. You are getting all upset and for nothing, your imagination has run away with you. We will have to stop the talk about the sea and the ship. It has evidently upset you far more than any of us realized. I don't know why you have built up such a fear of the ocean. Your fear is really quite unfounded, you know." John said, still trying to console my trembling body.

"I know John, but I can't seem to stop feeling this way. I can not even put my thoughts to rest when I sleep." I answered. I really wanted to do what John was asking of me. Yet I could not, but I would try for John's sake and for my sanity. I put my head against John's, shoulder and listened to his soft soothing voice.

"The next few months will be filled with our move to Suckiaug, so you will have your mind and body quite occupied for some time to come. Maybe that will keep your fright of the sea out of your thoughts for awhile." John said, with a sigh. Hopefully with time you will learn to love the sea and conquer this abhorrence you hold for it.

"I want that very much John, I truly do. But John, I think my dreams are trying to tell me something. Something that I can not fully understand right now." I answered him, trying my best to explain an inner feeling.

"Elizabeth, that is nonsense. You are letting the devil take over your mind. The elders and the Reverend would have harsh words for you if they were to hear you speak in such a manor as this. You are worrying your pretty little head about things you have no control over and can do nothing about. Just close you eyes and think nothing but happy thoughts and I will not take my eyes from you until you fall back to sleep." John requested, as he fluffed the pillow under my head and laid me down to rest upon it.

"Yes John do, hold me close, keep me safe. I beg of you not to tell anyone of my dreams John, I would not want anyone to think I am possessed of the devil." I begged.

"I do not discuss our private life with others Elizabeth, but you have got to get yourself under control. This is becoming an obsession with you. Please close your eyes now and get some sleep." John requested, patiently trying to sooth my fears.

I close my eyes, and try to do as he says but there seems to be a picture etched on the backside of my eyelids. A picture of flashing eyes, of grotesque horror burned permanently into my brain by the hand of Satin.

162

Was I possessed of the devil? Was I really letting him take control of my mind? I do not want this sea monster, so vivid and clear, to take over my life. I want to be rid of him more than John could even imagine. As horrible as the picture in my mind is I force myself to keep my eyes closed and I finally drift into a sound sleep.

The morning light brings calmness to my nightmarish world and with the shadows of darkness vanquished I open my eyes to the delight of a beautiful morning. I am more than a little tired, do to my exhausting tussle with the underworld of the sea, but seem to be none the worse for ware.

John is right, I am going to be much to busy getting ready for the move to Connecticut to think, let alone dream of much else. I wonder what I will have to leave behind this time? I do not have near the amount of things to go through, as I did when we left England. Yet, I do have to sort through our belonging before I can pack.

This time it is not a matter of space available, but a matter of what we can carry. I have become complacent in our new world, thinking we were settled for good. I have conveniently forgotten how hard it is to pick up and move. Our brief respite here in Roxbury has not eased the accumulation of loads of extras, and once again I find myself sorting, and piling and hem hawing, through our possessions. Once again there is a pile for this and a pile for that. Oh how I miss having dear sweet Katy to help me. She did so much for me and had taken such a burden off my shoulders. Not to mention, having someone to talk things over with.

Having a daughter old enough to take over some of the household responsibilities does a lot to free up some of my time for packing. I really do appreciate her. She has become quite a homemaker. Her willingness to step in anywhere she is needed is a true blessing.

As the day for our departure grows nearer, I both look forward to it and dread it. Departure day is a day that I will look upon with many mixed emotions. I know that I will find the strength from God to survive any trial or tribulation that might crop up along the way. I have come to a peace within my soul that will somehow allow me to deal with what is thrust before me and I know by my faith that man does not readily see the plans of God. I will take each day and each task as a command from God for my life and with His guidance and grace I will trudge down the path He had seemingly set forth for me.

The day of our parting from Roxbury has finally arrived and with all my resolve I am finding it no easier than our departure from Caswell Manor. The tears still flow down my cheeks and my heart still aches and time marches on and so do our lives, and what has really changed? I cannot believe that we are now on the move again, this time to Connecticut.

Our goodbyes are said and portions of our belongings are loaded on sleds pulled by two of the boys. Some of our things are carried in flaxen bags and the animals are tethered to a rope, as are our two goats. We have a few of our chickens in wood cages and our two trunks piled on a horse drawn wagon. So with our worldly positions surrounding us we start our long arduous walk to this place they call Connecticut.

After only a day or two of walking on the narrow trail forged in the forest by the animals, I found myself exhausted and tattered. The growth under the big trees snatched at our clothing. It rips and tares small bits and pieces of the cloth as we pass by. At times it reaches through the cloth to tear at our skin, causing little rivulets of blood to trickle down our arms and legs. In these few days of long hard walking it has become very apparent that this path to Connecticut is a very rough and unrelenting one.

It is not a well-trodden path we are taking and it has a way of crisscrossing back and forth through the forest. Sometimes we seem to be backtracking over our own steps as we trod over the fields and meadows, going up hill and down as we wind our way along valleys and streams. Occasionally we see a sign of another humans passing. Trampled down grass and broken trees and brush are a tell tale sign that something or someone has traveled this way before. I am sure by the looks of things it has surely not been many humans.

We see few animals during the day but hear their cries long into the night when we stop for food and rest. Sleep is almost inconceivable with the night noises about us. And day light hours are trod with great awareness of the dangers that lurk behind almost every tree in the forest about us. The area we are in right now is full of briers that are tearing at my legs and arms. My dress and petticoats are being ripped to pieces step by step as we steadily trudge forward on our journey.

The mountains and meadows are many and I find myself tiring easily. I am finding as we constantly push forward I hate the rushing rivers the most. Some are so full from the winter snow and storms that I fear for our lives and the lives of our livestock as we board these rickety hand crafted rafts that carry us from one side to the other. It sometimes takes us days to just cross one river. They are so vast and each time we come upon one the process of making the rafts, loading our supplies, our livestock and our families is a daunting task. If it weren't for the sight of land on the other side and the prospect of a better place to live I would feel like giving up. My weary and tired bones ache and the rolling of the rafts on the fast rushing water makes me feel as if I were upon the ocean again. A feeling I hate with a passion.

No matter how many times we cross one of these large waterways we never seem to get it right. No matter how hard we try we are never exactly in the right spot when we finally reach the other side. The swiftness of the current takes us far down stream and we have to climb steep embankments and retrace many rough miles to reach the path again.

I am constantly holding tight to Liz, for fear of her falling into the dark, white-capped waves splashing about us. No matter how often the men go through this routine of tying the logs together to build the rafts, they look and seem so unsteady to me. At each crossing it is always the same routine. We always had to leave the rafts behind. The men retrieve our ropes and we head on our way. It sometimes takes hours and hours and patience wear thin. I wish we could transport them to our next river crossing so we don't have to go through this time after time but the rafts barely make it across one river. They are just too fragile. We are thankful when everything including us safely reaches the other side. The animals fear shows in their eyes as we tug and pull them onto this floating contraption. Thus far, we have somehow succeeded in all of our crossings with out much loss of beast or belongings. A few close calls have reminded me that it is best not to hurry. Safety must come first no matter how anxious I am to get to our destination.

We just never have any time to rest. I am so tired today, more so than any other it seems. I feel ready to collapse. Our leaders are prodding us along very fast now, or so it seems. We have come to a very dense green forest with a slushy cold swamp. Very little sunlight is penetrating through the thickness of the trees. I feel as if I am running from a hidden enemy. We have walked for weeks now and many days long into the night before we were allowed to stop. I do hope that today is not another of those long days on the trail. What once seemed a delightful adventure to a wondrous new home has become drudgery. We are a driven people, driven by our desires. At the brink of exhaustion I try hard to remember what our desires are? What are our reasons for doing this all over again? In circles my life seems to be swirling almost out of control. We push on, day after day and week after week. Daylight and dusk have all been scrambled into one. We have no time to waste; no time to spare, and certainly I have no time for thoughts of regret.

As I push myself to put one foot in front of the other I heed the instructions of our elders to be every alert for anything out of the ordinary. Our eyes constantly on the move and our ears listening intently for the slightest rustle in the brush and stubble that is more than abundant in the forest. We are cautioned to be ever alert for Indians or wild animals. A sense of security seems to not be within our reach. At night one of the men stands guard and each man and boy takes his turn at sentry duty. Our stops during the daylight hours are brief, limited to taking care of our bodily needs and to have a drink of fresh water when it is available.

Our dried meat, biscuits and perhaps a small chunk of cheese are our sustenance. It is a real treat when we come upon a wild berry bush and are able to pull a few fresh berries off as we pass by. Our leaders seem to ignore all signs of approaching nightfall. They try to make use of every available ray of daylight. Today I saw the signs of nightfall many hours back but our leaders are pushing us on telling us we will have a better place to stop a little further up the trail. We need to reach our destination as quickly as possible, is always the answer given to almost any question.

What I once thought to be cool early summer days have sure turned out to be more like long hot summer days. The fouls we brought along seem to be suffering in their cages as they are bounced atop the wagon. Their beaks are wide open as if they are gasping for more air and their feathers are falling out leaving large chunks of exposed skin. Some have died from the extreme heat and confined conditions. The few cages of chickens and the larger of our trunks have become a very cumbersome burden. Our cow is pulling a crude sled now and she has provided us with some much-appreciated fresh milk. I am very glad that my determination to bring the cow, horse and goats along was not overruled. It is the only concessions made for me. Some of our people thought the livestock should be brought at a later time, when we were finally settled in this new place, but I insisted that it come now and I am so glad I did. Others also insisted that theirs be brought too. Liz has taken charge of leading the goats and I sometimes relieve her to give her little arms a rest. I have heard grumbles from others about the animals but they are plenty willing to drink of the milk at the end of a long day.

Today my flaxen satchel of necessities, which seemed quite light at the beginning of this journey now feels as if I have packed it full of rocks. I will carry it until I drop if necessary for in it is my lives possessions, or at least what is left of them. I have become very possessive of our things. The only time I will allow our horse out of my sight is when it becomes necessary for one of the men to mount the mare and ride her ahead to check for any hostile situations and make sure we are still on the Connecticut Path and headed in the right direction.

Every once in awhile a slight smile tugs and curls at the corners of my mouth. Just to think of the situation I find myself in is amazing. Even more amazing is the fact that I can find any laughter at all inside of me, but I do. One thing that will always bring a smile to my lips is the thought of our direction. It is a good thing that leaders and scouts have not left the leading up to me. I have felt lost since I first turned and looked back and there was no more Roxbury in sight. Knowing that my since of direction is probably the worse ever, I always make sure I keep up with everyone else in our group no matter how tired I am. I would surely not want to get lost now for we have long pasted the last bit of anything remotely connected to what I would call civilization.

The last bit of human life we detected was a half fallen down lean-to, perhaps belonging to a couple of trappers. It has probably not been used since last year, or by the looks of it maybe even before that. If I would have been directing us, we would have probably walked for a day and found ourselves right back at the edge of Roxbury. I seem to have a knack for walking in circles, when I think I am on a straight path.

Becoming very familiar with what to do and how to walk along this trail, I have time to wonder to myself. This is not always a good thing for me to have too much idle time. I seem to do it anyway and at this very minute I am wondering if our reason for taking this journey is really valid one? John, really did a tremendous job of convincing me, that this was right for us? Today I really don't know if it is right or wrong. This long hot walk, day after day has given way to, a great deal of time for idle thinking. It is true that we left England for not only the right to believe as we wished, but also for the opportunities to better our lives. Then while in the Massachusetts Bay we found that the theocracy kept us very much in the same situation we had left far behind. Sometimes it is hard to really keep focused on what started us on this journey. I wonder if our desire to have a more democratic way of life will ever be a reality.

As I walk along thinking, I concede to myself that I am making this move completely of my own free will, or almost anyway. John had a lot to do with the making up of my mind. But what if it is not as it was described, his Connecticut John told me about. John told me that the rivers were broad, and the valleys rich. There was room for large farms that would yield large lush crops. Would I find this to be true? Only time will answer this question that tugs at my heart and makes me doubt. Determination to have an answer to all of the many unanswered questions that roll around in my head is what forces me ever onward.

166

As I pull my muddied feet from the grip of the quagmire of slush I find myself in, my questioning thoughts stop. I am to the point of giving up. I have to stop wondering so much and concentrate on the here and now. My feet have become bogged down almost up to my ankles. I must remove my shoes, as it is imperative to preserve a commodity as hard to come by as these shoes are. Looking around I find almost everyone in our company in the same drastic situation. We are all stuck in this muddy, swampy marsh. With each step the grasp of the saturated earth sucks so hard it feels as if it is ripping my limbs from my body.

It was near to impossible for the horse to make its way through this terrain and the men were coxing the cow on as they tug at her rope almost choking her. As I wipe my brow, I'm trying to find the best way to free myself and I wonder if we will have to leave both of the larger animals behind. If we do they will have to be killed, as I would not leave them to the whims of nature. I blink and quickly put that thought out of my mind and try to hurry forward to see if the mare at least would bend to the command of my voice. We had only a little ways to go to be on more solid ground. I must try to save our animals before the leaders think we are taking to much time in getting them across this bog.

My many concerns about this place called Connecticut only increases as I work hard with the animals. Was it going to be worth all this effort? Finally, as if by some great miracle my feet hit solid ground. The horse and cows pace pick up as did mine and before I was aware of it we are all almost running at a fast trot. The horse especially does not want to slow down for anything she seems to sense something over the incline ahead.

My questioning thoughts as to what was ahead of us could not have been answered any more decisively or with more impact then what was taking place this very minute. Just when I felt our destination could and would never be reached. There the beautiful Connecticut River appeared before my very eyes. A glorious sight as we approached from a high bank above the rushing blue waters.

The day had been long and hot, and the last half of the day through the mud bog, a test of our determination, but the beauty of the landscape below gave us added vigor to rush forward and not stop until we had reached the rivers edge. The long days of travel seemed worth our efforts. We had arrived all safe, all together and in fairly good spirits. We had arrived and my heart is pounding with joy!

"Oh John, this is a lovely sight! I truly had my doubts as to our making this move all in one piece. I am glad that we did, for this does look like a wonderful place to build our home. The air is clear and refreshing and the river so big and beautiful. The water does seem to be awfully high; it is almost to overflow its banks. Is it always like this?" I asked, as I viewed the roughness of the sprawling waterway.

"This is a very big river, Elizabeth, but it is extremely full right now from the winter runoff. It will take us many long hours or even days to ferry all of the company's belongings and livestock across this wide, swiftly flowing water. I am afraid the awful dangers are still very much with us." John explained, as he and other members of the party

167

surveyed the best possible crossing place and safest approach to the situation.

"I am so pleased to be here at last that I think I could swim across all by myself." Exclaimed our Liz, as she found a rock under a big shade tree to sit upon and rest her tired feet.

"That would not be to good of an idea even in the best of seasons. The current here is much too strong. We will have to cross with care." Replied her father. Warning her not to even consider such an idea.

"What ever you say, we will do. Let us just hurry and get to the other side. I will not feel like I have reached home until I put my two feet upon that bank way over there." I interceded in their talk, before John, in his tired exhausted state took her comment to seriously.

"Yes, yes, Elizabeth, it is good to hear you so enthusiastic for a change. We will proceed on, but with caution, and I must say how very happy I am to know that you are looking forward to our new home here so much." John answered with a broad smile creasing his mouth. He even seemed to relax that rigged persona that had taken over his personality, after only a few steps had been taken on the trail.

Reaching the other side of the Connecticut River was a true test of our wills. But when we finally reached the other side I released a deep breath that had been pent up inside me from the very beginning. "Another body of water conquered." I sighed out loud.

John looked at me as if to say, "What is the matter now?" Frowning to warn me not to display my thoughts so that others could hear. I really don't think he knows what a fear I have of this pure liquid stuff that we so need for our existence. He loves it so, it is hard for him to imagine anyone not liking it. I can appreciate its beauty from afar with no problem. I just don't like this close, personal contact.

It was pure pleasure to me to see the last of our group come up the steep embankment. We all sat for a well-earned rest beneath the willows along the rivers edge. My what a pretty sight! I had grown used to the small babbling brook and beautiful Jamaica Pond, back in Roxbury, but this is really quite a different sight.

I never dreamed the rivers would be this big. It looks to be almost the same as an ocean, except for the land showing along its sides. Not a lot different than coming into Boston Bay, through the beautiful harbor, with its rocky cliffs bidding us welcome. Is this river bidding us welcome too?

It moves past us so swiftly could it even know we are here? I wonder where it is running? Or what it might be running from? What ever the case may be, it will soon reach its final destination, and tussle for its own space for existence mists the wonders of the oceans depths. It would eventually embrace the mouth of the sea, the fresh water of the river mixing with the salt water of the ocean to become one and move on with the current to who knows where and to what end?

There were even waves upon this river, just like the ocean. I am sure if I had known of its greatness before I left Roxbury I would not have made the decision to come here. And if John could have talked me into it I am sure I would have had a lot more reservation than I did. I am glad it is over and we are all safely on the other side.

The sun beating down on my face feels warm and soothing. I am feeling relaxed as I lean against a tree and let my eyes take in the full beauty of this new home. It is good to see the small children run about, playing a game, enjoying the freedom of the tall grass and cool breeze, to romp in. The cattle and horses had been watered and are resting their weary bodies. And I take this opportunity to do the same, even allowing myself to drift off into a light sleep.

The voice of our leader has awakened me abruptly, as he informed us that we must move on. It was time to once again be on our way. We were wasting precious time by setting here so long. I really wanted to stay here much longer. It was so relaxing here in the shade of this giant tree and the lapping of the water against the shore made a rhythmic hum, as if singing a soft lullaby, caressing me into a state of drowsiness. It was probably a good thing when Mr. Hooker called us all together for a prayer and we were on our way once more, for a few minutes longer and John would have to build my house right here around me.

When we finally reached Suckiaug it was a great relief to all of us. The few people that had come here the spring before met us with open arms and warm greetings from the heart. Everyone seeming so happy to see new faces and to spread cheer to us weary travelers. Many who greeted us were already friends from many years past and we were always happy to make the acquaintance of new friends. We brought messages from family and people they had left behind. Seeing these old friends filled my heart with joy and I found myself loving this place even more than I had first thought possible. In this great expanse of wilderness it is not always likely, that when one says goodbye, you will ever lay eyes on them again, to issue a hello.

This time we were experiencing, getting reacquainted with old friends, giving me renewed hope that someday I would again be able to talk with Sarah and William and enjoy that new baby girl that was born just hours before we left. Hannah, they had named her, how pretty. She would be a great comfort and help to her Mama some day. I was happy that she was born before we left so that I could at least hold her one brief moment, and place a gentle kiss upon the darling dimpled cheek and turned up button of a nose, and feast my eyes on the perfection of God's creation, before our lives separated us for who knows how long. Once I had thought forever, but maybe not. I never expected to be here, so maybe I will be back there someday or maybe even they will be over here. We will just have to see if our lives will come together one more time. Who knows what God has in mind for our destiny?

We seem to blow in the wind, like a leaf at his command, and plant our feet firm, sometimes for only a brief time. Then once again with another puff of air, up we go and move on a little further in life.

God is ever prodding us in his direction; to do his will in all things. We think with our great minds that we are making the decisions, but that is really folly, for God's hand is ever on our lives and ever present in our decision. That is if we listen to him. Sometimes we push forward in our own will and find that we have become bogged down in the quagmires of life with no direction at all. Much like we had been bogged down on the other side of the river.

I shall pray that what we have undertaken is within His plan for our lives and that we can now settle down and try to fulfill our dreams, our destiny here is this land called Connecticut. I pray that His blessings will always be with us, as we look to Him for guidance and care. I do hope that it is also in His plan to once again in our lifetime, let us set eyes upon our loved ones far away. I do not want to dwell on the possibility that I will not see Sarah again, for she is as close to a sister as I will ever have. I will miss her greatly.

"So this is Suckiaug? It is nothing like I thought it would be. I had expected that the company of people that came last spring would have accomplished much more than my eyes see right now. It does not look like they have really done much of anything. John, we did so much in our first year in Roxbury. What has happened here? Surely they could have at least started some sort of a town. I don't see much more than we saw when we landed in Boston Bay. This is very disappointing, don't you think?" I stated, much in dismay at what I saw. "The people are friendly and seem as happy to see us as we are to see them. But what have they done with their time?" I continued to converse with John as we walked along.

"Don't be so hasty to criticize for you do not know what has gone on here in the past year. We have got to find out all the details before any judgment can be made. It is very difficult to get supplies in and out of here right now and that is where we are going to be able to help, the river people. We cannot expect the same accomplishments to have taken place here. It is really quite a different environment than Massachusetts Bay and Roxbury. Time will make the difference Elizabeth, time." John explained.

"I know you are right John and as we move around a bit and get used to things I know it will get better. I cannot get used to the houses that do exist though. They are just dug into the muddy banks of the river, with a thatched roof. It is the very same as what we left. There is barely room to stand inside and the area is cramped and stuffy. Hopefully this is not your idea John, of my dream house, for if it is we will have to have a long talk. I might even have to sleep out under the stars." I chided.

"Now lets not jump to conclusions about anything. We have hardly been here long enough to make a foot print in the mud, let alone build a dream house." John responded with a laugh.

"You are right John, I am anxious for you to finish your business so we can talk about what we are going to do and get going with our lives. Hurry along now and quickly finish up what you need to do. Liz and I will just roam around and wait for your return." I said, knowing I was being much too impatient.

"My Mama, when they called Connecticut a wilderness area they only had the description half right. It is almost deserted. A few buildings

170

standing here and there and they seem to be in no special order. I don't think there has been enough planning here to call it a town. Why, it is only a few shanty's thrown together, there is much less here than in Roxbury. Is this really going to be our home?" Asked Liz, amazed and showing disappointment in what she saw.

"I know Liz, but as your father says we must give it a chance. That is only fair don't you think?" I suggested. "Yes, we will give it a chance, what choice do we have anyway?" Liz stated bluntly. I could really detect her ambiguousness at being here. She had never shown any of her feelings for the decisions we had made for the family. I wonder why she has chosen now to display her own thoughts and will so openly?

"Now Elizabeth, I want to hear no talk like that from you. What ever your father decides is for our good. He is only trying to provide the very best for us." I replied sternly, never quite seeing Liz in this kind of a mood. She knew by the use of her full given name that I meant business.

"Yes Mama, I am sorry. It just looks so awful, the most awful place I have ever seen." She answered with a large sigh. Her downcast look told me she would obey, but with reservations.

As I paused briefly to look around I felt much the way Liz did and I know she is just growing up and feels she has a right to voice her own opinion.

I really wanted to voice mine a little stronger myself, yet I knew it would be to no avail and besides I really didn't dare. I must heed my own words. "John knew best."

What have we come to? Will we ever be able to call this place home? My thoughts keep reeling, but I kept them and my observations to myself. I know that being by the river, gives John more advantage for trade than did Roxbury, but I do not want my children to live in a place of filth and mud like this.

How will I ever convey my thoughts to John without him thinking me ungrateful? I don't mean to be so mixed up, I just am. How can I be so happy and ecstatic on one side of the river and so dubious and depressed on the other? I am beginning to think that there is something wrong with me. I can't help myself, this is just so drastic, and so, I can't even find the words to describe it. I must do as I told Liz to do, give it a chance, I will make up my mind right now, no more doubts, and I will love my new home!

Several hours pass and John is still gone. We had tended to the livestock and poultry and we freshened ourselves by the rivers edge. It was beginning to show the first signs of days end when John came down the path toward us. A broad smile upon his face showing his pleasure at whatever he found. He really is an optimist. I don't think he could ever be disappointed in anything. He always has the ability to find good in everything about him.

171

As for me I fear that too much time has elapsed and the ugly fears and doubts have crept back into my head. I hardly gave John a chance to say hello before I burst forth with my first volley of questions. One after another they came spurting out of my mouth faster and faster. I hardly gave myself time for a good breath in between questions. "Oh John this is a dreadful place, there is nothing here! Where are we going to live?" I pounced on the chance to relive my mind of pent up questions.

"Slow down Elizabeth, one question at a time. That is all I can handle. It is not really even a town yet. This past year has been hard on the company that came ahead of us and they have hardly had time to do much more than keep themselves alive through the winter." John explained.

"I know John but there is no place for us is there? Now tell me the truth John, is there?" I continued my barrage of thoughts.

"Well, yes and no." He said, standing his ground and looking down at my upturned face, with a stern look on his.

"What kind of an answer is that, yes and no?" I replied just as firmly, placing my hands upon my waist in a motion of defiance.

"What I am trying to tell you Elizabeth is that yes we have a place to stay, but no there is no real home for us. I have talked to all the men in the company and set the wheels in motion for our real home." John smiled as he explained or tried to.

"Our real home John, where is our real home and where are we to build it? Up here overlooking the river is this where it is to be?" I questioned, looking about. Now starting to get excited myself.

"Elizabeth if you will just stop asking so many questions and let me talk I will tell you everything. What I am trying to say and fear doing a very poor job at explaining to you that Suckiaug is not to be our permanent new home. I have been trying all the way back here to find just the right words to explain all of this, so as not to upset you. I fear you will hate me and not want to go on. The more I think the worse it gets so I just won't think any more and I won't try to surmise your reaction, I will just tell you what is to take place and we will go from there. Just promise me that you will not get upset until you have heard me out. Please Elizabeth, can you promise me that?" John requested sounding exasperated.

"Yes John, I promise! You are trying to tell me that we are not going to stay in Suckiaug, aren't you John?" I answered, not quite being able to keep my, just stated, promise completely.

John ignoring that fact said. "Yes Elizabeth, how do you already know? How can you know what I am going to say before I say it? How do you do it, tell me how do you do it?" He said, almost demanding an answer now.

"It really isn't that hard John, it is written all over that honest face of yours. It is very hard for you to hide anything from me you know. You should have realized that by now. Now that you have the worst part

172

over with would you sit down beside me and start from the beginning and explain just what the plans are for our future." I said, as I lowered myself to the ground and leaned against the tree. I patted the ground next to me indicating a seat for John.

"Oh Elizabeth, I love you so very much. You always know just how to handle the most awkward situation and you make me so happy and proud. There are not many women who would climb aboard a dream and follow her husband like you have done. Thank you Elizabeth, thank you for being my wife." John smiled his sincere appreciation.

"John there is no thanks needed, you know that my love is so strong that it would never truly falter under any circumstances. Sometimes it does question, but it is always there and always will be." I told him, reaffirming how I had always felt and always would.

"Well Elizabeth we are going to be staying with Mr. John Talcott. He sent a group of his people out last year to build a home for him so it would be all ready when he arrived. It is a beautiful home high on the hill that overlooks the river. You will be quite comfortable there as will and so will the children. It will only be for a few months. Then Elizabeth, we will be heading for Cupheag and there we will build our dream." He went on to explain.

"Cupheag, where is that? That is such a strange name. Do we have to go on another ship to get there? Is that why I had all those bad dreams? I think I won't like being on a ship again John." I stated, concerned that another ocean voyage was to take place.

"No Cupheag is only a short distance from here. It is on the neck of water that separates the landmasses. We will have good shipping lanes there and will be able to secure many acres of land for our farm. We will have the best, for the both of us. It will be perfect. When our ships pick up cargo in the ports of Salem and Boston we will sail around and up the Connecticut River and supply all the towns along the river. Then we will sail back down the river and over to Cupheag and bring supplies home. It is really a wonderful place and I know you will love it." John said, and the vibrato in his voice revealed his desires.

"John, is there a town there already? A real town, at least as real as the one we left?" I questioned.

"No Elizabeth there is not a town at all we will be the first ones there. All that is there now is a small Indian village along the water. The river is called the Housatonic and we will land at Mac's Harbor. It will be up to us to plant are roots deep and construct the town to our liking. Several of the families will be going along with us and John and William will be able to build a fine life for themselves. Thomas and I will work the shipping lanes and you and Liz will have full charge of the farm and animals. Does that sound exciting enough for you Elizabeth?" John questioned as he took my hand in his and looked deep into my eyes.

"John what it sounds like is a lot of empty space, with no people, no buildings, and no houses! Am I correct so far? It sounds like a tremendous amount of hard, strenuous work and a long time before we will

173

ever have a house to live in again, let alone my dream house. Am I still correct, John?" I questioned sternly and held my eyes on his steadily.

"Elizabeth where is your spirit of adventure? I thought you would jump at the chance, to not only build our house the way you wanted, but we can build the town the way we want it too. I think that is a great way to start out. There is no one there but Indians and the decisions will be up to us. We have been given a chance to truly take over and build our future the way we want. The minister will come with us and we will work for the Lord every day of our lives. The King, will be pleased to hear that his subjects have planted their feet firmly in the soils of the Connecticut Colony and are building for the future." He explained with enthusiasm.

"Well as usual John your mind is made up and I seem to have very little say as to what we are going to be doing. I will welcome a real home to stay in if only for a few months and will be very grateful to Mr. Talcott and his family for their hospitality. Please tell them we accept their kind offer with grateful hearts. I will gather the family together and we will be on our way. You go ahead and express our thanks and return and help us with the livestock. Would that be to much to ask John?" I said, my tone rather sharp. I just couldn't help it. I was tired of trying to figure out what was going to happen next. For now I would do as John wished. I had no choice.

Now Elizabeth, your tone sounds a little sour, you are being a bit unfair to me. I am trying to do my best. Would it please you if we stayed here in Suckiaug? If that is your wish I will tell them we are not interested in the opportunities of Cupheag and we will settle here. Is that what you want?" He continued questioning me.

No John, that is not what I want; I don't know what I want right at this very minute. I am tired and hungry. We have had a long hard journey to this Connecticut and a most trying day. I quite expected something very different than what I found. Please just give me a few days to rest and regain a bit of strength and perhaps I will see this Cupheag in a totally different light. Can you at least give me a few days to adjust John or is that too much to ask of you?" I retorted back at him.

No it is not too much to ask Elizabeth, I am sorry I always bring news to you in the wrong way. I feel excited inside and automatically think you feel the same. I will go ahead now and will probably meet you half way up the hill on my way back." John said as he walked away. I knew I had disappointed him that was not my intention. I just wanted to stop and be permanent for a change. I just can't understand why that is so hard for John to figure out.

As we climbed further up the incline from the rivers edge we found a path that looks to be much more traveled and more likely it will lead us back to the center of this place called Suckiaug. As we walked along I let my mind take over my thoughts even though I know it is not in my best interest. I should really have more control over my mind but I am far too tired to fight even against myself. I just want some peace for my family and some place to rest our weary bones. Please, dead Lord, let some kind of security return to our family life, I plead within my brain. We are always in a state of suspension. We are a family and yet not quite a

174

unit.  We are almost settled, but never fully established.  I vow at this very moment to take responsibility for my own destiny.  I will go with John to this place called Cupheag and there a dream will come true.  It doesn't matter if John makes the dream come true or if it is I who brings it to fruition, all I know is that it will be completed.  This I vow to myself and to my children.

# CHAPTER 11

The Talcott house was a small, thatched roofed cottage, with a shed at the back. The weathered shingles on the outside were showing signs of the past winter with large streaks of dark brown smudges running from the wood to the dirt beneath it. All these ugly smudges were from the muddy waters that ran off the roof during the past long hard winter.

The dirt floor was damp, even wet in places and packed hard from the trampling feet of the family. This caused a pungent musty smell that nips at my nostrils as I enter into the dimly lit house. My toe snagged momentarily against one of the many protruding rocks showing through the packed earth. In places a table had been positioned over stones, to large to remove.

The walls were covered over with a white plaster like substance made from oyster shells. Mrs. Talcott, was explaining how the collection and grinding of the shell was becoming widely used in this area and that the shells were a plentiful commodity here. She continued telling me how they were ground into a fine powder then mixed with grass and small twigs and stuffed into holes to keep out the cold of winter and the heat of summer. She was quite knowledgeable on the subject and very proud of her home. As well she should be. Her efforts in settling here in this wild Connecticut country have been great and show in her home.

As we continued our conversation she explained how a more refined substance was mixed to cover the walls. Places between the logs, where the mixture had been stuffed, oozed out and had dropped to the earthen floor, to be ground and mixed with the existing dirt. The strange mixture looked like worms lying in the dirt. As my eyes become more accustomed to the dimness of the room, I can see more clearly what is lying under my feet. The soft soles of my shoes were not much protection against the rugged edges of the concoction. No one had bothered to pick up the messy left over debris and it was just about everywhere.

Mrs. Talcott pointed out a nice large loft area, above the parlor room, where the children slept. Scraps of materials from the fields, mixed with this shell mixture had also been used in the loft area to block large cracks between logs. Their sleeping area looked to be quite comfortable and cozy. With the heat raising from the parlor fireplace, I am sure all who slept up there were quite warm.

As my eyes roamed from wall to wall and from ceiling to floor I wondered where we were to fit into all of this? There was hardly room for the Talcott's, let alone the six of us. It was a secure enough shelter, but it was not like our home. There would be absolutely no privacy.

My mind drew me back to the awful musty, stuffy quarters we had on the ship that had brought us from England. My throat tightened and my stomach revolted in the memory. We would not have much more room here, I thought to myself. John has a way of finding us the most unique quarters, without apparently any forethought to our personal comforts and needs. Granted there is really not much available to anyone in this primitive land. I should be more than thankful that we have any kind of a roof over our heads. Will I ever have a real home again? My mind questioned but my mouth knew better than to speak.

Mrs. Talcott is a lovely woman, jolly and happy, trying her hardest to make the best of a bad situation. I wonder how much say she has had in this decision? Probably none! You would never hear a complaint from her lips though. You can just tell that complaining is not her way of handling things. There is always a smile upon her plump round face. Her rosy cheeks and clear blue eyes give her a look as if someone has just stuck her with a pin. Her little puckered mouth comes wrinkling together as if she is all ready to be kissed. She is just a person that God made to be happy all the time. I marvel at her good nature and genuine warm expression of friendship. I wish I could be more accepting, like her. My cheeks flushed at my own thoughts of my discontent and grumbling, here lately.

I hoped no one has noticed how uncomfortable I am, for I would never be so rude as to let my thoughts and feelings tumble out of my mouth and go hurting someone else's feelings. No I could never do that. I do realize these kind people, are only trying to help in any way they can. I should not even let thoughts of this kind, into my mind.

If I could talk to John it would be better. But he seems to think we have fallen into the greatest situation ever. He would just not understand my needs. He is perfectly happy now that he has his ship and has set forth in a direction he sees as the ultimate, for our future. It is beyond me why I feel so much discontent. I must pray harder for I surely need a greater understanding of why things have worked out the way they have.

Everyday when I say my morning prayers I ask for guidance from above. Some time I feel that I would settle for just about any kind of a shelter as long as we could call it ours. When I look around I know that thought is not really true. I have greater visions for our home, tucked far back in the recesses of my mind. Seeing what has been built and settled for in this wilderness area thus far, just gives me more of an incentive to strive even harder to achieve my dreams. I have waited this long and I will just have to figure out a way to get John moving in the right direction again.

The Talcott's generosity is greatly appreciated and I will welcome it gratefully for a brief time period, but the time has come for some decisions to be made. I will bide my time and wait for just the right opportunity to talk to John about my plans and my concerns.

Actually, being here in Suckiaug might be to my advantage after all. While we are staying here I will have more free time to work on the plans for our house. I can hardly wait to set my thoughts in motion. This little breathing space will be welcomed in fact. John's, announcement that the building of the house would be my responsibility, came as a great surprise. I wonder if he knows what he has done? I accept the challenge with great anticipation and hope he will not be sorry. It is too bad he feels he will be to busy too oversee this project. But I know that I will enjoy working on the plans, I need something to keep my mind occupied.

177

I will just show John Curtyce that if his ship is more important than our home that is all right with me. If he wants to be bobbing up and down and tossed to a fro out in that great furious ocean, then so be it. I will plant my feet firmly in this Connecticut soil and just show him, what Elizabeth Hutchins Curtyce is made of.

My determination to see this project through to the end is undaunted by the fact that there are few supplies here and much of the material has to be engineered right from the very earth you are building on. This is not a deterrent to me it is a challenge, one that I accept readily.

We settled into our new temporary quarters and time passed, and day after day it grew hotter and hotter. The moisture filled the air and it became heavy and hard to breath. Only along the waters edge could I find even a small bit of comfort form the scorching sun. An occasional breeze off the water was all that kept me from disintegrating.

Today being no different than any of the previous ones I find myself looking for any excuse I can find to go out of doors where the air is fresh. It is far to stifling in the close quarters of the house. I will do a little gardening today, a special time for me, as I love the cool earth between my fingers, and find such joy in the plants that seem to spring up from nothing. Asking Mrs. Talcott's permission to work awhile in her garden, she gratefully gave me the opportunity I needed to be outside. Kneeling down in the garden and proceeded to thin out some of the smaller plants my mind whirled on and on. I want to build my Caswell. I started to push the thought quickly out of my mind. For it seemed an impossible dream, at first that is.

The thought of even trying to duplicate the structure here in this place seemed preposterous. Then I thought to myself and why not? Everything else here is a remembrance of England, even to some of the town names, even the style of the cottages that had been built already. Yes, my ideas were already starting to formulate in my mind, a way to re-create beautiful Caswell Manor.

The design could be very much the same, only perhaps a bit smaller in scale. The need here would be for our living quarters and not extra wings for guests. Extra rooms would just be wasted space for we do not anticipate having the visitors we did there.

Here in Connecticut the house will be built for efficiency. Yes I am sure I can scale Caswell down to fit into a more presentable perspective for here. Perhaps we can secure some land here in Suckiaug. Now that I have gotten used to the surroundings it is not half bad. Even though John thinks Cupheag would be best, I cannot see anything wrong with right here. We are on the river here and it runs to the ocean. Of course it would be perfect. Along the river would be nice. I have always loved watching the water roll by with its voyagers of logs and leaves, traveling off too far distant places. I could be so content as long as I do not have to travel with them. I must talk to John about this possibility.

As I continue digging in the garden my mind formulates idea, after idea into finished pictures. My spirits were lifted already. Just a little imagination and I am on my way. I can hardly wait to get started

178

now. This will help me survive this time of uncertainty in my life. I would have never thought in my wildest imagination that I would be expected to live under conditions like we find ourselves in now. No I never thought it would come to this. When I was told about this new land before we left England descriptions were sometime sparse. Now that I have experienced things here for myself it was probably better I did not know what it was exactly like for I know I would have surely refused to make the journey in the first place. The sun must be getting to my brain out here and I tell myself to be careful what I think for I know perfectly well that if John Curtyce, wanted me to follow him to the ends of the earth, then to the end of the earth I would go. And I do feel that that end is right here in Suckiaug. My first inclination was to run to John and spill out my every thought. Then I thought better of that. I know my limits with John. I will have to approach him on this subject with care. I do not want him to change his mind now that he has given me the authority to create our home.

I suppose he thinks I will settle for just a lean-to as long as there is a fire pit and a place to sleep. I wonder what he will think when I inform him that I intend to build Caswell. No, a lean-to will not do. I have been uprooted, carried across the ocean, dropped off the ship in Boston Harbor and now traveled over rough wilderness paths, muddy and thick with thistles tearing and ripping my clothing and slashing into my skin until it bled. I have had the sun beating down on my head and searing like a hot poker into my brain and the wind and rain trying its best to sweep us off the face of the earth. And through all that a place called home dangled out there in front of me of which I never seem to be able to grasp. After all that I still find myself once again in a strange environment. This time I will not settle for less than I am promised. I will have my home!

I know not to expect miracles. I am prepared to work hard for what I want and a little Caswell, it will be. Yes my Caswell, with the rolling hills and rock fences and my beautiful rose garden about me. Perhaps a horse or two in the pasture land to finish the picture. Oh and right here in Suckiaug will do just fine.

John might want to keep on wondering about. Moving here and there, but not me. He brought me all the way across the frightful ocean, miles from my home and now he hesitates to settle. John cannot seem to find anywhere that suits him. I want this to be my last move. I need to have a permanent home. It might take me the rest of my life to do all I have in mind. But do it I must so I will talk to John and tell him of my thoughts and explain to him that I want this to be the last stop, on this long journey.

Slowly I get myself to my feet and stretch to ease the cramping in my muscles and bones from bending for so long. I realize my mind has been rambling on an on. Taking a few of the larger herbs in my basket I returned to the kitchen. My mind still deep in thought I hardly noticed anyone else in the room.

"Is something on your mind Elizabeth?" Mrs. Talcott's voice brought me back to the realities of the present.

179

"No of course not. I was just going to tell you how nice it was to tend to the garden a little for you. I needed something to do to occupy my mind." I answered her. And oh how it had occupied it. I kept those thoughts to myself. "It is getting very warm out there already, Mrs. Talcott. I bet the men are very hot out in the fields today." I was chatting aimlessly just to make conversation. I felt like all of my inner secrets were written all over my face.

For all my planning I knew it would not be an easy task to convince John, of anything he was not in favor of. I knew that it would not be a matter of deciding and it taking place. John is much stronger than that. If for an instant he thought that I was trying to run our household he would rebel in a flash. I will have to show some patients, and bide my time a bit longer. John and the boys will be able to help Mr. Talcott get his fields cleared and ready for planting and even the barn built if everything works out right. Perhaps that will help repay the Talcott's for the most appreciated hospitality they have extended to us.

"The day is so lovely," I sighed. "Look out at that beautiful clear air. I do love the out of doors so much. I would like to look around a bit more. The area here is quite pretty." I commented, wanting Mrs. Talcott to know my thoughts. Mrs. Talcott looked up with a questioning look and glanced toward the open door. Little did she know I was already working on my secret plan for stability? I wondered if she might have heard of any land available near the river. I was afraid to question too much for fear of giving too much away. I decided to ask anyway.

"Mrs. Talcott, do many people live down closer to the river?" I inquire, trying to make my question sound like general conversation. "No, why do you ask?" She responded.

"No special reason, it is just so pretty down there." I said, hoping I had not said too much or given her cause to suspect what I might be thinking. She would surely tell Mr. Talcott and he would in turn tell John. Then all my plans would be brought out in the open before I wanted them to be.

"You see a lot of the land close to the river is very marshy and wet. That type of soil is not at all good for growing corn or flax. We need to develop farms so we can support ourselves. The only ones that are near the water are the clam diggers, the fisherman and of course the Indian's, who come and go. I guess a few of the fur traders have some shakes near the water too." She continued with an explanation of the situation as she saw it.

"That is interesting," I commented just to keep the conversation going. Mrs. Talcott's next question startled me.

"Elizabeth," she quarried, are you thinking of looking for a place here in Suckiaug?"

I hoped that the surprised look on my face did not give all my thoughts away. I hesitated a moment and then answered. "John has not advised me of his plans yet. I am really in the dark as to what he has in mind. The last he mentioned was the plans to go to the Indian village of

Cupheag." I explained trying to convince her I had no other plans. I gazed out the kitchen door and once again let my mind drink in the warmth and beauty of the afternoon splendor. "My," I stated again, the sun is as big and bright as I have ever seen it and from the warmth it is already generating it promises to be a real scorching afternoon. The men folks should be coming in at any time now for their mid day meal. "What can I do to help you, Mrs. Talcott?" I asked, as I wanted to get the conversation off the subject of land and back to something general.

I was glad when she said. "Why don't you get the trenchers down and get some warm biscuits out of the oven. I think I can hear the voices of the men now!" I moved to do what I could and was relieved for a few minutes of silence.

Late afternoon was upon us before I knew it and the men had eaten and gone right back to the fields. The air within the little house was stifling. The heat of the outdoors and the heat from the cooking pit have become almost intolerable. There was no breeze coming in the door. I decided to take a little walk.

Mrs. Talcott had gone out to tend to the chickens so I took the opportunity to slip out the kitchen door. As I walked past the little kitchen garden, I had the greatest urge to open the little half gate and plop myself right down and start digging in the fresh warm earth. Mrs. Talcott had many fine herbs planted. I envied her the garden. I had a real yearning for one of my own.

Now was not the time to be thinking of a garden. I needed these few minutes alone to explore some possibilities for our home. As I walked along a path in the tall grass I let my mind go on dreaming and planning, working at ideas and plans for our future. Maybe I can only formulate them in my mind for now but I will at some point be able to hire the best of the artisans from England and they will take my dreams and turn them into a reality.

Since John and Thomas will be traveling about here and there in that ship of theirs, they can most likely bring me all that I might need to see this project completed. I really don't know what John is going to think of all I have in mind. I do know that if it is to his liking, he will get me anything within his power. Of course I have to ask him in just the right way.

I had to smile to myself at my devious thoughts. He just doesn't realize how much that shipping company is going to work to my advantage. I think he has a notion in his mind that I will not like taking care of our farm all by myself. But he is wrong, very, very wrong. I was taking care of horses and livestock long before I ever met John Curtyce and I can do it again. He will just have to remember that I am the daughter of John and Maria Hutchins Curtyce. They raised me to be a gentle soul, but one that could take care of herself and her family if the need ever arose. I have been far too lax in letting myself be tossed and turned around. Going here and running there at the whim of John.

Here of late, John seems to always be in search of what he calls, "that better life." What ever that is? I know now that life is what you make it and I intend to stop running and make something of what we have left. Neither of us is getting any younger. Before we know it, time will have passed us by. If it is up to me to put a stop to this adventure then I will.

As I continued down the path my mind once again reminded me that caution was needed to achieve my goal. A smile lights upon my face, for how true I knew that to be. If John, ever thought he was not in total control of his family he would be most distressed. Oh, I don't mean to imply in any way, that he is not the head of this family. I just want a little say in the direction of our lives. John started out our marriage giving me an equal portion of the decision-making. It has just gotten lost somewhere between there and here. I just have to find it and implement it again.

The days and weeks have passed quickly in some respects and very slowly in others. I steadfastly formulated my ideas into a working pattern. I could do everything in time and time was on my side. I was actually getting excited. Thus far everything was in my head but I knew time was getting close when I would have to brave the storm and talk to John.

The first order of business now is the barn and it is to be started right away. They will be working on it for a while but I really think it is time to talk to him about his plans with the shipping company. That will break the ice, then I can just ramble right into my plans. I will see if we can find a few minutes alone for that purpose. It is very difficult to be alone long enough for even a brief conversation under such confinements. Perhaps we can take a long stroll along the river this evening after supper. It has been such a long time and surely he will be receptive to the idea. I will make my plans carefully as to not raise any suspicions with the others. They will think it only natural that John and I should want to spend a small portion of our evening alone. Yes, I will bring the subject up at supper. He would not refuse his wife a special request in front of our hosts.

As I walk on toward the river area I thought of how sad it was that I had to resort to a scheme to have a few private moments with my own husband. But since everyone and everything else seem to come first in his life, then a scheme it shall be. It only makes me more determined than ever.

I looked around a bit more and deciding not to get to far from the Talcott's house so I quickly turn about and scurry on back. I busy myself during the rest of the afternoon with things about the house just little things that I could help Mrs. Talcott with. I need to keep very busy so the time will go fast and evening will come more quickly. Now that I have decided to finally talk to John, I want to do it as soon as possible. I am getting more and more excited by the minute about my thoughts for our future. I keep asking Mrs. Talcott for something more to do. She must think me awfully anxious today.

With insistence I finally was able to convince her that I really needed something to keep me busy. She reluctantly gave me some mending to do. Good I thought, now my mind and hands will both be occupied. Mending and sewing would be just the thing. The children could use some new things and some of Mr. Talcott's shirts had become too tattered for him

182

but if cut down would make a nice petticoat for Emaline and maybe even a couple of shirts for young Patrick. I was quite anxious to get started.

It had been such a long time since I had put a needle to a piece of material. This would be fun work. I remember how it was making little things for our children when they were young. Auntie or Katie made most things but I occasionally managed to put a few items together. I often stood by Auntie's side and watched intently. She would say to me in her sweet, patient tone, "Elizabeth, darling why on earth do you have to stand so close? If you insist on getting any closer to me I will most likely sew you right up in this garment. How do you think you would look as a pocket on my apron?" Then she would laugh in her happy jovial way, give me a big hug, a kiss upon my cheek, and move me gently out of her way. Oh how happy those times were with Mama and Papa, Auntie and Uncle and all the cousins. Why doesn't time stand still so that we can enjoy those special moments forever.

I hardly ever let myself think of home any more. It is so far away and it only makes my heart ache more when I do think of the family in England. I hope they know that they are never far from my thoughts. I do love them all so very much. It is always nice when a message is brought from someone just coming over to the new lands. Cousin James has such a unique way of getting the sea captain's or one of the crew to bring us a message from home. We have not been so lucky in efforts to send them messages. It was much easier when we were near to Boston Harbor for many more ships came and went. Now I suppose we would not be able to hear from home at all. This thought made my mood change and I once more felt alone and sad at leaving England.

They must think something has happened to us. I wonder if they worry about us like I worry about them? I suppose they do. They probably miss us just the same. At least they have the familiar house and familiar friends and the beautiful rolling hills of England to envelop them in comfort. I sigh a deep sigh and then think, what is the use I could sigh all day and it wouldn't take me back home.

Sometimes I think that John feels that since the children are grown or almost grown that we no longer need to have a house. He would be happy to roam around and around. I am surprised he has not asked me to make his ship our home. Oh my! What a terrible thought. Not I, if there is anything in life I want, it is my home. Deep within the bones that make up my very being, is the need to be settled, to have my own things about me and to make permanence in our existence. This seems so hard for John to understand. He is adventuresome and I can understand that, I only hope that he can understand my needs too. I will see, won't I?

I returned my thoughts to my plans for this evening. Tonight is the night I will propose my plans to John. How will he perceive my ideas? How will he respond to my decisions? It is only a few more hours before supper and then I will have the answers to my questions. I hope against hope that I will not be disappointed.

"This is a fine meal Mrs. Talcott, you are a very fine cook." John said, in his finest complimentary voice.

183

"Why, thank you very much Mr. Curtyce, I am most pleased that you are enjoying it." Mrs. Talcott smiled as she replied.

"We are very grateful for all the hospitality you have shown our family, Mr. Talcott but you have played the host long enough. It will just be a matter of a couple of weeks now and we will be on our way to the Indian village of Cupheag!" John's voice rang forth and the words clanged in my head and reverberated again and again in my brain.

My mouth flew open and I half screamed out. "Cupheag, so you still plan to move on?" I was choked with emotion. All my plans, all my dreams, yes, and all my schemes, gone, what would I do now?

"Elizabeth," John questioned. "Are you all right? I didn't mean to give you such a fright. That has always been the plan. It is just that the time is right now. It should be of no surprise to you."

I tried to find my voice, somewhere deep down inside me. "No John, no surprise at all. I was just not suspecting that now was the time you had in mind."

John's statement had put me in total shock. I was kept informed about nothing. His specialty these days seemed to be to thrust his wishes upon me without even the slightest consideration as to my feelings. It was always at a most inopportune time. When to react in any way but positive would have caused others to be concerned. Even when I asked directly about what was going on I received a most evasive answer. This was not at all like the John I had married. I was used to a much more shared existence. I found it hard to cope with this, matter of fact, you will accept, what ever I say attitude. What has come over him? I could just not figure him out.

John's glance over at me, caused a small smirk to come upon his face, as if to say I surprised you again didn't I. Well I am sure the flush of my cheeks, gave him a glimpse of the seething within me. What does he think he is doing? I am going to get to the bottom of this attitude of his, if it is the last thing I do. I will not only inform him of my decisions, but will make sure that he absolutely understands it. We are in this country together and I will ask for an explanation as to his actions.

I tried to calm the furry that raged within me. I could not keep my mind from flying from here to there and all over the place. How could John think I could just get up one day and move on without any warning at all. Does he really expect that of me? He must realize that things have gotten unpacked and I intend to leave nothing behind. Nothing!

Mr. Talcott, looking around and seeing the discomforting look upon my face, suggested that he and John retreat to the out of doors. At home there would have at least been a parlor to go to. That thought is petty and I regret thinking it. I am ashamed of myself. Our differences have not one thing to do with anything the Talcott's have done. I must control my temper and if it does get loose make sure it is vented against the person it needs to be aimed at.

184

I sit still on my bench, stunned beyond words. What is wrong with me? Leaving might be what I really want. I want to get on with our lives. So why does John's announcement, anger me so? Is it because once again I have had no say in any of the arrangements? Maybe I really don't want to move anywhere. Building my dream house here in Suckiaug had become so real to me. Oh, I am so confused. I am afraid of what lies ahead and not really sure in my own mind that I can accomplish what I intend to. Maybe, it is a little bit of all those things, I think to myself.

The thing that bothers me the most is that John and I are growing farther and farther apart. Does he not love me anymore, has this new way of life changed him so much that he no longer wants us to be a family, a family in the since of sharing. We had always shared our hopes our dreams, was that to be no more?

I was so lost within my own thoughts I had completely forgotten my manners. Mrs. Talcott had already cleared the table and was cleaning the trenchers.

"Oh, forgive me Mrs. Talcott. I seem to have been lost in my own little world. Here let me help you get these cleaned up and put away." I apologized.

She waved off my offer. "That is alright my dear, why don't you go outside for a spell and get a breath of fresh air. The cool, clear, evening air sometimes helps to clear the cobwebs out of a persons mind." She said, as she waved toward the door.

I glanced up at her, "thank you for understanding. I will grab a wrap and take a walk along the river. It is always so peaceful down there." I said, as I got up from the bench. "That is a good idea. Be careful and don't go to far. It will be nightfall soon." She warned, trying to ease my hurts.

I knew that she was just trying to be as kind as she could, but her words hurt. Was that my problem? Did I have cobwebs in my head? Was I the one that was all mixed up? These actions of John's were beginning to cause me to doubt myself. What is happening to me? The thoughts kept rambling over and over in my head. There is not a woman in this new land, which has not given up her heart and soul for this adventure. I bet Mrs. Talcott, often feels the same way as I do. She is just a more submissive creature of God, than I am. We are all made different. She is much to kind to let anyone know just how she really feels or thinks. She must keep a lot of her feelings locked up inside herself. I think she is just a very special person. So what does that make me? As I grabbed my shawl and leave the confinements of the house I take in a big deep breath and proceeded down the path toward the river. The clear blue sky is just starting to show the signs of a beautiful evening sunset. The clouds are streaked across the slightly darker blue horizon and the horizon takes on a bright red and gold hue and the big red sun is sliding closer and closer to the thin line that divides heaven and earth. What a glorious sight. I think this is my very favorite time of day. A special time when the last gasps of light kiss the day gently goodbye and night rushes in to engulf the earth in total darkness.

185

The total black, dense nothingness is only dispelled slightly, by the bright curve of the crescent moon, as it breaks the horizon in the other direction. For a brief moment in time, all of existence seems to be balanced ever so delicately, held in the palm of Mother Nature's hand.

I pulled my shawl closer about me and walked along the path. The trees make it seem much darker than it really is. They drape their great; giant arms out over the waters edge, as if they are taking a quick peek out of their forest door. I had to duck at times to keep from hitting my head on a branch. I walked on and on, time meaning nothing to me. Distance being put between the house and me and I seem not to notice or care. I was completely lost in my thoughts. I was so mixed up inside. I felt as if I was loosing control of my life. I was not mad anymore, just confused. I really didn't know what to do or who to turn to. There is no one here that I can talk things like this over with. John would not be happy if I were to talk to Mrs. Talcott about our personal business. Before I always had Sarah to talk to. We relied on each other and knew we could say anything that was on our mind. If only she were here.

I sat down upon a rock near the edge of the water and picked up a stone and tossed it into the crystal clear pool below. I loved to watch the circles as they grow and expanded, getting larger and larger until they disappeared. The water looks like it is in a panic, trying to run from the rock. It is so relaxing to set here in the coolness of evening under the river willows.

I have always wondered what makes the waters circle pattern so constant every time the pebble falls? I picked up another and another and throw them out further and further, always with the same results. First the splash then the tiny circles, my eyes strain to study natures work. Constantly I see them repeat the same sequence.

Why wasn't life like these circles? They seem so equal, so smooth and steady in their pattern. I wonder why my circles of life have so many bumps along their pathway? Why couldn't it be smooth and stay the same? I want my world to come back to me    I am tired of the constant upheaval that has taken over. I want my Caswell back, big Blacky, Cousin James, Auntie, Katy, Anna and all the people that made up my contented world. I have no one here, no one at all. God did not put me on this earth to live as a recluse. I need people and I enjoy them. John has got to understand this need of mine? He cannot expect me to live like this forever, can he? The questions kept coming, but never an answer.

I sit here by the waters edge just drinking in the beauty and I am not conscience of the darkness as it envelops me in its clutches. A squirrel springs above me on a branch and brings me out of my thoughtful day dreaming world. I look around me and become aware of a light river fog swirling in. I have been warned many times of the danger lurking behind the trees and dense foliage. I really didn't have any idea of how long I have been setting in this spot and was so unconcerned until the squirrel scared me out of my wits. Looking around I cannot see a thing that looks familiar. The sun has gone completely down and there is no light about me anywhere. I stand to walk back but I can no longer see the path. I take a step forward only to stumble over a large bolder. I turned the other way but find a tree in front of me. Hmmm, I think to myself. I am closed in by everything; the only other way to go is into the water and that is not an option I want to take.

I glance around once more, but the few minutes that have elapsed have not changed my predicament one bit. What am I to do? I am afraid to move for fear of falling into the water. I must not panic; I must keep control of my fears. If there are Indians out there they can probably see me better than I would ever be able to detect them.

Tears began to stream down my face. I think to myself, stop it, just stop it Elizabeth, this is no time to let your emotions get the best of you. Quit feeling sorry for yourself. The reprimand streaked through my mind.

How far have I really come and where is the house? Were my first frightened thoughts? I don't know, my mind answered its own question. How long had I walked? I really didn't know that either. Maybe I will just sit down again, it will be better than falling into that dark water down there. I pulled my shawl closer about my shoulders and feel around for a rock that is big enough for me to sit upon. Finally I feel one behind me and carefully eased my body onto it. I guess if I have too, I will just stay here until someone either comes for me or the dark night gives way to the sunlight. Which ever it is that is what I will do.

Hours and hours seem to have passed before I see the small glow of a lantern coming toward me. I could have cared less if it was a friend or foe. I was just glad to see that there was a spark of light in my dark world. "Over here, over here." I call out as loud as I can. Finally I hear an answer!

"Elizabeth is that you? Where are you? I can't see you?" It sounds like John's voice.

I yell again. "I'm over here. John is that you? I am here by the river on a rock. I am afraid to move for fear of falling into the water." The sound of John's voice seems to be coming closer. I listened but can only hear the crackle of the twigs under foot. Then I hear his instructions.

"Keep talking Elizabeth, I will find you by your voice. Can you see the lantern?" John's voice projected concern.

"Yes John, I can see the lantern. It is straight in front of me. Just keep walking, that's right, straight ahead and you will run into me." I instructed him. I knew John was close yet in the blackness I could not tell just how far or close he really is. I keep talking until the lantern shown right in my face. Then I calmly say, "Look down John, or you will step on me." I was teasing of course but I needed a bit of laughter. I was so happy to see John that I had forgotten all about being mad at him. I sprang to my feet and fairly flew into his arms, almost knocking the lantern from his grasp.

"Be careful Elizabeth you will knock the lantern out of my hands and then both of us will be lost. You have given all of us such a fright. Why did you not come back to the house when it got dark? We have been nearly worried sick about you. You know it is dangerous to be out here alone at night and you are much to far from the house. What in the world were you thinking about? I am beside myself Elizabeth. Mrs. Talcott said you were going out for a bit of fresh air and should return soon. When you didn't come back I didn't know what to think. I am so glad that I found you and that you are safe. If I hadn't have come upon you just now I was going back after the boys and Mr. Talcott and start a search for you." John spoke and his concern showed in his voice.

He hardly stopped for a breath between words. He was ordering me to follow him and return to the house instantly. He was treating me like a child again. My first instinct was anger but I quickly pushed it from my mind. All I could say was, "I am sorry John, and really I am. I did not mean to cause such great concern. I am truly grateful that you found me too. But couldn't we spend just a few more minutes here alone. It has been such a long time since we have even had the fewest of moments together. We need to talk John, we are growing apart and it scares me." John seemed shocked at my statement.

"Growing apart, what kind of talk is that? I feel as close to you as the day of our marriage. Have you changed your feelings for me Elizabeth?" He said. Now he was questioning me.

"No John of course not. My feelings for you are as strong as ever. It is just that our new life here in this place has driven a wedge between us. We never discuss things together anymore. All of the decisions are sprung upon me and I am just to accept them. That is not how it used to be. We always shared everything, the good and the bad. Now we seem to share nothing. I don't know what to do about the situation or if anything can be done. All I know is that we do need to talk." I answered him, trying to emphasize the urgency of our situation. As if not having the slightest idea as to what I meant, John continued talking.

"What brought all of this up right now? Was it what I said at the supper table tonight? I didn't mean to surprise you but we do have to leave sometime. You knew that didn't you?" He asked. I think he is actually trying to make me think that I am to blame for this whole problem. He followed one question with another and another. Was he trying to throw me off guard?

"John, you seem to be enjoying hurling these decisions at me from out of nowhere. What is it? Are you afraid I will try and talk you out of something or what? Please tell me what it is that is causing you to be this way?" I pleaded. John just shrugged.

"I really don't know what you are trying to say Elizabeth? Decisions have to be made quickly here; we don't have the luxury of mulling things over and discussing then for months before making up our minds. I would have talked our leaving over with you, but it didn't seem important since we all knew we were going to leave anyway." John's statement half stunned me. I honestly think he really believes what he is saying. Could he really not know that I had no idea, that the plans had remained the same? A lot of time has passed between our arrival here in Suckiaug and now. Further more the subject has never been brought up again. Am I supposed to read his mind too? I have dwindled my days away dreaming of a home here in Suckiaug. No one told me any different. I really have got to get through to him.

With a deep breath I try once more to make my point. "Well that is where you are wrong John. We all didn't know that we had to leave. It isn't just a matter of getting up one day and going off toward the blue horizon without a thought. We have been here for many months now things have been unpacked. It will take time to re-pack our things and make sure we have not left anything behind. These things are just a part of it. I would just like to be considered a little more. You seem to have forgotten that I am a part of this family too. I am your wife John, could you treat me with a little more respect? I feel like some hired hand that you expect to jump at your every command. Yes in the beginning you said we would be moving on then it never happened and you said no more. So I just supposed we would stay." I turned to see if my words were penetrating John's mind or not. It was to dark, I couldn't see his expression. John reached out for my hand. He was trembling as he spoke.

"I have really hurt you, haven't I Elizabeth? That was not my intention at all. I will have to try and do better and see if that won't help to make both of us a lot happier." He said as he drew me close to him and began rubbing my back. He nuzzled close to my ear and whispered his love and gave me a long lingering kiss.

"Let me see if I can start right now and see just how happy I can make you." I pushed him away gently, saying, "John this doesn't seem to be quite the right place for actions such as this. What if someone comes looking for us? How will we explain to them?" My question did not seem to deter John.

"Elizabeth, no one will be coming for us. Just close your beautiful eyes and rest your head, here on my chest. I told everyone I would find you. They know that we need to talk." John assured me in a quiet soothing voice.

This little rendezvous here with John was not the answer to our problems and I knew it all to well and I am sure that John knows it too. Yet I wanted to be in John's strong arms so very much. I need once again to rely on his strength to carry us through these difficult times. My strength or what little I have left is waning fast.

John's voice seemed to be barking out at me, trying to penetrate my dazed state. "The only thing that matters is that I love you Elizabeth and you and I are going to spend some much needed private time together. Living with someone else has been comfortable but has not allowed us our time. This is our time." He murmured to me as we rested quietly the on the rock.

Well I think to myself, John has finally realized that we have been living with someone else and have had no privacy forever it seems. I am tired of the fight and want to surrender to John but I do not fully believe that John understands my thoughts and desires for our future. I break the silence of our solitude with a profound statement to him.

189

"John, don't think this lets you off the hook in any way. We are still going to have to work at letting each other know what is going on and not just guess that each of us knows what the other is thinking. Do you agree with that?" A nod indicated acknowledgment. But John did not really give an affirmative straight answer.

"Being here with you like this and feeling the closeness of you and the love you inspire in me I would agree to most anything. Just ask and it is yours. What would please your heart Elizabeth? I am ready to conquer the world for you." John stated smugly, with a sinister smile on his face.

"John Curtyce, you are not taking anything I am saying to heart. I don't think you realize just how I really feel. You are just not taking any of this seriously. But I really mean what I say" I quipped back at John in as stern a voice as I could muster up. "Listen John, I think I hear voices over there. I am sure I hear someone calling out our names." I said. Straining to listen more intently.

"I can not hear anyone," John insisted. "It is just your imagination Elizabeth."

"No really, there is someone coming." I said, being even more positive now. We had no more gotten to our feet, and turned around, when we ran smack face to face with Mr. Talcott and the boys. Their lanterns blazed right up against our faces.

"Oh, you startled me, Mr. Talcott. John found me and we were just starting back for the house." My words tumbled from my mouth as if I had to confess to someone, my wanting to be alone with my own husband. No one seemed to be embarrassed, but me. Mr. Talcott, winked at John and directing the light down the path. He motioned for me to start walking. I flushed at his suggestive wink and hurried in the direction he indicated. I don't know what the wink was for. Was it for John's, thoughts maybe, but not his actions. Men and their strange sense of humor, I think to myself as I walk on.

Even the merriment in Mr. Talcott's wink could not tarnish the brilliance of our few brief solitary moments together. We were once more able to talk and discuss our inner thoughts openly without strangers near by to listen it. For a small portion of this night John and I were back in our own special world where we can retreat to where the two of us can leave the cares and discords of everyday life far behind. I know everything was not settled tonight but it's a start toward the rest of our destiny.

# CHAPTER 12

It took some days before I could fully comprehend that we were going to be moving once more. But when I did I conjured up so many new pictures in my mind, it was amazing. I just let my imagination run rampant and dreamed on and on about my new home. The whole idea of a new place soon began to acquire that same edge of excitement that had existed, in Roxbury. That is after I became adjusted to the whole idea of picking up and packing up and moving on once more.

We all looked forward to getting started. Especially me, I didn't want to sit around and talk any longer. A fault I have! No need to fool around once your mind is made up and mine was. For a fact, the time can't come soon enough for me.

I am so anxious to get to this new place that I have even conceded to making the trip by ship. And without too much coaxing from John, either. It would be a lot easier on my feet and I knew that from experience. I am also told a lot faster, which added greatly to my decision, to withstand the feared water, one more time.

No one wanted a long walk after the exhausting trek; we made to get here to Suckiaug. Living in this area for even a brief time period had not shown me any noticeable difference in the terrain, foliage, and undergrowth of the forested area or the thickness of the wooded areas. They all seem to be just as treacherous as any we experienced in other parts of the land we crossed. These were all factors on the positive side of my decision.

As the plans were implemented and started to unfold for this new and latest adventure of ours, I realized that John had done a lot of planning far ahead of time. I just never knew just how far ahead of time. For things seem to be revealed to me in dribbles and drabs, as questions or decisions arise. It became apparent that John's thinking and arranging had started long, long before we ever left Roxbury.

My thoughts were that I had not been consulted on a few things, now I am finding them to be many things. During an early morning visit to see the ship the question came up as to a captain and crew. It was not until then that John, told me about his hiring of a captain many months ago. The fact is that he had been hired even before I knew of the plans to own a ship. It seems that upon our leaving for Suckiaug, permission had been given this new captain, to hire his own crew, with the promise that if everything worked out to John's, satisfaction a permanent job with the shipping firm would be his reward.

The orders from John were to hire a crew, outfit the ship in Boston Harbor and leave for Suckiaug precisely on John's, schedule. The Captain and crew should have already left the safe confines of the harbor and be on their way here, for John, had stated his expectation of their arrival any day now.

The short sail to the Indian Village of Cupheag from here will be a kind of trial run for John, this new captain and the crew. John, on explaining all of this to me, seemed to be leaving a lot of the decisions up to this man. I wondered if that was really a wise thing to do? John is so used to being right on top of everything, yet it is impossible for him to be in two places at the same time, especially with him wanting the shipping company to start business immediately upon our arrival in Cupheag. He really has no other choice, I suppose.

I surely hope the Captain has chosen his men carefully for John, will be a tyrant if things don't happen as he expects them to. Time is not a commodity to waste in any instance as far as John, is concerned. Especially when supplies are needed so desperately in this new area. Delays of any kind could make this shipping venture unprofitable, or others will surely see the need for a business of this type and John, would miss out on getting his started first. That would upset him, more than I could ever convey. He has his heart, and mind set on this all falling into place. For his sake, I surely hope it does.

Putting all thoughts of the possibilities of fate aside, we rush ahead with all are plans and on the day of our departure from Suckiaug the whole town is out to say their good byes. I find it not as hard to say good-bye this time. Perhaps I am becoming callous in my feelings toward others? I hope not, for I have made many good and loving friends here. I'm sure my reason is none other than; I am just ready to move on and get started on life.

My part of this partnership in life with John Curtyce has been in a somewhat circling mode. I move, we move and things change about us, yet what is most important to me in life, the stability of my family, has not been accomplished. I need a permanent home in order to make that happen and in order to have this home, we need to stop traveling on and on.

I have still not had the opportunity to talk over the plans of the house with John, but I will find the time before we land at the Indian village. I will keep the promise I made to myself. I will also keep the promise we made to each other. To be open and not keep our thoughts locked away, to smolder and grow into a blaze of anger. I do hope John, agrees with what I want in the way of a dwelling.

The time has finally come and we are finally casting off from the little dock area and start down the beautiful Connecticut River I am finding that the motion of the ship upon this water way has lulled me into a thoughtful, passive, frame of mind. I rest against the brass railing of the ship and plead to myself, inwardly: Please, please John; want the same things I do. Please for me, for us, for our children.

The early morning sun, beating down against my back is warm and soothing, yet the lingering crisp sting of the fresh spring air, as it is thrust against my face, is cool and sharp upon my cheeks. I do not mind for this is one of my favorite times of year. It is a time when the seasons seem to fight for supremacy, one season retreating with regret and the other advancing with tenacity. In this particular case I find winter trying, desperately hard, to hold on a bit longer before giving in to the strong persistent clutches of spring.

As the ship moves slowly through the clear, ice sprinkled, river below, the evidence of this struggle is apparent. Spring has arrived, yet what snow and ice still remains is a reminder of the past, bitterly cold, winter. As I look about there are places which look as if the warm spring season could not possibly melt what is packed in the deep crevasses along the rock strewn, river edge.

The trees along the bank are turning their branches toward the sky, hoping to soak up the hot rays of this beautiful sunlit day. A delicate hue of soft light green, showing about the branches of the trees, as if they have dawned a light, springtime cloak, to ward off the chill that lingers as they anticipate and look forward to the coming summer heat. These first new leaves hatching out of their tightly folded buds are a spectacular rebirth of nature. Now they start a new journey through their life cycle. Soon they will cover the tree branches, where today tiny clumps of snow are still resting waiting for a warmer day than this, to melt and make its final departure for this season.

My, how I love to look upon this beautiful scenery as we pass by, the sharply distinct lines and unique blend of colors. There are small very brightly colored flowers, popping up here and there to aid to this masterpiece. I don't think I will ever grow tired of, the artistry of nature.

The time passing by as I stand here enjoying this glorious day doesn't seem to matter at all. It is just too enjoyable out here on the deck of the "Elizabeth," soaking in every drop of sun and every bit of the graceful beauty of the landscape, to let any negative thought spoil it. Leaning against the railing, I permit my eyes and mind to rest and enjoy the moment.

I'm so relaxed and enchanted with the view from the bow of the ship. John's approaching steps can't even disturb me. I know it is John, I am far too familiar with his walk not to recognize it the second I hear his steps. Even if I had not recognized the sound behind me I surely would know it was John the moment he tapped gently on my shoulder, with his strong hands. I let them envelop me in a strong grasp without so much as a blink of resistance. I would know John's touch anytime.

"My Elizabeth, anyone could be standing here with their arms around you and you wouldn't even be objecting." John chided.

"Really John, I would not expect anybody but you to put their hands upon me so boldly. Surely none on this ship, lest they wanted to be looking for work somewhere else, and swimming for their life, to find it." I responded to his teasing.

"You are sure of that Elizabeth? You can never trust a sailor, you know. They are a different lot." He stated boldly.

"John Curtyce, is that what I have to expect of you when you start sailing out into the great beyond? I surely hope not. Besides these men on this ship respect you, above any, and you are a big tease." I reprimanded him for even thinking anything else. For in just a short period of time I could see the devotion and dedication the men had for John.

193

"Your right, I am very lucky to have such a good crew. They seem to be doing a fine job thus far. I think the Captain has done a good job for me. I look forward to working closely with them in the coming months. We have lined up some interesting work ahead. I really think this new venture is looking better and better all the time." He replied.

"I know you are looking forward to everything John, you seem to have a deep seeded lust for adventure. As for me I am looking forward to our family, finally being settled in one place. This is going to be our last move, isn't it?" I asked, looking up at him from the corner of my eye.

"Yes Elizabeth, this is it. We will make Cupheag our home, for better or worse." He stated profoundly.

"My that sounds ominous, John. Do you anticipate it not being the right place to settle down?" I inquired, almost afraid to ask a question of that nature.

"Oh, no Elizabeth, I really think it is a perfect place for all of us. It will not be an easy place to settle in. I suspect the Indians here are, or can be, as unpredictable as they were in Roxbury and the surrounding areas of Boston Harbor. Here we will have fewer families about us for protection. Most of our success will come from our own initiatives and the great protection of God's watchful eye." He stated thoughtfully.

"I will pray then for this to be God's will, for more than anything, I want this to be our home. The last few months, were for the most part very pleasant, but as seems to be our lot lately, they lacked the privacy that I wish we could once again have. John, we are always in the midst of people. When will we ever be able to recapture our private times together? They are few and way to far between for my liking." I said not trying to hide the flush of my cheeks at being so wanton of John's attention.

"Why Elizabeth Curtyce, how bold of you! Speaking out loud of such things, right here in the open, for all to hear." John gave a hearty laugh as he spoke.

"There is no one around John, only you, and the words from my lips are for your ears only. If anyone else is listening then they are ease dropping and should be punished." I said. "You will punish them won't you?"

"You are a hard task master Elizabeth. I bet my crew is mighty glad you are not their Captain." John's deep throaty chuckle put a smile on my face. He turned me around to face him and tipped my head upward and placed a bold kiss, upon my lips and held me much to close for the openness of our position.

"John, behave yourself, someone could really be watching us." I said, fretting that we might really be detected out here on the deck.

194

"Well if they are out here spying on us, they would dare not speak a word, lest they come by your, previously spoken punishment." John said, in a burly voice, enjoying the playful manner of our talk.

"You are teasing me again John." I said, and squirmed from his arms.

"Yes, I am guilty of that. You are easy to tease Elizabeth. You are far to serious at times." He said, pulling me back within his grasp.

"Well I must try and change that so you will not think me stuffy and unapproachable." I said, determined not to let him get in the last word.

"Not to change the subject, but I did seek you out for a specific reason." John announced, candidly.

"What's that? Is something wrong with Elizabeth or the boys?" I turned to inquire in earnest.

"No, you always expect the worst. I have someone down in our cabin I want you to meet. As a matter of fact, I hope he is still there. We have been out here for sometime and I told him to stay put and I would find you and return in just a moments time", John explained, as he tried to hurry my steps.

"Well, if you told him to stay put, I am sure he did. Who is he and why is it of such importance for me to meet him? Surely he is not so important that you have to shove me down the stairs." I said, as I tried to keep my footing.

"No, more questions Elizabeth, just hurry along and see for yourself." He replied. As we scurry along the passageway to the cabin, I just have to stop for a brief moment to admire the brass plate on the door that said, JOHN CURTYCE. I touched it with my fingertips as I passed through the opening. I felt so much more comfortable here than I had in the long months of crossing from England to this new land. I really liked John's new ship, but am quick to admit I would not want to be on it for any long period of time.

The oil lamps along the wall of John's cabin give off enough light, so that going from topside to the cabin area below is not difficult at all. There are even enough candles placed close along the passageway to provide a fairly well lit effect. It is nice not to have to grope along and feel your way until your eyes grew accustomed to the lighting. I was grateful for that, for my mind remembers, with horrified clearness, the mishap on the deck of the "Lion" as I tried to traverse from lower to upper decks. I surely didn't want to have a similar mishap on this ship. That embarrassment was enough to last me a long, long time.

Upon entering the room I let my eyes rove around so I could locate this mysterious stranger. Wondering all the while why it was so important that I make his acquaintance. My first impression I must confess was only that of curiosity. John followed me into the room and proceeded with the introductions.

195

"Mr. Clarke, may I present to you my wife Elizabeth Curtyce." He said, gesturing with his hand in my direction. Mr. Clarke immediately came to his feet as we entered the cabin, walked to within a foot of me and taking my hand, which I had positioned at my side, proceeded to press it gently, but firmly, to his lips. I tried to defuse the flutter of emotion that seemed to serge through my body, culminating in a blush upon my face. It had been a long time since etiquette of this manner had been displayed before me.

Finally finding my voice I uttered. "Pleased to make you acquaintance Mr. Clarke. I can not offer much more than that as John, has kept your reason for being aboard his ship very secretive." Trying conversation to cover up my uncomfortable feelings, was really not working to well.

"Well hopefully Mrs. Curtyce, you will find the reason very much to your liking." Mr. Clarke replied, keeping the gaze, of his deep set, clear blue eyes, directly glued to mine. He had not so much as moved an eyelash or blinked a lid.

Somewhat befuddled at his arrogance, I answered him. "I hope so too, Mr. Clarke." Then I waited a long while for John, to step in and take this conversation in another direction. There was something about this man I found very disturbing. I was in a very uncomfortable situation and John seemed to be enjoying every minute of it.

When I looked over in John's direction, I was willing with all my might, that he would see my distress and free me from Mr. Clark's clutches. John, made no motion in that direction and when I looked down I suddenly became aware, that Mr. Clarke, was still in the possession of my hand. Pulling it away rather abruptly, and staring directly at John, finally led him to the realization that he had better say something before I made a scene that he would have to explain to his guest. He knew just how far he could push me with his fun, and right now it was over that limit.

"Well now." John spoke clearing his throat as if to make a big speech of some kind and then he continued. "Now that you two have met, we can proceed with the business at hand."

"I will just retreat back up to the upper deck and let you two carry on with what ever business that you need to talk over. It was very nice meeting you Mr. Clarke, perhaps we shall meet again." As I spoke I turned and retreated toward the door. I was more than anxious to be out of the sight of this new acquaintance, for he disturbed me far too much and in a way I was unfamiliar with. John grabbing me by my arm pulled me to an abrupt stop, before I could make a hasty retreat.

"Not so fast there, Elizabeth. This piece of business very much concerns you and I think it is of a subject that is very important to you. Come over here to the desk, I have something to show you." John commanded more than requested and I obeyed without resistance.

We all moved over to the desk at the side of the cabin. It was situated just under a small window that really did nothing for the lighting in the room. John pulled an oil lamp closer to the center of the desktop and started to unroll a large piece of parchment. Setting a weight upon each corner he motioned for me to take a closer look. He then stepped back and stood there very coyly, his arms folded across his chest.

My eyes searched the breadth and depth of the paper that lay before my eyes. I turned my head first one way and then the other, taking in every line upon the paper. I did not try to hide the enormous surprise and happiness that poured forth from within me. Finally finding an opening from my inner being to my outer being, the pent up emotions poured forth from my eyes. I could hardly see the paper before me now and the tears dripped down my cheeks and off onto the desk below.

"Now, now dear, we don't want to ruin this wonderful work with your tears, do we?" John said, as he offered his sleeve to me.

"Oh John! What is this, what kind of a surprise is this? Are you an artist, Mr. Clarke? This is beautiful; it looks so much like my home in England. How did you come to draw it?" I asked, looking up at Mr. Clarke.

"One question at a time Elizabeth. We will tell you everything in time. The important thing is that you like it." The expression on Johns face seemed to be questioning my response.

"Like it, I love it. It is beautiful and I will find a perfect place for it in my new home when it is built." I exclaimed, as I wiped the tears from my eyes. "This is a lovely piece of art work and I will treasure it of course." Now I felt foolish for the thoughts my mind had conjured up about Mr. Clarke. He had done something beautiful for me and I had been too quick to judge him. Both John and Mr. Clarke burst forth into a fit of laughter. I looked quizzically at the both of them and then back to the beautiful drawing lying on the desk. There before my eyes was my beautiful Caswell Manor. In almost every detail it sat before me, recreated on a piece of parchment paper. My heart pounded loudly in my chest and I felt as if it was about to burst. For the life of me I could not find anything funny about this whole situation. What did John and Mr. Clarke, find so amusing? Were they laughing at my very noticeable sentimentality? I hope not for that would be very cruel. Maybe Mr. Clarke, does not know how much I miss my home, but John, sure does and I would hope he would never think me foolish for my feelings. Once again I looked up at the two of them with their broad grins lingering on their faces.

"What is so humorous John? Are you finding me the center of your merriment?" I responded, not knowing quite what to say.

"Oh Elizabeth, you know I could never do that. It is just that I have been planning on this special moment for such a long time and I am genuinely pleased to see your reaction. This is not a picture of your old home Elizabeth; this is to be your new home. Mr. Clarke has been commissioned to design and build for you, this house, which is your hearts secret desire. I only hope you are happy with what we have brought about thus far." John explained.

"Happy, I could not be more happy than I am at this very moment, but what do you mean, this is to be my new home?" I didn't quite understand and questioned first John and then Mr. Clarke.

"Well, I think I am going to have to leave the explanation up to Mr. Clarke for I have some other business that is quite pressing and he is more than capable. If you will both excuse me I will leave the rest up to you Mr. Clarke, and leave my wife in your good hands." With that John, quickly hastened to the door and left the room. I just stood there, feeling a bit more than slightly uneasy, to be left alone in this room with a total stranger. Especially one that made me feel the way this one did.

I turned toward the picture on the desk, trying hard to hide the discomfort I felt. When Mr. Clarke spoke to me, he demanded that I look straight at him. The sound of his voice as he spoke, is what gave me cause for concern. I wondered how John, could have put me in this situation? How well does John, really know this man? Thoughts race through my mind. Mr. Clarke continues to speak, but my mind is only hearing parts of words. I had to get control of my thoughts and concentrate.

"Excuse me, Mr. Clarke, I was still studying the picture and did not hear all that you said." I stated trying to cover my uncomfortable feelings.

"I was only asking if you truly like the drawing Mrs. Curtyce? I only had the description, the one Mr. Curtyce gave me to go on and was not at all sure that it was going to come out right." He explained. I felt he was trying to be friendly and I had no real cause to be uneasy with him at all. I was almost ashamed of my thoughts.

"Well I would say that you have captured John's description of Caswell Manor, as perfect as anyone could. It is a marvelous drawing. I am very curious to find out how all of this came about, Mr. Clarke. How long have you been working on this and what does all of this mean?" I asked, feeling more and more at ease. Mr. Clarke had a way of making you feel as if you had known him for years.

"Mr. Curtyce came to me some time ago. It must be near to a year ago since our first meeting. He had inquired of someone that could both design and build his home. A mutual friend of ours brought us together. I think it has proven to be a very special meeting for me, Mrs. Curtyce, for I have had a great amount of pleasure in just putting this drawing together for you. From the conversations I had with Mr. Curtyce, I have felt that for a long time now I have known you. Now that we have met face to face I find the picture in my mind far unworthy, from what I see before me." His response caught me off guard once again; he has managed to start the strange stirring in my stomach.

"I am sorry if I am a disappointment to you Mr. Clarke, for your drawing is surely not a disappointment to me." I reply.

"Oh, not a disappointment in the least Mrs. Curtyce, quite the opposite. It is very much a pleasant occurrence, this finally meeting you after all this time." He answered, reaching for my hand in a friendly gesture.

"I feel that you have the advantage there, Mr. Clarke, since until a few minutes ago I knew nothing of your existence." I said and stepped back a goodly distance from his reach.

"I am looking forward to working closely with you in the weeks and months to come Mrs. Curtyce, I am sure that the pleasure of this acquaintance will be all mine." As the words came forth from his mouth he licked his lips and let a broad grin curl the corners of his mouth. Once again I turned toward the drawing, trying to break away from this conversation, for I felt it becoming much too familiar.

What is it about this man that bothers me so? I stare directly at the paper on the desk, but it is not the house I see it is the cynical, sinister image of Mr. Clarke's face.

He was tall in stature, with coal black hair; his eyes look as if they have been sculptured from the finest blue crystal. They were deep in color and piercing as they look at me. His skin is smooth and clean-shaven and when he smiles the dimples deep within his cheeks accentuated a warm broad grin that makes his eyes sparkle like the jewels in a night sky. His teeth are straight and as white as the fresh, first snow of winter. What was it about this man that made such an impression on my mind? I could not remember ever in my life taking such notice of a human being. I once again feel so uneasy in his presence.

He stepped behind me, so close that my dress is pushed against the desk and I can feel his warm breath upon the nap of my neck. I stood paralyzed, frozen to this spot, as he talked.

"This area here Mrs. Curtyce, has been set aside for a garden. I understand, it is roses that you are so fond of, is that correct?" He questioned.

I muttered an affirmative answer and continued to stare down at the desk. He was not interested in my answer and kept right on talking. "Over here Mrs. Curtyce, will be the door to the back side of the house. I have set aside a place there also for, a kitchen garden, if that is to your liking?" He paused and I nodded, still unable to move, both from uneasiness and from the fact that this man was far to close. He seemed to be enjoying my predicament very much, I thought. I think the situation is getting very much out of control.

Trying to break from this caged in positioning, I turn myself around and find that Mr. Clarke has not moved an inch and I am looking up into his smiling face. Mr. Clarke seems to be standing his ground and not yielding one iota away from me. If anything my movement made the situation worse. Now we were face to face, without a breath of space between us. We were so close that my eyelashes were in peril of rubbing against his chin. My heart skipped a beat and my face grew flushed. I did not know what this man was going to do next. His breath was whisper soft against my face and I feared he was going to take me in his arms. I froze, afraid to move and afraid not to move.

199

Much to my relief, after a moment, he stepped back and began to roll up the picture before me. Securing it tightly he reached behind the desk and pulled out another very long roll of parchment.

"What is that?" I ask, finally retrieving my voice from somewhere way down deep inside me. Even thinking my words coming out a bit choppy.

"This is another plan of your house." He answered, as he unrolled the paper and placed it on the desk for me to look over. Again, as I stepped forward to look at the plans, Mr. Clarke, positioned his body close behind me, pressing gently against me, he reached over my shoulder and proceeded to talk about the plans. I could not concentrate on what he was saying.

Could this be my imagination playing tricks on me, or was this man up to no good? I was sure it was the later. I had to figure out just what to do. He leaned forward once more pressing even harder against my body. His stance now is just much to close for comfort. I was being squeezed between the edge of the desk and Mr. Clarke. I had to keep my wits about me. I wasn't aware of what he was saying to me, for my mind was racing, desperately trying to find answers to its own questions. I felt I had to do something and I had to do it now.

"Excuse me Mr. Clarke, you are standing much to close. The air in the room is very limited." I said requesting more space between us.

"I beg your pardon Liz, as you can see here, this is the main part of the house, the great hall." He continued to explain the plans. Making no notice of my request or seemingly not letting it disturb him in any way, for he made no comment and deliberately choose not to move in any direction.

I thought it best at this point not to make too much of the fact that he addressed me in such a familiar manner. If my request to stand at a greater distance had been ignored, I was sure a request to be called Mrs. Curtyce, would be too. Not even John called me by any other than my given name, Elizabeth. This Mr. Clarke is quite arrogant, I thought to myself, but I will not let him throw me off guard, if that is what he is trying to do.

Perhaps if I do not make notice of this uncomfortable position he has put me in, he will just give up and nothing will be said of it. Besides, what would he dare to do here in John's cabin?

He was persistent in making sure that I noticed very detail of the drawing. I felt he was trying to keep me pined in this position for his own convenience. I hope he is not that persistent in all his actions, for if he is I might have a fight on my hands.

"I can see that is the great hall Mr. Clarke, I am more than familiar with the house, I grew up in it. If you have followed Johns, description as you seem to have, then there is no need to point out every room to me. I know where they are and can see your fine detail quite clearly." I remarked, hoping an explanation of my own would detour him.

200

"Good! I only pointed out the fact thinking perhaps you were unfamiliar with house drawings." His statement was so calm, yet he did not move to release me from the pressure of his body, against mine.

"I thank you for your consideration Mr. Clarke, but knowing the house as I do gives me a good idea as to where you have placed the specific rooms, on the parchment." I said, feeling like I was in a duel of words and knowledge with this man.

"That is perfect, I knew we would work well together. I just had that feeling from the very beginning of this project." Mr. Clarke sputtered out, with a jubilant clap of his hands, as if he was terribly thrilled at his discovery.

Then he immediately leaned over to unroll the drawing a little further placing a weight to hold the corners down. In doing so his movement pressed my body sideways over the table. All the time we conversed he kept me pinned against the front of the desk. Now he reached over and placed his hand atop mine and moved it to the right of the paper, continuing his description of the drawing.

"Then you will recognize this as the buttery with the kitchen directly in front of it." Then moving my hand, held tightly within his grasp over to the left of the page he continued. "Over here we find then the stairway to the upper chambers and on over here the library in front of which is the front parlor." He paused momentarily for a breath, but kept my hand tightly within his grip.

"Mr. Clarke." I jumped at the chance to say something. " I would prefer you not to stand so close and please release my hand." I requested as firmly as I dared. I did not want to be rude but I was to a point of either telling him straight out or jerking my hand abruptly from beneath his. Either way he would have to notice my irritation with him. I could not believe what I was hearing.

"Do you see this lovely cooking area right here Liz? I hope it meets your requirements. I will be glad to change anything that does not meet with your approval." He bent down and now his face was almost touching mine and his warm breath blew gently close to my ear. Once again my heart began to pound and I am sure he can hear it. I tried with all my strength to regain my composure. I tried to find my voice. I finally forced a sound out rather high pitched and squeaky. I cleared my throat to cover up my nervousness and tried to speak to this insolent, disrespectful man in a civil manner.

"I think I will have to study these drawings a lot longer than I have time for right now Mr. Clarke, but I do thank you for what you have done thus far and I am sure that after John and I look them over, John, will get back with you." I stated in a clear strong manner.

Mr. Clarke moved away quickly, as if startled at my husband's name. It was as if he had been in a trance.

"I was under the impression that it was you I was to be working with Liz. Mr. Curtyce was very specific in telling me that. He said, whatever you wanted you were to have." A broad smile crossing his face as he spoke.

"Well I am sure that John meant what he said, Mr. Clarke, but I will talk to John, about this project none the less." I explained.

"As you wish Liz." He replied with that familiar tone back in his voice.

I had to take this opportunity to stop him at this game he was playing, right here and now. This had gone a bit to far. Maybe he felt he had known me for a year but I had just met him and he was taking this familiar attitude, a mite to far. Before I could chastise him on this subject he requested boldly. "Liz, I must ask you to call me Eustace as that is the name I prefer to go by.

I feel that through the next few months we will become very close friends and be working in such close proximity it would be much better if you would use my given name." His request came as a shock and I stammered out my reply.

"Well thank you Mr. Clarke, I mean Eustace, if that is your wish then I will comply. However, I do not feel that we have been acquainted quite long enough for your referring to me with such familiarity. I have never been called Liz, in my life and find the sound quite strange to my ear. I prefer that you do not use it when you are addressing me." I tried to sound jovial as I explained my preference to him.

Nothing, absolutely nothing seems to faze this man. He immediately responded to my request with his jovial laugh and the insidious clap of his hands.

"Oh you will get used to it in no time Liz, but if that is your wish I will be most happy to call you Elizabeth. I feel like I have known you all your life." He answered, with such a smug look, I wished with all my heart I could slap it off his face.

His easy manner was hard for me to deal with. I have never quite met any one like him. One part of me detests him and the other part admires him. What in the world is wrong with me? I must be feeling and seeing things that aren't really there. My uneasy feelings must stem from not being acquainted long enough with this man. I certainly feel at a disadvantage. He has known about my existence for at least a year and I of his only a couple of hours.

One thing I know for sure, Eustace Clarke's, presumptuous behavior is wearing my nerves very thin. I have no strength left to argue with this strange, arrogant, and I must admit handsome man. I finally gave up, not wanting to bandy back and forth with him any longer. The tiny sparkle in Eustace's eyes led me to believe that he was a bit of a tease. I am sure he felt that he had won the first battle in this war of words.

I could not quite figure out what this game was he seemed to be playing or why he wanted to play it at all. Why would it be so difficult for him to call me Mrs. Curtyce? As if he were reading my mind he

202

interrupted my thoughts with another bold statement." I hope you really don't mind me calling you Elizabeth, for I just hate formalities. I always think that the friendly way is the best way. Don't you agree Elizabeth?" His warm smile was even more convincing than, the irrationality of his words.

How could I tell him that the familiarity, with which he expressed himself, caused me to feel uncomfortable? Could it just be my imagination? What if it is? Then I will just be making a fool of myself. Anyway, I am afraid that what ever I say now will only lead him to believe that I am enjoying his attention.

I paused in my mind for a moment for if I were to be truthful with myself I would have to admit that I have enjoyed this game of his, just a little. The challenge of trying to outsmart him was stimulating and I was not one to back down from any kind of a confrontation, not from him, not from anyone. Besides, I guess I could get used to Elizabeth, if he used it only in our private conversations.

I have to admit; Eustace intrigues me for whatever the reason. I am just not accustomed to being in such close proximity to a strange man, especially as close as he insisted on us being. I know I will have to be careful and not let him get within arms reach of me. If I can do that I think we might be able to work together on a friendly bases. But if not, I will have to speak to John, about it. I will take a wait and see attitude for now, since this is our first meeting. Caution will be my next move. My intuitions are usually very good but Eustace Clarke has peaked my curiosity. My summation of his character is very mixed up.

I was relieved when the door opened and John, walked in. I was exhausted from our war of words. "Well how did the plans for the house work out? I am sorry it took me so long to get the other business taken care of. Are you happy with everything Elizabeth? Has Mr. Clarke done a good job with what information I gave him?" John kept asking one question after another. Before I could answer Eustace, broke in.

"Mr. Curtyce, please, as I have told your lovely wife, I would much prefer to be called Eustace. I had a hard time convincing her, but please, I really would prefer it." He made his request sound so simple. I felt almost ashamed of my thoughts.

"Very well Eustace, first names it will be. I think we are all friends here and will become even closer in the near future. Yes lets do mince with the formality. Elizabeth, is that agreeable with you?" John asked, looking over for my approval.

"Well, yes John if that is what Mr. Clarke likes, I mean Eustace, that will be fine with me." I answered, not knowing why I just didn't blurt out all my concerns and get them out in the open right now.

"Well, now that we have that matter settled we, should see to some refreshments." Suggested John.

"Oh, none for me at this time John, I really need to go to my quarters and make a few more sketches while the light is right.

203

Elizabeth, it was very nice making your acquaintance and I look forward to working with you on the house." Eustace smiled his broad, captivating smile, bowed as he spoke and retreated to the door. A perfect gentleman!

I hoped the surprise on my face was not apparent to John. For he was not privy to the conversation Eustace and I had pertaining to him addressing me by my given name. I think he knew that his calling me Elizabeth, especially in front of my husband, would startle me but I tried not to fall into another one of his traps. It had been decided that first names were best. He had very smoothly gotten exactly what he wanted and with my husbands approval. What would he come up with next? I have a feeling I will constantly have to keep my guard up when he is around. He was still carrying the sparkle of mischief in his eyes, even as he reached the door and my mind was still trying to figure him out as he slipped quickly out, with no fanfare whatsoever.

"Elizabeth, did you really like the house? Was the surprise worth the wait?" John asks, turning me away from my thoughts about Eustace.

"John you know you don't have to ask that question! How did you ever keep this from me? I am so anxious now to get off this ship and get everything started. Will it take us long to get to Cupheag?" I enquired. I now wanted to know every move the ship was going to make and wanted to be sure it went right to our final destination.

"Not really very long at all. A couple of days at the most, but we will have to stay on the ship most of the time until a dwelling place can be put up." He explained.

"That is alright John, I can stand anything knowing that I am to have my home. I love you so much John Curtyce, this is such a happy day for me.

As John and I prepared for bed my thoughts kept slipping back to the afternoon and the plans for the house. Finally, not being able to contain my questions any longer I ask John, some of the things that were on my mind.

"John, have you picked out the property on which this home is to be built?" I questioned.

"Yes, it sits high on a knoll overlooking the water below. The house will be situated so as to have a beautiful view of all the surroundings. I have put in quite a large compliment of windows and as you can see, I have put in many small gardens around the house. You like gardens so much I really thought you would enjoy seeing one from almost every window." John explained to me enthusiastically.

"John, you are so thoughtful. But how could you possibly have found the perfect piece of property with out going and seeing it first?" I knew that John had not been away from home or had time to be out looking for property in another area of the country.

"Well, you know Elizabeth, these things come much later after the house is completely finished, but I just wanted to touch upon the whole completed picture. I do hope that Eustace filled you in on all the details of the house. And he should have told you about the land he had found to build the house on" John said.

"Yes, he tried hard to make sure that everything was to my liking. I could see how beautifully everything had been laid out and agree that the gardens around the house will add greatly to the beauty of the structure. Yet I do not remember him saying anything about the land." I said, continuing on an on. I just couldn't stop talking about the plans for the house. More and more questions kept flowing from my mouth. It even took me several minutes to realize that John was no longer answering me. I looked over, to find him sound asleep. How could any one sleep with so much excitement in them?

I didn't even get a chance to question John, as to where and how he came to hire Eustace Clarke, for this job and to tell him of my apprehension as to his character. John had obviously picked the very best man to build our home and turned over all of the responsibility to him. I must not let anything interfere with this judgment John, has entrusted to Eustace and also to me. I will just have to learn to deal with this man myself. I turned to face the wall and closed my eyes to shut out the thoughts of the day. It didn't work. The picture of Eustace burned brightly in my memory. I closed my eyes yet tighter and tossed and turned in a restless fight for sleep.

# CHAPTER 13

So far this voyage down the Connecticut River is not only a unique experience but also a very pleasant one. I feel a certain security having the sight of land on both sides of the ship at the same time. The monotony and fear etched in my mind of the crossing from England, to the New Land, is buried deep in the recesses of my brain in a dense, shadowy fog, almost completely obliterated from my memory, at least for now.

This is not at all like those long days and nights, rolling about in the rough angry sea, with little sight of anything but a bird or large fish from time to time. Yes, this is much more to my personal choice. I have a lot of things to occupy my mind. Most of it being just thinking of what this new area will look like and what a difference it will make in our family life. When I do allow my mind to wonder, I try hard to contain my thoughts to the realistic and not let my wild imagination go off and dream up dreams that will be impossible to bring to fruition.

With the prospect of our new home growing closer by the day, I am able to take control of the majority of doubts that once consumed almost every wakening hour. I have conditioned myself to look at this newest experience in my life with as much positive thinking as I can come up with. The fact that we will finally be in our own home keeps me going. Just knowing that it will be up to us to do the rest and to make the area into whatever we want it to be, is a great challenge. With the grace of God, we will make it a fine place to live. Keeping that thought foremost in my mind eliminates a lot of needless agonizing.

Even with determination there is still that little voice deep inside, nagging me on to try and predetermine and prearrange everything in my life. Keeping that under control can help keep disappointment away. I am determined that I will for once in my life accept things as they are and work from there. I find that this attitude makes me feel more at ease with myself, with John, and with the world about me.

Knowing that we will soon be docking in the harbor at Cupheag lightens my spirits immensely. I feel as if a big burden has been lifted from my shoulders. I can take a deep breath and finally relax for the first time in years. I don't know why I feel such a relief, for this is really no time to think of relaxing in any way, for there is so much work ahead, work on our home, fields, gardens, and the business must be established. A town will be built with a meetinghouse and so many more things. All this and much more would have to take place before we can call ourselves a real Township.

It will not be just our family, but all who have signed on to work toward these goals; we will all take an active role in all phases of this latest colonization. There are many families, and our survival and success depends on each of us doing our part. There have been many meetings about this new charter and just how to go about developing our town. Our leaders are careful not to let us expect too much, but we are determined and undaunted by the overwhelming tasks and projects that lie ahead. Permanency, a place to finally rest my feet, has indeed induced in me a great feeling of superior confidence that we can and will accomplish all our goals.

I will welcome this stability in my life, with a very grateful heart and a prayer of thanks unto my Lord for guiding me this far on our quest. I know that for many, this new land has become their home. I am happy for them, truly I am. Maybe someday I will be able to call it mine also. Now it is still very much just another place. A very strange and different place compared to my England. With the roots of my heritage left far behind, I find it difficult to give my heart and allegiance to another place. These thoughts that would be considered heresy by our leaders are the ones locked deep in my soul. To bring any disgrace to my family because of my feelings, I will not do. I must deal with my own demons, in my own ways. Seeking to find and follow God's direction for me will not be an easy path to follow. My questions are still many.

It has been many several years now since we left the shores of England-since we watched the thin line of earth disappear and merge with the sky and water. Liz was such a small child then. I wonder in my heart if this change in our family has made her have to grow up way to fast for there are times when I look at her and see the blossoming of a beautiful young lady. It is difficult for me to look at her or the boys and see anything but my little ones. This image exists only in my mind, for to they are all maturing so fast.

Since the majority of my life was spent in England it is reasonable that the majority of my memories are of there. But for Liz, I see her memories as a much larger, more faceted world than mine is or was. I do hope, when all our children are grown and have families of their own, they will see this change in their lives as a good one and a positive one. They have slipped into this new land much easier than I. That is a fact I have to admit at least to myself. Their acceptance has seemed to be total and without compromise. I wish I could have been blessed with the ability to make this transition with such apparent ease. I try to convince myself that it will get better and just to give things a chance and not expect too much so quickly. As I awake each day I pray for an understanding of what is expected of me even though my feelings are a mixture of a little of the new and a whole lot of the old.

In the beginning, the feeling was much like the tide rushing onto a virgin beach. It was the thrill of the unknown, the thrill of a chance to start anew, the privilege of being amongst the first to create these new colonies that was so enticing to us. None of the original facts that led us to this adventure have been changed, only the timing of how events have taken place. I still look forward to the challenges ahead and the prospect of a great future with only the slightest of apprehensions, for John gives me the assurance that everything will happen as it is suppose to. His word is gospel to him; he would not state it if he did not believe it.

As I look out across the water toward the shoreline, my eyes fall upon a sight of great splendor. The big ship has now turned its sharp, pointed bow inward toward the land mass--its green marshes and stands of trees contrasting against the indigo blue of the ocean. The land, at the head of the sandy, rock-strewn beach, is a crowning point between sky and sea. My stomach churns with anticipation, as the crew maneuvers the ship toward the harbor. The massive sails are groaning as the wind whips them in one direction and the hard work of the crew demands that they take another. I watch the scurrying about of the sailors and keep saying to myself, "don't expect too much now Elizabeth; you will only be

207

disappointed if you do." My mind must stay steadfast in its resolve and not conjure up an impossible dream.

The closer we come to the shore, the more detailed the landscape becomes. Large boulders lie away from the land's edge and are stuck in the shallow water with the foam-topped waves lapping over them-the waves looking like a mother cat cleaning her young. The rocks are in no particular order-looking as if they had merely gone to play in the sand and had gotten stuck. Perhaps in their hasty retreat from the onrushing ocean they had fallen. Now they are half buried-destined to stand guard, to protect the shore, giving the ocean waves something to splash against with their fierce, explosive, aggression.

I do believe, as an onlooker, the waves are losing their great battle, as they forge ahead and then retreat, only to roll back, again and again, in another futile attempt to conquer the land. They leave a small amount of their frothy foam spewing in frustration as they try to leap past the great huge boulders. These large broken-off pieces of the immense land mass look, too me, like sentinels on constant alert for the approaching enemy-ever watchful for the attempted destruction by the aggressor. The aggressor hits again and again, bumping and grinding only to make its swift retreat and regroup for another charge. On and on the battle rages and I am enjoying the privilege of watching this game of nature as we glide seemingly effortlessly into the small harbor.

We were up early this morning, had our family meal, our daily prayers, the reading of the Bible, and our day had begun. When I finally got myself looking presentable, I looked forward to coming up on deck. I have enjoyed this quiet time as we approach this place called Cupheag.

William and John Jr. are really grown men now, very capable of taking care of themselves. I should not leave out Thomas, since his journey out to sea; he too has matured into a man. If anything keeps him a boy, it is I. No matter how hard I try, I still see him in my mind as a small child. My heart does not want to fully let him traverse into manhood. All of the children have really taken to this new life quite well. They have all given their full support to the needs and decisions of their father. We have so many wonderful blessings to be thankful for. We have such a fine family. John and I both realize that the children too have sacrificed much for this unique adventure in life. I wonder, if we had known over five years ago what we know today, if we would have ever left our beautiful Caswell. I hasten to think for myself, I would not have.

There are many of our acquaintances that have not had the family unity that we enjoy. I can only think that this journey is hard enough without a constant conflict within the family. I feel saddened when I come across the separation of mother and son, or mother and daughter, or sons and fathers, over a difference of views and feelings. Life seems far too short to carry on with stubborn views that separate one from another. It does happen and the wounds from these kinds of hurts are slow and hard to heal. Sometimes they can never be completely stitched back in place, leaving an ugly scar to remind one of past differences.

As I turn my head to see what the commotion is, I see John approaching from the cabin area. With a smile and a wave you can just tell how very excited he is. He is enjoying every minute of this voyage. As I watch him approach I think to myself, what a handsome man he is, and these few days with the sea and sun beating down upon him has made his skin take on a warm copper color. The color of his skin accentuates his strong handsome features. He looks not a lot different today than the day I first laid eyes on him, and it is no wonder I grew to love him so totally, in such a short time.

I saw him then as a handsome young man and I see him today, his face etched with the maturity of manhood, as a handsome husband walking boldly across the polished deck of his very own ship, to greet me, his wife. The only visible difference from that first day to this is the maturity that grew with years, from that young man to this one, who is very much in charge of his life, his family and his company.

"Well Elizabeth, here we are, what do you think thus far?" He asked, not being able to subdue his excitement.

"I think the rocks at the waters edge are spectacular. This whole scene set against this beautiful blue sky with the emerald green waves, and their frothy white caps dashing wildly about, is breathtaking John, breathtaking! It looks to be a very wet and marshy coastline from this angle. I wonder what it is like when you are up on higher ground? The colors of the water seem to change quite often from a deep blue in some places to a very light green in others. I wonder why it changes seemingly for no reason from one color to another?" I questioned, not really expecting John to have an answer for any of my questions.

"I think you will find the view to be even more spectacular than the one you are seeing from here. As a matter of fact Elizabeth, the second part of my surprise for you is right before your very eyes," he said, as he pointed toward the shore line to our left.

"What do you mean by that John? All I can see is a line of what looks to be grassy areas, with a few trees sprinkled here and there and a very large salt marsh area. It doesn't look like there is much more," I said, squinting to see if I had missed something of importance.

"Well, there is a little more than that Elizabeth. Once you are atop that grassy area, right over there, you will find a magnificent parcel of land and when you stand upon it you have a view of this waterway that is incredible. If it impresses you like its description impressed me, I think you will feel as I. It is that piece of land I have chosen for our home." John burst forth with his surprise.

"Oh John, really, really, right over there? Will it be safe for a house? It looks like it would be right in the middle of the water. Are you sure the house will be safe that close to the ocean? It might be overtaken by the waves, just like they are trying to overtake those rocks," I said, not being able to imagine anything beyond the large rocks and sandy beach.

"Elizabeth, would I ever put you or our home in a place of danger? Of course not! It is really much higher than it looks. It is the angle we are at that is deceiving to our eyes. You will find yourself a great distance from the water's edge, when you are up there. It is perfectly safe and just wait and see, you will love it," he questioned and then answered his own statement before I could put forth any comment.

"When will we be able to go and see it John? I have waited so long. Can we go as soon as we dock?" I inquired, hardly able to contain my excitement.

"Well, shortly Elizabeth. There are a few matters that will have to be taken care of here on the ship and at the dock area, but I promise that as soon as I am free I will try and secure a moment in time for just us. We will view our future home plot together." John quickly explained the order of business and then gave me a coquettish wink as he started to walk away.

"Oh John, you will hurry won't you? I don't know how much longer I can wait. I want to get started on the house right away," I shouted, trying to be heard above the wind and the flap of the sails.

"Slow down now, my love, it is going to take more than a few days to put up a house of the kind and size you want." John walked back to my side as he talked. "We are very blessed to have the lumber from William's mill. His mill will be of great use to the new areas being established. The other supplies we brought will help too, but we were not able to carry everything. Other supplies will have to come from Boston Harbor, and we will have to make many trips before it is all finished." John had his brow wrinkled up and was looking at me as if he was seeking some sign of dissatisfaction.

I pressed my lips together and wrinkled up my nose and questioned. "Are you trying to tell me that I have to wait a long time? You are, trying to do just that aren't you John?"

"No, not a long time Elizabeth, I just want you to be realistic about what things have to be done first. You have to realize that everything can't happen the instant we arrive. Besides there are other families we have to think of too. Our meetinghouse, has to be built, you know what it was like in Roxbury. When we arrived there many things were already built or in the process of being built. Here we have nothing." He responded, sounding a bit exasperated.

"I know John, you don't have to explain what we went through, I am well aware of what happened in Roxbury. I did think that this would be a little different though, since we are to start our own settlement. I will not let you discourage me, I am just excited." I answered, but John, continued talking. I was so insistent in our talk, before leaving Suckiaug, I think, he is trying to make sure I am advised of his every thought, especially since I had complained of feeling left out.

"Have you talked to Eustace, lately and gone over any of the other plans with him. I think he did finish some more drawings and sketches of the upper portion of the house. You know, I really want you to put forth your own creativity into our home Elizabeth. Eustace has been instructed by me to comply with your every wish. I am afraid that since the shipping business will keep me away from home, for sometimes-long periods of time,

210

I will have to leave a lot of the decisions and problems of the building of our home in your hands. Very capable hands and very pretty ones, I must say."

"Oh John you are teasing again, but I love it. I will do my best. I do have some reservations about Eustace, though." I said, my statement catching John, off guard.

"Oh really! Why is that? He questioned. "He has not done anything to offend you has he? I will not tolerate that from any man, no matter how highly recommended he is." John looked down at me and I knew he was concerned about how I was being treated.

"No, it is not that, I just feel uncomfortable around him and I really don't know why. It is really nothing he has either done or said. I felt uneasy with him standing so close to me in the ships cabin, as he leaned over pointing out portions of the house drawing. It was just a feeling." I drew in a deep breath, feeling relieved that I had was finally talking to John, about Eustace.

"Well, I would want to stand as close as I could to someone as pretty as you, if I had the chance. I surely hope you can over come this feeling Elizabeth, for he is the best there is when it comes to planning and completing a project like this. Do promise me you will try hard to get along with him."

I would honor Johns request of course but I wondered if he had heard all I said. His off handed compliment gave me little security for my feelings. Perhaps he chose not to make an issue of it at this time. I had chosen not to at the time it happened, why did I expect John, to come running to defend my honor now? I decided to drop the subject and handle it in my own way, if it ever occurred again?

"I will of course try to over come this obstacle John, for all our sakes. I would not want to cause any delay in the building of our home. I am sure Mr. Clarke and I can reach an amicable agreement." I stated, with a renewed air of confidence.

John turned and walked away wanting to get the ship docked and everything accomplished in short order so we could go see this new home site, as soon as possible. He promised to hurry and I knew he would. But I am sure it will take far more time than I really want to share with the duties of this ship, but wait I will because I don't have any other choice. This ship is becoming Johns, other priority. Now I wonder if the ship is first and I am second or do I still hold a slight edge over this massive, structure of polished wood?

It will be special, a special time, whenever we can spend a few moments alone together. It has been such a long time. When we first met we would take long walks and pass away many hours alone, discussing all our thoughts and dreams. Some have come true some are still waiting. The only thing I know for sure is that our time together has never been quite like that, since our marriage.

211

For now I will do as I always have done, just bide my time. I at
least don't have to pack before getting off the ship, for the ship is to
be our home for at least a short while. I will just look forward to being
alone with my husband and planning our future together. From what I can
see from the ship the land around this area looks peaceful and quiet. It
will be nice to finally get off the ship and look around. Patience
Elizabeth, patience, I remind myself.

It was mid-afternoon before John, returned to get me and we walked
down the plank and off onto land once more. The pathway up a small hill
from the shore was covered with crushed, broken pieces of white shells.
It was hard walking against the bottom of my feet.

Upon reaching more level ground, I saw a vast panoramic view of the
countryside. There were far more trees than I imagined there to be. It
was surprisingly appealing to the eye. The path we took across the meadow
was soggy and wet, with small patches of ice here and there. Occasionally
in shaded areas a bit of snow. I wrapped my shawl close about me and
shivered at the coolness in the air.

Being in the open, near the water, the wind seems so much stronger
and much cooler than I anticipated. It feels very warm and comforting as
John slips his arm around me and draws me close to him. His warm body
close to mine is very soothing. It has been so long since we have had
time alone to share our love for each other. We always seem to be in a
cluster of other people. I am so enjoying this quiet solitude with John.
As John draws me even closer a slight murmur of contentment escapes my
mouth.

"There is that better my sweet? It is a bit cool up here but we
are almost to our land now and we will not terry to long and we will hurry
back before you catch a chill." He said, squeezing me to his side as
tight as possible.

"No John!" I protest harshly. "Please don't hurry back. This is
so beautiful. The birds are singing and the wind is blowing through my
hair. I love the smell of the fresh salty breeze and I especially love
the freedom of being totally alone, for the first time in many, many
months with my husband. I want this moment to last as long as possible."
I beg of John not wanting to give up one moment of our privacy.

"You are trying to distract me from my obvious duties aboard my
ship, Elizabeth Curtyce." He said jokingly.

"Well, maybe I am at that John Curtyce, but we deserve a little
time to ourselves. Don't we?" I retorted, looking up with a mischievous
look in my eyes. Knowing full well that John, would not want to hurry any
more than I did.

We walked along in silence, just enjoying each other and the lovely
countryside around us. About half way up a slight incline in the road
John turned and we started through a small wooded area. The trees are so
tall and the foliage so thick, it almost looks like nightfall has come
upon us. As we approached the other side of the wooded area a lovely
meadow appeared. A small stand of trees stood at our far right and as I

turned in a complete circle, so as not to miss any of the beauty that is surrounding us, I let my eyes stopped at the edge of the clearing where the earth just seemed to blend in with the sky. John, urged me to walk on toward that fine line of grass, the one that seemed to divide the sky and land.

"Now not to much further Elizabeth." John instructed. "It is marshy over here so be careful. Here hold my hand and come across these rocks and you can view the whole area." I followed John with caution keeping a tight grip on his hand.

"Oh look!" I said in amazement. "I thought that was the sky out there, but it is water. How beautiful, what is that way out in the water John?" I questioned as I pointed toward a thin gray line nearing the edge of the sky. It looked to be a very long island.

"It is the land we sighted as we turned west out of the Connecticut River into the sound, heading toward Cupheag. Isn't it something that you can see so far? Now come over here, look down, see we are at the top of a little cove and that is where I will be able to dock my ship. It will be perfect and when the house is built up here, you will be able to look from the window and see my ship come sailing in. Now what could you ask for, more than that Elizabeth? Do you like it so far? You have hardly said a word." He exclaimed. I could not remember John, ever being this happy. At least not in a long, long time.

"I don't know what to say John. It is really beautiful from up here. I can see for such a great distance. I think if that stand of trees was not there I could see all the way back to England." I exclaimed, expressing my disbelief in the crystal clear air.

"I doubt it seriously Elizabeth, you couldn't see England even if the trees weren't there, for you are looking in the wrong direction." John, chuckled, knowing that I was probably the worst ever in knowing which direction I was looking in, or going in. I blushed with embarrassment but John, just gave me a tight squeeze and kissed my up turned face.

"You are wonderful Elizabeth, you see everything with such enthusiasm. I am so grateful for that. You never seem to restrict my dreams and always support what I feel is right for our family." I shrugged my shoulders, replying. "Isn't that what a wife is for John? That is what I am told anyway. It is my duty to follow, follow, follow!" I teased back at John, enjoying the freedom of not being overheard by half the crew on ship. Now we need to incorporate the reasons we came to this new land and the reasons we needed to leave the shelter of Roxbury and give birth to our own Colony.

"Do I sense a wee bit of sarcasm in the tone of you voice, my dear?" John asked, as he turned his head slightly to the side, as he awaited my answer.

"No, not really, you have done a fine job thus far, I am just really very ready to settle down and am glad to be here. I will leave the decisions up to you and just sit back and enjoy every minute of the rest of our life together." I said, breathing a deep sigh of contentment.

John and I sat down on a large outcropping of rocks that seemed to be placed just right in this specific spot for our comfort. His arms held me close, as he tipped my face upward to meet his, in a long lingering kiss. My senses reeled and my skin tingled at the touch of John's embrace. The light sigh that escaped me let John, know just how receptive I was to his touch and, our midday walk passed into a beautiful day of special memories.

We spent the afternoon walking around the great expanse of meadows and fields. We placed the house here and there in our minds, trying to decide on just where the right place was. I knew John, had already decided just where he wanted to situate the house. He was just letting me take in the full extent of the wonderful view, and go on and on, about this and that. And I really think he was enjoying all of it. We were like young kids again setting out, fresh and new. How happy I am making these new plans. I am very, very content.

As the sun passed further and further toward the west, we knew our time of solitude, was coming to an end. The big round, gloriously red sun, was fast on its way to disappearing. John and I looked at each other, not needing to say a word. Neither of us wanted to give up one minute of this special shared time for we knew there would be a long void, before we would be able to do this again.

John's voice broke the serenity of the moment. "We need to return to the ship. It is not only quite a walk back; it would be unwise to be caught out in this wilderness after dark. Besides the rest of the family will be wondering if the Indians have captured us. We have the other families on board to consider and a lot of arrangements for their shelters have to be made."

The trail we had walked up here on, is not a well-worn one I think perhaps it has been made by wild deer or other animals searching for water. As John and I walk in silence for a long way and then John broke into my dreams with a question that I knew had to be faced, at some point. Although it surprises me that he would have chosen this particular time to bring it up.

"Elizabeth, I have been thinking a lot about our future and the future of our family while on this trip. I feel that it is time for the boys to start considering the probability of a family and homes of their own. Since we have required so much of their time and efforts, don't you think a wife and children for them and some grandchildren for us would be nice?" John's, timing of the question surprised me, but not the question itself. I had often entertained the same thoughts. But since he brought the subject up first I would let it be his idea, not mine.

"My John, you really have been doing a lot of thinking, haven't you? I knew this time had to be reached someday, yet I still have the desire to hold on to us as a unit. Has someone approached you about the boys or have they said something to indicate, that is what they want to do John?" I asked, thinking perhaps one of the families had talked to John, about the boy's future.

214

"Well, in a way, John Jr., has mentioned quite an interest in Eliza. Even William has that special look in his eyes when he looks at Mary. They are both nice young girls and from well founded homes. I would have no objection to either of them, would you Elizabeth?" He said, looking down and putting his arm about me as if to shelter me from a blow. I appreciated the tenderness in his approach to this subject.

"No, of course not John. Have you approached their fathers as to your thoughts? Or is this just something you have been mulling around in your head?" I questioned. Not knowing just how he expected me to react to this conversation.

"No, but I will just as soon as all of our feet settle a bit more upon this new area. I want our family, and the families that have come with us and the ones that will join from the overland route to have time to settle in." I had to agree with John that was the wise thing to do. We would see if the boys really were showing an interest toward these girls or had the closeness on the ship just made it seem that way.

The days passed quickly and one by one, all that had sailed with us left the confines of the ship. They were all on their own parcels of land, and soon the little settlement of people started to resemble a town. We held many meetings and had more than a few discussions on the best way to do one thing or another. It was a wonderful time of hard work and great rewards. There was so much to do to start a settlement and get housing underway for everyone. We once again had to work hard and fast. Long, long days were in order. Protection had to be provided from the elements and also from the Indians in the area. We always seem to be racing against something. It is either the weather, the season or something else I guess that is what keeps us going, the ever-present challenge of survival.

The constant commotion left all of us with a feeling of intense churning inside. It was like something contagious, we fed off of each other's energies. Eustace, started almost immediately on the house and John Jr. and William helped as much as they could. Both of the older boys had decided on plots of land for themselves, this fact making it even more evident that the two of them would soon become four. Eliza and Mary appear to be the picture of young women in love, looking forward to a happy and full life. Both being capable and willing workers, they pitched right in and worked with both their own families and when over on our place, offered to help wherever it was needed.

Thomas is spending most of his time by the dock area doing anything that is needed of him. Other times he is in John's shop fixing and polishing and just in general enjoying what ever he is doing. He doesn't think anything that has to do with sailing is work. He had become a right hand to his father, able to take a lot of the responsibility of the shipping business upon his shoulders and leaving time for John, to set up a small shop that would be a supply house for incoming goods. These goods were desperately needed to sustain life in our new home. "Our new home." The words rang forth from my mouth and I said them out loud as often as I dared for they sounded good as they trailed through my mind, and out into the openness around me. "Home, home, home at last."

I watched with great eagerness the building of the house. John was right. Eustace was a master at his craft. Everything he did, he followed through, with great precision. It would not be long now until the living area would be completed and we could move off the ship and into the completed portion. John and Eustace have warned me not to expect too much at first. It was a beginning not an end product that I would be moving into.

I must admit, I was very anxious and excited and could hardly wait for that day to come. It had been so long since we had a place to call our own and so many things had happened to keep a real home just out of reach. Sometimes I would feel like my dreams were so close that a quick snatch of my hand and they would be mine. Then like always when I did try to get them in my grasp, they would disappear into thin air.

As I watched from afar, my eagerness grew and the excitement today at going to see the house was almost too much for me. It is not that I hadn't seen it before this, it is just that John, has kept me away from the house these last three weeks, telling me he wanted to surprise me. I am more than ready now and can't wait for the noon meal to be completed so we can go and I can see this surprise for myself.

"John, you are eating so slow. Any other time you would be finished and back out in the fields or down to the ship by now. What on earth is taking you so long?" I questioned, squirming in my seat beside him.

"Nothing is taking me so long, you are just more than a little anxious to go up and see the house." He said, as he gulped a big swig of warm ale, to wash his food down faster.

"Well do you blame me John, we have all waited quiet a long while to have a real home of our own again. After all John, I have not even been allowed up there forever so long. You must be trying to hide something from me." I voice my opinion, hoping he will get tired of hearing me complain and hurry.

"So be it Elizabeth, you win, we will go right away I can see that I can not hold you back another bit of a moment. Grab a rap and let's be on our way." He said, as he pushed back the trencher and stood to his feet.

As we approached the little knoll at the property's edge John, put his hand upon my shoulder and with a broad smile upon his face exclaimed. "Elizabeth, you are just like a small child. You get such pleasure out of such small things in life."

"Well John Curtyce." I retorted. "I don't call this a small thing at all this is one of the biggest things that has ever happened to me. I feel like we have finally arrived at the end of a long dream. I am comfortable and content and am just looking forward to moving in and settling down with you at my side. It is a peaceful feeling John, a feeling that I have longed for, for many years now. It is the feeling I had when we first married and moved into Caswell Manor. I think that Caswell has finally caught up with me. You probably find me foolish

216

thinking such thoughts as this, but I can't help it the only thing that hampers my joy is the fact that the boys will be going out on their own soon. Finally we have a home and no one to enjoy it with us. Our children are all grown or almost grown."

"Now, now Elizabeth, don't let unhappy thoughts creep into your mind. You know that Liz, will not be leaving home for a few years yet and the boys will be here with or without a wife for a bit longer, as their homes are not even started." John said, knowing my sentiments ran deep. I know he is right and I will just be borrowing unhappiness and trouble if I continue to think along these lines. I will put these thoughts right out of my head, for now anyway and just enjoy the moment.

As we rounded the top of the knoll and the meadow and fields spread forth in front of me, I stopped to draw in a deep breath. The climb had not been a hard one, but all of a sudden I felt out of breath. I guess walking and talking so much used up all the air in me. Upon getting my second wind I motioned for John, to come along and I started to run up the path. My feet fairly flew. Faster and faster I ran, tugging at my skirt trying to keep it from getting tangled beneath my feet. John was surprised at my swiftness. "Hurry, hurry!" I shouted, waving him on faster. John caught up with me in just a couple of strides and grabbed my arm pulling me to an abrupt stop. When my eyes focused ahead of me there stood our home. Without even seeing the inside of it I felt a surge of joy start at the very bottom of my feet and swiftly race through my body and out the top of my head. I shrieked with happiness for it was a sight grander than any I had dreamed.

The vision before me was more than I had ever hoped for. There before my eyes stood my Caswell. It was all my dreams of the past seven years, culminated into a single structure. We paused to view its magnificence. My heart was racing as fast as my feet, as I flew toward the front stoop and broad front door. I paused momentarily to rest my hand on a beautifully crafted, brass door handle and feast my eyes on a knocker fashioned like the head of a lion. John, catching up with me opened the door and we entered the great hall. I let my eyes slowly, drift from floor to ceiling, from wall to wall, finally resting on the magnificent carved fireplace mantle. The beauty of this massive fireplace, with its stones of native rock is just breathtaking. They were gathered from our land and used in its construction to the fullest extent of their grandeur. My mind immediately started placing pieces of furniture here and there. I wondered about the room feeling the warmth of its embrace closing in on me. I moved in silence from room to room fixing in my mind every corner and every board. There was a fireplace in every room and an abundance of windows to look out. John followed me from place to place not speaking a word.

As we walk about the house in and out of each room I am amazed at the great detail Eustace, has put into this house. He has spared none of his talents. Everything was finished with wonderful craftsmanship. Eustace is truly a great artisan; I finally let myself admit this fact. This I had to admit and he had been a great source of help with the details of my home. As I paused, John took my hand in his and gave it a gentle squeeze, and with his other hand he tilted my head upward. Our eyes locked and in his rich deep voice, echoing in the vast emptiness of our home, he said, "Elizabeth, I give you, your dream."

217

# CHAPTER 14

Sandy Hollow, it is our own little settlement, appropriately named for the tiny little niche, carved out of this Connecticut shoreline. The sand and rock that has been eroded away by the wind, and rain has left this lovely peaceful area for us to create our own abodes. Time and the elements have done such a marvelous job I only hope we can do half as well in our endeavors to colonize here. The area has engulfed us in its beauty and the cove protects us from the strong gusts of wind that blow off the water and can sometimes make this a very cold and foreboding place. With each passing day we manage to accomplish more and more in this majestic Connecticut Country.

Every moment that elapses from time, brings the gratifying fulfillment of more and more of our dreams. Life here is much different than that in the Massachusetts Colony. Living on the water's edge or on the cliffs above has a uniqueness all its own. That is how it has been for me anyway. It is an experience that I have grown to love more and more as each new day merges into nightfall and embraces the beauty of a new dawn.

We all left the confines of the ship so many months ago and all of the families have secured land, built mud dwellings along the river embankments or put up more permanent houses than the mud ones. Some of the people seem to me to still be in a very temporary situation and I am sure they are as anxious as I was for their permanent structures to be completed. I hope that those in a temporary sod house will soon find a nice new log structure completed for them. The experience of living in the damp sod with earthen creatures always visiting is not a pleasant one. Not to speak of the cold that penetrates your bones and causes them to ache unmercifully. I remember far to clearly how dirty, drafty and uncomfortable our sod home was, in Roxbury. I also remember how I longed for what I had left far behind in England and the beautiful land I had called home for most of my life. Sometimes it is unbearable to have to wait for a permanent home to be completed. The priorities of this company, we have signed on to, are many and our permanent dwellings were put far down the list.

It is true that many people turned back from Boston Harbor, returning to their native lands but here in the Connecticut Country it would not be easy to leave. The distance alone from a larger harbor to Sandy Hollow would make a person think twice before deciding to turn around and go back. Hopefully the ones here with us now have come to terms with their discomforts as I have tried to do with mine and the building of our settlement will continue.

A lot of concern from our leaders and the people has turned to the subject of John's shipping business. The need for more supplies for the new dwellings and staples that cannot be grown here yet, are very low and we will have a real disaster on our hands if something isn't done soon. It seems like there is one problem after another that confronts us. We continually take our wants and needs to the Lord in prayer and ask for a speedy answer. I hope His tolerance of our requests is substantial.

219

As a Company, we have taken one concern at a time and tried as a group to meet the need of everyone. For ourselves, as individuals, we are trying to be as self sufficient as is humanly possible. Even the best of intentions and thoughtful planning is not always enough. We have found that to be a fact in so many instances.

Getting here safely was the first priority for everyone. I must confess, that getting a home built and moved into quickly was first on my personal list. Now I am torn between duties, that have to be done for the good of the settlement, and the ones, I want to do, to put my home in order.

The families that took the overland route to the Indian village of Cupheag arrived in disarray after several delays along the trail. They were tired and worn out, some sick and others just plane weary of the whole idea of this new land. The few who were able to come on the ship with John were mighty glad to greet the ones that had come overland. Hearing of their delays and sickness along the trail saddened us immensely. I am afraid they will find no rest here. There are just far too many tasks to be taken care of. Only those who are grievously ill can be given temporary time to overcome their sickness. Others are expected to rely on the Lord for strength and commence daily participation in the urgent work and creation of this settlement.

John's need to secure some kind of building to house what supplies he already has for his business was taken care of in record time. This was accomplished in quick order with the help of the crude lean-to built by the fur trader Wooly Jack. It had been his home and where he stored the hides he had collected for trade to the Indians and some of the newcomers in this area. We are told that he has moved on to greener pastures or at least moved on to the Canadian country. John being very insistent upon using as much of the exciting structures as possible added a small building attachment using some of the wood he carried on the ship from his brothers saw mill in Roxbury. With this he was able to put up a pretty presentable building quite quickly. Of course a large portion of the lumber he brought will go to the Company for its building projects. And of course a lot of it went into our permanent home, of which I am ever grateful. John's store building is nothing to compare with the shops of London Town but there is not one thing here to compare with London Town or even our small village of Nazing for that matter. So I will just call it adequate. At least it will take care of the needs of storing what is here and give him a small area to put more articles and foodstuffs when he returns after his first excursion, as a shipping company. If the necessity was not so great for these staples he would not have been allowed to put up any kind of building ahead of the settlements needs.

I again find it hard to believe that there is really not much here in Sandy Hallow. I never know what to expect and the only comparison is my beloved homeland and Boston and Roxbury. I do see many choices as far as a sight for our settlement and our homes are concerned.

Now that the first shop building has been completed John and Thomas have only one thing on their minds. At this time it is the launching of the shipping business. To just say they are anxious to get started would be an understatement. It is on their minds every waking hour. Both of them want very desperately to get going on their first real sailing adventure as a company. Patients are definitely not one of their virtues at this moment.

With all their ardent wishing, to ride the waves of the high sea once more, their immediate departure is to be delayed, by at least a month, or maybe more, by Rev. Blakeman. Rev. Blakeman is our spiritual leader and elder in the company. He called a meeting and in doing so, put a damper on John's, and Thomas's plans to set sail. It seems we are never really able to make our own choices. There is always someone or something standing in the way of what we want to accomplish for ourselves. There were many disagreements at this meeting and John voiced his opinion on several of the subjects that came up.

Rev. Blakeman explained the set order of business for each new plantation. Ours being no different than any other, we will strive to follow the rules, as closely as possible. Our leaders are men of high learning, selected for their positions with a lot of thought and prayers. Several of them were sent here two years ago to secure this land from the Indians. It was very important that all the land in the Pootatuck River region was obtained from these Indians in a legal manner. They were to make a treaty with the Indians and make sure that all the river area was within this treaty. This would prevent the Dutch from taking any of our land and would give us the area needed for the many Englishmen that hopefully will follow.

The Paugusset Indian's, which include the Pootatuck, Cupheag, and other tribes, have summered in this region for generations, fishing and clamming in their small river encampments. They find the abundant supply of oysters and clams a good source of food for their people.

With plenty of fish in the ocean, the river full of fresh water, and the wild animals in the forest, the Indian people are kept from hunger as they live a semi-nomadic, peaceful existence. It is only on rare occasions, that a dispute has momentarily disrupted their pure, simple way of life. I am afraid that our arrival here has been one of those occasions. At first it took some time for the word to reach all the Indian tribes, of the settlement that was to be established here. Once it did, everything seemed to calm down and we rested more easily. We had seen the effects of angry Indians in the Massachusetts Bay area and did not want to experience that again.

When the English of Connecticut were sent forth to make this treaty with the Indians, the Sachem and the others were happy for the English friendship. Mr. Goodwin and Mr. Hopkins were instructed by their hierarchy to make a payment to the Sachem. The Indians have seemed pleased with this payment for their land and we see them or signs of them, only occasionally, in or around Sandy Hollow. There is still a small encampment down by the river in Cupheag that number, anywhere from a few to many, depending on the time of the year.

In the little over two years since we left for this adventure to the Connecticut Country, a relative calm has been the order of existence here. With little communication and such long periods of time between messages, how could anyone really know if an area was war like or calm before arriving their in person. So much of what we find we just have to

accept.  I wonder if there is really any use in being told anything.
Nothing seems to be like we imagine it anyway.

There are none of us who venture to far from home though.  Just the
fear from seeing and hearing of the attacks on settlers in Roxbury and the
surrounding areas in Massachusetts, is enough to remind us to keep a close
and watchful lookout.  Many of us still consider any Indian, to be hostile
and unpredictable.

My mind is relieved by the calmness of the area and the differences
between my life in England and this new land is finally coming together.
For my children, in comparison to the way I was raised in the beautiful
English countryside, this is absolutely a completely new world.  These
past eight or so years from planning to arrival have been very unsettled,
topsy-turvy years.  I do feel now that we have become practically settle
that I have finally landed, right side up.

My concern for my family always makes me wonder what affect all
this will have on their future, mostly for the two younger ones, Liz and
Thomas.  I question in my mind, if the love of the ship isn't Thomas's,
way of striking out at his mixed up emotions.  Maybe the confines of the
ship, give him the security he requires, and the vastness of the ocean,
gives him the freedom he desires.  He has sure become complicated to
figure out, since we left our homeland.

Liz, on the other hand is really experiencing life right here, for
her memory of England and our home there has, nearly been erased by the
new life around her.  I fear she, most of all, will loose touch with the
generations of the past.

What thoughts and fears do exist in my heart?  Like the scale of
life, I precariously balance the old teachings and ways, against the new,
in a never-ending struggle, for what I believe to be the best balance for
my family.    There  is  such  a  fine  line  between  our  guidance  and
interference.  John is always quick to remind me that you learn by doing.
You can't succeed in life if you don't get in there and try it.

John's theory is that, we are like babies all our lives.  We will
fall many times as we seek to walk the course of life, and many times we
will have to struggle back to our feet and try again.  There will be times
when we have help from others and times when we will have to do it on our
own.  His reasoning is it is not always important as to how we achieve
something, but that we continue trying until we have succeeded.

I wonder if our purpose for leaving on this great adventure was
really as we have stated so many times for the betterment of the
children's future and for the betterment of our own life.  I imagine John,
is perhaps wondering right now too, with his schedule for sailing being
opposed by the settlement leaders.  He wants to leave to go get supplies.
The leaders feel that it is more important to secure our area and have the
meetinghouse built before anything else is put up.  We are told in every
worship service that the agenda, set forth, is what God has in his plans
for us.  We come to this new land so we would have the religious freedoms,
which had been taken from us.  So now we must do as our elders request.
Yet each day finds more and more of our house supplies being used by our
leaders for the common areas.  I can in some ways understand the need for

222

this togetherness and yet the selfish part of me wonders why and when our individual needs will be taken care of.

It is extremely hard on John, for he believes with a strong and faithful heart. Yet, he wants and sees other things needed for our existence here, of equal importance. His views are dismissed with very little consideration from the elders and it is decided that the stockade around the common area and the meetinghouse will be built right away. John's insistence backed by the fact that we have had no trouble with the Indian's, is to no avail. Nor that what he could supply would be of help to all these projects. He is told that plans will move forward, as ordered. John and Thomas have no choice but to comply.

When I see these conflicts going on inside John, I do begin to doubt our opting for this life, over what we had. We already had a strong foundation built in England and here in the new country we can hardly get a foundation started. We must pray about this situation more each day, until an answer is found. Especially for John, he needs to have the patients to wait a bit longer, before returning to Boston Harbor. I do pray he will be granted those patients, from God.

I'm not looking forward to the day he sails off. It will be hard having him away from home. I will have to face it when that time comes and I know that it eventually will, for it is inevitable that the direction of his life is definitely out to sea.

I just want the children to be able to look back on their lives, as John and I do ours, and hopefully realize the true love we bare for them. I want them to know that their happiness was truly, all John and I ever wanted. We would have braved most anything for them even if there were only one small slim chance, that their lives would be fuller and more prosperous. Whatever risks were apparent and the ones that were not apparent were still risks we were and are willing to take for a better future for them and for us.

For now, we'll have to put our lives and plantation together as quickly as possible. There are a lot of regulations for this Connecticut Colony. I am very unfamiliar with all of them. We have had the requirements explained many times. Each of us with our own portion of land, land set aside as a common area for the use of everyone. This area would also be used for the training of our men and their military duties. On and on goes the list of the regulations. We must comply with the orders of business or risk punishment and possible loss of our charter. Not wanting that to happen, we all work long and hard to achieve whatever it is, we are supposed to achieve. We do as we are ordered to do and ask few questions.

With a blink of the eye we have rushed and worked our way right through spring and find that late summer is upon us. John is just about ready now to take his ship out to sea. The time has finally come and the watchtower, which is built at the north end of the common, will be a great spot to view the departure of his ship, "The Elizabeth." William, will be on watch, when it embarks, so I will at least get a very good description of the event, from him. He is taking quite an active part in the military settlement and the protection of our area.

223

Each man in our company takes his turn at watch. When the General Court met, they appointed Sergeant Nichols to train the men and exercise them in military discipline. These training days are long and are a requirement for the Colony. From dawn to dusk on most days, we will find our husbands and our sons, marching to the beat of the drums.

We have turned these days into festive affairs, as we all enjoy watching our men do the drills. Watch House Hill, as we have named it is a perfect spot to keep an eye out for trouble and watch our men execute their aptitude for these military maneuvers. It is a great place to observe the Train Band as they are called and socialize with our fellow towns people.

The first Congregational Meeting House. Has the honor of being our very first real, town building placed in the center of our settlement. This is where we will seek to absorb the teachings of God.

If it wasn't for the sadness that has befallen us, with the loss of some of our loved ones, this could be said, a perfect place to live. The area of ground, surrounding the meetinghouse, is filling up much to fast, with the deaths and burial of many of our people that contacted the fever on their overland walk to here. We fervently pray for their souls, and especially for our dear friend Samuel Dennison, who is being laid to rest tomorrow. He was killed when a tree fell on him as he was cutting lumber for a new home. He will be greatly missed by us and especially by his young wife and two small children he leaves behind. Somehow they will have to try a make it on their own at least for a while. Perhaps a kind and gentle sole will take pity on her and take her for his wife and care for the children as his own. Then there is little Jamie Gibson, newborn son of Daniel and Bessy, only living a few days after his birth. We only buried him last week and these tragedies break the hearts of each and everyone of us.

Rev. Blakeman and his wife Jane are ever present to be of assistance in our times of bitter grief. What would we do without them? They meet our spiritual needs and nurture and care for us with such love and patients? The land they picked for their home site, borders ours, and has afforded us a special, loving friendship. We are a fortunate settlement, to have such endearing people as this, for our leaders.

With John sailing now I find even more things to be proud of in our boys. Both John Jr. and William have really taken over since John and Thomas departed for the supplies. This first voyage will be a short voyage, I am told. They must get back before winter with the things we all need to get us through until spring. While William works with the military, John Jr., keeps an eye on the business for John. William helps at night and whenever he has time off from the military drills. These drills keep William very occupied but it is something he seems to love.

We are trying to get a few fields of flaxen and corn planted and harvested which will help stock the commons building a great deal. With all we have to do there is very little spare time. The boys have acquired their father's talent for meeting and greeting people, who came to the shop. I know that anyone that enters the door will be treated with honesty and affection.

224

I am already missing John so very much. He will be quite surprised, at the orders the boys have taken in his absence. It looks as though he will have to turn right around and go for more if he has not anticipated all these needs ahead of time. Knowing John, as I do, he has probably thought far ahead and will be bringing back many of the items that are wanted and have been asked for.

Just keeping up with the books seems like a full time occupation. The boys are busy far into the night. I wonder where they get the energy to keep up with all the things that are required of them. I'm finding, that my energy is running very low, here of late. I enjoy having Liz, at home. Except for helping one of the other families, she spends most of her time with me. It is very important that she stay close to home to learn the tasks that are required of a homemaker. She is very good at sewing and doing needlework and has acquired quite a knack for preparing meals. I wish I had learned more about cooking when I was her age. Caswell Manor never afforded me the privilege of learning to really cook; Anna always did it. I want Liz, to be fully prepared so when the time comes for her to marry, she will be able to not only cook for her family but will be able to take charge and fully manage her household, under the supervision of her husband, of course.

I am ever grateful to my father for providing me the opportunity of seeing a small corner of the business world as I grew up. It has made this transition from England to the New Colonies, perhaps a little easier. At least I can understand John when he speaks of the urgencies of his business.

My adjustments and learning experiences in this new land are many and in the area of cooking for my family and myself has been very challenging from the very beginning. But I have become quite adept now, and when the fresh garden vegetables are ripe, I will enjoy putting them into a succulent dish. I'm proud and happy to see Liz, enjoying these simple duties of womanhood, as I know she will be in need of all of them to carry her through life.

Today I have decided to stay close to home and begin to thin out my garden and plant a few new seeds. Some of the plants have come in much to close. Then there are a few that have already matured and I can pick them and also some of the matured herbs. John and Thomas will still be away for sometime and there are definitely many things around here that need to be taken care of. I can't wait for the children to have a little more spare time to help around here. Any spare time has been depleted with their other tasks.

As I kneel down in my garden, gently turning the dark brown, rich, moist, soil over and over, I pick up hand full after hand full, letting the dark granules slip through my fingers. It cascades in a tiny stream back onto the ground. I pick up one hand full after another and feel the warmth of the morning sun deep within this beautiful earth. Again and again I let the damp earth sift through my fingers. Occasionally I came upon a clump of hardened soil. I gently massaged it, breaking it up and mixing it together with the finer particles. How I love this time in my garden. I marvel at how warm the earth feels and how soft and gentle it is.

This love of mine, for gardening, is something that was nurtured in me from early childhood. I caress every little seed as I place it with care into the hands of Mother Nature. I silently pray it will grow into a fine young plant bearing for me, the luscious vegetables for our dining pleasure. I do not take my plants for granted, for they need the same nurturing, as does a small child.

This vegetable garden is wonderful and I am enjoying getting it started; yet I yearn for the time when I can plant the first of my flowers. I pray it will be soon so when next spring comes, I can enjoy a beautiful bouquet, like the ones in my memory. I want a beautiful flourishing fruit orchard and many different kinds of berries. My flower gardens will border the broad walkways and give pleasure to all our friends, as they came up the walk to visit us. The little lantern holder at the end of the walk will always be there to light the path and guide their steps.

Being totally engrossed in my planting and planning. I completely blanked out the rest of the world around me. Each little seed has to be planted, just so, and spaced, just right, and watered, just enough. Then I cover them with a small portion of fresh, sweet smelling, earth and give them a tiny pat of love and then on to the next row. On and on I go not minding toil or time, just enjoying the complete unity I feel with nature. How wonderful it is here in my own little garden world.

I am so engrossed in what I'm doing that it has kept me from noticing footsteps coming up from behind. It is just a feeling deep within, at first, that I am being watched. Slowly I turn my head as my eyes seek to identify this being that has crept up on me with such stealth. I am startled at the first sight and realization that it was a man who is standing here. My eyes are fixed on first the bare feet, then I let them travel upward to the small loincloth tied about his waist, on past his bear chest with strings of shells and animal teeth, clinging to the moist glistening sweat on his body.

Upward my eyes travel, finally resting on the face of one of the area natives. The shock of seeing one of the native men up so close causes me to gasp with fright and the realization that I am looking into the deep-set, coal black eyes of one of the Indians stills my heart and body. He has eyes that seem to be expressionless. I cannot tell if he is friendly or intends to do me harm. He just stands before me with his arms folded across his chest making no motion in any particular direction. My heart is pounding so loud I am sure he can hear it and I fought to keep control of my senses. In my mind I am running and screaming for help, but in reality, my feet are stuck here beneath me in my garden mud. Not a sound has escaped from his mouth or from mine. Our eyes are just locked on each other like we are both waiting for the other to make the next move. I have no idea what he wants no idea how to talk to him.

I want to run for the safety of the house, but something tells me to move would be very unwise and if I am to move to make it happen very slowly and not give him any provocation to attack me. I am trying with all my heart to keep my eyes as fixed to his face as he is keeping his on mine. Neither of us has dared to blink or make any sudden motions. He is much taller than me and would be looking at nothing but the top of my head if it weren't for my up-tilted face. The look on his face could be called

226

ferocious, with a somewhat quizzical scowl. I try to find my voice feeling that this standoff needs to be broken. But when I try to speak nothing will come out. With more force a tiny squeak escapes my gapping lips. I clear my throat and try again to communicate with this unpredictable native. I have already decided that a scream would not be a good thing to do. The boys were in town and Liz was helping another family with some sewing. I am even far too frightened to cry. All of a sudden, and very swiftly he reaches out and touches my hair. The reddish blond strands tumbled from the ribbon that had loosely held it, tied at the nap of my neck. I feel the ribbon slide past my hand as it falls to the ground.

Total black silence envelops my world and for a brief span of time I am falling, falling, down, down and around and around, swirling and tumbling into a dark deep pit. Then I can remember nothing else happening. My first vision that comes into my frightened mind is that of walls surrounding me. There is a damp musty stench in the air about the room. As my senses start to return I am aware of being on a bed in a very dimly lit room. I open my eyes and blink them and my skin feels cool. As I reach for my forehead I feel a damp cool cloth that has been put there. Again I blink my eyes trying to clear my mind and make it remember so I will know where I am and how I got here. Holding the cloth tight against my head I try to sit up hoping for a better view of my surroundings.

"No, you must stay there. You must not try and move. You have had a terrible fright." The voice I'm hearing seems to be coming from the shadows beyond my vision. I cannot quite make out who is speaking, but there was a slight familiarity in this voice from beyond. I am thinking to myself, who can this be? Where am I and who am I with?

Now my memory is starting to return to me and I remember with terrifying fear, the Indian. My whole body is trembling and shaking violently. My mind is telling me to think fast, you are still alive as I see the shadow of the man in the room moving over closer to me. The apparition came closer bending over me and tucked a coverlet up around my shaking body, pulling me close with his strong muscular arms. I shut my eyes upon his touch and keeping them closed hoped to blank out the fear of what he was going to do to me. Was he now going to kill me this strange Indian person? What had he kept me alive for all this time? And why had he brought me here to his mud hut? I kept my eyes locked shut hoping to close out the horror that had befallen me. I could not bear to look upon this wild native. The only words spoken in this dim existence had been, "don't sit up". I suddenly realize this native man could speak English. He is talking to me in my own language and I am surprised and stunned. I am confused and shocked. My eyes fly open as I turned my face upward to secure a look at my captor.

A more frightening realization than that of being captured by a native floods my senses. I am being held excruciatingly secure in the arms of Eustace Clarke. This situation is more distressing to me than being carried off by the Indian. It takes me just a few minutes to fully comprehend what was taking place and with all the force I can muster up I pushed against the chest of this awful man with all my might, begging him to release me. My extreme fear of Eustace Clarke has brought me back to my full senses.

"Eustace let me go, turn loose of me." I demand, squirming to free myself. "What am I doing here? Am I in your lean-to? How did I get here? I must get home." I continue to talk and struggle for my release at the same time.

"Wait a minute Elizabeth. You are in no condition to go back up to the house right this minute. You just stay right here. I will hold you in my arms and protect you from any harm. I would never leave you to the dangers of life, like your husband has. You are like a fragile flower and need care." Eustace's speech was slurred and he was paying no attention to my request.

"Eustace let me go immediately. John, will never stand for any person, he has put his trust in, to act like this toward his wife. Unhand me at once!" I demanded in as strong a tone as I could manage.

"Now, now Elizabeth, why should you worry at all about what John, would think or do? He is not here to protect you, I am. Besides, all I did was save you from the sureness of death at the hands of a native. Do you really think John, would be mad at me for that?" He continued to speak as he pulled me even closer, tilting my head back.

As I scream in protest he continues to hold me in place. His eyes are glossed over and he keeps running his tongue back and forth over his lips, with a crazed look of passion and lust, on his otherwise expressionless face. He is holding the blanket tight about my body. I struggle and try to fight my way from within his grasp. It is no use, he is much stronger than I, and he has me not only in the confines of his arms, but the coverlet is wrapped much to tight about my body. It is impossible to get my legs and arms free.

"Eustace, I plead, stop, don't, please let me go." I cry out, trying to convince him that I am all right and need to return to my garden. His mind seems to be far away and he looks as if he cannot even hear my words, let alone understand them. He has a desperate look about him that only adds to my fear.

"Come, come Elizabeth, you know you are very grateful and appreciative of my attention." He is speaking nonsense! "You have to know Elizabeth it is my nature to care for and protect lovely ladies such as yourself. Especially when their husbands have deserted them. I feel for you like a family member and I want to protect you, as John would expect a friend of his to do for his wife. John believes me to be a very close friend."

"Family, friendship, you have no idea of the meaning of the words, this is pure unacceptable behavior on you part Eustace and you are a disgusting, vile man. John, will surely see you shot for this or hung from the yardarm of his ship." I said, turning my face from side to side in an attempt to avoid looking at him with his smirk of a smile on his face.

"Elizabeth, my dear. I am trying to save your life." He spat the words out at me, as if in a rage. He held me in the grasp of his strong arms as he tried to keep me from fighting and struggling any further.

228

Scream after scream escapes my mouth. I feared him above anything else in life and I didn't know what his next move would be. Twisting and turning I finally free my face from against his chest and start the incessant loud screams once more, screams of displeasure, screams of fear, screams of hate. They all fell on deaf ears. My trying to fight Eustace seemed to excite him more. I fear for my life, far more from him than I had the native intruder, in my garden. His body is heavy against mine as he tries to quiet my screams. I scream in agony for my strength is no match for his. "John, will kill you for this, he will kill you, Eustace Clarke." My repeating that to Eustace does nothing to him for he just ignores me.

"I doubt that my dear Elizabeth, I think quite the opposite. I have just saved his darling wife from a sure fate of torture and death. I am due my just rewards." He said, with a smirking grin on his face. I am fighting against his tight grip with all my strength but I know it is of no use. I am no match against his strength. My screams grow as loud as I can make them and yet they seem to be heard by nothing but the still air in the room and my own ears. It was as if Eustace, had gone mad and nothing could reach him.

Suddenly, a voice broke through the air. My mind told me it was William. I am sure it is William and the thought spurred hope into my soul. Just this small spurt of hope gave me the strength to break from the death grip that Eustace held me in. Now I was screaming for my life.

"William, here, I am, in here." The door flew open with a crashing thud. Upon hearing William's voice Eustace, released his grasp on me and jumped from the bed. He smoothed back his hair and greeted William, with a concerned look on his face. He left me in a crumpled, rumpled disheveled heap, upon his bed.

"William, your Mother is in here. Come and help me. I am glad you have finally returned." He spoke in a curt, demanding voice.

William, running inside and shouting, "What is she doing in here? Mother, you look awful, what has happened to you? Please explain what has happened?" William continued to question the sight he saw before him. I opened my mouth to tell William what had taken place, but Eustace broke in.

"William, I found your Mother lying in the garden. One of the natives had attack her and when she fainted he had left her for dead. I brought her in here and was just wiping her brow with a cool damp cloth, when I heard your voice. She is in a terrible state. She was trembling so; I rubbed her arms and legs to comfort her from the chill and covered her. I was trying to make her warm and revive her from her faint. She has been so frightened she is not even making sense." He continued, just ignoring the fact that I was even present, and perfectly capable of speaking for myself.

"As I drew in a deep breath and started to explain once more, he immediately interrupted again. I opened my mouth to protest Eustace's, explanation for my disarray and for being in another man's bed, but he would not let me speak. He was determined to continue on. "I hope it was all right to bring Miss Elizabeth here. I just didn't know what else to do! I didn't know the extent of her injuries and my place was closer than

229

the house and I knew there was no one at home to care for her. She has been a bit delirious and imagining all sorts of things. She even thought I was the Indian." He told William.

"You did the right thing Eustace. I am very grateful for you taking care of my mother and I am sure my father, will reward you greatly on his return." William said, looking at me with pity and sympathy. What was I to say now? All of a sudden this rough, vile, shameful, disgusting man has become a hero. I am stunned into disbelief. What would my explanation sound like now? What was I to do? I lay there still on Eustace's bed in total consternation. William and Eustace, standing there, talking as if I were not even in the room. Finally William turned to me and asks.

"Mother, are you really alright, are you hurt in any way? What did that Indian do to you? We will find him and punish him. I am so glad you are still alive. We will have to take more care while father, is away. Can you stand up or should I carry you into the house?" William asked, trying to determine the extent of my injuries.

There never seemed to be an instant between his words to even answer one of his questions. The next thing I knew there was Eustace beside the bed. "Here, I will carry her for you, William. Let me help you." Eustace interjected and proceeded to bend over the bed and was about to lift me into his arms, when I fully realized what was going on. At the sound of Eustace's words, every bit of strength that had left me came rushing back, seven fold. I sprung to my feet in an instant and bolted for the door. Demanding that I walk to the house under my own power. Furry raged inside me and once on my feet I did not hesitate one more moment. I pushed past William and rushed for the house, straightening my skirt as I went. I flung open the door and did not even bother to close it.

I run as fast as I can straight to my room and began tearing the clothing from my body. I want to burn them, I want to wash and cleanse myself in the cool water from the china basin. I needed to wash the dirty filth, of Eustace and his dingy shack from my body and from my sole.

How would I ever face John? The thought of having to tell John what had happened in the garden and in the lean-to sickened my stomach. Even if I could do nothing about it, I shall still feel the shame of being in the lean-to of Eustace Clarke for the rest of my life.

The worst part, he has turned his disgusting act of taking me there instead of to my own home some kind of an act of heroism. I will never be able to convince John or any other, that it was Eustace, who had attack me, not the Indian. What was I to do? I threw myself across the bed letting the tears flow until no more could escape my eyes. I finally fell asleep from pure exhaustion tossing and turning with violent dreams of Eustace.

I find myself awakening in a cold sweat and I notice that the late afternoon shadows are ascending into my room. Hearing a light rap on my bedchamber door makes we come fully back to the present.

"Yes, who is it?" I asked, feeling fear overtaking my body once again.

"It's me, Mama! Liz. Are you all right? Can I come in? I have a cup of tea for you." Liz's sweet voice was soothing to my tattered nerves.

"Yes, Liz, please come in. I guess I fell asleep." I explained, as she entered the room with a tray of tea and biscuits. The look upon her face is like a big question mark. She came quickly to my bedside and sat the tea tray down on the table beside the bed.

"Mama! Mama!" She cried, "I was so frightened when I returned home and heard what had befallen you this morning. It must have been such a terrible fright. When John Jr. and I got home, William told us about what had happened and how the Indian, had attack you and that Mr. Eustace, had saved your life. We are all so thankful that he was here to help you, Mama. Are you really all right? Is there anything else I can do for you?" My blood boiled to even hear the name of Eustace, let alone that he had saved my life. But, by now it was probably spread all over the settlement, the great hero, Eustace Clarke.

I shutter at hearing Liz tell me what Eustace was spreading all around the settlement. I must assure Liz first that I am fine and in my mind I think that this is not a matter that she should have to hear or deal with. I will freshen up and go down in a few minutes for our evening meal. Hearing my intensions does seem to relieve her mind and Liz goes back down to the kitchen area to put the food on the table. I wash my face and pick up my silver hairbrush from the dressing table and begin to brush through my tangled, snarled hair. Finally I tied it back with a pink bow, put on a fresh white waist and black skirt. I slip my feet into my black leather slippers and take a big deep breath. As I let the deep breath out slowly I instinctively know that I have to face whatever lies on the other side of my bedchamber door.

I entered the eating area with a big smile and greeted the children as happily as I could muster up. I try to answer their questions and put their fears to rest. I think they were more afraid of what their father, would think of them, if he had come home to find me dead from an Indian attack, than they were of anything else. I assured them it was no fault of theirs and that their father would not be upset with them in any way.

I quickly change the subject to what their day had been like and what was new in their world. Liz, chattered on and on about the Nichols children and how cute they were. She said, she had made the boys some new breeches and the girls a new petticoat each.

"Are you all through with the sewing for Mrs. Nichols now Liz?" I asked, hoping she would not have to go away from home for a while.

"No, not quite. There are still a few things I have to finish up on the skirts for Mrs. Nichols and she indicated that she could probably find more for me to do." Liz answered.

"Well, it sounds like she is quite pleased with your sewing." I said, not wanting her to suspect my thoughts.

"I do hope so, I enjoy sewing and playing with the children. They are really quite amusing." She said.

"It is nice that you love what you're doing so much." I told her, knowing Mrs. Nichols really appreciated her help with the children and the sewing.

Turning my attention to the boys, I inquired. "John, William, how was your day?" I knew what I was doing; I was just making small talk. I did want to know how the children's day went but more important than that was the fact that I did not want them to ask me about my day. That's what I didn't want. I could not face any of their questions now. Somehow I just need to get through this evening.

As I smile in the boy's direction, John Jr., finally starts talking. "We had a very busy day at the store. It seems as though everyone, needs everything, right away. I sure hope Papa is back from Boston soon." William echoed his sentiments.

"We are at a loss without him. We hardly have a moment to spare all day long. It looks as though we had better close up the shop and stay close to home until father comes back, after what happened to you today mother. There is no shop, or anything else, that is as important as your life. I fear to think what father would do to us if he was to come home and find that harm had come to you or Liz." William's, concern was written all over his face. I could tell he had many more questions he needed answered but was afraid to ask.

"William, you and John, must not neglect any of your duties at the shop or in town. I know this has been a frightening day for all of us but your father needs us. I am sure he will be glad to hear that we needed him so desperately, and I also know that there are going to be many, many times when we are left alone. We will just have to make the best of it. We will take more care and be more watchful from this day on." I replied, assuring them that their father would be quite proud of how they had handled everything, while he was away.

"Mother!" William continued speaking, "When do you think he and Thomas will be sailing back into the town harbor?"

"I really cannot say for sure. It shouldn't be too much longer. This was to be a very short trip. I don't think your father is planning on going out any more now, until next spring. That is why he wants to make sure he brings back as much as he can now. It will have to last us all through the winter and keep the store in good supply until he brings another shipment in. I really hate that he has to be away so much. Perhaps after he gets things started he will turn the shipping over to Thomas and he can spend more time here at home and in the shop." I replied, hoping in my own heart that he would be home soon and stay home.

The children all agreed that they would much prefer to have their father here at home. Then Thomas would be gone most of the time and we would be missing him. Seems like we never find a time for all of us to be here at once, anymore.

"How did you find Mary Wilson's health to be, Liz and the Wells family? Did you see them while you were in town?" Before Liz, could answer my questions a sharp rap came from the door. I freeze in my place. I thought I was beginning to get over the fears of the afternoon, but the knocking brings back the fear in me with a force greater than I could have ever anticipated. It was very late for anyone to be calling and especially to be coming to the back of the house. Both boys jump to their feet at once and head for the door. The musket stands next to the door and quickly William grabs it and John reaches for the latch. As the door swings open I can hear the boys greeting Eustace.

I reached for my chest, for I thought my heart has surely stopped beating. My skin begins to crawl and the palm of my hands turn cold and clammy. I look up as Eustace rushes to my side. He is so brash coming into our eating area and standing here beside me with a grin across his face, as broad as the sea.

"Good evening Miss Elizabeth, I was just stopping by to inquire as to your health. After your terrible shock this morning I wanted to see that you had recovered and were doing well. You still look a bit pale." He said in a most soft and concerned voice.

I can hardly believe my ears. This man has to be an idiot. I dare him inquire about me. I dare him, to set foot in my home. After what he did today taking me to his lean-to. Just what right does he think he has? He has none and I want him out of my house immediately. I almost gave way to my rage, but remembering that the children knew nothing of what had really taken place, I replied with as few words as possible. "I am quite fine. You need not be concerned about me."

All I want him to do is leave, to get out of my sight and out of my home. I dare him he is so arrogant. Of course William and John couldn't stop thanking him and Liz was full of all kinds of questions. "Did he see the Indian? What did he look like? Do you think he will come back?" On and on, they all went question after question.

Finally thinking I was about to the end of my wits with this guise of his, and not to mention it was turning my stomach I stood and hopefully not seeming to impolite, said, " good night, I am sorry to be so abrupt Eustace, but you are right, I have had a very unpleasant experience today. I have had an experience that for as long as I live I will never forget. I am sure I will carry a hate for the man that attack me, until my dying day." I was very careful not to say Indian and I hoped that the meaning behind my statement would sink into his thick head. With that short but sweet statement I turn and go to the stairway and pause looking to make sure the house would once more be secured.

The boys ushered Eustace, to the door, thanking him once more. I was never so happy to hear the door close behind someone in all my life. William and John returned to the room muttering something about they wondered if they should have asked him to stay for tea. That was about all I could stand. I glanced in their direction and excusing myself and started up the stairway to my bedchamber.

233

Feeling that my actions were a bit abrupt, I paused about half way up to say good night, indicating that with all that had happened today, I felt I should turn in early. They all agreed and didn't seem to think anything of my apparent rudeness to Eustace.

Once in the empty silence of my own room my furry overtook me once again. What does this man think he is doing? I wonder if he is afraid I talked to the boys and told them the real truth about how he had treated me. Maybe he is worried now, I hope so. As a matter of fact I hope he is scared to death. Nothing would please me more than for him to be as frightened as I was. Just thinking of him was making me more and more upset. I know I have to put him out of my mind, at least for now. I will figure out how to handle this situation in the morning. I really am far too tired and worn out to think anymore tonight.

My thoughts turn to John and my needing him to be here at home so badly. I need him to be here to listen to me, to defend my honor. I need him to hold me and assure me of his love. All the words Eustace, had said during our encounter came back and they seem even more vivid now than when they were first spoken. Each and every word is haunting me and rolling around in my head. "I would never leave you to the dangers of life, like your husband has. I am only trying to save your life." Over and over the words rang loud and clear in my head.

I cried softly into my feather pillow. I sobbed the words out loud. "What if when John, comes back and I tell him the true story and he hates me or doesn't believe me. What then? Oh! John, what will I do? How can I tell you? What will you think?" The questions flowed forth as did my tears. I had to keep the faith, to know that no matter what had happened, John, would always believe me, of course he would, wouldn't he? More unsettling thoughts!

My night's sleep was a restless one. My dreams were a haze of grotesque figures, coming at me from dark places. I would wake up sharply, sweating profusely; I would fall back asleep almost immediately and continue to dream horrible dreams. I wanted to sleep, to blank out my thoughts, but sleep had brought me no relief. I longed for the light of day to chase the gray shadows away. I was grateful for the morning sun. Somehow the bright light of day gives me courage and security that I could not find in the darkness of night. I still fell tired and I am moving very slowly just taking my time at this getting up process.

As I splash my face with the cool water in the basin I try to push the thoughts of yesterday far back in my mind. There is nothing I can do now until John, comes home. Nothing that is, except stay as far away from Eustace Clarke as possible.

Eustace is still working on one of the upper wings of the house so I know that it will be hard to stay completely away from him. I am so thankful that the house is almost completed. If he could only have it done by the time John, gets back he would be leaving for good. That is if John, doesn't really kill him for what he did. It is just unthinkable and against all of our religious teachings to be in another mans home being a married woman. What an awful thought, I would not want John, to have the blood of another man on his hands. Especially knowing that it was because of me he had to kill him. Yet I knew full well that when John, hears the

234

real story of what took place that there would not be a place in this land called Connecticut were Eustace Clarke, could hide or from which he would be able to escape the rage of John Curtyce.

As I ready myself to greet the day I turned over and over in my mind the thoughts of the past day and the possibilities for my future. I descend the stairway slowly, I seem unsure of what to expect in my own home. I feel intimidated by my own family and these familiar surroundings. What a strange feeling.

The warm fire in the cooking area has taken the chill from the early morning air. I lift the heavy kettle and place it over the flame and hang a pot on a hook over the coals so I can make some porridge. The bread from the day before was in the warming oven and would be sufficient for our breakfast, then I would have to make some more. That is all right I thought to myself. I will spend the morning baking and not go out to work in the garden. I shudder at the thoughts of the Indian and then of Eustace.

Before I can let myself dwell on my memories, Liz and the boys come into the kitchen all declaring they were half starved. I doubted it seriously but I play along with their fun, knowing that their laughter was the best thing for me. I love them all so much. I smile and think just how special each one of them is to their father and I. Breaking my thoughts before they had time to take over my day, I inquired as to the children's plans for this beautiful new morning.

"Well!" William said, "John and I have to go to Watch House Hill and drill for the better part of the morning. Then we have things to do at the store. We will be away for most of the day."

"Are you concerned about staying here alone all day Mama?" Asked John. William interrupted saying. "It will be all right. Eustace said he would be over early this morning and be working in the upper part of the house all day." I felt terrorized at hearing these words. All I could think was no, please dear God, no, I silently prayed. I cannot be alone with that man. I was almost stricken with panic so I keep my face to the fire, not wanting the children to see the fear that I know will show on my face. I could not respond to William's statement. I softly ask Liz, if she would be home today. My heart was beating faster and faster and my ears were ringing as I heard her response.

"No Mama, I told you last evening that Mrs. Nichols, had some more new sewing for me to do and I had a bit to finish up from what I had started. Don't you remember?" She replied almost apologetically.

"Oh, yes I do remember you mentioning it at supper last night. Do you think it would upset her if we sent word by your brothers that you were unable to come today? I really need you to stay home and help me with some baking. I didn't realize last night that we had run plum out of bread and biscuits. You wouldn't mind would you? You could plan to go over to Mrs. Nichols, another day. Maybe I could even go with you then. I would love to spend a few minutes visiting with her and then go and see the shop. John and William can ask her what other day would be good. I am sure she would understand." I was almost pleading with her, hoping that they would not detect my apprehension at staying home alone. I didn't really know if it was a good idea to have Liz, here. What if Eustace was aggressive toward Liz? I am sure he is crazy. I just don't know what this man is capable of doing but I could see no other choices, I knew that I could not stay in this house alone with him. Not for one minute.

"I don't mind at all Mama. Especially if you think it will be all right with Mrs. Nichols. John, will you and William stop by her house on the way to town and deliver the message for Mama and me?" She asked of her brothers.

They both replied at once. "Of course Liz." William, urging John, to hurry for fear they would be late, they both rushed out the door. I breathed a sigh so loud that Liz made a comment as to why I was so out of breath? I just explained that I had not slept well and was just a bit tired. This seemed to ease her concern and we immediately started the baking.

I managed to stay as far away from Eustace, as humanly possible. Only speaking to him when he approached me as to the plans on the upstairs area. I always made it as brief as I could and did not encourage any conversation at all. He didn't seem quite as cocky as he had before.

By evening when the boys returned from town they had unbelievable stories to tell. It seems that Eustace, had spent the previous evening in town making sure everyone herd all about his heroics. No wonder he came to our door so late. He must have just been returning. How proud the townspeople were of him, came the word from William and John. Telling of how they patted him on his back and congratulated him for his bravery. The story had gotten more out of hand than I could have ever imagined.

The account of what had happened as told by Eustace, was that he had fought with the Indian, had injured him and saved my life. The lies kept getting bigger and bigger. I will just stay at home, I don't think I can face anyone let alone listen to them brag about Eustace, when I am in town. How much more can I take? I really don't know!

# CHAPTER 15

The air is warm and the sky is a crystal clear blue and John is coming home! My world will be back right side up and complete once again. How I hate, his sailing off and being gone for such long periods of time. No matter how many times I tell myself that this is necessary, it makes it no easier to endure. Now at last, his ship had been sighted a few days back and today I expect it to dock in the town harbor. I wish our own dock were ready for the ship. It would be that much closer and that much sooner that John would be in my arms and I would feel whole again. I will have to keep myself busy today so that time will pass quickly.

As mid-morning slowly moved toward mid-afternoon, I think how foolish of me to have anticipated time passing swiftly when I had waiting so anxiously for such a long while. I don't know why I thought dusting and cleaning for hours, would make time fly by? As far as I can tell it is standing still or maybe even come to a complete stop?

I want everything to be perfect when John walks in the door. He will be surprised to see the house finished. When he left it was barely started upstairs. I straighten the table beside the entry door and gently hum a country tune. I look around making sure everything is in its specific place. I really have enjoyed putting the finishing touches on the window dressings and arranging the furniture, even though it had taken many hours. At least they were hour's will used and not wasted away doing unproductive, needless tasks.

John and William had been so patient as I moved things from one side of the room to the other and then back again. I was never quite sure just where it looked the best. I really think they said, " Everything looked just perfect," so I would finally stop and they could have a rest. There really isn't that much furniture to move about. I was just so indecisive as to where it should be placed. First over here and then over there, back and forth across the rooms, until one of the boys would say, "Mother." Then I knew it was time to stop.

I was finally feeling a part of this beautiful country. My memory of life in the quaint English countryside seems faded and far away. I am adjusted now to this new way of existence and have become a part something once again. Sometimes when I looked back on our life across the ocean, it seems like only yesterday that I was packing for this long adventure. Then, at other times it seems like it has been an eternity since we left our beautiful home. Has our life really changed? I often wonder if it has really been for the better? Sometimes I can't help letting doubts clutter my mind. When I contemplate the past versus the future, the hardships endured by all of us that have made the sacrifices, and the present state of our lives and the lives around us, I just can't help but question our decisions. I think I would have to say that some has been good and some has been bad. We have only changed locations not our principals and for the sake of our religion that has been for the best. I must say though that enduring all the hardships that this change in our lives caused, some have been unbearable.

Basically it is a good life, I think to myself as I try to keep my mind occupied with positive thoughts. If I stop and look around I find the seasons are similar, the countryside is looking more and more like that of an English countryside and now that there are more people I don't feel so isolated. The cottages and homes look very familiar and the names being given to the new towns and settlements are names of places we left behind.

I do not want anyone to misunderstand me. I am grateful for the freedoms I am enjoying here as much as anyone. It would be impossible for people to go to a new location and not institute a great majority of what they had in the other location into the present one. I like other people might have thought I was starting over but in reality all I am doing is continuing my life in a new setting and putting all that is familiar to me back around me. Of course to be perfectly honest I do hope that we left behind most of our bad habits.

The names of the towns in the Massachusetts Colony are starting to come over to Connecticut too. AS more and more of our countrymen and other new arrivals spread out into the vastness of this new territory, I can see that we are truly making this a "New England".

I just hope and pray that, as we incorporate the new laws into our settlements that the oppressions of the past are not interjected into the present laws. I have seen so many of our leaders, interjecting orders that were used in England and that is frightening to me. Just where would we go from here? We have surely reached the outer limits of the land by now. We must be careful to keep our reasoning just and our thinking straight. The future for our children and our children's children depends on us. Our dreams of a better life for them must not slip by the wayside. We must not let the sacrifices we have made be for nothing.

Now that the house is finished and John's business is at least started, I feel much more settled. My thoughts turn to the passing time as I look around and try to find something more to keep me occupied. I feel a few pangs of hunger, churning in my innards and a nice cup of hot tea would be wonderful. As I take a deep breath and let it out with a big sigh some of my many apprehensions seem to ease. I look around realizing that we have no tea. I will just have to cut me a nice piece of fresh Johnny Cake and get me a cup of fresh goats milk. That will just have to do for now. Oh, how wonderful it smells, coming fresh out of the oven. It must be its delicious aroma that has been taunting me every since I first slid it onto the warming area. Tonight will be a very pleasant evening for our family. I have fresh greens ready to cook, the boys will bring in fresh fowl to roast, I have this delicious Johnny Cake, and a scrumptious baked custard. This will be a very special meal for my very special family!

The tiny flutters in the pit of my stomach are a sure sign I am having a hard time containing my excitement. I think I will glance out the window once more toward that great expanse of water and maybe I can see the large white, bellowing sails of "The Elizabeth" coming in close to shore. As I reach the window and scan the horizon my heart nearly jumps right out of my mouth. Could that be John's ship? Oh how I hope so. I will be so disappointed if the ship does not dock today. I must calm myself for even if that is John's ship, it will be hours before it reaches the dock and everything is unloaded and he is home. I sigh another sigh this time in disappointment at my thoughts and realizations. My inner self tells me to have patients yes Elizabeth patients. I know that no amount of wanting will make that ship get here any faster.

Looking again toward the water I ascertain that from where I am the ship is just not moving at all. At least it sure isn't moving fast enough for me. When last I peeked out until now I would think it should have reached shore but it hasn't. I think perhaps my eyes are playing tricks on me. The wind is blowing strong and steady, so that should make it get her quicker, shouldn't it? I seem to be questioning myself in my mind and then reprimanded myself for being so impatient. I know that all these questions in my mind do not do me one bit of good. I know it, but I can't stop my mind from speculating. I can't stop thinking even if I want to. I am like a small child waiting for a special, promised treat.

The sun slowly moves across the sky as the hours of the day sweep away. The dust from the floors has also been swept away and I continue to keep a watchful lookout. If I still wasn't so frightened about being out of the house alone I would walk to the edge of the clearing so I could watch the big ship, with its bellowing white sails drift casually into the dock. My thoughts and imagination caused me to stop and listen and see if I could here the sails snapping in the brisk wind. I wanted to be at the dock when it did come in and yet I knew I had better stay close to the house. My experience with the native was still too fresh in my mind and chills of fright shutter down my spine just thinking about it. No I will just wait here in our wonderful, beautiful home.

After checking the fire and making sure all was tidy and neat on the lower level, I start up the staircase carrying in my arms the freshly pressed curtains, for the upstairs windows. I was anxious to see how they looked. I wanted them to add just the right finishing touch to our cozy new bedchamber. I pull the dressing stool over to the window and climb up on it. What a breath taking view from way up here. Oh, it is so beautiful! The placement of the house gives us such a wonderful look at the ocean and shoreline below. I am glad I decided to use a delicate material for these curtains. Not that I had much choice in the matter. They will allow a lot of light to come in during the day and frame the beautiful scenery below. Maybe John will bring back some more material and I can make curtains for the other windows and dress up the rest of the rooms, a little bit more.

I grab the curtains from the back of the bedpost and put all other thoughts aside as I proceed to hang them. I adjust the ruffles and fuss with the tiebacks. Then stepping off the stool I back up to get a better look. I have a real sense of pride and accomplishment for I have created something all by myself and they are very pleasing to the eye. Climbing back up on the dressing stool I fuss a bit more over just the right twist here and there and then jump down and step back and look again. I know I am just creating busy work now. But I am having fun, and it is keeping my mind and hands occupied until John and Thomas come running in the door.

Looking once more out the window I come to the conclusion that the ship has put down anchor way out there for it doesn't look as if it has moved an inch. The more anxious I get the slower the time seems to pass. Ho hum, what to do? I wonder to myself as I take on last glance out the window and around the bedchamber before going out into the hallway.

Proceeding to the top of the stairs I suddenly stop. For just one instant my mind flashes back to Caswell Manor and I can see a vision of the beautiful portraits of Mama and Papa on the wall of the entry hall. I still miss those familiar things from my past so very much. No matter how I try to deny myself that fact, it remains within my soul.

I dusted off the beautiful staircase as I go down to the landing. As the landing stairway turns, I stopped momentarily to admire the beautiful stained glass window, that let in beautiful colored light beams from the outside. They danced about in the air and found a resting place upon the walls, giving a rainbow of glistening light crystals, to delight my day. Yes, the house had turned out to be more than I had dreamed it ever could be.

The rooms in the upper level are very large and square. A fireplace for warmth stands against the inner wall. Two sets of multi pained windows grace the outer wall. These large windows give the rooms a feeling of vastness. The windows are my favorite part of this spacious house. I can look out of them and see forever, or so it seems. Maybe that is why I wanted our bedchamber built so much like the one at Caswell. I could not see the ocean, at Caswell, but I did have my colorful, beautiful garden below to look at and enjoy. Here I have the best of both settings. A smile creases my mouth for my flower garden has not even been started. Oh well I will have the best of both settings as soon as I get my roses in the ground. I just checked the bare root plants the other day and they look good. I know I will enjoy looking out all these windows just as I did those in England. I will open the curtains in the early morning and look out upon my beautiful roses and will remember my homeland with fond memories.

Again as the thoughts travel through my mind, I realize even more that what we were creating here is so much a replica of what we left behind. Our dreams were to start anew. What is anew? Our new creation is nothing but our remembrances built in a different place and in another time.

As I turn and go back up the stairs to our bedchamber I feel almost giddy at the prospects of John's homecoming. I take just one more tiny moment to make sure that everything in this room is just perfect. I had placed my rocking chair close to the window, just as it had been at Caswell. A small table next to it replicated, what I had left behind. I will someday be able to sit here and have a nice cup of hot tea. Surely they will not keep this ban on tea forever. I don't seem to understand all the complications of this new life. But being a female, it is best if I don't ask about these bans. That thought makes me feel so very frustrated. Why should being a woman, eliminate anyone from questioning and having thoughts of their own? Maybe John, can explain these new laws to me better when he gets home. Anyway this will be a nice bright spot to sit and sew. The bright light of day will lend itself to helping me see better as I stitch a fine new shirt for John, or perhaps a new apron for myself.

It doesn't matter that everything that has been done both in building the house and decorating, is copied from our home in England. There was nothing at Caswell Manor that I wanted to leave behind anyway. If I could have I would have brought it with me, just as it was. It is a

240

compliment to recreate something that we love and care about. If we hadn't loved it, we wouldn't want to duplicate it. I'm proud of my family and my home. My memories are all I have and I never want to part with one small particle of them. I want my heritage to always be a part of my life and a part of my children's lives.

As I approach the landing once more I think to myself, this window on the landing would need nothing. It is beautiful just as it is. As I lifted my foot to ascend down I almost lost my balance. I stop in mid step and turn quickly and I found myself going back up to take a third look at the bedchamber. Was it really as I wanted it to be, for the return of my husband? Was it perfect or at least as perfect as I could make it? I stood in the middle of the room and turned my head first one way and then the other.

"I wonder if John will like it too?" I hadn't realized, I had spoken out loud and I was startled when a voice from behind answered me. I jumped, as I was so startled when I realized that there was someone else in the room with me. It took a moment for me to comprehend what was happening.

"Well I think he will like it just fine. As a matter of fact he likes it very much." Came the familiar sound of John's voice.

"Oh John, your home, I can't believe you are really here. I have been watching for you all day. How could you have crept up on me like this? You have been gone far to long and so much has been done and so many things have happened and I missed you so very much and I love you so very much. Please don't ever go away again John. Please, please, don't leave me again." My words tumbled uncontrollably from my trembling lips.

"My, my Elizabeth, why the tears? You are supposed to be happy that I am home. I hope they are tears of joy, for if they aren't I shall just have, to leave again." John smiled as he pulled me close to his body and enveloped me in his strong, caressing embrace.

"John, don't make fun of me. I have missed you so very much and have needed you home with me. You know how easily I cry." I stammered forth an explanation.

"I know my dear Elizabeth, I am as joyful at being home, as you are to have me. I am only sorry that you have had so much trouble while I was away." John said, moving me out to an arms length and looking me over.

"Trouble, what might you be speaking about John?" I questioned, holding my breath.

"The trouble with the Indian, Elizabeth. You didn't have more than that did you? I should think that would have been enough for a lifetime." He answered, once again pulling me close to him.

"Yes John it was more than enough for a lifetime. I was frightened near to death. I have stayed very near the house since then and haven't even tended to my garden, the way I should. I am afraid to be alone out

241

there. How did you hear about it so quickly?" I questioned, wondering if he had already seen his boys.

"You know Elizabeth, there is nothing that escapes the ears of the men at the dock. Also Eustace met the ship and walked back up home with me. Thomas stayed aboard to tie things up and keep an eye on the unloading. Eustace told me how he had come upon you in the garden and that one of the local Indians was attacking you.

Were you hurt in any way, Elizabeth? You look so beautiful to my hungry eyes, it is hard to perceive the picture Eustace, painted of how he fought off the Indian and shot at him with his musket. He said, he thought he had wounded him but didn't have time to take pursuit, as he had to attend to you. I am ever so grateful for his quick actions and alertness. I am especially grateful to him for saving the life of my beautiful wife. I don't know what I would have done, if I had come home to find that some harm had come to you. I want you to tell me all about it Elizabeth, now that I am home we will try and find the Indian.

I will need a good description of him and I will get the best trackers to pursue him. We will make sure that he is unable to bother any of our people again. Let alone pray upon our women and children. We must not tolerate any hostile or aggressive behavior from these natives." John said to assure me he would do everything in his power to make my world safe once again.

Yes, I could give John a description of my attacker, but it would not be the description he is expecting. "It was Eustace, he took me into his lean-to and when I awoke I was lying upon his bed. I don't know what I would have done if William had not come in when he did. I was so frightened. I screamed, and cried out, and screamed again. Finally William heard me as he was coming home. William saved my life John. It was so dreadful and so horrible and I have his face burned in my memory and I will never be able to forget it or his hands touching me. How I hated him being so near to me. I will always, always be afraid of him and I hate him John. He is no good, no good at all." As I spat out my feelings, I felt an instant release of my fears, now John, knew the truth.

"Hear! Hear! Elizabeth, you are shaking all over. Here let me hold you close. You have had such a terrible fright. You will never have to see him again Elizabeth, never, I promise you that. I will stay close to you and protect you. I am sure as long as I am home there will be no more trouble with the Indian. He has probably gone many miles away by now and you have nothing to fear from him." John assured me.

"The Indian, nothing to fear from the Indian?" I screamed in my mind as it raced faster and faster. John thinks I am speaking of the Indian, but I am talking about my fear of Eustace. I am speaking of, waking up in his lean-to with his arms wrapped about me. The coverlet keeping my arms and legs restrained. Suddenly I realize what John, was saying and that he was not even really listening to what I said. With all of my strength and determination within my sole I looked straight into John's eyes.

"John will you please listen to what I am trying to say. I fear you do not understand where the blame lies in this matter. Won't you

242

please listen? I am not nearly as afraid of the Indian as I am of Eustace Clarke. He is a rough, crude man." I tried once again to explain what had really happened that nefarious day, to John.

"Now Elizabeth is that any way to talk about the man who saved your life? He told me that you were in a state of hysteria when you awoke and had lashed out at his attempts to comfort you with great fierceness. That is understandable, under the circumstances. He said, you must have thought he was the Indian and it took a great amount of strength and restraint, to calm you down." John continued to speak, his words sounding like something out of one of my bad dreams.

"John, I was afraid of him, I was." I stammered, please believe me, I begged.

"Yes, I can understand that Elizabeth, after all you had been through, you would naturally be frightened of anyone at that moment. Eustace understands perfectly and knows you were reacting out of fright and holds no ill feeling toward you. He was just glad to be of service in my absence. You know he really thought you were dead. He said, he had rubbed your back trying to bring the life back into you and had put his ear close to your lips to listen for your breathing. He was quite frightened and very relieved when you finally recovered.

"Enough of that talk for now. You seem quite fit and a beautiful sight before my eyes. We will just be thankful for the kindness of our friends and a lot more careful in the future." John stated, giving me a broad smile and loving kiss. My body curled into his and I caressed his face in my hands and thanked God, for returning him to me. Further attempts to explain were brushed aside. I knew he really didn't understand at all. Eustace had done a thorough and convincing job of lying. John, put an end to our conversation by declaring we would never speak of this incident again.

"I rushed home from the ship to see my beautiful wife and home, not to talk of unpleasant things. Now show me around the house Elizabeth. From what I have seen so far Eustace, did a beautiful job of building it and you have done a magnificent job of decorating it. What a pair you two make." My ears revolted at his statement. I couldn't find any part of it a compliment. I started to protest so that I could tell John, what Eustace had really done to me, but his lips were upon mine in a passionate, loving kiss, once more. My mind went blank and the only thing that mattered was that John, was home and I loved him and he loved me and we were together.

We spent the afternoon walking around the grounds and I showed John the garden spot where I had been attack. I tried desperately not to let my memories spoil our walk. Some of the small plants had already popped their little heads up through the soil and in a few short weeks we would have another few rows of fresh beets and greens on our table. Life was starting to look fresh and new.

John suggested planting some of the corn seeds we had brought from Roxbury in one of the far fields and he would work with the boys to build some fences to keep the livestock in. He informed me that he had managed to bring a few more little animals on the ship. There was so much

243

excitement in his voice, I forgot the past and dreamed with him, our dreams of the future.

When early evening arrived, we were upstairs looking over the newer part of the house when we heard the door open and the familiar voice of Thomas, calling out. I rushed to the top of the stairs and hoisting my skirt so as not to trip, went scurrying as fast as my feet would travel to greet him.

"Thomas, Thomas, here we are, welcome home. You have been greatly missed. It is so good to see you. Oh my, you have grown a foot since you left and your hair is streaked with golden strands from the sun." I commented as I gave him a hug.

"My Mama, you sure don't miss a thing do you? How are John and William and Liz? I have really missed them. Many of their friends in Roxbury and Suckiaug send them greetings. I have so much to tell them. Where are they?" He questioned as fast as the words could escape his mouth.

"Well, Elizabeth is at Mrs. Nichols doing some sewing and the boys are in town taking care of the store and practicing their drills on the Common. They should be home any time now and we will all be able to get caught up on the news of the family and friends, around the supper table. Put your things away and just enjoy being home. I will take care of finishing getting something ready to eat for our evening meal." I said, as I moved to the cooking area and checked on the progress of the food I had already started. I tried to fix something for everyone a kind of everyone's favorite food supper. Yes, this was a very special day that deserved a very special meal.

When the rest of the children arrived from town I quickly had John Jr. and William prepare the fowl they brought with them. When it was placed on the spits we all gathered around the table and the chatter was so loud and constant it is a wonder that anyone could understand the other. Of course we had to know how William and Sarah were doing and how all the family was? Thomas had messages for everyone and stories about everything. We talked on and on I even accomplished putting supper on the table without missing a bit of the conversation. We ate and talked so much we were surprised to find the only light in the room was the dim glow from the cooking area. John finally realizing that we had been so engrossed in our conversation that we were almost in total darkness. He quickly got up and taking a small twig from the wood stack he caught a fire on its end and lit the candles on the table, he tossed the stick into the fireplace and sat right back down.

This was a wonderful time, the voyage had been a good one and John was able to bring many things back with him that would be needed for the store. John Jr. and William, told him about the orders and what people were asking for the most. I could see by the look on John's face, that he was pleased with the way the boys had handled things while he was away. He advised them that he looked forward to going into town early in the morning and looking over the books and orders for himself.

Yes, we were in our new home, and the scale was tipped more toward the settled side, than the unsettled side and we were happy. What more

244

could a mother ask for than to have her loving husband and wonderful, happy children surrounding her. This was indeed a very memorable day, to put in my memory book.

Bright and early the next morning we found ourselves on the path to town. Even if town was not in any way the grand gabled roofed buildings of our English villages, it was ours. To be exact it is a confused, conglomerate of half thrown together shacks. It is getting much better day-by-day though and from the time of our arrival until now there have been many good changes and the merchants are fixing up the buildings to look more orderly and pleasant to the eye. At first it was a matter of just having a place to work or sell out of, for other needs of our community were of greater importance than what the place looks like.

We greeted our neighbors as we passed, many asked if the ship had been unloaded and if special items would be available. John, had not really anticipated such a response to his shop and was very pleased when the boys showed him what they had accomplished while he and Thomas were away. They had not only managed to put a presentable building together but had arranged what little stock we had, very neatly and tagged every item with a price tag. I could tell that John wanted to go over the books with them so I made an excuse to wander around and see some of our friends.

I had not been in town for some time and it would be nice to just stroll about and see what was going on. I told John that I would be back in an hour or so. I wanted him to enjoy this time with his sons. Liz had wandered out earlier to visit with some of her friends, perhaps I would meet her along the street and we could walk together. A quick kiss on the cheek and I was out the door. This excursion was going to be pure, pleasure for me. I had no schedule, no timetable, no cares or fearful thoughts. It would be just a leisurely walk around my very own beautiful town.

Lets see where shall I go first? I know I want to see the ship. I wonder if it looks the same? The men will be busy for quite a while so I don't even have to hurry. I turn the corner and start down the slope from Sandy Hollow toward the town dock. I think of how nice it is to just be able to take my time and enjoy my walk. It would also give the men plenty of time to look over the books and what ever else they want to do.

The early morning sun is warm upon my cheeks and the fresh smell of the sea air invigorating. The cool crisp sea breeze blew gently and as I enjoy my stroll I find at times I even had to pull my shawl about my shoulders to ward off the chill of the afternoon air. I am surprised when I looked back up the hill and find that Sandy Hollow is really beginning to take on the looks of a real town. More and more the town is spreading out and the little hollow we first sat foot in was winding its way up and out, growing more and more each and every day.

Cupheag the Indian village, sat quaintly at the waters edge with a dug out canoe, bobbing in the water and a few of the smaller Indian children playing about. The banks of the Pootatuck were crowded with the temporary mud dwellings that had been left vacant. It gave the appearance that Cupheag and Sandy Hollow was somehow, intertwined.

Lost in my own thoughts I find myself saying good day to this one or that, as I walk along the path. Without even realizing it I was speaking or nodding to people and not even paying one speck of attention, to which person the voices belonged. The changes are many and there seems to be so many more people than I had remembered being in town. The familiar faces were interwoven with faces of strangers. Had it been that long since I was in town? The boys had told me of several new ships that had come into harbor, but I never realized that so many new people had stayed. I must take more notice from now on and keep up on what is going on. Everything is happening so quickly. In this short span of time we seem to have over crowded ourselves on the banks of this beautiful river. It does not seem as open as before.

I am amazed at how comfortable I am. I feel free and unafraid. I walk on even venturing down to the middle of the dock. I stop to enjoy watching the men unloading the ship. My heart swells with pride at seeing John's ship, sway to and fro in the light current. It sure brings a surge of pride to my heart just to know that it is his very own ship and it has given him so much pleasure to finally be doing the things he had dreamed so long of doing here in his new homeland.

I had really kept myself too cooped up while John was away. I was surely enjoying this new unrestrained freedom. People along the way were probably wondering what I was doing walking around without John or one of the boys at my side but I really didn't care. I finally felt as if I belonged somewhere. This was our town, my home, I belonged, and I finally had a place to call home once again. Remaining in my own little world gave me cause for alarm when a light tap on my shoulder interrupted my enjoyment and brought me back to reality. As I stopped and turned to see who was seeking my attention I was surprised to see Eustace standing there.

"Good day Liz, and how be you this fine morning? I trust you are feeling fine and that the family is doing well. I am surprised to find you walking about the dock area unescorted. Have you lost your husband already?" Eustace greeted me with an air of superiority. A cold chill ran down my spine and I tried to calm my heart, which was pounding so hard inside my chest that I was sure Eustace, could here it. With my insides shaking I tried to answer him without showing the emotions that were running through every inch me.

"Good day Eustace. Thank you, for your concern of my family. Yes, I am pleased to say they are all well and doing just fine. And to the other question, no, I have not lost my husband." I said curtly.

"You must be pleased to have John back home with you, Liz. He shouldn't leave one as lovely as you alone so long at a time. It could be very dangerous you know." He stated with that sinister grin, curling his lip up around his pearl white teeth.

"Eustace, please refrain from calling me Liz and I resent your familiar tone in this unexpected conversation. I also did not appreciate you telling John about the Indian at the house, before I had a chance to explain the way it happened in my own words. I am very appreciative of your concern for my family but John and the boys are most capable of taking care of their own people. John is grateful that you were near by

246

when the Indian came to the house but you did not have to lie about what happened. The Indian did not hurt me in any way. You gave me much more of a fright than the Indian ever could have." I lashed out at Eustace, letting all my pent up thoughts tumble out of my mouth. He responded so quickly I hardly had time to think. "Now, now Liz you know, I am only trying to sooth your tattered nerves and make sure you are doing well.

"My mind was quite alright Eustace Clarke and I am perfectly aware of what was going on. If you are worried about what John thinks of you, you needn't. He is grateful for your friendship, such as it is. If he ever finds out the truth he will be after you within the blink of an eye. You had better watch you step Eustace Clarke or I will tell him every detail of what went on in your lean-to and make sure he understands the difference between a so called friend and a friendly Indian." I spat out my words with furry in my voice, for I wanted Eustace to know, that I had no intention of letting some poor Indian take the blame for his acts.

"Liz, you sound a little miffed at me. I was only trying to take care of you for John. That is the least I could do for a good friend." He continued to speak, taunting me with every word.

"Stop calling me Liz. Your arrogance is unbelievable and this conversation will cease right now. You just better watch your step, if you know what is good for you." I said and turned and briskly started back up the hill.

"I would rather watch yours, my darling Liz, much rather." Eustace words carried on the wind as it blew past my ear. All I wanted to do was get away from this vile man. He was impossible. I almost ran all the way back up to the store. I was completely out of breath when I arrived at the front door of the shop. I opened the door quickly and rushed inside as if a wild animal was running after me and very close to me.

"Elizabeth, what is wrong, you are as white as a ghost and so out of breath. What has frightened you so?" John demanded an answer. He looked so fearful he almost scared me.

"Oh, frightened, I'm not frightened. I just must have walked to fast up the hill from the dock area. Here I will just sit down here on this crate and rest a few minutes and then I will look and feel better." I said as I pulled the crate under me and sat atop it very thankful that it was close at hand. I tried to compose myself for I am determined that I will not let this dreadful man spoil my day, not this day or any other.

The men were so engrossed in what they were doing and didn't really give me much more notice. But while setting on the crate trying hard to compose myself, I had the time to wonder as to why I could not make John understand just how much Eustace bothered me and how he was always insinuating things. Why couldn't I tell him that I felt that he was being suggestive and far too familiar? Was it because I was afraid I would look like the fool and John would believe Eustace over me? Where had all my confidence gone? Why would John not believe me? What was wrong with me, why did I let this man bother me so? All the questions that were stuck in my head just kept rolling round and round and I had no good answers for any of them. I took a deep breath and my heart finally returned to a

247

normal beat. I had tried; perhaps there will be a time in the future when John will be in a more receptive mood. Maybe I will try again then.

I was glad when John and the boys started closing up the shop and we were ready to return home. I was tired and after seeing Eustace again, I wanted the security of my own house. The shadows were beginning to get long and the daylight is about to be snuffed out by the oncoming darkness of nightfall. We hurried and locked the doors to the shop and started up the hill. We are going home! What a good sound that word has for me. Home, a real home! Did I really dare to plant my feet firmly on this soil and let it creep deep into marrow of my bones? Could I count on this to be our final settling place? I want so to believe that it will be. I really do, but some little part of me is afraid that if I fall in love with this place called Connecticut and really settle in, that the day will come, when I will once again have to get up and move on. I must be honest, I don't know if I could. I don't know if I could ever pick up and totally start all over again. I have such a great big need within the very fiber of my being, too belong and to be steadfast and secure, with the love of my family about me. That is all I want from life.

I cling tight to John's arm and we walk silently up the darkening path, the boys and Liz, running far ahead of us. Oh, the spirit of youth, how wonderful it is. Where has my youth gone? I must try and find it or at least find its memory and secure it firmly along with my feet in this the land of our choice.

248

# CHAPTER 16

ALPHA & OMEGA

The Beginning And The End

"Thank you so much for all you kind words, Mrs. Blakeman." I said as I glanced around the room. "Everyone has been so kind to our family." My, I have repeated the same sentence over and over, I think to myself as I continued to smile up at Mrs. Blakeman. I speak first to this person and then to that one. As I breathe in deeply and release it slowly letting a long lingering sigh escapes me. Mrs. Blakeman looks concerned but neither of us continues the conversation. I have this nagging desire to be alone, alone with my thoughts, alone with my sorrow. The time seems right and if it isn't I can't do anything about it, for my feet seem to have a mind of their own and without thinking of the consequences I find myself running, fleeing swiftly from the crowd in the parlor. I neither look left or right as I pass the well-meaning town folks who have come to our home today to pay their respects. Up the stairway my feet trod. I feel like a giant hand is pushing me from behind. I stumble into a room. Stopping to catch my breath I realize I have ended up right in Mama's bed chamber with a stack of tightly held, black leather books clutched close to my chest. The flaking worn leather edges of the tiny books are sticking to the palms of my sweat-laden hands. I wipe at a trickle of perspiration on my brow. I can feel the flakes from the leather merge with the sweat and slither past my temple to my chin.

I know that my actions have left a black smudge on my face but I have no desire to stop and clean it off. The beautiful blue delft china pitcher and bowl on the bedchamber washstand has no water in it anyway. My mind seems to be questing why I have ended up where I am, for some unexplainable and unknown reason I seem to have rushed into this room rather than some other room in the house. I am just too tired to search for an explanation. My swift forward motion just seemed to drop me here and here I stand clinging to a bedpost for dear life. I let the entire weight of my body rest upon the massive mahogany bedstead and listen to my heart pound wildly in my chest. I again rub my hand across my moist forehead. I am so hot I anticipate a searing hot skin, but find a cold clammy brow instead. The tightness of my throat makes it hard to swallow and is like a warning bell, letting me know that the room has been depleted of fresh air far too long.

My mind is talking to me as if it is an entity unto itself. The thoughts in my head cause me to move as if ordered to do so by some mysterious person, I cannot see. My chest heaves as I inhale as much air as I can possibly hold. Slowly I try and calm myself and walk toward the large double window. The window is tremendous in size and looks somewhat out of place in accordance with the rest of the room. My eyes caress the darkened wood with the exquisite hand hewn casements, rubbed smooth through time, by the loving fingers of Mama's grandchildren. They have been nicked and marred, scratched and dirtied all by loving little fingers.

I let my own fingers move aimlessly to and fro, retracing a previously used route along the sills edge. Perhaps I am subconsciously hoping for an explanation for the turmoil I found myself in today. But it isn't my mind; it is a splinter of wood that is pricking deep into my fingertip that brings me out of my thoughts and back to the realities of the moment. Picking at the tip of little sliver sticking out I grasp it with my fingernail and feel it ease its way from beneath my skin and the flow of blood rushes forth to spurt out at me. I inhale allowing myself a moment of time, to indulge myself and try to relax. I wet the stricken area with the tip of my tongue and press my thumb hard against it trying to stop the bleeding. All the while I let my eyes rove the expanse of the breathtaking seascape that greets me far below and I know instantly why Papa had positioned the house just this way and with such a large window in this very spot.

My mind takes over my will once more as I remember how often the children have stood here in this exact spot, gripping the edges of the window, steadying their bodies on tipped toes, as they tried to balance themselves hoping to secure a better view of the beautiful rolling fields, wooded forest lands, elegant garden and this breathtaking panoramic scene of the gorgeous waves crashing against the rocky shore, far below. The little ships bobbing up and down in the small harbor always caused great excitement amongst them. A smile crinkles my face, for I can still envision the children in my mind, all jumping up and down, each jockeying for a coveted position to spy something before the other saw it. Oh, they were so little then and that time seems so long ago. Yet with a blink of my eye I can transverse back to rekindle in my soul the smell of the freshness in the newly cut timbers and the excitement in our hearts when this home was first completed. This wood was light in color then with each grain showing through in a magnificent, distinct pattern. I know of no other place in this house that pleased Mama more. Yes, Papa had chosen the perfect spot, giving Mama such a breathtakingly splendid view of this beautiful blue-green ocean below. Today the frothy, white capped waves are crashing furiously against the jagged rock strewn shoreline far below. They seem to be in empathy with my mood. The ships are sloshing to and fro looking as disorganized as my thoughts. I pull back the massive, tightly woven paisley drapery, and securing them with a braided gold, tassel ended cord I marvel at how beautiful they still look and how wonderfully they have stood the test of time. They gave the shear tie backed curtains that Mama had made into a framed picture. Mama was so proud of her accomplishment.

The light the window emits into the room amazes me. The glare from the afternoon sun hurts my eyes it is so bright. But I do not want them closed right now no matter how bright the sun. Everything put into this house or built into this house, has a purpose. Very little was left to chance. The thick cloth of the draperies was to keep out the cold of the winter when shut and let in the warmth of the summer sun when needed. This allowed Mama complete and total control over what she desired in her bedchamber.

I think I prefer it as it is now with the bright rays of sunlight streaming through the bubbled, hand blown glass panes. Papa had ordered a shipment of this hand blown glass from England, a request that was not easily carried out. There was no glass to be had here in the new land and the oiled paper cover that was normally used was not what he wanted. He had to wait many months for his window glass to arrive but it was well worth the wait.    Our Papa was never one to use something that he considered second best.    When he set his mind on something he was heaven bent on making his wishes come true, not minding the wait as long as the end result was what he wanted.    The glass was hand blown and etched along all four sides of the tiny panes and as the sun pierces through the glass it gives this room a lovely sparkle as little rainbows appear hear and there on the ceiling and walls, dancing around and around.

As I let my eyes drift to the horizon far off in the distance I discern a few white fluffs of clouds starting to peek up at us.    Perhaps in time they will produce some much needed rain and it will help to cool the air.    I am not willing to wait for the rain for my needs are more urgent.    I must have some fresh air right now.    Reaching out I push the sash up a crack.    It moves only a little but with that small opening comes a gentle breeze.    As refreshing as it feels it is still not enough of a breeze to move the sedentary, dank air with the pungent fume that hangs heavily in here since Mama's death.    I strain to raise the sash a smidgen higher giving the humid outside air more space to flow through hoping to bring some freshness in.    The humidity from outside mixing with the damp air from within is only causing a musky odor to cling to my nostrils.    The smell of sickness still lingers and nauseates my innards.    My stomach wrenches in revulsion.    The stench has a tenacious hold on these surroundings.

Being so intent on getting some air into the room I totally forgot about the little books that I still held tight under one arm.    I must have shifted them to one side as I pushed against the window.    The moisture was now beginning to run down my skin.    It traveled past my wrist, down my arm, making its own path to my elbow and then aimlessly dripping onto the floor.    Realizing I must put the books aside for the moment, I do so, before I ruin them with my own body fluids.    I gently place them on the side table to Mama's bed and raise the window as far up as it can possibly go.

The fresh sea breeze rushes in as if it has been waiting for just such an opportunity.    It's impact into the room bellows out the curtains and sends loose items spilling around the floor.    I let things fall where they may and greet the cool air with gratitude, breathing deep, filling my lungs to capacity.    I can feel the winds soft cooling effect as it flows ever so gently through my moist hair.    I stand silently and steady, enjoying the freshness of the moment.    I am not willing to allow either thought or deed to interrupt the pleasantness about me.    For a brief moment I revel in this quiet solitude.

Like most things in my life this was to be but another fleeting moment in time, for my mind would not let me pause for long from the reality of the present.    As my eyes move about I glance down at the small books lying upon Mama's bedside table.    It takes me only a moment to remember what had brought me to this place.    I pull the old rocker close to the open window and sit down.

Pressing my toe gently against the warped, aged wood floor, I feel the familiar motion begin.    The distinct creaking friction between the worn rungs of the rocker and old boards, marking out that familiar rhythm, like a song from childhood being replayed over and over in my mind.

251

I close my eyes tightly and in my isolated reverie I can feel the security of my mother's arms about me. My mind seems to be making me remember just how it felt to rest my head gently against her shoulder. Oh how often through the years she had cradled me in her strong, loving arms. This very chair had always been a comfort as long as it was Mama who sat in it with any of us on her lap. The beautiful little baby face carved, gracefully into the back of the chair. "An angel it was," she always said. Watching over her babies, guarding them from the forces of evil.

No matter where she was in the house, when one of the babies needed to be comforted or held, Mama always retreated to her bedchamber and this rocker. We all knew that the chair with the little carved face was her favorite.

As I sit gently rocking back and forth, I too, have a feeling of great comfort. The high back and the gently curved side arms wrap around me, hugging as if protecting me in some way. Her children and her grandchildren had been rocked many a mile in this old chair. It was one of the few pieces of furniture she had with her from England. She prized it above all her many possessions. I had heard the story so many times of how her mother had rocked her just the same way she had rocked our children and us. In a way I think she felt she had been born right in it. Yes, this weathered old rocker, darkened with age, marred from use, is a piece of family history, inanimate, unable to tell the tales it must have soaked up in ever grain of its fiber. It had traversed the ocean wide and within its grasps it holds tight the secrets of generations past. The chair was hand carved by Mama's father, before she was born, just for the purpose it had always been used for, to just rock babies. And that it had done and it has served well through the years, I can attest to that.

It is here in this room, in this cherished chair, that I found Mama, weak and tired, barely able to communicate. Her mind sharp, but her body tired and weak. Cameron, her hired man, had rushed to our farm and summoned me to come fast. His words still ring clear in my thoughts.

"Miss Eliza, Miss Eliza, our Miss Elizabeth is very ill." He was out of breath and could barely say more.

I donned a bonnet and grabbed my shawl and followed him as swiftly as possible. I found Mama, pale, the normal pink blush of her cheeks faded to an ashen white, she was sitting in this room, in this rocker with an old dress clutched tightly to her bosom. I tried to remove the faded garment from her arms. She drew in a small breath and clutching the tattered cloth even closer, she looked at me with glazed eyes and tried desperately to speak. Her words were almost inaudible. I bent close and brushed a wispy strand of graying hair from her forehead. I gently kissed her upon her cheek. She gave no real recognition as to who I was only to the fact that she knew there was someone else in the room with her. She seemed dazed, lost deep within her own mind, so transfixed, deep in her own world that my words could not penetrate into her conscious or seemingly even her subconscious state. I was puzzled watching her clutch the rotting clump of material in her arms. Large glistening tears flowed down her pale, thin face. I wiped them away with the hem of my skirt; letting the ones from my own eyes, fall aimlessly to the floor.

Here she sat, with her head tilted back against the side of the chair, eyes trained on the distant water in the bay, with a tired exhausted look, haunting her frail face. She tried once more to speak; nothing came out but a whisper. She seemed so weak. I tried to coax her to her bed but when I touched her she flinched and coiled tighter into the chair, bringing the cloth she held, up to her lips. I offered a sip of cool water from the pitcher by her bedside table. More dripped to the floor than down her throat.

"Mama," I said, "let me lay you down in your bed. You are too tired to sit here, you need to rest." She did not move her eyes from the window. Again she tried to speak. I put my ear closer to her mouth. I could barely make out the words that came in strange tangled spurts.

"This was for you Eliza, it was to be yours! Your father is coming for me I can see his ship. I wanted you to have this before I left, but I must wear it myself. I must get ready now."

She drew in a deep hard breath and closed her eyes. It had taken all her strength for those few brief words. She now seemed agitated and distraught. I talked on, trying to sooth her with calming words. Her breathing became erratic and she drifted off into an uneasy sleep.

"Don't talk now Mama, it is all right, Papa will be here soon. It is all right." I continued to talk as I rubbed my hand over the top of her head, as if patting a puppy. It was an automatic motion, a caressing move, knowing she didn't even realize what I was saying or what I was doing for that matter. I have the feeling she perhaps didn't know who I was, at least part of the time.

What words I could distinguish made me think that the past was very much the present to her in her sick, weakened condition. She was speaking as if the news of Papa's ship, being lost at sea had just been delivered, when in actuality it had been several years past. She never really wanted to recognize that fact and she never gave up hope that his ship would come sailing into our beautiful little harbor at any given moment. She always told us that someday he would return for her and she knew in her heart, he would.

I remember being totally lost in my own thoughts and I had jumped at the sound of Mama's voice when suddenly she opened her eyes and recognized me. What a relief to my soul. She seemed rested and alert questioning me as to what I was doing setting in her bedchamber. As clear, as a fresh spring day, she started conversing with me. She had a smile upon her lips and a twinkle in her eyes as she talked on, telling me of how she looked forward to this journey with Papa in his big sailing ship and the good times they would share as they sailed about the ocean discovering new places and seeing new things. The islands they had only glimpsed from afar on their crossing from England could now be explored and enjoyed.

She would finally be able to return to her beloved England and return to the home she had left behind. Just the thought of seeing her house and animals gave her a glint of strength.

253

"I saw the sails of your fathers ship, the Elizabeth, they have come closer, is it at the dock yet?" Her questions had come quickly, but as fast as the spurt of energy had come it waned.

Then as if the moment of departure with father had arrived she looked at me and said.

"It is time for me to sail away my dear, remember I love you, good-bye Liz, good-bye. Please understand, I love you my darling daughter but this is one journey I must take with your father, alone."

Her voice trailed off, she closed her eyes and slumped forward in the chair. The shock of the moment caused me to react instinctively. I quickly stepped on the back rung of the rocker to keep Mama from falling on the floor and yelled for help. My brothers John and William rushed in. Cameron had run swiftly to the fields to tell them of Mama's condition and they were so out of breath as they entered the room that they couldn't even speak. My brothers gently picked Mama up and laid her on her bed. I sat beside her, our hands with fingers entwined. Something in me rejected the thought of letting go. At times her brow would wrinkle up as if she were musing over something and then a smile would return and she would seem to relax momentarily. Time passed and for several days she remained much the same. Some days I had hopes of a full recovery and others I resigned myself to the situation at hand. Eventually her breathing became more and more shallow and then labored and finally there was no breath at all. I held tight to her hand and it took me some time to fully comprehend what had taken place. I quickly released my hold on her, then just as quickly picked her hand back up and gently wrapped her fingers over mine, rubbing them ever so easy in a massaging motion. I felt her hands became cool and then cold to the touch and knew I was witnessing the very life being drawn from her body. It didn't matter to me. I did not have the strength or will to let her go.

I continued to hold her fingers around mine forcing them to intertwine, willing with all my might for them to grip mine when there was no grip left. I persisted until the pliability was no longer there. Still sweeping my other hand over her thin, gray hair, muttering how much I love her. My motions were repetitive, without thought. The void in the room was overwhelming. There was no conversation, no answers to the questions rolling around in my head, and no way to fix the hurt in my heart.

For that brief moment in time, my life had stopped along with hers. I could find no answers to the questions that raced through my thoughts. I only know that at some point I was finally able to make a physical break in the bonding of our bodies, yet I do not know how long it will take me to make some kind of a more spiritual break with my soul.

I have been setting here a long time with my eyes misted with tears as I remember with too much vividness this past week. Or has it been longer? Time somehow has no meaning at the moment. My motions seem meaningless for here I am walking to the window once more. What am I looking for? My eyes are strained and tired. Am I too looking for the big sails of Papa's ship? Is that it out there somewhere just over the horizon? Without realizing what I am thinking, my mind questions. Could it really be Papa's, ship?

It seems as if all my sadness started an eternity ago, when in reality it has only been a matter of days. My mind is wondering today, just as it did the day she died. Here, there and everywhere. It jumps, conjuring up memories, memories of childhood, of growing up, happy times, sad times, memories, and memories. Is life nothing but memories I wonder to myself? Where is my future going to lead me? Can I make it without Mama? Life seems so unfair.

Mama's life was far to short. She wouldn't have died if Papa had been found. I know that to be the truth. In my heart of hearts I know that Mama's life would have been different if he would have only come home. If he only could have known how Mama, grieved for him and watched each and every setting sun for some little sign of his returning ship. If only the big sails could come clapping and blowing in the wind, sailing "The Elizabeth" into the harbor. I find myself right at this very minute; doing the same thing she had done so often. Looking out the window hoping against all hope that what I am seeing way out in the great blue ocean is my Papa's ship. I want it to come sailing swiftly home and into our safe harbor just as she had dreamed it would. But what could it change now? Perhaps it is just my way of putting off the inevitable. I cringe at the thought of facing my tomorrow without Mama. The stark, horrible reality causes the tears to flow once again and they tumble out of my eyes and drip down my face as if they are a river rushing to the sea. I retreat to the rocker and as much as I try, I cannot stop the avalanche of emotion from plopping itself directly into my lap. Even trying to divert my thoughts does nothing. I can find nothing pleasant to divert them to.

Looking down into my lap reminds me once more of the reason for rushing up here in the first place. The books, tied ever so neatly with the pale, blue ribbon. I don't even remember picking them up from the side table, yet here they are lying in my lap. Again I let the questions of my mind ramble on. What is in them? What do they say? I watch the faded bow as it wiggles atop them, as I hold the books in my trembling hands. Why had Mama, given them to the Reverend for me? What is written on the little pages that she wanted so much for me to read and understand? I wonder, but I am not ready to untie the bow and unlock the answers to my questions. No, not just yet. I am not ready to do anything. I want my mind to stop thinking. I want to close my eyes and wake up another day, another time, maybe even another place. A change, I think I would like a complete change in my life.

The pain within my chest is unbearable, and the tears that had started to fall earlier were back. The pain welled up inside my body, and cried for release. There was no holding the tears back this time. I could not control my sobbing. My body raked with the grief I felt. My emotions had finally broken through and had taken complete control of me.

It was a harsh steady sea breeze that brought a slight chill to the air and roused me from my crying spell. The wind is so strong in fact it is bellowing the curtains almost straight out from the curtain rods. But before my conscience mind has time to ponder the actions of the breeze the strong gust seems to die down. Its action is much too quick for my liking. I would like it to stay longer here for there is something about it that is calming to me. For just a very brief moment I feel the soft gentle air, brush gently past my wet cheek. And with it the marvelous scent of the beautiful lilacs and roses from Mama's garden waft past my nostrils. As the air mingles with an escaping tear it feels ever so much like one of Mama's moist gentle kisses.  The nearness of her is at hand and somehow I feel Mama has come to say goodbye.

As the air drifts ever forward through the room my thoughts drift ever forward through my mind.  I remember with such pleasure the wonders of Mama's talents as she fixed a special bouquet to brighten the parlor table, or a fresh bunch of dried roses, in the midst of a dark, dreary winter day, bringing freshness to the stale, damp, smoke filled living quarters. "Yes," she would say, "the heavenly scent of angels breath." Then she would smile her special smile and hum a gentle tune and go about her day.

I wonder how long it will take before I can think upon all my many memories without them tying knots in my stomach and welling up tears in my eyes?

My rocking motion has become erratic like my thinking and I stub my toe against the wide wood plank floor as I slow the rocker to a gentler pace.  The faster I think the faster I seem to rock.  I know my reasons for being here are purely selfish.  I had sought just the right moment to escape from the well-meaning townspeople downstairs.  I don't mean to be rude, but I fear I have been.  I just need so terribly much to be alone. I desperately need a refuge to sort out all these confused thoughts, or to not think at all.  I also need a refuge from all the sympathy givers, with their sweet smiles and gentle hugs.  Their words are meant well but seem hollow in a strange yet sincere way.  I find it hard to explain even to myself.  I hope they will forgive me for my abrupt departure from the parlor for I need a place of utter empty silence, to find some quiet comfort of my own.  I still do not understand why Mama had to leave this earth for the so-called better place.  What did that mean?  What was wrong with right here where her family is?  Here where she was loved and revered by everyone who knew her?  Our neighbors' words of comfort, though coming from the heart fell empty upon my ears.  I realize that at some time in the days and months ahead I will come to grips with my feelings, at least I hope I do, but for today I have to put everything away in a space within me to be retrieved and dealt with later.

The pressing duties of the day had to be taken care of and endured with little time to think of anything else.  A lovely service, with many kind words was presented in loving memory of Mama.  Then we had left the little meeting place and walked in silence behind her hand carved coffin to the burying grounds.  There we were John, William, and I following the elders as we trudged our way up the rocky path to the little cemetery that would become Mama's final resting place, here on earth.  The members of the congregation were all there following behind in silent tribute to Mama their friend.  Mama had now traveled on into the heavenly home she always believed in and left this home here on earth empty and in despair with her passing.  I kept my eyes on the ground as we walked along watching the puffs of dry earth burst from beneath my feet.  The dust reminded me of a passage in the Bible.  I kicked at the hard ground, as if in rebellion and instantly knew I would receive a harsh reprimand for my actions.

Upon returning to the house, I greeted each and every person with a grateful thank you and a smile that was permanently etched on my lips.  I was acting out of duty, out of impulse, because this is the way people act when a loved one dies, this is what you are suppose to do, these are the

256

words you are supposed to say. But in my heart all I really wanted to do was bolt and run. Run like a wild stallion, and not stop until I reached a cliff where I could run no further. So when the time seemed right I seized the moment and rushed from the room with hardly an utterance.

This was not an easy day for me, nor had it been an easy month. Mama's illness had caused me to rush to her side and try as best I could to comfort her in her last hours. Wishing with all my heart that I could wipe away her pain and anguish, as she had done for me so many times in my growing up years. The silent tears, that slowly trickled down her thin, white face, and the gentle, but firm grasp, of her delicate calloused hands around my fingers, a memory ingrained so, so, deep in my mind. The one last shining droplet of water that escaped from her questioning eyes still glistens in my thoughts. I have relived the moment, again, and again, seeing myself, as I bent over her, my tears intermingling with hers, the one last soft kiss upon her cheek as I brushed her eye lids gently down, and with a deep sob, told her good bye. Finally, I had been able to untangle our entwined fingers and I slowly pulled the covers up over her.

As I looked upon the body, lying there upon her bed, I knew I had lost, not only my Mother and my teacher, but also most of all, my friend. We had shared laughter and sorrow, and the void, her departure from this life leaves in my world, can never be filled. I know that many things will touch my life, with meaning and love, but none as my mother has. The hole in my life will exist, until the time comes when we once again meet, in that far distant place, where eternity is found. I do not remember the loving words Rev. Blakeman said, at her bedside that day, or much else that happened in the hours that followed. I was in my own world, moving about, without much thought as to why or what. Just doing what needed to be done. Really I just kept busy so that I didn't have to think.

Today seems to be a day just the same as that one. I am in a fog, moving about mechanically. When Rev. Blakeman handed me the books, I took them without question. He gave no real explanation, just said, "Elizabeth, these were your Mother's and she entrusted them with me, to be given to you upon her death. She said, you would understand, and murmured something about; you were so young, you had to know from whence you came, in order to know where you were going. I assured her I would care for them and give them to you at the first opportunity. So this I do. Your mother was a fine and righteous woman and a loving servant of God," he explained, and then paused. There was nothing more he could say.

This day was as hard for him as it was for any. He and his family live on land that borders ours in this place called Connecticut. Being not only our friend but also the minister of this small company of ours, his duties are sometimes unbearable.

Today he finds them especially heavy for he was burying one who had traveled from England and braved the hardships this new land had brought to most that climbed upon her rocky shores. I smiled up at him not knowing one word that would help either of us.

"Thank you Rev. Blakeman," Is all that I could utter. I knew not what her message meant, nor what lay within the pages of the tiny books. All I know is that they were from Mama, and they are for me. It should

257

not surprise me that I found the first opportunity I could to excuse myself. When the moment arose I seized it and left the room. I quickly ran up the stairs. Without even realizing where I was going, I found myself standing in Mama's bedchamber. Why had I come here? Somehow her room had drawn me like a magnet. I needed to be close to her. I guess I felt her presence here. Perhaps I could, somehow, absorb some of the inner strength she always displayed.

Here I am, sitting in her rocker, with a little stack of her books upon my lap, and the sadness of her parting welling up inside me, causing my breath to catch in little gasps. My eyes are transfixed on the little books as I reach down with trembling fingers to untie the tiny, neatly tied bow. I can't help staring at the books. But as the bow slips gently away and falls to the floor, I open the cover page and let a tear from my misty eyes fall upon the page. I recognize immediately the neat handwriting of Mama. There were many women, who could neither read nor write, and men for that matter, and her being able to do both gave her great pride. She was always most insistent, that all her children learn these lessons in life. She taught us with much love, but sternness. Reading and writing was as important to her as walking and talking. We all had learned well, and this made her proud.

The pages are neatly dated, but I find my eyes fighting not to focus as if they are too tired to try and decipher the dim writing. I aimlessly leaf through the pages and stretch my neck to stare out the window. What does all this mean? This is all in Mama's own hand, what could she tell me in these little books that she could not share with me in person? What did she mean when she spoke of my future and my past? I was perplexed, tired, devastated by her death.

I can hear the movement of the people down stairs, and I know some are leaving. They are saying good-bye, and I know I should go down. Yet I find myself making no attempt to move. Mama would be appalled at my manners. I know that, but it still makes no difference to me. I can hear John and William, talking to the friends and families that have gathered here today. Their voices are all a blur of noise. As I rest my head against the back of the chair I feel my body vibrate from a long drawn out breath. The noise from below becomes a swirling picture of sight and sound in my mind, blurring together, making no sense at all. My mind is agitated wondering aimlessly through the years. I seem to be somewhere in a state between twilight and dawn.

Suddenly, I am back many years, my mind winding itself tight, tight like a clock, back to the day the news came, that Papa's ship had been lost at sea. The news had come with no warning, no time to prepare. Just a strange sailor, running up the garden path, bellowing out:

"Master Curtyce his ship sank! Master Curtyce his ship sank! Everyone was lost at sea! There was no sign of survivors and no one could find a trace of either Master Curtyce or Thomas."

What a way to deliver a message of such immensity. Who brought the word of the great disaster I really don't remember and it really doesn't matter. What mattered was Mama, and the shock that message had upon her. I can still visualize in my mind seeing the blood draining from her face and her body slump to the floor. She was in total disbelief that any thing as awful as that could happen to Papa and my dear sweet brother. This was a tragedy I could never quite deal with and I'm really not sure Mama ever dealt with either. There was no recovery of the bodies and no funeral; the reality never quite sank in. I preferred to push their disappearance far back into the depths of my inner being. I had always pretended they were just away. Maybe Mama had dealt with it in a similar way, for, from that day, until her dying day, she lived as if Papa's big ship would come sailing into the harbor at any moment. At sundown on days when she was not kept in the fields longer than normal, the trenchers were placed on the table in anticipation of his arrival and a lamp was lit beside the front stoop, the lamp swinging back and forth on a rod iron post as a signal of hope and welcome home. She believed, he would come running up the lane, and she would drop whatever she was doing, and run with outstretched arms, down the garden path to meet him. I am sure this was the scene, enacted many, many, times in the privacy of her mind. Did it happen that way for her in the end? Did her fondest dream, finally, come true? Had Papa really come for her?

I know my questions will remain unanswered as many of Mama's were. Her life was full of surprises. One of the biggest was her finding that Thomas was married and that he had sailed with his father on that last voyage. Until the word from the sailor she had not known. There was hardly any way to get messages from town to town, unless someone was going or coming from the place you needed to get in touch with. Thomas had left Cupheag many months before his and Papa's final voyage and had gone to Suckiaug, along the beautiful Connecticut River. When Papa had gone to sea that last time, he stopped in Suckiaug before leaving for Boston Harbor and evidently Thomas had climbed aboard, for the news of the ship going down included Thomas as missing. It was not until Mary his wife, had come to our door shortly after she had received the news that Thomas was lost at sea. It was then we learned he had left his new bride, of only a month, and succumbed to the call of the sea, his real true love. It was then and only then that we were apprised of their marriage and the obvious fact that Mary was with child. She had no place to go and felt her only alternative was to come to Thomas's family.

Mary's family had died on the voyage over from Scotland and a kind family had taken her in. She was indentured to them for her keep but they were unable to care for her and the child she carried. It broke Mama's heart to see the sadness in young Mary's eyes and to know that Thomas would never see his darling baby. The news of the shipwreck had put Mary to bed, and even after little Patience was born, many months passed before she seemed to have an interest in life. Mama had prayed, many nights, for God to give Mary the strength to accept what life had dealt her, to take care of, and love her precious baby girl. Mama knew that it was just grief that was destroying her newly found daughter-in-law and with caring and love she would regain her strength. How many times I heard Mama say, "God is our strength, and he will provide us the answers in time." Do we really ever totally understand or do we finally give up our quest for an answer, for the sake of sanity and muddle on down life's path? Whatever it is, by giving love and assurance to Mary, Mama gained strength from it also.

I must say, taking care of Mary and the baby did give a sort of peace and calm to our household. It was like a kind of filling stuffed between the crusts of our lives, taking up the empty space left by the disappearance of our loved ones. I know, for Mama, it gave her a reason

259

for being alive and a reason for hope. It gave her a reason for getting up each morning. John and William were busy with their own families. The work on their farms and all the work in the family store, took up all the hours allotted in their day. It is not unusual to find a man and his family with both a farm to work and a store to keep. Everything here in this land of dreams has taken on greater dimensions than in England. People seem to ware many hats for there is a great need for so much. There are so few of us scattered over such a vast area that what would be considered impossible has become normal. The tasks here is this new land are many.

As I watched Mama trudge through each day, after the word of the ship wreck, I felt like each day was to her like a giant quilt that had been torn, leaving a wide gaping hole and she was stitching her life together one small piece at a time. Bit by bit she was trying to make it whole again. Everything, about her life was a scrap, another patch in her tattered existence. She tried hard to find something to hold together the outside edges of her world and fill in the loneliness she endured without Papa. She once said to me, "Eliz, the loss of your husband is one of the greatest losses you will ever have to endure, and the loss of your child, is a loss greater than any you will ever experience. Whenever you loose a child you loose a part of your very soul. A portion of your very being dies too." That was the closest she ever came to admitting that they would never be back. To her dying day, the loss of Papa and Thomas showed heavy, in the lines upon her beautiful oval face. The twinkle in her beautiful eyes had lost the luster they once possessed.

It was Mama's great determination and tenacity that allowed her to carry on with the plans and dreams that had brought us to this new country. Nothing could stop her. She worked from early dawn to dark. She was a hard working and sometimes very stubborn person. Many days when neighbors came to call, their conversation was made over the handle of a hoe instead of over the handle of a teacup. For they would almost always find her in the fields, even way after the sun had kissed the day good bye, tending to her crops, checking on the corn or the animals to maybe feeding the chickens a bit more meal.

There was much to do and her determination to get it all done, and done properly, was a fierce drive within her. The only time she even let down her guard for a moment was when she was with her grandchildren. They were the bright rays of sun in her cloudy days. She loved them with a deep and passionate love. For each was a beautiful jewel, full of effervescence, wonderment and joy. She would always give them a kiss atop their little heads and would say.

"I love you little ones; you are the fresh new flowers in my garden of life." Then she would give them all a piece of fresh baked Johnny Cake, and send them out to play. They loved their Munna, as they called her with all their hearts.

My children's loss is as great as mine and at some point in their young lives they too will become conscious of the fact that her presence is with them no more. They will realize that Munna is not around to play those special games, or to sing her special songs. They will hear the joy of her laughter no longer, or be cuddled and spoiled, as only a grandmother can do. They will now have to rely upon their memories to sustain them in their personal time of grief. Grief they would surly experience at some point in time.

There always seems to be such a special bond between a Grandmother and her grandchildren. A secret bond of love, granted a grandmother, from God. I hope someday to achieve that same special bond with my grandchildren, as Mama had with hers.

As I let my downcast eyes rest on the journals in my lap, I can't stop squirming in the chair. As much as I want to read the books there is something that holds me back. A shiver runs down the length of my spine and curiosity overcomes indecision, as my eyes search and focus on the writings on the first page. It simply says. "To ELIZABETH, WITH LOVE"

I turn the page to continue, my hand trembling as I do and the fragile pages chatter at the shaking, but now I know I must read on. Mama has neatly noted all the important dates of her family. Though I know them by heart I read each and every entry as if seeing it for the first time.

Elizabeth Hutchins Curtyce, daughter of Lord Byron Hutchins and Abigail Hutchins. Born, the 26th day of September in the year of our Lord, 1560.

The pages of the tiny journals are colored with age, and no matter how carefully I turn the fragile pages small fragments of the crisp brown edges flake into my lap. I turn each page with more care, trying not to tremble as I look upon my mother's words. I feel my emotions surge within me as I read the dates that signify the arrival into, and the departure from this life, of all her loved ones. My eyes are blurred with tears as I wrestle to keep the memories I hold inside from taking over my senses. I need to keep my feelings pushed, as far back in my mind as possible, for if one drop of them emerges and mingles with the present grief in my heart, I fear I will not be able to stand it. I must force my mind to continue to read this my inheritance, line by line.

Married, John Curtyce, on the 19th day of April, in the year of our Lord, 1610. Parish Church, Nazing, England. I know the entries that followed on these pages so well, yet I scrutinized each and every one of them as if I am seeing them for the very first time. Perhaps I am trying to will them to jump off the page and give me some kind of an explanation and help me to make some sense of what is going on in my world today. The information on these pages is inscribed ever so neatly, and ever so clearly. Mama had carefully and very methodically placed them in chronological order beginning with the marriage and ending with the deaths of her loved ones.

Seeing the information in the written form brought more moisture to my eyes. It seemed to dispel the belief I had so long held, for them just being away. It brought the facts and the finality of the facts forcefully forward. Mama had added just the word DEATHS: And then notated the death of John Curtyce and Thomas Curtyce. I know these were two deaths that Mama never quite accepted.

DEATHS

John Curtyce, my devoted husband and loving father of my children and my precious son Thomas Curtyce, both lost at sea in the year of our Lord 1655. They sailed from this life together, as they had sailed together here on earth.

My life continues here in the Connecticut Colony, while my memories lie in England and my heart lies lost in the vastness of an ocean.

I know how Mama always had a deep fear of the ocean and had refused many sailing adventures. My eyes scanned the words and my heart burst into a hard rhythmic pounding, growing louder and louder, causing my anticipation of what lay in the pages of these precious books to grow and grow. I let my fingers nimbly and eagerly turn the page, for I was committed now, compelled to read on. As I adjust myself into a more comfortable position in the rocking chair, I anticipate a joyous adventure.

I remember vividly how all of us loved to hear Mama tell of her trips to the big city of London when she was a very small child, and of her house and horses and her life growing up. She spoke of everything with immense love, and yet there was a slight emptiness in the telling, as if there were always parts left out on purpose. Maybe the books I hold in my hand or the ones lying on my lap will fill in those untold parts. As her writing continues, I inhale deeply and resolve to read on.

I am Elizabeth Hutchins Curtyce and these are my thoughts and feelings as I have traveled a strange and sometimes puzzling path while on this earth. When my life seemed set and complacent something always came along to set it back in the main current. I was carried swiftly through this life sometimes being shown wonders my eyes could barely conceive.

Though life has been sometimes smooth and sometimes rocky it has always been interesting. I entrust these book to Rev. Blakeman to be given to my daughter Elizabeth upon my death. With the closeness and unspoken understanding that only mother and daughter share, I pray that through love and wisdom she will glean a bit of humor, a bit of love and a whole lot of understanding into the why's and way's of my life. They are just thoughts, hopes and dreams, a spattering of my journey into unknown and uncharted lands. Peoples from the past and peoples and places of the present, jotted down to merge into a portrait, that is my life.

Mama's bedchamber has become dark and gray. Shadows creep about the room. The chill of the night air causes me to shiver. I rub my eyes to clear the blur from my long hours of reading and looked down upon the empty pages in front of me. I turned to the next page it was blank. I turned to the next and the next and wistfully I think, Mama's writings have stopped, there is no more.

I had come to the end of her journals. She had taken me on a journey through time. Carried me along on the fragile wings of her dreams. She had shown me through her little journals, the fulfillment of her wishes and the tragedies and happiness's of her life. I had looked through a gossamer veil, deep into the innermost part of her heart. I was

a part of her world and she a very special part of mine.  Now I must
return to this world, the here and now, the happenings of today.  I must
find the family and somehow face my tomorrows as Mama, so eloquently
written to me, showing me, how she had faced hers.

I know in the years to come I will put many moments aside and
reread these pages.  I will digest the thoughts and try to learn from her
experiences.  Yes, many more times in the future, I know I will seek out
her wisdom.  I look down on my lap and see the blank pages before me, and
yet I know am not ready to close them, these little remembrances from
Mama.  I feel a need to find more of her writings.  To close these pages
now seems too decisive a decision for my tired mind to undertake.  No, I'm
not quite ready in my heart to take such a final step.

Many years have past between the last of her writings and today.
Why had she not continued to keep up the journals on a day-to-day basis,
as she had started from the first?  Perhaps she felt I was old enough to
form my own memories.  Or maybe after fathers and Thomas's deaths she
could not bear to write anymore.  Whatever her reasons, the pages are now
void of her beautiful handwriting.  As I continue to search, looking for,
I really don't know what?  More writing?  Perhaps!  Whatever it is causes
me to leave them open upon my lap.  I need the journals to continue, for
in my mind I feel that as long as I hold them open, Mama is still here
with me.  To close them is like closing the lid on the casket.

The devastation of the day once more consumes me.  I draw in a deep
breath and release a sob.  I find myself looking almost frantically
through the pages of the journals.  I finally find success far back in the
last little leather bound book.  Here Mama had inscribed a poem her ode to
New England, her welcome to her friends.  I didn't need to read the words,
for I knew them by heart yet I find myself intently looking over each and
every word and my lips moving to form the words aloud.  As I read I let
them swim through my mind lingering for brief moments as I remember back
through the years to the time she had written this poem and had given it
to her friends as a welcoming gesture as they visited our home.  I let my
eyes move over the words and my voice took flight as I read them aloud.

Welcome To Our Home

Within these aged walls, there is a warmth that only years could obtain, and in the tradition of Old New England, the welcome lamp is lit, and will shine through the window and light the path to the door. The humble hearts within will wait till the sound of your voices, and the presence of your smiles, lights the room. Welcome to our humble home. May the friendships shared, and the memories lived, be everlasting. Friendship is a great privilege afforded man and with this thought we hold out our hand.

Yes, Mama had felt that way. Every one of her friends was a beautiful flower in her garden of life every friend very special in his or her own unique way. The old friends had become precious jewels and the new had become cherished treasures, and her life cycled on. The rocker creaks, as it slowly rocks back and forth across the wide board floor. I close my eyes and slowly drift back through the years. I want to see just how far back my memory will go. I discover that within my own mind I have volumes of memories. I reach back in my mind and let it carry me as far back as it can possibly take me. Perhaps I am grasping for that lifeline, she spoke so graciously about. I wanted to capture it, stretch it just a little bit further, let her grab hold of it and pull her back to this side of life. I want her to take hold of my hand and jump the chasm of space, hold on to the tail of my memories and let me carry her effortlessly as she had so often carried all of us. We could live on together; discuss her thoughts and dreams, face, to face. I wanted to talk with her, tell her how much I love her. Say the things, that in life, I might have left unsaid.

I want to see Caswell Manor and run through the fields of lush green clover. Smell the sweetness of her garden, the aromas of the kitchen hearth. I want to ride Big Blacky and see the pictures on the wall. I wanted to take her back to the land of her birth, to the dreams she had left behind. I want to give back the happiness she had so willingly given up for us. No it could not happen. Turning back the pages of these books would not make my world whole again. I could not stop the progression of time.

The darkness here in my mother's bedchamber has engulfed me. It has come upon me with such stealth. The darkness has invaded my little sanctuary from the present and time has once again slipped away. I reach over and without much thought light the small oil lamp that sits on the bedside table. I am oblivious to all the activities downstairs. Or is it the lack of activities down there that has attracted my attention. Now that I stop to listen, I hear nothing. I wonder what has become of John and William? They must think I have disappeared. They probably needed some time of their own to adjust to the loss we have in our lives. How selfish of me to have left them to face everyone alone. What must they think of me? I guess I will find an answer to that question later but for now I cannot seem to give up this special private time with my mothers memories.

I flipped through a few more pages and find nothing, there seems to be no more of mother's writings. As I start to put the little books down my eyes momentarily glimpse some notations far back in the last small book. I quickly adjust myself in the rocker and start reading once again.

For a brief moment, I feel as if I have received a second chance, a reprieve of some kind. Whatever it is I am grateful and I continue to read.

"My dearest, darling Elizabeth, it begins; these few thoughts of my life, I have entrusted to the pages of these tiny books, so you might know from whence you came. Be patient with life Elizabeth and true to your maker, for you may find rough seas ahead and without God you have nothing. It is only by his strength we survive on this earth at all and by his grace we find everlasting life. I have always felt you were denied something in life by our journey to this new land, and yet, there was no way to stop it from happening. I cannot go back to my beloved England, my book of life was written long, long ago and I have lived it the only way I knew how. It was not for me to change or challenge, only to do my very best. Carry your heritage with pride, Elizabeth, for a woman tends to loose her own identity when she becomes a wife. Just remember a small part of you will always remain a Curtyce and with future generations the bloodline of your father will flow in the vanes of your children. Tell your children the stories you remember and let them know that no matter where they are in life, they can draw on the strengths that were so abundant in their ancestors, and have been passed down from generation to generation. Your father will be coming for me soon Elizabeth, and no matter how hard it is for me to leave you and the family behind, I will have to go. I will board his ship with pleasure and join him on the rest of his voyage through time. I have let the monsters of the sea separate us far to long. We will sail the seas of eternity together and no more will parting come between us. Without regret of the past, nor fear of the future, I eagerly look forward to your fathers return."

I pause to ingest what I am reading. Now I know what the tattered, faded remnant of cloth was. The one she held to so tightly. It was her wedding dress! She somehow thought in her tired, worn out mind that she would put it on and meet Papa upon his return. In her dream of dreams, she would greet him anew, the fresh new bride, eager to explore his universe with him. So like her, I thought even in her last hours, thinking of giving up all that might mean anything to her, for the dreams of my father. I silently hope that she did have her wedding dress on and that, as she had wished, it would somehow bring to her in her new world, a tie, a closeness with her past. Yes I pray, at least in her mind, she was able to dawn the dress and greet Papa as she did on that beautiful April day, so many years ago.

I turn my eyes back to the book and read on: My will provides for my grandchildren. Elizabeth, you received your portion upon your marriage. This little memento of my life is my special gift to you. May my journals bring you joy and understanding and I pray in some small way, they can breach the miles between your beginning years in the land of your birth and the ones spent here in this new land. I pray they will serve to connect the two.

As I gently turn the very last piece of tattered parchment book, I find tightly pressed between the pages, a crumpled, faded, deep red rose. Mama's favorite flower! Though weathered and darkened with age, with the pedals crinkled and the edges flaking away, it still holds the sweet fragrant scent of its youth. That wonderful fragrance of early spring, when life is new and rebirth is generated. This little crushed flower is passing up to me from the stained brown pages of an old book its heritage, its fingerprint of life, its beautiful smell.  So like the bloodline of man, so passes the heritage of a rose.

TEMPUS

FUGIT

TIME

FLIES

266

Made in the USA
Lexington, KY
16 May 2018